UNKNOWN PLEASURES

Unknown Pleasures

JASON COWLEY

faber and faber

First published in Great Britain in 2000
by Faber and Faber Limited
3 Queen Square London WC1N 3AU

Photoset by RefineCatch Limited, Bungay, Suffolk
Printed in England by Clays Limited, St Ives plc

A CIP record for this book is
available from the British Library

ISBN 0–571–20233–0

2 4 6 8 10 9 7 5 3 1

For Sarah.

And in memory of
Anthony Frank Cowley, 1935–91, and
Salvatore Morreale, 1966–98

The author wishes to thank Sarah Kernohan, Lilian Cowley, Jon Riley, David Godwin, Emma Platt, Penny Jones, Martyn Bedford, Sergeant Mark Hussey, Brian MacArthur, Peter Wilby, Alison Hibberd and Victoria McHugh.

And special thanks to Phil Whitaker for his superb support and encouragement.

Why do you seek the living among the dead?
  Luke, xxiv, 5

With autobiography there's always another text,
a countertext, if you will, to the one presented.
  Philip Roth

Searching for England

A wood in darkness, empty city streets, a woman alone with her baby in a sombre room, and then the body of a man lying dead in my flat: the events of the past fortnight replayed themselves like a video nightmare controlled by an unseen hand. Since returning to London at the end of August my world had been turned upside down in search of a man I'd never really known. The choice seemed simple now: to run and keep on running, to run somewhere – anywhere – or to take my chance in the courts. The phone in my pocket which I dared not lose was quiet. So I lay there slumped in the carriage of a train speeding north towards Manchester; and lying there I began to mourn the lost warmth of the English summer through which I'd just passed, a summer which had wrapped itself around me so completely – like a safety blanket – that I'd been lulled into thinking that my search was at last approaching an end, that I'd finally returned to a country I once called home. And now? Nothing but the slow desolation of early winter . . . and the mistakes we repeat.

Later, disturbed by the sound of the train as it rattled into the station, I opened my eyes on to a sullen Saturday afternoon, a long way from summer now. Through the smeared glass I saw thick-jacketed soccer fans massed on the platform outside, their verbal agitation muffling the platitudes of the senior conductor's apologetic farewell – we were more than forty minutes late. Leaving, I submitted myself entirely to the flow of the crowds heading for the exit: the shoppers, the weekend commuters with their cases and holdalls, the beery West Ham fans whose movements, under the supervision of a police escort, had all the spontaneity of canned laughter.

1

This time, as I left the station, I was certain I hadn't been followed.

Outside litter swirled in the wind. The pavement was salted and my breath hung suspended like a frozen cobweb. Across the way, my uncle was waiting for me, a tall, familiar figure I found reassuring after so many days of living under extremes of isolation and threat. Yet, wary of approaching too soon, I watched him through the glaucous light – the hustle of Manchester Piccadilly– as he leaned against his car, a newspaper or magazine rolled up under one arm, his long stone-coloured coat and black scarf cracking in the breeze. For a moment, I thought there was someone with him in the car, but as I looked again I saw nothing but the gathering shadows of the life I'd never had the chance to lead, the absence that was always there.

Then he saw me. 'Joshua, over here!' His voice reached me on the wind, above the engines of the dirt-splashed cabs, as a warm and welcoming thing. As he approached, low blue-bruised clouds were passing rapidly overhead, the pale disturbance of a turbulent northern sky. In the distance, the glare of an overlit mall, and colonies of shoppers scuttling like ants.

We embraced spontaneously – and how the missing years had grown like a forest between us. In truth, I scarcely knew this near-stranger pulling me towards him with all the familiarity of a close friend, scarcely knew what to say to him. Except to say hello.

He had aged more than I'd expected in the twelve or more years since our last meeting. Time had stripped the once-florid colouring from his face and his hair had receded alarmingly. What was left was dark grey, swept back in frayed, wiry strands and clipped neatly at the sides. The skin around his neck was loose and there were swollen pockets of tiredness under his eyes.

'Joshua,' he said, inspecting me at arm's length, as if I were one of his disgruntled pupils. 'You remind me so much of your father.'

My father! If he'd said that two months ago I might have felt differently. For as long as I can remember I've been searching for my father in the gaps, omissions and ellipses of my mother's conversation, in her hesitations and sighs, in her laughter and verbal slips, in her unspoken questions, but above all in the troubled distance of her gaze. But always searching for him without any conviction, without believing that anything would ever be resolved; convinced that the riddle of his disappearance would remain forever precisely that. For a start, there had been no word from him – or of him – for more than a decade. No new leads or paths to follow, stray threads to unpick. All those years of waiting.

My father disappeared twelve years ago, this month: November 1983. He was forty. Not that life had begun for him. No, he walked out of our lives one winter weekend like any other, having lived an apparently ordinary life like any other. He walked out trailing nothing but thin streams of gossip, innuendo and accusation behind him. That was merely the start of it. There then followed the long lassitude of aimless days, as we stumbled blindly around in the spaces he'd left behind, into which we poured our own slurry of words and hopes – the conspiracy theories, the frightened speculations, the forlorn appeals. All of which amounted to ... Well, what did they exactly amount to? He was absent without leave; in time, he was metaphysically absent, too, for in their hearts my family had abandoned him as dead.

So Mum, by the end of 1984, began the train of events that would lead to our eventual emigration to Toronto. There was nothing to keep us in Dorset any more, she told me. More accurately, there was nothing to keep them: Mum and Dan and Rachel. The wide avenues and tall apartment blocks overlooking High Park, the rattle of air-conditioning on long summer nights, the exotic chatter of the immigrant communities – the Poles, Ukrainians, Italians, Irish – among whom Mum grew up, the sob of her father's cop car as he nightly returned to their underground parking lot, the high windows of the glass towers of the downtown financial district – these were Mum's memories of growing up in Toronto, her home city. It was where, in late adolescence, she'd first met my father when he'd washed up as a young man in Ontario in search of work and adventure. In search of something. To me, though, talk of our departure from England was the definitive moment, the psychological moment. I feared then that he'd gone for good.

So at the beginning of 1985 we stopped waiting for him to come home and left home ourselves instead. We left our small town in Dorset, a slower, quieter, more amateurish place than Toronto – and I still can't bring myself to forget it, even though I've tried, just as I've tried to convince myself that Anthony Winter died the very first day he disappeared. So why believe, through all those years of waiting, that he was actually alive and well, perhaps even planning to re-enter our lives in a style as startling as his original disappearance? Bang: the absent magician re-emerges from behind a cloud of smoke. Now you see him, now you don't. Just like that.

Or something like that.

There have been times, though, when I've believed that his disappearance was nothing more than an elaborate stunt, the purpose of which would perhaps one day be revealed, like the meaning of the universe. There were other, darker times when I've found myself so caught up in the clotted loops of my own consciousness, moving between the past, present and the dreaded future, working my way through drab days, that I've felt as isolated from the world as an astronaut adrift in deep space. And the worst thought of all: what if my brother was right, what if I'd actually been in denial all this time, what then? Would the search for my father, which began the day I returned to London at the end of that unnaturally warm English Indian summer, amount to nothing more than a self-dramatizing wrong turn? The quest of a fool . . . heading for a fall.

London Calling

My search really began the morning I arrived in London with nowhere to live. The search for a home, that was, not for my father. The overnight flight from Toronto had been sleeplessly uneventful. Dehydrated and grappling with a mild hangover, I took the hot, crowded Piccadilly Line tube into the West End, where I'd naïvely hoped to check into a decent, cheap, centrally located hotel. First mistake: there was no such thing as a cheap, centrally located hotel, at least not one my mother would have considered decent, with vacancies. So I ended up, on my first night back in London for more than a decade, in the YMCA at King's Cross, with my luggage propped up in a chair at the end of the single bed like an admonishment. I felt anything but deflated; in fact, I felt euphoric at finally being back on home soil, as it were, after so long away. How different everything seemed and yet how unchanged, too. I couldn't wait to get out there on the streets, to get in among it all: the crowds, the clubs, the bars.

A couple of days later, I began my trawl around the West End property agencies, searching for a flat. I eventually found a property agency in Soho which specialized in cheapish, short-term rented accommodation: summer lets, short leases, shared housing, that kind of thing. 'We're popular with tourists and wealthier students,' said the manager, Binoo John, or more accurately Binoo K. John, MA, as he reminded me by dropping his embossed card on the desk when I asked how I spelt his name. The time I spent with him in the small, exceptionally well-ordered office he shared with his partner, Mr Colin, whom I was never to meet, was slow but profitable in unexpected ways. We struck up a rapport.

Binoo John was a fastidious, stooped, plump-fingered man

with narrow eyes and a spirited tongue which seemed somehow too big for his mouth, so frequently did it show itself,
tracing the outline of his lips or flicking hungrily like a lizard's.
He intermittently brushed back his fringe, revealing a smooth,
pale forehead; his silvery goatee beard prospered wirily. In
conversation, he cannily assumed a tone of spurious deference.
It was spurious because unconvincing; he was always pausing
to chuckle to himself as if recalling a private joke, as if he didn't
believe anything I said.

The flat I was most interested in renting, from the details,
was in Nassau Street, which turned out to be just north of
Oxford Street and a short walk from the office. On arrival, I
discovered there were nine apartments in the three-storey
block, three on each floor. The apartment I wanted was on the
second floor of a scruffy, stuccoed Georgian terrace, perhaps
once part of a grand house that had probably been converted
long ago into flats. It was a shabby yet expensive central urban
location: no green spaces, a constant hum of traffic, an off-
licence with windows obscured by metal bars, artless splashes
of graffiti and slogans daubed on walls – private messages
publicly displayed. Binoo John explained that the flat was
owned by a City financier – a 'corporate finance man', he called
him – who, from the relative dereliction of the property and
anonymity of the surroundings, was not altogether a success.
Either that or he owned the entire block. There was, from the
beginning, something about the area I liked, something sug-
gestive of more than the usual inner-city grime and lost lives.
The pubs, the multi-purpose stores, the offices and shops, the
church, the venerable hospital: all this must have meant something once, must have seemed like the threads holding
together the larger canvas of community life in a huge, devour-
ing city. I doubted if it was like that nowadays. Too many
people were, like me, passing through; no one was rooted.

Looking round the flat, I found it hard to believe that there
could be anything smaller in the block. Room one: bedroom/
sitting room, furnished with a sofa that folded into a narrow

double bed, a wardrobe, a small TV and video, a polished teak dining table and four hard chairs. Room two: a small fitted kitchen, which had the usual kettle, bread board, cutlery, sharp and serrated-edged knives, pots and pans, toaster, gas cooker with an eye-line grill and small washing machine. Room three: bathroom with an enamel bath but predictably no shower. This being England, there was, naturally, no air-conditioning unit.

'How many?' Binoo John said.

I followed him through into the cramped kitchen, where I heard him muttering to himself about the rent.

'How many?' he said again.

I had no idea what he was talking about.

'How many tea bags?'

'Oh, one of course,' I said, surprised that there should be tea bags in an empty flat.

'Of course?'

'Well, isn't one normal?'

'No, no. I have two in the afternoon, one in evening, but three in my first morning cup.' He looked up. 'Milk?'

I nodded.

'You know the writer Anthony Burgess?' he said.

'*A Clockwork Orange*?'

'Yes, that and many other good books besides. I find them in the library sometimes. Most recently, *Mouthful of Air* – very witty study of origins of language acquisition. I especially like his books set in Malaya. D'you know them?' He peered at me expectantly, awaiting my answer, then continued. 'Anyway, I read that Anthony Burgess started each morning with cup of tea made from five bags. *Five*.' He raised his plump hand as if in celebration. 'With the tea he smoked large cigar, taking all smoke down. Did same thing every morning, like a ritual. Can you imagine!' He once again readjusted the knot of his tie, smoothed his recalcitrant fringe with a neat lick of spittle across three fingers. 'Are you a smoker?'

'I stopped,' I said.

'Very good. I used to smoke far too many cigarettes,

sometimes two, three packs a day. Began getting heart palpi-tations – these little butterfly flutters in the chest. One day, doctor said to me, "Binoo K. John, you're going to have to stop smoking if you want to make old bones." Put like that, I panicked. I thought, Yes, I want to make old bones.'

He expertly flipped my single tea bag on to a spoon, tossing it into the sink; he did the same with his several tea bags. He passed me a chipped mug darkened by tannin stains. I allowed the tea to cool. We were sitting on the sofa now, side by side, like nervous lovers. He asked what had brought me to London, and I told him about my two-month placement, beginning in six weeks or so, at a City law firm.

'Which one?'

'Clifford Chance. D'you know them?'

'Heard of them, very famous firm.'

'I used to live over here, you know,' I said, changing the subject. 'When I was younger.'

'In England?'

'Yeah.'

'How long ago?'

'More than a decade ago, actually.'

'You must see changes.'

'I only arrived a few days ago. On first impressions, every-thing seems, well, more modernized, high-tech, like I'm still in North America. They've even got Starbucks here.'

'What's Starbucks?'

'A pretty good coffee chain.'

'I don't drink coffee myself, makes my heart race, and we don't want any of that. Old bones, Binoo, old bones.'

I winced as I sipped the tea.

'It's OK?' he asked.

'Sure, it's fine.'

We relaxed into conversation. He told me more about him-self: that he was from Calcutta but had won a place as a mature student in his mid-twenties at Keele University. He decided not to return to India when his younger brother also followed him to England. 'My brother married a Welsh girl,' he said. 'They're living in Swansea now, where he works for DVLC.'

'What's that?' I said.

'DVLC, it's the vehicle centre, where ownership of all the cars on the road is registered.'

We talked about Canada on the way back to his office, the reasons for our emigration, and he seemed genuinely fascinated. 'Have you ever thought about trying to trace people who knew your father, who worked with him?' he said.

I explained that my mother had offered me no such encouragement, so committed had she been to starting all over again in Toronto, to starting without him. In fact, only recently had she begun talking about him again, once we'd accepted her decision to remarry. 'She worked so hard to let him go,' I told Binoo John. 'I guess it's too painful for her. Anyway, she's happily married again now.'

'It's a very strange story,' he said, opening the door of his sun-stilled office.

Specks of dust were illuminated by thin light streaming through the shutters. As Binoo John prepared the papers on his desk, he began telling me about a fellow mature student, a Greek-Hungarian he'd known at Keele. This guy's father, like mine, had disappeared when he was a boy. The family were then living in Budapest, having escaped from Greece, and there were rumours that the father had been murdered by the Greek secret police.

'They'd pursued him to Hungary. My friend's father was communist, member of underground organizations. He'd fled from Greece following nationalist coup. He was very involved in dissident politics, with revolutionary groups. He kept dangerous company. My friend was obsessed with it all.'

'Some people think I'm obsessed with what happened to my father, too,' I said. 'Well, maybe I am obsessed with it. And when my brother tells me to stop fretting, I shrug now. I don't give a damn what he says.'

9

But Binoo John didn't appear to be listening. Instead he smiled and wiped his forehead once again, before draping the handkerchief across his legs. 'So what's it to be? Are you going to take it?'

A short period of perfunctory wrangling followed before we agreed a monthly rent of £750. I was to move in at the end of the week. Although I didn't start work for a while, I wasn't badly off. I had more than enough money to cover the rent – money I'd saved in my years working during and after law school, as well as what I'd been given by Mum and my step-father, Al, which they'd secreted into an envelope for me and left on my pillow the night before my departure to England. I'd found the envelope when I'd gone up to bed, a little alcohol-clumsy, after the garden party held on that last night in Rosedale, the shadows from the willow tree stretching across the still waters of the swimming pool, the smell of burning coals and barbecued meat in the air, merging with voices, light laughter, the hilarious chatter of a fountain. And somewhere from a nearby house came the sound of a baby crying.

Leaving Binoo John's office, I said to him, 'If you were in my position, Mr John, if you maybe wanted to track down your missing father's old associates, how would you begin?'

He ran his fingers through his hair, picked at his goatee, plucking several silvery threads from it which he inspected intently, like an ape plucking fleas from her baby's scalp. 'I'm sure there's somewhere in London – St Catherine's House, I think – where you can look up death certificates, or Companies House for business records. Or what about the old police files? You never know what they might turn up.' He again raised his hand – as a form of farewell. 'Until next time,' he said.

From the office, on a whim, I took the tube straight up to Belsize Park, where my father used to have his London flat. He'd lived at 6 Belsize Avenue, on the third floor of a white-painted Victorian mansion block. I wandered down from the station, feeling a bit like an amnesiac returning to a place he'd once called home, and sat on a wall outside the block. His old flat was in provocative darkness. Sitting there, I could visualize every detail of how it had once looked to me, and I recalled the bright shock of all its many disappointments.

A couple of people came in and out of the building. I went over to inspect the names on the intercom, intensely curious as to who was living at number six. No name was listed there. Then, as I turned away from the door, I almost collided with a young woman returning to the block. I smiled at her but she responded with a look of haughty boredom, her white-as-if-bleached teeth striking in the pale light of dusk. She had straight shoulder-length blonde hair and smelt faintly of perfume and cigarettes. She exuded a kind of distant metropolitan cool, and you could see that she was relaxed in the city, at home here – and yet how wrapped in defensive armour she was, too. She pushed past me, letting herself in. Through the frosted glass of the door I watched her walking up the stairs and I just knew, instinctively, where she was heading, knew that she lived in my father's flat, even before the lights came on upstairs in his old front room, which overlooked the street, even before I saw her shape silhouetted against the glass. I watched as she drew the curtains.

At the bottom of the road I turned to look back, and doing so I felt as though my father were watching me through the distorting lens of all those lost years; and it was as though, if I dwelt long enough outside his place, I might see him rise again from his chair and cross the room to the window, from where he would look down at me sat on the wall below. He would raise his arm in a formal gesture of recognition and then turn again, a restless, inscrutable figure withdrawing into the darkness of his flat, withdrawing into the past.

From there I took the tube to Tottenham Court Road and headed down to Trafalgar Square, and then, after asking someone the way, I went west to Piccadilly Circus. I scampered across the road and stood on a traffic island, leaning against the famous statue of Eros, which I'd only ever seen in photographs and movies, cars, taxis and buses hurtling scarifyingly around me. I stared up at the neon dazzle of the billboards, at the glare of lights. I wanted to drench myself in the atmosphere, to breathe in the invigorating air of change and renewal, to preserve that moment before my experience of London and of England inevitably became devoured by habitualness and familiarity.

Time stand still, I whispered to myself, time stand still now.

Two men must have heard what I said, despite my lowered voice, for they regarded me with a kind of pity and then deliberately barged into me, jostling me aggressively. I staggered back a few paces before regaining my balance. When I looked for them again they'd been absorbed by the crowds, and there was only a red wash of neon light on the pavement. Before my accident, when I was fitter and still playing rugby, I would have gone after them, fancied my chances. Now all I did was feel for my wallet in my back pocket. It was gone, and with it some cash and my credit cards. Welcome to London.

On the way back to the YMCA I called an emergency number to put a stop on my credit cards. I'd left my passport, driving licence, Canadian ID and some traveller's cheques in the room.

It was past eleven by the time I arrived back at King's Cross and the pubs were emptying. I didn't feel much like returning to the hostel after what had happened, so I began aimlessly circling the station, intrigued by the gangs – the blacks, Asians, the shifty hard-faced whites – clustered around it. There was an obvious police presence on the streets, and the foot patrols monitored you as you walked. I hung around for about half an hour or so before returning to the hostel, from where I phoned home. Mum was out and I spoke to Al. Our conversation was as perfunctory as ever: yes, I had found somewhere to live; no, I hadn't visited my employers in the City; no, I hadn't contacted my uncle David in Manchester but would do so soon; yes, I would call Mum regularly; no, I wasn't fretting about the accident; yes, I knew how she worried about me. The money ran out before I could say goodbye. That was it. Tomorrow I'd invest in a mobile – which I did.

I climbed the hard stone steps of the YMCA to the fourth floor. Turning into the strip-lit, bare-walled corridor, I heard music from the adjacent bedroom. I paused outside the door, where I heard a giggly girl's voice and laughter; and I was tempted to knock, wanting so much to be part of what was happening in there. I lingered for a while outside, willing the door to open – but it did not. So I slipped into the dispiriting emptiness of my own room, with its single bed, solitary wardrobe and basin in one corner, its hard carpetless floor. I tossed my linen jacket on to the bedspread, went over to the window and opened the curtains in an aggressive sweep – light spilling into the room from the street. Dust had settled on the window-ledge through which I swept my hand, tracing feathery patterns with tensed fingers. I wrote the word 'lost', and another word I don't wish to recall. Then I stared out at the traffic below and wondered why I'd returned for a job I didn't want, to a city I didn't know, in search of a life I'd never lived.

The lights in the high-rise block opposite shone dimly. The air was fragrant and petrol-scented, and I felt the weight of the low ceiling on me. There was nothing for me here: London wasn't my patch, never had been. I was a country boy. I knew no one in the city, had no contacts. I wondered if I could even properly call myself English any more, despite clinging stubbornly to my accent, to my artificial sense of self.

Outside the city moved: sirens and engines, the lights from traffic brushing the curtains. I closed my eyes and dreamt; later, the small-hours hush was interrupted by the hiss of a passing car and by whispered female voices from the adjacent room. I stumbled over to the basin, where I'd submerged a couple of cans of lager. I drank a can of the now-warmish beer, then another. The hours passed more easily after that, except that I couldn't stop thinking about the girl I'd seen earlier in Belsize Park. I pictured her alone in my father's old bedroom, turning restlessly under thin sheets, her tanned skin loosely covered by a T-shirt that belonged to . . . I fell asleep before I ever found out.

In the morning my small room filled oppressively with sunlight but I lay there in a kind of lethargy, and there was also that old familiar sense of perplexity creeping up on me. I stayed in bed beyond noon that day, and the next day and the one after that, just as I had on returning home, last Christmas, to Rosedale, where Mum and Al had lived together in affluent seclusion for more than a year. I'd returned home after being injured in a road accident. Two of my closest friends, Amy and Tom, both young lawyers from Ontario, had been killed. We three were on a short break in the States, visiting another friend from law school in Boston. We were hanging out at an all-day party in the Italian quarter of the North End. I'd had a couple of drinks and snorted some coke; and then I got it into my head that we must drive out to Concord, Mass., and go down to Walden Pond, where Henry David Thoreau had lived in his remote cottage in the woods.

Amy and I loved his book *Walden*, and his desire to live intensely, far away from the crowd. 'I look upon England today,' he wrote in 1854, 'as an old gentleman who is traveling with a great deal of baggage . . . which he has not the courage to burn.' The raw truth of that observation, read from my Canadian exile, electrified me; and how I longed, unlike Thoreau's England, to shed my own baggage which I'd never had the courage to burn.

Of course, it was a crazy idea to go out to Walden Pond, but at the time it had a kind of rough beauty. It wasn't hard to talk Amy and Tom into coming with me. They were pretty pissed. On the way out to Concord we collided with a truck. The police said that the driver had fallen asleep and drifted across to our side, but my reflexes weren't sharp enough. I could have avoided it. We smashed off the road and into a tree, an old doughty oak. I can still hear the hiss of the busted engine, and see the crumpled metal of the bonnet, and the deadening lack of human movement around me. My memories now of the time before the accident are of a vanished world, one through which I moved freely and with purpose. It's all long gone.

I was left in bad shape: a collapsed lung (since inflated), ruptured spleen (since removed), broken left wrist (sporadically aching), torn knee ligaments (healed). As the driver, I was burdened with no blame, neither by the parents of my dead friends nor by the police. I'd had a few drinks – but not illegally so; I'd been speeding – but only just; I'd lost concentration – but then we all do that. I'd been cleared, not killed, but that was really the problem. It was then, once out of hospital, that I returned to Rosedale, abandoning the career in the law that had lucratively awaited me at the firm where I'd worked well through two previous summer vacations.

Those initial months of recuperation – as I lay listlessly around the house, curled up on various beds and sofas like an aged cat – were made strange by Mum's obvious delight at her forthcoming wedding. A few months earlier, she'd finally had my father declared legally dead, freeing herself, psychologically and administratively, to marry Al. Outside the window, the snow was thickly packed beneath startlingly clear blue skies; inside my mother's excitement – like an eloping teenager – made me feel old. Being back in Rosedale was like the end of the line. At the age of twenty-five, I felt the best was already behind me. The doors had closed.

I left the hostel just in time to prevent myself from withering completely into aimlessness.

My first week in Nassau Street was mostly a time of lonely wandering, of adapting to the rhythms of a new city, a new life. As the fume-choked roads were becalmed by a heatwave that was to linger even into October, I began exploring the tangle of streets around my flat, buoyed up by a powerful sense of expectation. What I loved most, at first, were the warm, breathless afternoons when the West End crowds caged me in the swagger of their embrace and hurried me along to nowhere. After the inertia of Toronto, finding myself at liberty in London felt like walking from darkness into a lighted room.

I had breakfast every morning at a little coffee bar I found in Soho. It was called Princes Cappuccino and was an intimate jewel of a place situated off Soho Square, a short walk from my flat. Princes (the apostrophe had long since disappeared, perhaps had never been there at all) was owned by two Sicilian brothers in their early thirties, Lilo and Roberto, both of whom wore white aprons over their T-shirts and shorts. I had a bantering acquaintanceship with Lilo, who never seemed to remember my name. 'Mate' was the best he ever called me. As for Rob, well, he was tall, dark-skinned, perhaps morose. The café had space enough only for a cold-drinks machine and seven tables pushed up against a mirrored wall; sometimes I shared one of these with other regular breakfasters, who nodded whenever they saw me. All this I enjoyed; all this made me feel more like a local, like a Londoner.

That first week I also spent an afternoon wandering through the wondrous green spaces of the capital's parks and an evening watching a blues band in a cramped basement club rancid with cigarette smoke. I took everything in; nothing escaped my furtive notice. My wanderings brought me briefly into contact with other young transients like myself, other backpacking travellers – Americans, Australians, Canucks, Kiwis and white South Africans – a confederacy of English speakers, but never with the English themselves.

But I soon grew tired of the sluggish heat of mid-afternoon, of the tug of tourists, becoming attached instead to the cooler shades of early evening, once most of the offices had shut down and the commuters had returned home. At such moments the West End seemed to catch its breath, suspended as it was between departure and arrival, between the day and night crowds. And it was at night that I most craved contact with others, that my thoughts seemed to rattle like coins in the empty tin of my head; and it was at night that I would wander through the big hotels – the Meridian on Piccadilly, the Dorchester and the Grosvenor on Park Lane. I relished the overlit anonymity of these places, with their interchangeable multinational staff who smiled 'hello' as you passed them and the discreet money-glamour – the feeling that you could be anywhere in the affluent world as you walked on soft carpets along empty air-conditioned corridors, past conference rooms and offices, past crowded dining rooms from which emanated expensive laughter. I liked checking out the gym and steam rooms, the pool-side entertainment, while all the time imagining that I, too, was one of the disappeared and could now be anyone I wanted to be – an actor, banker, diplomat, private detective or spy.

Sometimes, in spare moments that week, I took the Northern Line up to Belsize Park and wandered in the long late-summer sunshine down to where my father used to live. Why I kept returning, what I hoped to find, I didn't know; but perhaps if I hung around long enough the woman who now lived in his flat might invite me to see inside the place: 'Hey, big boy, I've seen you around. Fancy a drink?' Who was I kidding?

Then I'd always return underground again, travelling through stations I'd never heard of, along routes with which in time I hoped to become more familiar, through tunnels that had once been so much part of my father's and my grandfather's London – and would become part of mine, too.

I: November 1983

There are three of them in the room and they are arguing. A shipment of videos from Scandinavia has disappeared. Oliver King, who was to have collected the videos from the docks at Felixstowe, claims they were either never on the boat or have been confiscated en route. 'It sometimes happens,' he says. Nicholas Dundee doesn't believe him. Anthony Winter doesn't believe him either, although his disbelief is part of the game.

Oliver King, who is in his early forties, is divorced and lives alone in a small bungalow in the village of Thorpeness, Suffolk. He and Anthony met through the classified pages of a soft-porn contact mag. Oliver is a small-time porn dealer, having once run a sex shop in the Portman Road area of Ipswich, and Anthony, with his portfolio of interests, is confident that as more and more titles become available for the first time on video and more and more homes become equipped with the necessary hardware, there is real money to be made from the VHS analogue video-porn boom. He's convinced Nicholas Dundee of this, too, and together, working through Oliver King, they have invested in a huge shipment of hardcore material from Hamburg, Copenhagen and Malmö. Except that the order was never placed; Dundee is the victim of a sting.

Earlier Dundee and Anthony Winter had set off for Suffolk in an attempt to find out exactly what had gone wrong. They drove across the flat, monotonous, loamy landscape of the eastern counties. A low mist was settling in a blanket as Anthony looked out at the stone pines, oak and ash trees, at the odd pillbox in a field, a surreal reminder of a conflict that never quite reached English shores.

On arrival in Aldeburgh, a mile from Thorpeness, they stop for a drink, sitting at a wooden bench outside a pub which overlooks the North Sea. It is cold and there is no one else around. The light is fading and the beach is bathed in a hazy glow of artificial light. They can hear the weary rasp of the retreating waves. A wind is blowing from the east and they are aware of the rattle of the rigging of the fishing boats hauled up on the beach, their keels and hulls vigorously reinforced against the constant battering of the waves. Further along the coastline, there is the indeterminate shape of the Sizewell power station.

They drive along the beachside road to Thorpeness, a curious toy town of turreted houses, stilted follies, converted churches and an ornamental lake ... a seaside village reinvented as a kitsch theme park. Oliver's bungalow is at the bottom of a rutted dirt track. They drive down it, passing a disused water tower which has been converted into a holiday home called the House in the Clouds. They pass a windmill and further on, where the track widens, there is the entrance to a golf and country club. They pull up outside Oliver's bungalow, parking on the drive – in truth no more than a rough patch of stony soil. Anthony Winter presses the bell and a tall, angular figure moves behind drawn curtains.

Opening the door, Oliver peers out through spectacles held together at one end with black tape. He's a tall, spidery man, with short dark hair and wary eyes. He's dressed in a shirt buttoned to the neck, black jeans and white sneakers. He's unshaven and seems oddly fatigued. He leads them through into the garage.

There are three of them in the garage and they are arguing. Dundee is insulting Oliver, swearing at him, accusing him of lying. Dundee demands to know what's gone wrong. How? Why? He seems almost deranged by rage, as Anthony had guessed he would be. Oliver King remains calm, as Anthony hoped he would. He holds to the agreed story: that he himself has been duped, cheated; that the boat never came in. He tells Dundee that he's lost money, too, that they all have, but that they can quickly earn it back. Dundee isn't convinced. He doesn't believe Oliver's account. Nor does Anthony, as he and Oliver have pre-arranged. Anthony Winter also becomes threatening and agitated, and so Oliver spits at him, as pre-arranged.

Then Dundee surprises them both by pulling out a knife they never knew he carried. He presses the button of the flick. Oliver glances at Anthony when the blade catches the light, his eyes blank and uncomprehending like a frightened animal's, and then at Dundee, as if he still doesn't understand. Then he tries to kick the knife out of Dundee's hand to pre-empt any attack. But Dundee moves first, and fastest. He moves danger-ously. And the level of his dangerousness? Well, that was something on which Anthony Winter hadn't been prepared to wager.

Oliver lunges, flaps, then falls. One stab through the ribs and he falls. He falls heavily on the hard concrete of the oil-stained garage. Dundee seems to be in a frenzy now, stamping on the prostrate figure. He stamps on Oliver's face and chest, his wrists and shins. He drives his boots into his balls, head and stomach. Anthony Winter watches all this, awed, appalled, but above all motionless. He makes no attempt to intervene.

When it's over, Dundee staggers back against a wall, bat-tered by an applause that only he can hear. There's sweat on his face; he keeps wiping his hands on his trousers, as if they're wet. Neither speaks, and there is no sound from the fallen man. They're on the hard, metallic edge of silence – and there's noth-ing to show for weeks of meticulous planning and apparently smooth execution. Except a dead man.

Oliver's lips are grotesquely swollen. Blood leaks from his crushed nose. His eyes are unrecognizable. Anthony Winter walks over to him, crouches. He wipes some of the blood from his face. More flows into the grey spaces left behind. He knows he's betrayed Oliver, and these are the ashes of Oliver's life at his feet, to be raked over: the secrets he kept, the deals he did, the rural isolation he nurtured. 'He's not breath-ing,' he says.

Two days earlier, Saturday, Oliver had met Anthony Winter in London. They'd watched a few videos together – the kind of stuff that Anthony had tried selling. Anthony, in particular, didn't think much of *Teenage Lesbians*, or of *Piss Artists*, two best-selling titles. But he was delighted they'd made £10,000 each from Dundee's gullibility and eagerness to exploit the porn market; and they still had more videos to sell, with the market proliferating as it already was into niche preferences.

Dundee, meanwhile, is still leaning against the wall in the garage, gulping air. His shoes are splattered with white paint – a pot of emulsion has been unsettled and is leaking thickly across the floor.

'He's not breathing,' Anthony Winter says again.

Dundee approaches. He takes Oliver's arm. 'His pulse is very faint,' he says.

He rests his hands on Oliver's chest, pumping rhythmically. He pauses to blow into the open mouth, flooding his lungs. 'There's so much fucking blood, it's disgusting. We've got to stop him swallowing it.'

Anthony Winter cradles Oliver's head in his hands. 'Come on, Ollie, stop fucking us about,' he says, and adds, 'We'd better call an ambulance.' Everything has gone wrong, he thinks. It wasn't meant to happen like this.

Dundee looks up. 'What are you fucking going on about? How would we explain it?'

'We could call the ambulance and then clear off. Just go.'

Dundee slaps Anthony's face and an immediate change occurs in him as he calms, becomes more rational. 'We've got to do something for him,' he says, lowering his voice.

'It's too late,' Dundee says. 'Where were you when he needed help? Why didn't you try to do something to stop me? You could have fucking done something. You could have done . . . ' Then he says, 'It's too late. Feel his pulse.'

But then Oliver appears to stir. The death rattle?

'Look,' Anthony says, thinking he would exchange all the

money he will ever earn for that one man's life. 'Look at him – look at his lips. Look there.'

Dundee turns, and perhaps he, too, sees the near-imperceptible flutter of Oliver's lips. Whatever, he removes a packet of cigarettes from his pocket. He uses his unsteady left hand as a shield against the draught. He strikes a match. His nails are bitten and his right index finger is bent and swollen, as if once broken. Light flares in the gloom.

Outside the garage, litter and rotten leaves are being scattered by the wind. Dundee removes the cigarette from his mouth, runs fingers across Oliver's cheeks. He places the cigarette between startled lips; it hangs limply. For a moment it seems as though it will drop into the pool of blood gathered in the hollow of his throat. Then Oliver appears to pinch his lips together and drags on the cigarette; at least, the burning tip seems momentarily to glow.

Dundee removes the cigarette. 'Did you see that?' he says. 'He took a drag. The old fucker took a drag. Did you see it?' He rocks back on the soles of his paint-stained loafers, begins to laugh, gently at first but then with increasing energy. His face is distorted by his greedy laughter, which merges with the trailing cigarette smoke and with Anthony Winter's own slow, reluctant laughter.

What neither man hears, not far away, is the blowing of the bitter sea wind.

Pseudocide

I went to an office of Companies House in Bloomsbury Street, near the British Museum. I was shown to a corner desk by a short, prematurely grey Welshman, whose untidy whorl of hair sat uneasily on his head like a barrister's wig. He was probably in his early thirties, but he moved like a much older man, unsteadily, as if the soles of his feet were painful. I liked the earnest hush of his voice, though, and the patience and expertise with which he led me around the computerized files.

At the time of my father's disappearance there was much speculation in the local press about his supposed business difficulties, the false starts he'd made, the failed ventures and entrepreneurial stumbles. There was the story, popular among my classmates back then, that he'd owed money to a local gang leader and been murdered by a hit man, his body buried on Brownsea, the private island in the middle of Poole Harbour. A pal and I even rowed out there once in a hired boat, and began searching among the bushes and trees for his unmarked grave; but we became uneasy when we stumbled on a sign pinned to a tree: 'Trespassers Will Be Prosecuted'. As we rowed back to shore, I heard my head-master speaking the Lord's Prayer inside my head. That spooked me.

There were, inevitably, the false sightings of Pa, the spoofs, pranks and wheezes. I recall on more than one occasion different men – 'fantasists', my mother called them – walked into police stations in the Poole and Bournemouth areas, in the immediate aftermath of his disappearance, when he was still news, the talk of our town, and claimed to be him. They actually claimed to be my father. Even we saw the comedy in such madness. 'What drives them?' Mum asked us. 'What makes them claim to be someone else?'

I keyed my father's name into the computer. Anthony Winter. I wasn't quite sure how he had made his money. He always seemed to have plenty back then, to be scooping handfuls of loose change from deep pockets (his 'snow', he called it) to pay for our crisps and sweets and drinks and games. I never felt materially deprived as a child. I had everything I wanted, things my friends never had – such as a BMX, a racer and a fabulous stag-horn bike. I had the best Adidas Mamba trainers, Lonsdale track suits, my own bedroom, television and stereo system, six pairs of different-coloured stay-pressed trousers. I had two Harrington jackets, a leather jacket, a navy-blue blazer, Ben Sherman buttoned-down-collar shirts, a new pair of shoes every six months. My sister had her own horse, her ears pierced on her tenth birthday, despite Mum's protests, and six years later, as a special treat, she'd had the same ears pinned back as well (she must have tired of my brother and I calling her 'Dumbo'). My brother, a sports fan, had mountaineering and tennis lessons, a season ticket to watch Southampton play football at the Dell, kangaroo-skin sports boots and a Gunn & Moore cricket bat, as used by Derek Randall. Because Pa was seldom around to take him to football, he also bought a season ticket for Dan's best pal. As a family we had regular summer holidays in Spain, Greece, Italy, Yugoslavia, Tunisia, Florida and the south of France; we had a summer (and a tree) house in the garden of our whitewashed house in the hills above Studland Bay. I repeat, we had everything we wanted.

There were eight Anthony Winters listed in the register of directors, living as far apart as Oban and Shrewsbury. I wrote down each of their names and addresses before I realized that the listings covered only the period *since* 1986. I asked the Welshman about this.

'Which period are you particularly interested in, sir?'

I told him.

'We don't have computerized records for the seventies and early eighties. You'll have to look on fiche.'

'I'll be able to check, though, by individual names on fiche?'

'No, I'm afraid it's a manual system, catalogued by company name. You can only cross-reference on computer.'

I sighed elaborately.

'If you have the names or the numbers of the companies you're looking for?'

'The numbers?' I said.

'Every company has an individual number, like a personal National Insurance number. The name of a company may change but the number stays the same.'

I was ashamed to concede that I knew none of the names of my father's various enterprises and certainly not their numbers. All I knew was that he once described himself to me as an 'entrepreneur', long before such people were among the commanding presences of the modern scene. I relished repeating, when friends asked about my father, that he was an entrepreneur, even though I invariably stumbled over or mispronounced the word – the Frenchified flourish of it. Then I'd wait for their response, for the perplexity to show on their faces . . . because their fathers were doctors and lawyers, bank managers, accountants and engineers. Because they didn't understand. Because they were *conventional*.

So what, seriously, did my father do? At random, he was involved in an operation that sold fitted kitchens and later double-glazing; and a cleaning company that had the contract to clean Sainsbury's in Dorset and parts of Hampshire, as well as numerous struggling independent supermarket chains. I accompanied him and his staff once or twice on their early-morning rounds, washing and buffing the aisles and checkouts, sweeping the corridors and stairs, mopping out the deli, the kitchen, cleaning the windows.

My father also helped set up *The Classified*, an advertising free sheet delivered direct to people's homes. Like most of his later ventures, his involvement in the paper didn't last long.

And I could never understand why there was no news in *The Classified*, why its pages offered nothing except low-grade adverts and pages and pages of estate agents' blurred photographs of properties for sale. That, Mum said, was the point. I didn't quite get it.

For a period, too, he'd even bought and sold properties himself, in and around Poole, renovating them with his then partner, Bert Owen, one of his few friends we knew well enough to attach the epithet 'Uncle' to his name. My father, though, wasn't long in the property game. One afternoon he arrived home unusually early. Uncle Bert, he said, had suffered a heart attack that very morning, while working on their latest property – my father had returned from the hardware store to find him lying at the foot of a ladder, the stiff fingers of his right hand curled proprietorially around a paintbrush. I'd never seen my father so prostrate with grief as when he told us about poor old Bert. It was not long after Uncle Bert's death that he began spending more time alone in London – 'seeking out new opportunities', my mother euphemized it.

I became aware of a door closing behind me. I peered into the screen, at the glow of meaningless names; and as I did so an image of a lost Sunday in October 1983 came back to me slowly, like someone returning to full consciousness after a trauma. My father had arrived home that Sunday morning unannounced from London, on what was expected to have been one of his weekends 'away'. I can't exaggerate my delight when I rushed downstairs to find him at the kitchen table, drinking a cup of coffee, his dark hair more unruly than ever. Mum looked on from the breakfast room as he cuddled me, challenging me to 'shake hands', a little reunion ritual we always enjoyed.

'Go on, Josh, harder,' he said, but I couldn't break the thick dead hold of his grip. 'The day you beat me, boy, I'm finished.'

'You'll never be finished, Pa, never, not with me around to protect you,' I said.

'You're right about that. There's life in me yet,' he said,

26

crumpling my hand again painlessly for good measure. He may have looked tired and unshaven, as if he'd missed a night's sleep, but his voice was full of happiness – and he was strong.

After breakfast he suggested we visited the Isle of Wight for the day. Since Dan was due to play football and Rachel had ballet rehearsals, he asked if I wanted to bring a friend. I made several calls to boys in my class, none of whom was free. But I didn't mind going along alone with my parents; unlike most of my mates at school, I wasn't ashamed to be seen out with them, perhaps because I so rarely saw them together. That trip out to the Isle of Wight! The short journey across the choppy surf, the unusually warm October sunshine, the silent rust-coloured trees, the countryside scorched into a red-brown haze, the gritty sand between my toes, the shy delight on Pa's face when Mum jumped in alongside him in the front of the car. These images repeated themselves, like a series of slow-motion replays, as I worked my way through the files.

It was little more than a month after the trip out to the Isle of Wight that my father disappeared. In the weeks that followed I recall receiving a short typed note from Mrs Owen, Uncle Bert's wife, expressing her regret at what had happened. She mentioned how 'strange' – yes, strange, that was her word – she'd felt when her husband had died, leaving her alone with her son. About six months later, she wrote again to say that her son was progressing well at his new school and asked if I would like to meet him. I briefly considered responding to her invitation but there was too much happening in our lives at the time and Mrs Owen seemed an irrelevance, an inconsequential memo relegated to the bottom of a pile. I never wrote back.

Searching on the microfiche at Companies House, I was unable to find any record of Anthony Winter's activities; not even *The Classified* was registered as a company.

'Perhaps it was registered under a different name, as part of a larger publishing company?' the Welshman said. 'Does it still exist?'

'It folded before we moved abroad – years ago.'

'Pity. Since 1991, all directors of "live" companies are listed, and pre-1991 directors are asterisked, to mark the date at which they became directors.'

'Is everyone legally obliged to register their companies?'

'No. But the vast majority do to protect themselves, because if your company collapses then the creditors and shareholders won't have a claim on your personal assets.'

What were Pa's assets? The house in Poole? No – we were swiftly forced out of that when Mum calamitously discovered that, even in the event of his having been declared dead (the insurance companies were determined that his absence should be treated as suicide), he was insufficiently covered through his endowment mortgage to meet the entire debt on the house. The flat in London? Rented, as it turned out. His smart car? Mechanically flawed, alas. Pensions, tax-free saving schemes, shares? All cashed in during the middle to late 1970s. And yet if he was buried under a landslide of trouble, he never let it show. If everything in his life was spinning out of control, becoming increasingly yellowed and tatty – like an old newspaper – if there were dense, labyrinthine financial problems, multiple overdrafts, credit debts, defaulted mortgage payments, he never let on.

Mum sometimes hinted that he didn't have as much money as he'd led us to believe, that he didn't even have what she'd thought he had. He didn't, for a start, have a pension, or sufficient life cover to pay off the outstanding mortgage debt. He was declared permanently missing, not dead, and there was nothing Mum, in her half-widowhood, could claim on insurance while he was presumed to be alive, even if there wasn't anything to claim. But which of us, at the time, would have been prepared to let him die, let him float freely away like a buoy cut from its moorings?

It was only much later, once we were settled in Toronto, that Mum began speaking of how he'd broken promises, must have had enemies.

'So we're better off without him, is that what you're trying to say?' I asked her once.

She quickly said no, but the guilty flicker in her eyes said – I knew – yes.

She was a strong woman, my mother, resolute in her independence and determination to bring us up without him, without the participation of any man. That's why she wanted to return to Canada, I think, to make a clean break of it, to demonstrate she could cope alone. She could, she could. And I admired the way she made a go of things in Toronto, although I was often hurt by the way she would sometimes reveal wounding things about Pa – about his 'recklessness', his 'irresponsibility' – as if she wished to diminish him in some way, to *humble* him.

In the spring of 1984, we moved out of our large house in the dusty lanes above Studland Bay and into a thin-walled annexe, one of three flats in a converted modern town house, which at least offered decent views over Poole Harbour. We had no garden, just a concrete yard we shared with another family. So followed another anxious year, played out against the background of distracted waiting . . . waiting . . . waiting for something: a chance sighting, a body being washed up on the beach, a suicide letter, a ransom note, a postcard from Hawaii. Anything to break the monotony and drag of dead days, the feelings of emptiness. But no – nothing happened, repeatedly.

I felt despondent that afternoon as I left Companies House: nothing seemed to be happening all over again. I bought a cup of coffee from an Italian café and sat opposite the British Museum, at a pavement table. The air was thick with fumes and dust and even the trees seemed to be perspiring. Even late on in the afternoon of that eerie summer the sun was hard, heartless. People broke for the shade as if dodging bullets. Sitting there, it was difficult not to accept that Mum might have been right all along: that Pa was demanding, deceitful and brash, that he'd broken promises, must have had enemies.

But was he entirely worthless? There was certainly an

element of self-savouring showmanship about him. He claimed to have influential friends – actors, musicians, TV stars, politicians, sportsmen, jet-setters – anyone influential, anyone on the move. 'You've got to cut a clean path to the top people as quickly as you can, then you've got a chance,' he once said. There was confidence in this claim, a chin-jutting defiance: doubt me if you dare. He was an accomplished, fluent talker – at times, a charged, tyrannical monologist and a talented mimic. Muhammad Ali, Jimmy Cagney, Humphrey Bogart, Clint Eastwood, David Bowie, Meatloaf, the men from ABBA, Prince Charles – he could make us laugh with his slightly deranged impressions of all these and more.

My sister, brother and I loved it when he read to us of an evening, even if his thoughts sometimes seemed to be gloomily elsewhere as he paused to look at his watch, poured himself another dry martini, made or took phone calls, or simply stared as if into a void. On those 'book nights', as we called them, the three of us would gather in Rachel's room to listen to him as he sat at the end of the bed, reading from *The Hobbit* and *The Lord of the Rings* (never finished). He had a different voice for every character. Such fun!

The city was shutting down and groups of tourists were leaving the British Museum. Watching them hurry across the road, I returned to that first weekend (his last weekend) we spent together at his flat in Belsize Park. As events stand, I'm happy to believe I was the last member of our family ever to walk with Anthony Winter, talk to him, joke with him – although Mum probably had the last glimpse of him, in the rear-view mirror of our car, as she pulled away from Belsize Park, having driven up from Dorset to collect me at the end of my long weekend adventure.

That damp afternoon I remember him pulling up outside the British Museum in his maroon Jag XJ6. I waited there for him, leaning against rusted railings beneath a tatty umbrella, after a slow afternoon on a school trip to the museum. I saw him first: the black glitter of his stare, the rough shadow of his late-afternoon stubble, the hair an untidy mass of lightly receding dark curls, the white shirt worn, as ever, open-necked and casual. Yet there was something distant in his expression that was hard to account for, a kind of lostness; but he cheered up when he saw me, dressed as I was in my absurdly uncomfortable uniform.

The passenger door opened and I climbed in. The air inside the car was hot, cigarettey; it made my eyes smart. He leaned over to kiss me and I relished the familiar, reassuring smell of him, the unmistakable scent of his Aramis aftershave.

'How was it today?' he asked, beating an impatient rhythm on the dash with his left hand, the band of his wedding ring a percussive accompaniment to the Stylistics tape which seemed always to be playing in his car.

I didn't – couldn't – answer. He asked again about the exhibition. I mumbled something about how my eyes watered whenever I looked at the glass-encased mummies. In truth, I was so overawed at finding myself alone with him that my replies to his questions hung, unspoken, in the sickly air. I think my discomfort must have amused him; he kept chuckling to himself and I kept noticing the shadows of his several fillings, like small dark currants. Then he mentioned my birthday. 'You're thirteen tomorrow, son, don't forget. What shall we do to celebrate? Shall we go to a football match?'

'I don't like football,' I said. I don't think he heard me.

The traffic was slow as we headed out of the clotted centre, our progress being delayed further by what Pa described as an 'anti-Thatcher rally' taking place outside a university building. I watched the massed ranks of students with blanched fascination as they shouted orthodox slogans of rebellion, their faces contorted by a rage I didn't understand. One girl, dressed in ragged army fatigues and a leather jacket with badges on the lapels, set fire to an effigy of Margaret Thatcher, the flames from its long nose lighting up the gloom like a firework.

'What are they so angry about?' I said, summoning the courage to ask Pa a question.

31

'They're junkies, communists and wasters,' he said, peering at his own reflection in the rear-view mirror. 'To think my taxes pay for their tuition – they're an insult to the nation.'

Once through, we began picking up speed and I looked out over the black rain-smeared streets, slyly holding my nose so as to block out the smell of his constant cigarette. And all the time I was secretly longing to be far away from him, back with my classmates on a steamy coach bound for Dorset, and then home.

In murky light we made our way up to his flat, our footsteps clumsy on the carpetless stairway. I couldn't wait to see inside his place, the gadgets and intricate hi-fi equipment he must have, one of the new touch-button CD-players I'd read about, the VHS video recorder with its own remote, the suntanning and water beds, the valuable paintings and thick, expensive carpets, the gold taps in the bathroom. So many treasures.

At the bend in the stairs, the lights cut out. Pa halted abruptly as if he'd slammed into a glass wall. A passing truck vibrated outside and I heard him cursing as he ran his hands across the bitty, paperless walls, feeling for a light switch. I continued up the stairs alone, trusting my good eyesight and using the handrail as a guide. Then my father found the switch and we were drenched in soft, appealing light. Approaching the door to his flat, I sensed that a fantastic adventure was about to begin.

But the flat was cold and damp; there were no paintings on the bare walls, and the carpets and curtains were frayed. Where was the promised opulence, the indicators of his wealth? He didn't even have a spare bed, although he did have a second bedroom, a model of willed turmoil, a riot of toppling towers of boxes, scattered box-files, careless piles of unironed shirts and empty suitcases; in fact, everything to suggest that he was in transit, on the move.

His own bedroom was perhaps the bleakest room of all. The only object of commanding interest was a black-and-white photograph of my deceased grandfather, Frankie, dressed in a boxing robe, his bare knuckles raised in mock fighter's pose. The sitting room had a scuffed leather sofa, a rocking chair, a small portable TV, several large bean-bags. There was nothing more, nothing I'd expected; why, in the kitchen he didn't even seem to have an electric kettle. At least he had his own phone and an old boxy answering-machine. And I thought he was meant to be a tycoon, super-rich, glamorous, *the* man. The Big Man. My rich father.

I went to bed early that night (I had his bed, he was on the sofa), but I couldn't sleep. A lump of disappointment was stuck like a crust in my throat and I couldn't swallow it. Lying on his creaking single bed, distracted by disco music that seemed to be emanating from somewhere in the building, I wondered about the strange desolation of the flat. What could have gone wrong there? The hours dragged after that and the light from the sitting room leaked distractingly beneath my door. So I withdrew further beneath the sheets, playing with my new digital watch (an early birthday present from Mum), the red figures on the black face illuminating the darkness as I randomly pressed the buttons, trying to forget the ruin of his flat.

I was woken twice during the night by the telephone. The second time, hearing Pa's voice again, I remembered where I was and began to relax for the first time that day. I climbed out of bed and went over to the door, where I strained to hear what was being said; but his muffled conversation was tantalizingly out of reach, like a face glimpsed and then lost again in an anxious crowd. Soon I was listening to him as if from the bottom of a well, or while under sedation: he seemed to be that far away from me, receding all the time, as if he were actually disappearing.

The next morning we had breakfast in the kitchen, at a smooth pine table, across which were scattered newspapers, magazines, cards and strips of torn wrapping paper. Pa prepared breakfast: strong coffee (too bitter to drink), eggs, muffins and strawberry jam, cereal, toast and more eggs.

'I love eggs,' he said, dipping warm buttered toast fingers into his soft yoke. 'Fried, poached, boiled, scrambled, coddled, pickled – you name it. Chopped up in mayonnaise, whipped up in a meringue – for breakfast, for lunch. I like them in a sandwich with lots of tomato and black pepper. I even like them raw sometimes, whipped up with milk and a spoonful of sugar. They do great things for your strength, son.'

He rolled up the sleeve of his dark blue Fred Perry, tensing his arm so that his bicep bulged. 'You not drinking that?' he asked, lighting a cigarette. Then he slurped down my coffee in three noisy mouthfuls, while I admired the junior golf clubs he'd given me, their heads specially weighted, he explained, to offer the beginner extra flight.

I watched him through a mist of cigarette smoke, his nicotine-stained fingers twitchily turning the pages of a news-paper. It was another damp morning, with patches of rain and a magnificently disturbed sky. You could hear the wind strengthening; the lime trees outside our window seemed harassed, their branches gnarled and twisted like arthritic hands. From the window, I watched fallen leaves being gusted into random piles before the wind hurried them along again, like a farm dog rounding up recalcitrant sheep.

Once he'd cleared away the dishes, Pa practised his short game, chipping imaginary golf balls from, he said, 'out of the rough'. He was dressed in a red baseball cap, red Fred Perry (he'd mysteriously changed out of the blue one) and beige chinos. Then, strolling a couple of paces, he began putting, elaborately stroking real golf balls, *my* golf balls – one, two, three – across the frayed cream carpet. If he was aiming for a hole, I couldn't see it.

'The trick of it, boy, is not to lift your head too soon,' he kept telling me, the shadow of his cap making bars across his face as he crouched awkwardly over the ball, his hands gripped low on the stem of the putter, his knees slightly bent. He did this for about half an hour, muttering, cursing, cajoling. He seemed to miss more putts than he holed, from his continual whooped annoyance. And he kept complaining about the cold, although the heating was up oppressively high. In fact, as he lined up a putt, I asked him several times if the heating could be turned down – I could feel the sweat gathering in the creases behind my knees – but he never seemed to hear.

His concentration was eventually disturbed by a phone call from Mum, wishing me happy birthday. She and Pa spoke briefly, and then it was my turn. Her voice was, initially, full of a brittle laughter to which I responded. Yet when I told her that Pa had bought me a set of golf clubs, her tone altered, darkened; she said something like, 'You don't even like golf!'

It was really no big deal; I wanted to do something that he enjoyed doing, to share something with him. I wanted to play golf.

'What did she say?' he asked at the end of my conversation.

'She, er, she asked what you gave me.'

'Well, did you tell her?'

I nodded.

'And?'

'She seemed . . . ' I felt myself blushing, not for the first time that morning.

'What is it? She seemed what?'

'I c-can't remember.'

He threw his hands up in exasperation, turned away and strode into the bedroom. The door swung shut behind him, leaving me alone with my golf clubs. So I began stroking balls across the carpet, but I quickly became bored. Where was the hole?

He re-emerged from his room wearing a long dark raincoat, a stiff, wide-brimmed Homburg and a red woollen scarf. 'Come on, boy, put your coat on. We're going for a walk.'

We turned right out of the door and walked pacily along the pavement, overlooked by bare trees and tall terraced houses, their front gardens scattered with fallen leaves. Cars were tightly parked on either side of the road; smart cars: Jaguars, big Fords, Alfa-Romeos, Mercedes, a Roller or two. There was money around here, all right. At the bottom of the road, adjacent to a pub, we turned right into Primrose Hill Road.

'Where're we going?' I asked.

'Not far, you'll see.'

He lengthened his stride and I struggled to keep up, passing the high-rise blocks on Adelaide Road, my lungs aching a little as I took in clean, cold air.

'This way,' he said, when we reached the neat perimeter fencing of Primrose Hill Park.

I followed, a couple of strides behind, but as we climbed towards the summit of the hill I sprinted on ahead across the wet grass, kicking a hurried path through the damp-heavy leaves. It was only a short, brisk climb to the top but it left me breathless. Pa called me over so that I stood alongside him, under the flat grey sky, looking out over the sprawling urban landscape below: the incessant movement of the city, the small, stick-like people. He took air into his lungs. I felt disoriented, clumsy even, as I looked out over the city, imagining myself to be a parachutist about to jump out of a plane into clear, blue nothingness.

'There, look at that . . . London,' he said. 'Fantastic, isn't it? There's the Post Office Tower and there – you see that big dome? – St Paul's.'

'You can see for miles,' I said.

'When I was younger, Josh, when I first got back to London with Mum, I used to come up here occasionally on my own, at night mostly. Looking out at the bright lights of the city, the small lights of the houses below – it took my breath away. It was as if the lights were on water or I was on a ship looking back at the city. Everything seemed possible then. The lights symbolized the future, what I was gonna achieve.' He paused, removing his hat, which he clutched tightly in his hands like a prize. 'That was before I realized the world's a pretty awful place.'

I looked up at him, confused. An awful place?

He must have sensed my incomprehension, for he let out a slight sigh, like gassy air escaping from a bottle. For a moment we were silent. A low-flying plane passed overhead and I heard the whine of traffic on Regent's Park Road. He placed his hand on my back. 'Come on, son. Let's have a cup of tea.'

*

It was growing dark when I stepped out of the elevator at Belsize Park tube station, having mooned away several hours at home since leaving Companies House. It was another stickily sultry night. There were people on the streets, standing outside pubs with bottles of beer. Two cyclists glided past on the road, their feet motionless on the pedals as they freewheeled down the hill, their lamps probing the gloom in cones of fragile light. I turned right into Belsize Avenue, heading down once again to my father's old flat. I reached the bottom of the road and looked up at the window, the same window from which I'd watched the wind chasing those leaves across the road that last weekend before he left us. The front gardens of the mansion terraces were as dry and stubbly as a farmer's field after the harvest. I sat on the wall opposite the flat and waited, waited for something to galvanize me from my latesummer torpor: an adventure, a change of fortune, anything new and different to free me from the trap of myself.

The afternoon spent at Companies House and looking for a death certificate at St Catherine's House had yielded nothing. The Anthony Winters, all directors of their respective companies, were not my Anthony Winter. I'd rung up all eight of them from home. There was no reply at three; three more were 'out', and the two I spoke to were baffled, even angry, when I introduced myself, whimsically, as their son Joshua. One of them replied that he didn't have a son; the other that his only son was called Gareth and was with him in the room, at that precise moment. I apologized.

Then I saw her, the young woman from the flat, walking along the street with a man – her boyfriend or husband, I presumed, from the ease with which they held on to each other, from the way they whispered conspiratorially like spies. I watched them approach my father's block. The woman punched out the code on the keypad. The door sprang open and they went inside. I closed my eyes and imagined following in behind them, up the narrow staircase, the cream carpet soft and new underfoot. I paused at the familiar bend in the stairs as the woman took out her key and let herself into the flat – *his* flat – leaving the door ajar as if she knew that I was there in the shadows and wanted me to follow. Which I did.

I was moved by how much the flat had changed since my father had lived there, how much smarter it was, with its cool, minimalist chic: stripped wooden floors and doors, sparse black furniture, white walls, spotlights, Mondrian prints on the walls in the bathroom, light jazzy music on the CD-player. The boyfriend was pouring himself a drink. I walked past him and stood by the open window, looking out over the hazy streets where I was, in reality, sitting. He didn't seem to hear me, or know that I was there. He was wearing a business suit and seemed older than I'd imagined, perhaps in his early forties. He had a professional distance, a reserve. He had money. The woman walked into the room. She removed her jacket, took her drink from him. 'Any ice?' she said.

He went through into the kitchen. I tried whispering to her but she couldn't hear. Instead, she rolled her diamond engagement ring along the length of her tanned finger, lifting it easefully over the thick crinkle of her knuckle, as though it were greased. There were glossy magazines on a glass table in the centre of the room. The guy returned, rattling ice in the glass. He put his arms around the woman, running his fingers across her bare brown arms. Embarrassed, I coughed to alert them of my presence there, but they were too caught up in the immediate thrill of the moment to notice who was watching. So I left them there together, opening my eyes as I walked downstairs, letting myself out of the block and then heading back towards the station. I was a little envious of the life they'd built together in my father's flat, the life and certainty they enjoyed together there, the comfort of each other, the security it brought them, even if it was, for now, an imaginary life they were living, within my control.

On my return to Nassau Street, I rang my mother. She was preparing supper. 'We're having barbecued lamb tonight, Josh, stuffed with garlic and smothered with rosemary – your favourite.'

And what had I eaten? Another bucket of Kentucky fried chicken, baked beans and chips.

I fell on a break in conversation to ask her, nonchalantly, if she remembered the exact names of any of Pa's companies, or of his partners.

'There was Uncle Bert, of course . . . But why d'you ask?'

'I'm just curious, Mum.'

'You're not brooding, Josh, are you? What's the point of digging up the past?' There was anxiety in her voice. 'Tell me about your flat. What's it like?'

'It's cool,' I said. 'Maybe a bit small, but it's pretty central.'

'What's the weather like over there?'

'Toronto-ish – hot and humid. It's as if I'd never left home.' I stopped short. I'd never referred to Toronto as home before – throughout my years in Canada, home for me had always been England.

'What about your job, have you been in to see them yet?'

'Not yet, no.'

'You will, though, won't you? It's for the best if you start to make a go of things.'

The next morning, before I dressed, I rang our old family doctor's surgery in Poole. The receptionist explained that our former doctor, Kim Kellor, had retired several years earlier. He was still living in Poole, but she refused either to give me his phone number or confirm whether he was at the same address as when I'd known him.

'But he was my old doctor when I was a child,' I said. 'He knew my family.'

'It doesn't matter,' she said. 'We aren't authorized to give out the doctors' personal details.'

I took a more oblique approach. 'My father died some years ago. I'm wondering if it would be possible to see his medical records.'

I could hear phones ringing in the background, the crackle of irritation in her voice as she explained that when a patient dies his records were automatically returned to the health authority.

'D'you think they'd be able to help me?'

'When did he die?'

'In 1985.'

'If you write, I'm sure they'd photocopy the relevant notes for you since 1991.'

'But he died in 1985!' I said.

'Oh, sorry, I thought you said 1995.'

'Why couldn't I see his records before 1991 anyway?'

'Under the Patients' Charter, that's when you can have access to medical records. That's the rule. If you're unhappy, speak to the health authority.'

Encouragingly, she took my numbers when I asked if she'd forward a message to Dr Kellor.

There was a repetitive tapping at the door as I replaced the receiver. Pulling on my gown, I glanced at the clock. Too late for the postman. I opened the door to be greeted by a hunched old woman, perhaps in her late eighties, dressed in a heavy winter coat. She was leaning on a pram. Her thick football-like socks ended just below the knee and the laces of her battered blue trainers were undone in unknowing imitation of urban cool. The gnarled tips of her fingers showed through the frayed ends of her woollen gloves. Her silver hair was thick and wildly long and quite magnificent. Her chin was whiskery, manly, stern.

'She's back,' she said, without introducing herself.

'Who's back?' I said.

'She's been away with them ramblers again.' She gestured towards the door of the corner flat.

'Oh, right, she's back.' I had no idea who the old woman was, or whom she was talking about.

'She's been on holiday. She's always going away with the ramblers.' Then she began to laugh, shrieking even.

I felt curiously exposed, embarrassed by her, unsure what she wanted me to do or say. Then the old woman turned and stumbled back across the corridor, using the pram as support. I watched her approach the flat, push at the open door and stumble inside. So she was one of my neighbours.

That afternoon I met our returned rambler on the stairs. She'd evidently been rushing and seemed a little breathless. She introduced herself as Katya Loktova. She told me she'd been living in Nassau Street for about eight months and worked as a researcher for the BBC Russian Service, at Bush House on the Aldwych. She was, I guessed, in her late twenties, slightly older than me. There was an exotic difference about her appearance, a foreignness, but she spoke with only a slight accent, a barely perceptible suggestion that she was not a native English speaker. Her blue-green gaze was startling. Her short skirt was pulled tightly across smooth bare legs and several buttons on her shirt were undone. I told her about the old woman.

'Oh, you mean Mrs Green. She's harmless. She's lived here for years, I think.'

'Katya, d'you want' – I hesitated – 'd'you want to come in for a coffee, or something?'

'I can't now, but maybe tomorrow . . . James.'

'Josh.'

'Yes, maybe tomorrow, Josh.'

I watched her go into her corner flat, wondering whether she lived alone; and I found myself admiring, too, the swell of her hips through her tight white skirt, experiencing the first real stirrings of sexual desire I'd felt for anyone since the accident.

It wasn't long before I discovered that Katya indeed lived alone, while white-haired Mrs Green shared her flat with her middle-aged son, a silent loner who moved in and out of the block at the oddest hours, neither once raising his head as he passed me on the stairs nor returning my greetings. His silence was curious, but Katya suggested that, like his mother, he was quite harmless. As I became more used to Mrs Green's eccentricities, I responded to her. She didn't speak so much as shriek at you in a tone of hectic accusation, with most of her sentences ending in that delightfully cracked, manic laughter.

Although I never actually saw inside her place, I sensed the pressure of its clutter. Her son seemed to be forever returning with another item of junk – an old chair, a ruined rug, a preposterously dated lamp. And whenever Mrs Green opened her door you could hear the forlorn chirping of caged birds. To the last, I was never able to work out what she was laughing about. She spoke a language that was entirely unfamiliar to me, a private language; but I tried to laugh along all the same, even when, in the end, there wasn't much to laugh about. She took that battered old pram everywhere she went, pushing it in front of her like a Zimmer frame as she made her way unsteadily towards the overheated frenzy of Oxford Street. How she got up the stairs one can only guess, but she did. It was the exuberance of the old woman I came to admire most, her complete disregard of conventional reserve, her splendid isolation. Her shrewd awareness of what was happening around her was also impressive and was something I came to ignore at my cost.

And all the time I was settling in at Nassau Street, getting to know Mrs Green and Katya Loktova, I was hitting wall after wall in what had become, to my surprise, an ardent quest for my father. Or, more accurately, a quest to discover something concrete about those last few months before he disappeared. I wanted to add some colour to his skeletal, monochrome outline, to make him less virtual, less of an archival presence in our lives, and instead something more vibrantly real, as a parent should be. So I wandered from St Catherine's House to Companies House to Belsize Park and back again; but with each new inquiry I seemed to be backing myself further into a cul-de-sac, becoming trapped in the circle of my own obsession.

I put him on the missing persons list at the Salvation Army and contacted the National Missing Persons Helpline, which, founded in 1992, might have been more useful to us in the early 1980s. I contacted the remaining Anthony Winters listed at Companies House, but one by one – surprise, surprise – they were ruled out of the hunt. I also rang Clifford Chance to arrange to visit them for an induction meeting; and yet, at the same time, I made no attempt to study English company law. Nor did I follow up on any of the letters I'd written from Toronto to those other City law firms which had once seemed to offer the door to a career of respectable Al-like wealth and hardened achievement and now offered nothing but containment and dull bureaucracy.

In truth, I'd committed myself to the following of a grail long ago and increasingly nothing else seemed to matter. But a grail, I began to understand, offers no possibility of a resolution; it merely lies before you like a long flat road winding endlessly through open countryside to nowhere in particular.

II

They begin searching Oliver King's house for the money one of them knows will never be found (ah, the putative pleasures of money, lost and gained). They search everywhere, including in the cellar beneath the garage, which turns out to have been Oliver's storeroom, his *dark* room. Amid the clutter and the junk, the deteriorating newspapers and old Joy Division and Killing Joke records, the smell of damp and the thick cobwebs, they discover more stashes of porno mags and cases of videos: hardcore and softcore, for fetishists and masochists, mags for spankers and spunkers. There are big-girl and big-boy mags, fat-girl, black-girl and gay-guy mags. Mags featuring shaven women, aged women, pregnant women. Mags for analists, cross-dressers, coprophiliacs and transsexuals. *Fist Fucking*, *Oral Sex Secrets*, *Anal Delights*, *Pregnant Asians*.

'We were on the right track,' Nick says. 'I've always thought there's serious money in this stuff.'

Money? Anthony Winter has had enough of money.

They continue searching the bungalow. They look in wardrobes, drawers and cupboards, in the attic and in the kitchen, in bins and books, in the oven and in the fridge, under mattresses and between the sheets. They search among his socks, pants, jumpers and pyjamas. They scatter his shirts and T-shirts all over the bedroom – then refold them. Under Oliver's single bed they eventually find a shoebox with some money in it. They count: £266. Nowhere near enough.

They search for diaries and letters, address books and notepads, for anything that might actually explain what went wrong, might help them to recover their losses. Nick Dundee curses Oliver, again and again, blames him for what happened, his peculiar death.

'He came at me first,' he says. 'What could I do?'

'You could have put the knife away, for a start,' Anthony says.

A brief, fierce tussle follows, and the two men touch foreheads, like rutting stags, before Dundee sulks away.

Later, Anthony Winter suggests setting fire to the bungalow, with the body in it, but Dundee wants to take Oliver away with them, leave him in woods or in the sea.

Anthony remembers the remote village of Stratford St Andrew, not far away, where there's woodland and open farmland, where he's been once before, to a pub in the village with Oliver King. When he was alive, he thinks, and he pictures himself and Oliver together, sitting by an open fire, the drinks they shared that afternoon.

When they finally come to load the body, its limbs bound, into the boot of the car, Dundee seems unable to look at what he's done. He sweats and pants; he mutters to himself like a drunk.

They are struggling to lift the body out of a wheelbarrow and into the car. Nothing has prepared them for how heavy a body can be – a dead weight indeed. Nor how unwieldy.

'This is a fucking farce,' Dundee says.

Anthony Winter reverses the car down to the open garage doors, where Dundee is waiting, the tail lights falling on his face in a curious glow. Time crawls as they bundle the body, the wheelbarrow and some garden equipment into the car. Then, at last, they are on their way, lights dimmed, as Dundee drives through cold, silent Thorpeness and then out on the open road towards Stratford St Andrew.

The car picks up pace and the two men wonder about each other: can he be trusted? They know, too, that a kind of doom inevitably awaits them, like tomorrow's sunrise.

Ghost Patient

Katya and I finally arranged to have dinner at a Thai restaurant she liked in Soho. There were no spare tables on the ground floor, so we were taken upstairs by a dainty waitress dressed in an Oriental costume. We ate, in a near-empty, echoing room, at an open window with views over the humid heave of the street. It was a fantastically calm night; heavy, fumey air rose from the pavement like steam from the Manhattan subway. Katya was wearing a pale-blue silk shirt – the colour of sea-gulls' eggs – casually unbuttoned to reveal her sunburnt throat and the sweat on her chest.

Over dinner I told her for the first time about my family, but not the accident, about my ostensible and actual reasons for being in London. She listened, and as she did so I noticed how impossibly fragile her hands were, and how she wore a soli-tary silver stud in her nose. We drank more wine and the tables began filling up around us. Katya herself spoke of how she'd come from a resolutely secular and artistic home, and how she and her family had always lived as 'perfect bohemians', even in the Soviet times. Her parents were both painters, although they'd earned their living as graphic artists working for state publishing companies. Yet, since coming to London and separating from her boyfriend last year – 'we were together for three years but it never seemed to be going anywhere' – she'd begun to feel 'the absence of spiritual rit-ual' for the first time in her life. Did I feel the same? she wondered. Had the disappearance of my father led me to seek the consolation of religion?

No, I said, there was no God-shaped hole in my life, and this seemed to disappoint her.

I could sense, meeting her blue-green gaze, a maturing

intimacy developing between us; once or twice she leaned across the table to touch my arm and I felt again, as I had on that first afternoon we met, a dim stirring of desire for her, quite unexpected in its intensity. Flirting, I told her when she spoke to me, particularly about Russia, I regretted being unable to free her to speak naturally, without inhibition and in her own language.

'So, you mean my English is no good then?' she said.

'Not at all,' I said, and my tone was defensive.

'Oh, Josh, I'm only joking. You're really too serious sometimes.' After a pause, she continued, 'You know, Joshua,' but her sentence was left hanging. There was the sound of shattering glass outside, followed by shouts and raucous laughter. She stretched to look out of the window. 'Silly boys,' she said, turning back to me. 'What's the matter now?'

I couldn't answer because I'd mistaken a green chilli for a slice of pepper and bitten robustly into it. An embarrassed decorum prevented me from spitting, so I swallowed instead. Which made things worse. I waved my hand like a fan in front of my mouth and began drinking water. Too quickly, alas – I began hiccuping. Soon I was scooping lumps of cold white rice into my mouth, but I was never much of a chopsticks man and I sprayed it everywhere. Katya was hugely amused. She had a teasing, girly laugh, which it was almost worth eating another chilli to hear. Well, almost.

Then we fell strangely silent. I knew immediately that something had been lost between us, in the way that an audience's applause at the end of a musical performance breaks a spell, interrupting suspended time and disbelief. Conversation became stilted. I asked for the bill; Katya insisted on paying half. We went downstairs, past the sweet-smelling kitchen, and out on to the street. After the air-conditioned cool of the restaurant, the evening felt almost tropical – and it was already around midnight. The heat's unnatural, I thought, a portent of something wrong.

47

We walked slowly back to Nassau Street, our hands never quite touching, although I wanted to hold her, to pull her towards me. I was lost, I realized, without the possibility of intimacy. On the landing, outside our respective flats, I almost asked her in, but she mentioned her tiredness, her early start the next morning. She wanted to be alone.

'Well, good night,' I said, offering to shake her hand.

'Don't be so formal, Josh,' she said, and leaned over, kissing me briskly on either cheek. I could smell the restaurant on her hair, the lingering sweetness of fried coconut oil.

We separated. She slipped into her flat without looking back. As the door closed I wondered if someone was waiting for her there in the darkness. I saw her being dragged towards a man. He lunges and fumbles, begins unbuttoning her shirt, the blue fabric on his heavy hands; she leans against him for support. He opens her shirt and touches her flesh. She's warm and willing – she's his. At least for one night.

I turned in frustration and kicked my door, then banged my head against it twice, making my eyes water. I heard a door open. It was not Katya but Mrs Green. The landing light was on but she was still holding a torch, which she shone straight into my face.

'What's all this lark going on?' This time she wasn't laughing.

'It's only me, Mrs Green.'

'Who's that then?'

'It's me, Joshua, your new neighbour.'

'How long have you been my neighbour?'

'A couple of weeks. We've spoken several times.'

'Leave her alone, why don't you? She's a good girl.'

'Katya?'

'You know who I mean. She's a good girl.'

Torchlight flickered, as if she was taking my photograph. Then her son appeared in the shadows behind her and stepped out on to the landing. He was wearing a dressing-gown and slippers, and swiftly withdrew when he saw me. I heard the

48

low murmur of his voice, then Mrs Green returned inside, saying nothing more.

All through the next week I spoke to Katya most days on the phone at work but saw her only fleetingly, on the stairs, in the street, by the church. She was always rushing, hectically absorbed. Had I upset her?

*

I was surprised when Uncle David replied to my letter by return of post. I'd belatedly written because I wanted him to know that I was in London, but also because there was much to ask about my father, ahead of our inevitable meeting. The brothers had grown up together in a three-bedroom Victorian villa of sombre interiors in Forest Gate, not far from where the East End puts on its smart coat and polished boots and swaggers out into the leafy urban villages of Woodford, Chingford, Loughton, Chigwell and Epping. Their father, my grandfather Frankie, was a bus driver, his entire career spent clamorously negotiating the London traffic at the wheel of a huge red double-decker. He hated his job; claimed the roar of the engines had left him with a low persistent ringing in his ears, later diagnosed as tinnitus, something I'd always dreaded contracting. I remember old Frankie, whose wife I'd never known, with his partial deafness and fondness for superstrong untipped Player's cigarettes, his anecdotes about his years as an amateur boxer, fighting bouts in East End pubs (I think these must have inspired me to pick up the gloves at university), his stories about driving buses during the Blitz, his recreational racism and complaints about 'insolent darkies'. But above all I recall his unstinting love and admiration for my father. It was Frankie who'd urged his son to move up and out, to keep on keeping on; to study at night school for a couple of O levels to offer himself a chance (he left his secondary modern, to work as an apprentice shirt cutter, when he was fifteen; David, more academic, had made it to the grammar school).

49

David Winter went on to make a decent career for himself as a teacher in the independent sector. He was now deputy headmaster of a Lancashire boys' school. Whereas my father went off in another direction altogether: at the age of nineteen he left the East End and went first to New York and then to Toronto, where a cousin of Frankie's had emigrated after the war. Those were the beginnings, or so I used to believe, of his money-making years, of buying and selling, hustling and touting. He chased money hard, Mum said, especially when they first returned to England as a newly married couple in the 1960s and my father began buying up and renovating near-derelict properties in unfashionable parts of south-east London. He sold them on for decent profits. It was a trick he later tried to repeat in Dorset, with scant success once Uncle Bert had died.

September 1995

Dear Joshua
What a pleasant surprise to hear from you – and from London! You should have rung in advance to say that you were coming. I would have come down to meet you.

For some reason which was never made entirely clear, my father had become clumsily estranged from his brother some time in the early 1980s. Before then, we used to travel up to Manchester every summer, and spent an occasional Christmas with David, his late wife Anne and their daughter Emily in his modest, book-cluttered house in Bolton. It was during the wet summer of 1982, I think, that my father announced that we weren't visiting Bolton that year. No convincing explanation was offered, although I recall once hearing him tell Mum that he missed 'the Professor', the nickname he used for his brother.

Pa's seemingly irrational decision to stop visiting David was part of his long withdrawal from intimacy. Increasingly inscrutable and cocooned in his own world, he seemed to grow ever more remote from us with each passing month, spending weeks on end at his flat in Belsize Park, from where he operated behind the dark curtain which obscured all that he did from us.

I continued reading my uncle's letter:

You asked about your father, Joshua. There's no easy way of understanding what happened there. There's also not much to reveal that you probably don't already know. You asked if the police contacted me. The answer is, yes, they did. They wanted to know if I'd heard from Anthony, if I knew anyone he was especially close to outside the family. I told them we'd virtually lost touch, for whatever reason this happens in families. I never understand to this day why your father and I grew apart. The enmity was not coming from this half of the country. I wanted to see him, to see you all. Your father could be a difficult man, as I'm sure you understand.

After he disappeared, I couldn't accept that my only brother had gone. Can a person disappear, cease to be, just like that? You hear about this thing they now call pseudocide: creating the impression that you're dead so that you can assume a new identity. But I never doubted for a minute he was dead, probably suicide (if it was pseudocide, why didn't he attempt to fake his own death, leave a car and some clothes by Beachy Head or something like that?). But ceased to be, for ever? That's impossible to grasp. I'm not religious – I'd call myself a dyed-in-the-wool North Korean atheist actually – but after he went I kept asking: what are we? Are we minds attached to bodies? Are we just bodies alone? Or physical objects that can think? If there is something non-bodily attached to our bodies, does this thing have an existence of its own, when the body ceases to exist? Does that separate entity live on in a series of different bodies? As you know, each one of those alternatives I have just expressed is believed by millions of people. Humanists believe one, Christians one, Buddhists another. Whichever of them is right – and maybe none of them is right – but even if one of them is right, the others must be wrong. That means most of us are wrong about what we are; we *don't* know what we are. Isn't it fundamental to one's own being, to one's own conception of oneself? It's also fundamental to one's own survival. If one of those alternatives is right, then I face complete and total annihilation; if another is right, the essential me is going to exist for all eternity. The difference between annihilation and eternal life for me – for you – depends on what the answer to that question is.

I paused from the letter to answer the phone.

'Joshua Winter?'

'Yeah.'

'Dr Kim Kellor here.'

'Dr Kellor, what a surprise!'

'Is it? I thought you wanted me to call you.'

His tone was as brusque as ever. I pictured him not as he must be now, but as he was then: a small, muscularly robust figure in his late forties, thinly bearded, with straight flat dark hair worn in a short basin-like fringe, and an edgy, confrontational manner as if permanently on the verge of irritation. A casual dresser, he had never once worn a tie and preferred open-necked shirts, V-necked sweaters, faded corduroy trousers. Not the attire you expected from a GP, at least not in those days. His manner and swaggering cavalier approach to medicine earned him the inevitable local sobriquet 'Killer' Kellor. He was certainly the one doctor in our surgery to whom rumour stuck like fertilizing spores: the missed diagnoses about which Mum gossiped, the over-enthusiastic prescribing of antibiotics, the women whose bras were removed when they'd complained only of leg pains – he was the one doctor no one trusted with their life.

'Well, thanks for calling, Doctor,' I said. 'I was wondering' – I changed direction – 'do you remember me? My family and I were patients of yours in –'

'I know, I know who you are, Joshua, for goodness' sake. That's why I called. How's everyone?'

'They're fine.'

'Your mother?'

'Fine.'

'Went off to the States, didn't you?'

'Toronto actually.'

'Yes, that's right. Very good. Now, come on, no one rings out of the blue for nothing.'

'It's a long shot, Doctor, but I'm trying to trace my father's medical records. D'you remember what happened to him?'

He did, and so I explained how I hoped his records would offer insight into not only his health, but his state of mind before the disappearance: whether he was suffering from a serious illness he'd kept from us, or exhibiting symptoms of stress, headaches, colitis, insomnia, stomach ulcers, depression or worse. Anything, really, that might offer a window on to the shifting, fluid patterns of his inner life.

'Bad business what happened to your father, very bad business,' he said. 'I liked Anthony a lot. Played squash with him a couple of times. Good, direct player. Hit the ball very hard.'

I knew nothing of their squash games but said, 'I know he did, Doctor, I know.'

'Never found his body, did they?'

'No, they never found his body.'

There was an uncomfortable pause.

'Anyway, Joshua, I'm not sure I can help.'

He confirmed what the receptionist had already told me, that my father's medical records would have been returned to the health authority.

'Is there no chance they'd still be at the surgery?'

'Before I took early retirement there were patients registered with us who never came in at all. Perhaps they were living abroad or had moved without telling us. Ghost patients, we called them. They're alive, but it's as if they don't really exist. But it's unlikely your father's one of those.'

'A ghost?'

'Yes, because the authorities tend to write to absent patients after a couple of years. If they don't get a reply they're struck off the list.'

'And their records?'

'As I said, returned to the local authority.'

Our conversation concluded with Dr Kellor inviting me to visit him 'whenever you're next in Poole'.

Talking to him had rekindled my yearning to see the old place. Those skies and that sea tugged at me. 'What about this weekend, Doctor,' I said. 'Are you free?'

He was – on Saturday morning. 'I'm still in the same house, Joshua, if you remember it.'

I did because it used to be on my early-morning paper round, which Mum encouraged me to do once we'd moved from Studland.

I rang the Dorset health authority. It was a similar story: my father's records ought to have been returned. If they had and were extant – medical records of a dead person were destroyed after ten years – I'd still be legally prohibited from seeing them. Two hours later a woman from the health authority rang back to say she'd located my father's file. His medical records had been forwarded on his request, in 1982, to a surgery in Belsize Park, for which they gave me an address. They'd never been returned from there. I found the number for the surgery in Belsize Park, but they had no record of my father. Once more it was recommended that I contacted the relevant London authority. Which I did, but there was no trace of my father ever having registered as a medical patient in London. So he had disappeared, all over again.

I returned to my uncle's letter.

Hundreds of adults disappear every year, and I've read that the most common time for vanishing is between thirty-five and forty-five. Your father was forty. Dante was thirty-five when he stumbled lost into the dark wood of middle age, half-way through the journey of his life. Three score years

54

and ten: our biblical span on Earth. But in this godless age the midpoint of the journey of our lives is not thirty-five, but usually forty. There's the old joke about life beginning at forty, but more often than not the only thing that begins then is a midlife crisis. Women have a biological change and it's a pity that men don't. It would help the problem to be understood more. The problem with a midlife crisis is that, by definition, it's an over-reaction. The whole thing can take grotesque forms. Otherwise perfectly sane men start jogging, or buying MG Midgets, or having affairs with young girls. In reality, a midlife crisis is all about structuring your life – facing up to things that haven't been faced up to before. The certainty of death, an unhappy marriage, professional failure – whatever. Then you can settle down to cope with the over-reaction, as I see it.

I myself don't have this sense of looking back at life with regret. Sometimes I meet men who say, 'When I was nineteen I was going to play football for England.' Or be a captain of industry, or write a great book. For some reason, it never happens. So there's this residue of disappointment. I think one of the reasons why people commit suicide is to escape this sense of disappointment, which can become intolerable. The feeling of meaninglessness must be the worst feeling of all. The feeling that nothing matters, that there's no point to anything – what a terrible insight that is. And there were times I nearly felt like that myself after Anne died.

Perhaps, Joshua, the truth is no more than that your father was locked into a midlife crisis and panicked. Took his own life to escape the burden of living. I can't think of any other explanation. Pseudocide would have been too selfish, even for him. He cared about you all and would have understood that it's always the ones left behind who suffer most.

He went on to lighten the letter with some passing refer-ences to sport, and to schoolteaching. He also invited me up to Lancashire, as and when I had the time.

III

They drive through the dense, swirling fog to Stratford St Andrew. They intend to dump the body in the woods on the edge of the village. They can't agree on whether Oliver King dragged on the cigarette, or whether they imagined it. They can't agree on what to do with the body, either. Except to dump it and quickly. Dump it anywhere wet and dark. Despite their disagreements, he is dead all the same.

The van bumps along a patchy, uneven track to reach the most secluded part of the woods, surrounded by flat, open East Anglian farmland. Nick Dundee is first out of the car. He opens the boot, inspecting the burden of their strange fruit. Anthony Winter joins him and they both stare at the body, saying nothing. Soon they are pushing Oliver King through the trees in his own wheelbarrow, using torchlight to cut an oblique path through the bracken, bushes and fallen branches. When the torch falls on Oliver's face it seems blue-grey, peaceful enough, consoled.

The woods are screaming with unfamiliar noises, some soft. They expect, at any moment, to be disturbed and released from the weight of their secret. Neither of them has control of his bladder or bowels; first Dundee stops to shit, then Anthony. They both wipe their arses with damp dock leaves.

Dundee still wants to bury the body in a shallow grave; but when Anthony stumbles on a pond, half-hidden by a thick ring of evergreens, he becomes more adventurous and begins tossing stones into the pond to assess its depth. Dundee crouches beside him, reaching down through the reedy chill of the water. He cools his hands and wipes them across his face. Anthony is searching for something heavy with which to weigh down the body. He moves, unlike the sluggish Dundee, with confidence. Their roles have been reversed. Anthony seems more composed, in charge now, and he thinks he can smell shit on Dundee's clothes, and thinks about pushing him into the pond, pushing him in and then holding his head under the black water until that smirk he'd seen in the garage leaves his face for ever.

'We can't bury him, you know,' Anthony says, his voice a mere whisper.

'Why not?'

'We'd never dig a grave deep enough. They'd find him. Bodies are always being dug up in the woods, by dogs or kids. No, better to weigh him down, sink him in the pond. It's our only real chance.' Anthony is surprised by the authority in his voice.

Dundee looks at him. 'What if he floats to the surface?'

'What if he doesn't?'

'Yeah, but what if he *does*?'

'Let's just make sure he doesn't.'

Anthony picks up a heavy branch, drops it into the water. 'What d'you reckon?' he says. 'It's either this, Nick, or we just give ourselves up. We've fucked up big time. Or you have.'

'Fuck off,' Dundee says. 'I think I'm gonna puke.'

The wind is rising. There's cold drizzle in the air. For the first time that night the half-moon can be seen through thick ribbons of cloud. Anthony looks at Dundee and sees the pain in his pale-blue eyes, the lingering disbelief which he still feels too. Dundee looks startled, as if he's awoken abruptly from a dream to discover that what he worst feared and from which he hoped to escape is true.

'What about this?' Dundee holds up the murder knife.

'Give it me here.' Anthony hits the button, shines the torch on the blade. There's blood on it. Good, he thinks.

'Are you gonna chuck it in?' Dundee says.

'Leave it to me. I'll get rid of it later. It'll be stupid to leave it near the body.'

Then they work together to topple Oliver out of the wheelbarrow. Blood is drying in clumpy patches on his face and in his hair. Dundee lets out a muffled scream when one of his hands inadvertently brushes Oliver's arm. He feels the coldness that remains when all animation has gone.

The rope with which they tied up Oliver has the texture of a banana skin and the handle of the spade feels rotten and spongy. They load stones into Oliver's pockets. They bind his arms so that he's clutching the spade to his chest like a ceremonial sword. Then they begin rolling him towards the edge of the pond. Over he goes and they watch as he falls clumsily into the shallows. Anthony uses the fork to push him deeper out into the water. He shines the torch on the sallow, ruined face. The body seems to float, or snag on something.

'The water's not deep enough,' Dundee says.

'For fuck's sake give us a hand then,' Anthony says, 'don't just stand there.'

They both struggle to force the body out into the water.

'Fuck this,' Anthony says, and he wades out into the water himself. He wrenches the body away from the mass of clinging reeds in which it has become snagged and tries to drag it out with him. Slowly, the body shifts. He heaves again and this time Oliver King begins to sink slowly beneath the surface of the feculent water, the torchlight flickering warmly on his disappearing face.

Anthony turns to Dundee, the dirty, stinking water almost up to his stomach. But he is checked from speaking by a kind of exhilaration which grips him like a cramp spasm, and it's as if he feels he has another chance in life – that he has more than the one life – and the means of doing something about it.

Dundee is sitting despondently at the edge of the pond, his hands covering his face. He retches twice, the second time vomiting. Anthony feels contempt for him, and then a curious pity.

Back in the van, sitting behind the wheel, staring out over the darkness of the fields, Anthony Winter accepts that his life is finally out of control. He's come full circle: he is there. He has nowhere else to go.

Upton Park

Fine rain was falling when Pa and I returned from our walk on Primrose Hill. Once back in the flat, he began hurrying through that morning's papers while I amused myself chipping plastic golf balls out of his 'rough', relishing the lofted flight offered by my new nine iron.

'I know,' he said, 'let's go to see that football match I mentioned. So who's it to be, boy? Who d'you support?'

I halted my stroke in mid-swing, looked at him. 'I don't support anyone, Pa. I don't really like football.'

'Good boy,' he said, stirring to ruffle my hair.

When he turned back to the paper, I flattened my hair down again with greasy palms.

'Who's at home?' he asked himself, pausing to light a cigarette. 'Chelsea aren't, nor are Arsenal, QPR or Millwall. But Spurs, West Ham, Fulham and Brentford are.' He poured himself a glass of whisky but forgot to offer me anything. 'Who did you say you supported?' he said again.

'I didn't, Pa.'

'What?'

'I didn't say anything.'

'What's the matter with you, boy? Can't you speak up?'

He returned to the paper and muttered, 'So West Ham it is, then.' He smiled to himself as he spun his Homburg across the room like a Frisbee.

I'd not been prepared for football and as we set off in his Jaguar I felt somehow guilty, as if I were snatching illicit pleasures on the sly. The autumn light was fading and visibility was wretched, but each time we were forced to pull up at lights or at a roundabout Pa braked dangerously late, as if relishing the hiss of his tyres on the wet roads.

We arrived at Upton Park in good time and parked in a secretive little side street – no more than five minutes' walk from the stadium but largely empty. Pa was wearing his Homburg, a red woollen scarf and a long, dark coat. He took my hand as we splashed noisily through the puddles. He bought a programme on the glossy cover of which was the picture of a footballer I didn't recognize but whose name Pa knew. To this day, I can't remember who it was.

It was the noise of the terraces I heard first from outside. Inside, as we took our seats in the West Stand, I was excited by the sight of so many people massed together under the floodlights, the orchestrated songs, the verbal assaults on the harassed clusters of away supporters, the roughness and secular abandonment of it all! The air was thick with cigarette smoke, and surrounding us there were men drinking coffee or tea from Thermos flasks. I tried to catch my breath in cupped hands but it kept escaping, like fog through a fishing net.

'I'm looking forward to this,' I said, and it was as if my words had startled my father. I looked up at him and his eyes appeared wild and saucerish as he searched the crowd, as if for someone he recognized.

The game was played on a clogged, swampy pitch, and the players were stumbling around like drugged elephants, their boots sinking voluptuously into the turf. Sometimes you could hear them shouting above the softening sound of the crowd, their voices carried on the wet wind, as intriguing as gossip.

'Pa,' I say, in one of the many breaks in play, 'Pa, if it was snowing today, not raining, how deep would the snow be by now?'

'What a funny question,' he says, swapping smiles with the woman who's just swivelled round, in the seat in front, to look at me. Her hair is wrapped up in an old-style factory turban.

'Pretty deep, Josh, I guess, pretty deep.'

'Like, how deep?'

'I dunno, maybe six inches.'

I open my hands to evaluate the depth and he nods approvingly. A struck match flares in the darkness behind us.

At half-time, Pa leaves me alone as he goes in search of drinks and, he says, to make a telephone call. The game has restarted by the time he returns with a coffee and a can of lemonade for me.

'You've been a long time,' I say.

'There was a queue.'

'Did you find a phone?'

'Huh-huh.'

'Who did you call?'

'It doesn't really matter.'

'Did you call Mum?'

'No, not her. I spoke to her this morning, remember?'

His voice is . . . I don't know how to describe it really – different, deflated. There's like a sigh in it I wish would go away. To engage him, I mention the snow again.

'How deep would the snow be now, Pa, because it's been raining all through half-time.'

He laughs. 'You still on about that?'

'Up to my knees?'

'Not that deep, no.'

'How deep?'

'Yeah, you were right first time, up to your knees. Now watch the game. Here's your lemonade.'

As he slips back into thought, I bash my can gently against his paper cup, coffee splashing over his nicotine-stained fingers. Our eyes meet and again there's something far away, not quite right, in his gaze.

'Thanks for the golf clubs,' I say. 'They're smart.'

'Good boy,' he says. 'Are you enjoying watching your team?' Then he laughs to himself, strangely.

'Are you all right?' I ask him.

'Course I am,' he says, and pats me on the back.

The second half passed without event, memorable only for

61

the intensity of the racial hatred hurled like garbage at the black away striker, who seemed pretty relieved to be substituted, his ears assaulted by a cacophony of monkey chants. By then, the optimism of the home support had long since hardened into a kind of gnarled resentment, and people were leaving early as the game slid irritably to a goalless close. But I wasn't bored.

'Pa?' I say.

He turns towards me, his eyes inflamed by a tiredness I couldn't see then.

'How deep is the snow now?' I ask him.

'The snow?' he says.

'Yes, the snow, our snow.' I hold out my hands, trying to collect the imagined flakes before they melt exquisitely into rain.

'Here,' he says, taking my arm roughly, 'look up there. It isn't fucking snowing. Now don't keep on, for fuck's sake, Joshua.'

I've upset him, I know that, and he gestures maniacally at the drenched sky. Against the red glow of the floodlights you can see the torrential rain.

'Come on. Let's go home. I've had enough of this crap,' he says.

'But the game, it's not finished.'

'Come on, Josh. Let's stop pissing around. It's freezing.'

I reached out for a hand that felt strong and warm.

Sometimes, I need only close my eyes to hear the screech of our car speeding away from Upton Park, and the sombre gasp of his lungs as he takes in smoke through an open mouth. I've since recycled the events of that afternoon endlessly, like a movie buff spooling through archive footage of films he once enjoyed in his youth as he searches again for a favourite scene he once knew so well but now seems doomed never to find again. So for him, as for me, only the silence is heard.

Closer

That night I watched the woman leave the flat in Belsize Park with if not a new boyfriend then with someone I hadn't seen before. I tracked them from a distance as they ambled up the hill towards Hampstead village, her blonde hair shining in the evening darkness. They seemed caught up in the happy languor of the moment, pausing outside a brasserie to read the window menu. They went inside. I approached and looked through the window after them. The interior was spacious, informal and bright. I went in and asked for a window table. They were sitting across the room from me, against a white-painted wall. Exposed wooden beams ran across the low ceiling, and the floor and the doors were thickly varnished. I ordered a beer. Their hands were touching across the table. The waitress brought them a basket of bread, and the young woman dipped a husk into the obligatory dish of olive oil. There was a bowl of olives on my table, two empty wine glasses. I looked over at her and our eyes made contact across the room, as they were to do several times during the next hour or so. I placed my order and waited, the restaurant filling up around me.

Some time had elapsed before she rose from her seat and walked across the restaurant. She paused to look back fleetingly in my direction before heading downstairs – a signal? I finished my third beer and followed her. The new boyfriend never looked up as I brushed his table on the way past. There were several loose hairs on the collar of his shirt and I imagined removing them. I arrived at the top of the narrow staircase as a young guy was emerging from the Gents' below. We crossed on the stairs, exchanging perfunctory nods. At the bottom of the stairs, I waited in the corridor for her to come out. The lavatory door eventually swung open and there she was, her usual casual *hauteur* replaced by an expression of genuine puzzlement. She was motionless, staring at me, a slight flush on the line of her cheekbones. She held a shiny black Prada bag in her left hand.

'Excuse me,' I said, unconvinced even by this lunge at friendliness.

She took several steps towards the stairs. The air-conditioning unit was rattling like a broken exhaust.

'Excuse me,' I said again, reaching out to her.

'What?' she said, evading my hand. 'What is it?'

There was perspiration on her brow, a dusting of powder on her cheeks and a startling slash of red lipstick across her mouth. As I approached, she retreated, defensively, I thought, and immediately I understood my mistake. She hadn't been looking at me in the restaurant, hadn't been sending signals at all. She had no idea who I was, nor did she want to know.

'Oh, sorry,' I said, 'it's all a mistake. I mistook you for some-one I knew. An old friend.'

She smiled coldly and turned towards the stairs, the outline of her knickers visible through her skirt.

I took the tube home from Belsize Park, at a baffled loss to explain my own behaviour. Alone in the dusty carriage, I reimagined how the scene might have turned out differently, disastrously. This time I saw myself grab her arm. She lashes out with her handbag as I draw her towards me, the buckle scratching my cheek.

'Leave it,' I say, kicking the bag.

She pleads with me not to hurt her.

'You don't understand,' I tell her. 'I don't want to hurt you. But why were you looking at me like that?'

'Looking at you?'

'Upstairs in the restaurant.'

'I don't know what you mean.'

'You don't know what I mean?'

64

She's broken free now and is running up the stairs, the outline of her knickers showing through the tightness of her skirt . . . the high, wide, womanly curve of her hips, her tanned legs. I make another lunge at her.

'Leave me alone, you freak,' she screams.

This time, I let her go, feeling that her departure is something fixed and irreversible, like a crack in a vase. Then I'm left to reflect on the futility of what's taken place, the impossibility of it all – and the heartbreak that lies ahead. At the top of the stairs, she collides with her boyfriend, who's perhaps concerned at her extended absence. He peers down at me. Looking up at him, I feel as isolated from their world as a lone hot-air balloonist. We're all inconsolable, I want to tell him.

The episode in the basement was, I knew, an aberration; a warning about what could go wrong if I continued to indulge this claustrophobic obsession with my father and his flat. I was becoming tired of myself, of always watching myself – the curse of self-consciousness. Hurrying back from the tube to Nassau Street, I knew I must never return to Belsize Park again, knew that I must do something – anything – to lift myself beyond morbid introspection.

So the next day, after an uneasy night, I phoned Katya at the BBC. We agreed to meet the next night for drinks at the American Bar of the Savoy.

I arrived early and ordered two glasses of champagne. These were served with a dish of heavily salted nuts by a tall Swede dressed in a pompous white tuxedo. I'd drunk most of my champagne and had begun sipping Katya's when she breathlessly arrived, her pale legs revealed by a long split in her black skirt. She was wearing three silver studs in her right ear and a tiny nose diamond gleamed. She wore a thick silver ring on her right thumb and a loose faded black-leather strap on her right wrist. She sat down, crossed her legs and laughed nervously. There was a rustle of background conversation, and a pianist began playing, on a sweeping grand piano, a piece of music I couldn't identify. I followed Katya's gaze down to where her red-painted toenails were visible through strappy shoes.

'I'm sorry I'm late,' she whispered. 'Are you angry with me?' Then, 'Can you hear that? He's playing Tchaikovsky's First like it was a pop song.'

The Swedish waiter glided over as if he were on skis and the carpet a blanket of fresh snow.

'More champagne for madam, sir?'

'No, not champagne,' Katya said. 'I once had this boyfriend – the one I mentioned to you – who kept bringing me champagne and chocolates every time we met. It was really awful.'

'Vodka then?'

'No, not vodka, that's a Russian cliché. A glass of red wine will do.' She looked at me.

'Is claret all right?' I said.

'I don't mind.'

'A glass of claret then,' I said, surprising myself by tipping the Swede a spontaneous fiver (something I immediately regretted). Katya sat impassively, inscrutably. How unimpressed she seemed by my jejune extravagance – the flourish of the boy with a rich stepfather.

The wine arrived. We raised glasses, chuckling as they collided musically. Soon Katya was discussing the dramas of her day: of how her office at Bush House was becoming a kind of 'theatre of the absurd', she called it, with an ensemble of combustible characters, warring factions and conflicting egos, all working against the backdrop of non-negotiable deadlines. As she began to relax, I told her more about what I'd been doing recently and why I was returning to Dorset.

'Are you driving?' she said.

'No, I don't have a car. I'll go by train.'

She sipped her wine, saying nothing more.

I began telling her how I'd returned to Belsize Park, in recent days, to check out my father's old London flat. 'He spent most of his time there in the end,' I said. 'That's why Mum wasn't surprised when her calls went unreturned that week he went missing. She only became seriously worried when he didn't turn up for the weekend as expected. Even then she went to the police without telling us first.'

Katya asked what, if anything, I remembered from the day I discovered he'd gone.

'Well, I remember being called to the headmaster's office. I thought I was in trouble for bunking off a couple of lessons the day before. As it was, Mum and a copper were waiting for me. I knew immediately something was wrong by the look on her face. I never dreamt it was my father. On the way home in the police car, she explained that something might have happened to Pa. That's how she put it: "Something might have happened to Pa."'

'What did you do?'

'I think I burst into tears. I immediately thought he was dead.'

'He was, though, wasn't he, in a way?' Katya said. 'Perhaps your mother should have told you the truth straight away.'

'The truth? Nobody's ever known the truth, that's part of the problem.'

I ordered a cold beer. Katya told me more about her life in Russia. In particular, she spoke about a 'favourite' grandmother who had died last year at the age of ninety-three. This grandmother was born into a large Jewish family in Odessa.

'Her name was Shaipiro – an international name, by the way. You know how many Jews in Russia have changed their names? My mother and I have this little joke about being Jewish in Russia. "I met this Jew the other day," my mother says to me, "who changed his name from Shaipiro to Petrov." Well, one day, Mr Petrov returns to the government official and asks to change his name again, to Ivanov – another very Russian name, of course. But the official says to him, "Why do you want to change your name, Mr Petrov, you've already changed it once?" Petrov says, "Yes, but people keep asking me what my original name was."

67

I smiled and slipped Katya's hand into mine, watching her eyes closely for a response.

'When my grandmother was dying,' she continued, 'I returned to Moscow to be with her. I visited her every day in the hospital. I spent hours with her, sitting by the bed. This little old shrivelled woman from Odessa could hardly see or hear. Sometimes, when the drugs began affecting her too much, she forgot how to speak in Russian. It was very strange, especially when she began speaking to me in Yiddish, bits of conversation I couldn't understand. Sometimes she sang Yiddish songs from her childhood in the small village.' Katya softened her tone and began gently to sing one of her grandmother's songs.

'You sing beautifully,' I said.

'Yes, but you should have heard my grandmother sing! I took my tape recorder to the hospital on my last few visits. I taped her talking about her life, and singing these songs in Yiddish. One day, Josh, I hope you'll listen to these songs with me.' She looked up, squeezing my hand. 'You know, my grandmother's husband was a Kazak ataman.'

'What, from Kazakhstan?'

'No, Josh,' she said, laughing. 'Not Kazakhskaya. A Kazak.' She rolled her tongue and made a guttural sound at the base of her throat. '*Kaaz-ak*. Or perhaps you would say Cossack.'

'The warrior people?'

'Yes, that's it, an ataman is a Cossack leader. A chief. So you can imagine, a Cossack ataman marrying a Jew. It's a very strange mix, even for Russia.'

'Russian extremes again,' I said, 'just like the weather.'

Later, as Katya and I waited on the Strand for a taxi, I pulled her towards me and into a speculative embrace. Dust spun up from the wheels of passing cars. Horns blared. Drunks shouted. Whispering men approached, touting, 'Taxi, taxi, taxi' – but they didn't add, 'unlicensed, illegal'. As we kissed for the first time, I felt the thickness of her tongue inside my mouth, tasted the red wine on her breath. I knew we should forsake a taxi for a slow, intimate walk back to Nassau Street.

'Katya, I want you to spend the night with me,' I said.

'What?' she said. 'I can't, no, not yet.' I could feel her nervousness and the hard hands of rejection on my chest, pushing me away.

She rushed towards the Savoy, where a taxi had just switched on its light. She hurried over to the car, and I pursued her quickening shadow along the Strand. I caught up with her, spoke to her through the open window, my words flowing maybe too quickly.

'What's the matter? Have I offended you? It wasn't that I wanted you to stay with me like that.'

Her expression remained fixed, as if she'd understood nothing of what I'd said. There were times, I was to discover, that if I spoke too rapidly or relaxed entirely into idiom, she seemed slightly lost in incomprehension. As the taxi pulled away, I saw her look back at me through the thick glass. A wounded light seemed to be streaming from her eyes.

I walked home through the crowded streets, the swarms of unknowable people around me, the faces glimpsed, the heat of the traffic, the threatening noise. The problem with cities was that there was no privacy, nowhere you could be alone; and as I pushed my way back to Nassau Street, I found myself longing for catastrophe, for an annihilating event to cleanse and empty these streets – the degeneracy I saw that night around me, the rootlessness.

Back at the flat, I opened the door, went up the stairs to where . . . Katya was waiting, sitting outside my flat. She had the forlorn air of someone against whom a great injustice has been committed. She also looked tired. Seeing her sat there, I immediately felt ashamed by the earlier arrogance of my thoughts, that wish for destruction.

'Hello,' I said. 'Are you all right?' I could see her legs

through the split in her skirt; her eyeliner had run across her cheek. 'Can I sit with you?' I said.

She nodded.

'Have you been back long?'

Again, she nodded. I wanted to stroke her legs, to hold her pale hands. There was sweat on her chest, where the buttons of her shirt were open, and I thought of the Thai restaurant again, the smell of sweet coconut oil in her hair, the noise from the restless streets, the incredible heat.

'Did I offend you?' I said.

She didn't answer.

'Why won't you say something?'

She sighed. 'I want to explain something to you, Joshua,' she said, 'something about trust, about how I really feel. I've been badly hurt before, you know, and I can't – won't – let it happen to me again. It's too painful. I've worked hard to start a new life here in London. I don't want to mess it up, I don't. D'you understand?'

'Yes,' I said, but I didn't.

How long since I'd felt the flesh of a woman beside me?

Then she giggled. 'You must think I'm crazy.'

I nodded, saying, 'A tiny bit.'

'Well?' she said.

'Do you want to come in with me?' I said.

'Right now, here?' she said.

This time, I shrugged my shoulders. Without saying anything, she took my hand and led me across the landing to her flat.

Once we'd made love – for the first time, silently and in the plain darkness – I asked her to come with me to Dorset. She suggested we took her car.

IV

Three days after the murder Anthony Winter leaves the country. He hopes to lie low, clear his head, at least for one day. He drives down to Dover and takes the ferry across to Calais, where he spends a lonely afternoon wandering around the rainy streets. Wherever he goes he keeps hearing the low Fenland winds, sees the flatness of that monotonous East Anglian landscape, struggles with the effects of the sleeplessness of the previous nights. Not an hour passes but he thinks, too, of Nicholas Dundee, of what he might be doing – has done.

Sitting in a harbour-side café, he watches the ferries returning across the Channel to England, and can't bring himself to board one. The temptation to fake his own death is like a dull ache in the chest he can't ignore. He fantasizes about driving deeper into France, to Le Crotoy on the bay of the Somme, perhaps, where he and his parents had their only foreign holiday. There he would leave his clothes and a note, in French and English, on the beach, and then simply disappear, heading down to the warm south and beyond, to anywhere he wants to go.

It's growing dark when he checks into a cheap hotel overlooking the ferry port. He has always enjoyed the soiled romance of transient locations – ports, airports, train stations – points of transition and intersection. The hotel has a vacancy sign in the window. As always, he asks for a view of the sea. He pays a supplementary charge and takes the lift up to his double room on the third floor. Asked in English about his luggage, he tells the woman he has none. The hotel smells of neglect and under-investment. There aren't many guests about; in fact, he sees none during his brief stay.

The wind is stronger by the sea and the flags along the front are flapping noisily. He watches an elderly couple looking out to sea, a boy walking his dog, and then the French television news. Someone must have missed Oliver King: a father, brother, friend or punter. Someone must have noticed he wasn't around. Someone must have seen them and their car in the village, at the pub in Aldeburgh, driving in the dark out to Stratford St Andrew. He goes into the bathroom and pisses in a steaming rancid stream.

After dinner he finds himself walking around town, half-looking for a woman. It's dark, windy and wet, and he can hear the sea turning in on itself, the threat of more rain always there. On his return to the hotel he encounters an old man playing the piano in reception, a piece of music that makes him think immediately of his wife.

Later, in his room, he begins writing a letter to her.

This is the hardest thing I've ever had to write, but when I've tried talking to you recently about what is going wrong words have always failed me. I'm disgusted with the way I've been treating everyone but I don't know what to do about it. I feel like I've wandered into a maze but can't find my way out. I feel stupefied. All that I've known before seems useless. I don't know anything. My coins no longer fit the machines. I'm in a land I no longer recognize. At times like this, I've tried praying, but even prayers don't seem to help me. If this note is found with my clothes, then you know that I couldn't see a way forward. I hope one day you'll forgive me for taking the coward's way out.

But I reckon it's easier to love someone who isn't there.

He breaks off, listening to the long sad blast of a night ferry's horn. Did the letter strike the authentic note of regret? Was it believable? Did he even believe it himself? He screws up the letter, drops it in the sink and sets it alight. The pages curl and darken; then there are flames.

Crossing the Channel, the next day, he sees the cliffs of Dover through persistent eye-stinging rain and thinks how spoilt and unwelcoming they are. Dull grey, not white. He prefers leaving England and looking back at the cliffs. Ahead is an entire continent of discovery. Newness. Whereas behind him there is only a small, damp, restrictive island. The past.

On the way back to London, he stops off at a sports shop to buy his son a set of beginner's golf clubs. By the time he reaches the British Museum the boy is already waiting there for him, standing against the railings, dressed in his school uniform. He seems out of place in the city, a lost boy. He smiles shyly when he sees his father. This smile moves Anthony more than he ever thought possible, and he feels again the burn of inexplicable regret in his chest.

Sleeping Partners

Katya and I left London at eight the next morning, stopping once at a service station on an anonymous strip of motorway, where we drank muddy black coffee and ate an all-day breakfast, sitting at a plastic table on flat orange chairs which were screwed into the floor, under the ruthless glare of hard twenty-four-hour-a-day lighting. By the time we arrived on the outskirts of Poole the morning had bloomed into sunshine, yet I felt bloated and dehydrated from the long, tedious journey – all that junk food and recycled air. We'd come south together because I was curious to discover what time had done to our whitewashed house high up in the sandy lanes of Studland, curious to discover if the picture of Poole I carried around inside my head was no more than a metaphysical conceit, nothing but a construct of nostalgia and lonely imagination.

We drove through the town, the roads already beginning to strain with traffic, and out towards the harbour, searching for bed and breakfast vacancies. Driving along the front, I was struck by how much had changed. Everywhere you looked there were new buildings and construction sites. Developments had sprung up along the waterfront: modish apartment blocks with balconies and decks overlooking the thicket of masts of sailing boats in the modernized quay. There were bars and restaurants, pizza parlours, burger joints and video stores where before there'd been nothing but an old pub or two. New, smarter roads had also been laid, and several hard-surface tennis courts, a putting green and a bowls club were unfamiliar to me. The drab prefab where we'd lived before emigrating to Canada had gone. On its site was another larger, more modernized apartment block. There was nothing to regret in its passing.

And yet I felt a something rising faintly to the watery surface of memory like an air bubble. In the first year after the disappearance, my mother, who by this time had found herself a part-time administrative job at one of the local schools, began keeping an audio diary of her experiences, dictated at intervals. I'd never heard those diaries, and didn't know if they still existed, but I've always assumed they were the mechanism through which she grappled with her loss. I recall once arriving home from school to find Mum sitting up at the breakfast bar in the kitchen, her elbows placed either side of a tape recorder, into which she spoke in short, rapid sentences. There were photocopied pages from a document headed 'Family Law' on the table beside her. I glanced at one of the pages, on which was written something I couldn't understand, let alone pronounce. I memorized what was written: 'Emigration and Leave to Remove from the Jurisdiction'.

Mum mustn't have heard me come in, since she continued speaking into the machine as if I wasn't there. The only thing I remember her saying exactly was something about 'the bastard not even having the courage to leave a note'.

'Who's the bastard, Mum?' I said. 'You don't mean Pa, do you?'

She turned, surprised to find me there, and it was strange to see her smiling (I'd expected tears on her face, a melodramatic dribble of mascara). 'No, Josh, I don't mean Pa, of course I don't,' she said.

'Did he leave a note?' I said.

'A note?'

'Yes, you know, like a sick note at school, to tell us what was wrong with him or where he was going?'

'No, he didn't do that.'

'Why didn't he, Mum? Why didn't he tell us where he was going?'

'Because he just didn't.'

'Does this mean he was kidnapped?'

'No, Josh, it doesn't mean that.'

She realized the tape was still running and pressed the stop button firmly.

'When is he coming home?' I said.

'I don't know if he's ever coming home.'

'D'you want him to come home, Mum?'

'Of course I do.'

'But what if he doesn't? What if he never comes home?'

She went through into the kitchen, not answering. 'D'you want a cup of tea?' she said.

With her attention engaged elsewhere, I secreted one of the photocopied pages into my pocket. 'Has anyone been up to the flat in London?' I called into the kitchen.

'The police have.'

'Have you been to the flat, Mum?'

'Yes, I've been to the flat.'

'I stayed at the flat once,' I said.

'I remember.'

'We went to football. It was raining.' I heard the kettle click on. 'What if he's dead, Mum?'

'Don't say that,' she said, coming through from the kitchen to cuddle me. She held me close to her but all I could think about was how warm and itchy her sweater felt.

Later, I went to my room and placed the fold of paper on my desk.

Other factors – Loss of heritage; Access

(i) *Loss of heritage*

The first and very important factor, which has played a greater part than the issues in the few reported cases might suggest, is the loss of the child's natural English heritage and identity; not merely in the sense of uprooting him from that which he has always known, but in the sense of turning him into something different from that which he would otherwise be. The point is a simple but fundamental one. Whatever the day-to-day needs may dictate in regard to care and control, whatever the wishes

and upsets of the child may dictate as to access, a good
other parent does still have a right to say, 'My English
child shall not become an American or a German or an
Icelandic one.'
In Dyer *v.* Dyer, 7 *November 1973*

Although I understood very little of what I read, I understood enough to know what Mum was thinking, perhaps even
preparing. Or, as it turned out, had prepared – for it was later
the same evening that she told us she hoped to take us to live
with her in Canada.

'I don't want to become an American,' I said. 'I don't want to
lose my heritage.'

'Whatever do you mean, Joshua?' she said. 'It's Canada, not
America, and you'll always be English, regardless.' I remember
her look of pained suspicion.

That must have been in the autumn of 1984, when a great
storm of change was blowing through the country in the form
of doctrinaire economics and industrial unrest. We spent hours
of an evening in our thin-walled annexe, watching the television news with Mum, hoping for a snippet on Pa. But there
was always nothing.

'Mum,' I said, 'why is Pa's case never on television?'

'Because he's not famous,' she said.

'But he's been in the paper!'

'Yes, Joshua, he's been in the local paper, but that's different.'

'Why? If he's in the paper, he must be famous.'

'It doesn't quite work like that, I'm afraid. You can say many
things about your father, but you can't say he was famous.'

There were images of violence on the news most nights back
then, in particular clashes between miners and the police. I
remember Mum tried to explain, more than once, the background to the dispute that had led to such extreme conflict, but
none of us was really interested. We wanted to talk about Pa

instead, but she seemed willing only to interest us in other things: our schoolwork, the harbour-side developments. In retrospect, she was right to keep us talking about the world outside our own small world inside the flat, about politics and the future, although then it didn't feel quite right. It felt disrespectful.

Katya and I parked up and walked down to the harbour, sprawling out on a bench. You could see Brownsea Island, the thick clusters of its trees, out in the middle of the harbour. The clean coastal air was a heady release after the prolonged staleness of the car. I'd returned to Poole with something approaching fear and trembling. It was there that I expected innumerable long-suppressed memories to come rushing towards me like a pack of wild horses, dragging the carcass of my younger self behind them. But no – it was the smaller, more local things that came back to me most urgently: the construction of a treehouse one summer in the branches of our yew tree (it was destroyed the same month in an electric storm); weekend barbecues in the garden; long walks up to Old Harry Rocks with Mum; a game of beach cricket in which I scored a rapid fifty with Dan's new Gunn & Moore bat – a feat of lasting pride, even if the stumps were no more than a bucket of damp sand, the ball a sea-soaked tennis ball and my sister, Rachel, the lone bored fielder.

We found a room in a modest bungalow offering bed and breakfast and a view of the harbour. I paid the deposit. When the old couple who owned the bungalow went out, I made two cups of coffee. Katya and I agreed to meet later for lunch after I'd visited both the library and Dr Kellor. I left her in the bungalow, dozing in our quiet corner bedroom.

The library had been modernized, extended and computerized and had lost that old musty attic-like smell of unread books and newspapers. It felt (and smelt) like an industrious office – overlit and rather noisy. I looked up some back copies of the *Poole and Bournemouth Gazette* from more than a decade ago on microfiche, and read again the patchy details of what happened: an urgent lead story in the week of the disappearance; a feature speculating on whether he'd been murdered; an interview with my mother in which she spoke of her sadness at having visited the local morgue ('the awfulness of all those poor unclaimed bodies'); an interview with a private detective who specialized in tracking down missing persons.

There was a front-page picture of Pa, republished in the following weeks in ever-diminishing size, beneath the headline: 'Fears Grow for Missing Local Businessman'. The picture was an indistinct shot, taken in our garden, of Pa standing beside the yew tree dressed in an open-necked Fred Perry. What was it about his expression that was so disturbing? The picture was published again the following week, above a basement front-page story, captioned: 'Business Worries: Mystery of Disappearance Grows'. The next week, the story had been relegated to the inside pages, under the headline: 'Police Rule out Kidnap of Businessman'. And so it went on, for more than six weeks, the story of my father drifting inexorably towards the back of the paper as its potential for sensation and scandal diminished.

The most striking images from that entire period, though, were from the posters of my father fixed to walls, trees and lampposts around the town; and the flyers distributed free with the local paper with which he'd once been associated. His pale, startled black-and-white portrait peered out from beneath the capitalized headline:

MISSING
Anthony Frank Winter, aged 40
Last seen November 1983
Any information please contact
Dorset 0966 366 366
Or your nearest police station

Reading through the reports, I felt myself again being buffeted by the winds of rumour and innuendo . . . the wicked

79

things that were said. So what of the gossip that he'd had other relationships, other women? Well, no one ever stepped forward to reveal themselves. That he was living a new, clandestine life in New York, where he'd always had a love child? No sightings on that front, either. Suicide, a death plunge off Old Harry Rocks into a truculent winter sea? No body, no sighting, no note, no long farewell.

I knew Pa was different, that he never went to an office as my friends' fathers did, that he wore his hair long, an untidy swirl of dark curls, that he was too restless for the conventional life. But surely he wasn't *that* different: the only man of his generation in our town literally to vanish, to leave absolutely nothing behind, no track to follow? Gone.

In truth, these reports added nothing I didn't already know. Most frustratingly, they revealed nothing about his motivation. The eternal mystery of Anthony Winter I was beginning to accept was his absolute incomprehensibility.

As I set off for Dr Kellor's, I realized what it was about the old newspaper photograph of my father that had so disturbed me. The expression on the man's face . . . He *was* inconsolable.

Dr Kellor's house was set back from the road but the gates were open. I swung on to the gravel drive, the tyres of Katya's car tossing up dusty chips of stone. He'd lived in that house for as long as I could remember: late 1950s, detached, red-brick with wood panelling at the front, a veranda and porch, and a long strip of front garden hemmed in on three sides of its rectangular plot by tall trees, the branches of which were thick and leafy against the blue sky. The slightly overgrown lawn was dotted with rusting croquet hoops, and there were a greenhouse and a weathered wooden shed in the far right-hand corner.

From an upstairs window a curtain flapped and I thought I glimpsed the pale blur of a woman's withdrawing face. Soon afterwards Mrs Kellor greeted me at the door. Her short hair was still dyed dark, and her skin had a worn, leathery glow. I introduced myself and we chatted briefly before she showed me into Dr Kellor's study. He was at his desk, apparently talking to himself. I thought he'd gone quite insane until I realized he was using a hands-free phone.

He smiled warmly, lifted his hand as if to indicate surprise at my height, before gesturing for me to sit down. A mild summer light streamed through the window behind him. Killer Kellor, like his wife, had aged very little. He'd kept his hair and possessed the same bulkily pugnacious demeanour as before: broad, solid shoulders, muscular neck, intimidating hands. The beard was fuller, if anything, and flecked grey.

'Sorry about that, Joshua,' he said, when he'd finished. 'Looks like you're keeping yourself well.'

'I've certainly been enjoying the summer,' I said.

'Phenomenal, isn't it? They say it's as good as seventy-six. I suppose you're too young to remember that one. Remind me, how old are you now?'

'Twenty-five. I'm twenty-six at the end of November.'

'That's a mighty good age for a man to be, Joshua, twenty-five. It's all ahead of you.'

He asked after my mother, then offered me a drink. I chose something non-alcoholic.

As he left the room I saw that he was wearing knee-length chino shorts and flip-flops and walked with a slight limp. He returned carrying a tray on which were balanced two glasses with ice and sliced lemon in each, two small cans of tonic water and a bottle of gin.

'Sure you won't have some of this to help it stand up a bit?' he said, unscrewing the gin bottle. He generously poured gin into each glass. 'That's better,' he said, settling himself at the desk. 'Now, how can I help?'

I explained that my father's records had been transferred from Dorset to Belsize Park and from there, disappointingly, they'd completely disappeared.

'Not easy getting hold of these things, is it? The Patients' Charter has changed all that now, but it's no good to you.'

I asked him directly about my father's health.

'I'd remember if he wasn't fit, Joshua. You remember the ones who are never out of your sight, the neurotic ones, the heart-sinkers. You remember the seriously ill, or those with something unusual like AIDS. If your father wasn't well, I'm sure he would have told me when I saw him. I don't think he ever came to the surgery.'

'Did you see him often?'

'No, not often. Played the odd game of squash, and there was' – he interrupted himself – 'Pretty good player he was, hit the thing terribly hard. Used to run out of puff after a bit, though. You know, bit of a tobacco man. But we all were back then. What about you, Joshua? A smoker?'

'I had a road accident last year,' I said. 'Haven't smoked since.'

'Serious, was it?'

I hesitated. 'No, it wasn't serious. But, Dr Kellor –'

'Kim, please.'

'Kim, OK, you were going to say something, squash and . . . ?'

'You're quite right. Your father and I used to occasionally have our little business chats. My wife and me not having children, you know, had a bit spare to play with, liked an investment.'

He paused, opened a drawer, removed something small from a decorative tin, rolled it between his fingers like a piece of fluff and then placed it on the fleshy inside of his lower lip. He must have read my surprise. 'It's snuff, old chap,' he said. 'Picked up the habit some years ago while on holiday in Sweden. Very popular over there, snuff-taking. I import these little tins – Ettan, it's called – from Stockholm.' Then he sneezed violently into his handkerchief. 'Now, what were we talking about? Oh, yes, quite a character, your father. Always had something on the go.'

'Were you involved in any of his projects directly?'

'I put up a bit of capital for that newspaper thing .. the, umm, oh dear, what was it?'

'*The Classified*?'

'Yes, that's right. So there was that. I almost got involved in a little wine bar thing in London as well.'

'Wine bar! Which wine bar?'

He must have detected the quickening tone in my voice. 'This little place in Camden he wanted to buy and turn into an upmarket eaterie. Asked if I would be one of the sleeping partners. I must say I was interested. Even went up to town with him once to have a look round. Not bad, but totally in the wrong area. Camden was a right dump then. This was before Maggie began sorting out the inner cities. Those little wine bar–eaterie places work best, I think, in stockbroker belts – the Wentworths and Sunningdales.'

The Camden wine bar was, at least, something authentically new and different. Dr Kellor had dangled a rope from the side of the boat and, like an exhausted swimmer, I grabbed it. I asked if he remembered its name.

'I'm afraid not. All this must have been, pfff' – he made a noise like escaping steam – 'back in the early eighties. Hold on, though. I can find out.' He went over to a metal cabinet and began searching through numerous files. He took several, clearly marked 'Investments', over to the desk and worked through them. 'Here it is – yes, Nick's Bistro. Got a whole section on it here.' He seemed absorbed by what he was reading, as if caught up all over again in the excitement and complexities of the proposed deal, in the potential risks of becoming my father's sleeping partner. 'There's even a couple of letters here, from Anthony.'

'May I see?'

He passed them across the desk. These were not so much letters as scribbled notes, written in my father's distinctive hand, every character idiosyncratically angular, like the electronic squiggles on a cardiogram indicating a heart in distress: erratic, wayward, a heart collapsing in on itself. Receiving these examples of his handwriting so unexpectedly, though the notes were of the blandest unimportance, moved me tremendously.

83

I asked Dr Kellor if the police had visited him after the disappearance.

'Yes, I believe they did come to the surgery,' he said.

'Did you mention the wine bar to them then?'

'I don't know. Maybe, maybe not. They were, like you, more interested in his health than anything else. As were the insurance people, who also contacted me. Think they were trying to find out if he had any medical reason to commit suicide. You know, being diagnosed with terminal cancer or something.'

'You never mentioned the wine bar to the police?'

'You know, I don't think I did.'

I met up with Katya and we drove to Sandbanks, where the car ferry crosses the harbour to Studland. At peak times in summer you sometimes had to wait as long as an hour for space on the clanky ferry, but there was only a short queue today. Nor was there much activity on the grey-green choppy water. We crossed the harbour and drove along the narrow lanes which sliced through the chalky heathland downs. We parked outside a pub from where you looked out across the sweeping expanse of the English Channel, a huge bowl of blue-green light which I saw reflected in Katya's eyes. The air was brisk and colder up in the hills and there was a distinct autumnal wind. The Indian summer seemed less oppressive here, much further away and seemingly as one with the urgent streets of London. We were high on the thin air of our own intimacy, and we were comfortable.

I closed my eyes and tried to summon up those distant summer days of childhood. And soon enough I began to smell the scuffed dust in the air, re-experienced the cool, burnished light of late afternoon as we hurried up from the beach after a long day's bathing, could hear the snap of dry twigs as we walked in the clustered shade of the trees which were banked either side of the narrow tracks leading up to our house, hear the languid murmur of insects.

Katya was dressed in a loose T-shirt and cardigan. She

clapped her hands together for warmth as she looked out to sea, the wind pimpling her skin. 'Is everything as before?' she asked me, her accent more noticeable than usual.

'It's almost exactly as I remember it. And yet everything seems somehow different, spoiled in a way. I don't know why.'

We walked briskly, following the road as it swung left up the hill towards ours and the other handsome houses elevated above the hot struggles of neighbouring Poole. As we approached, I was gripped by a kind of inexplicable gloom, as if I knew what lay ahead: the house derelict, the windows boarded up, the front door daubed with obscenities, the guttering busted and hanging loose, and the garden thickly overgrown. I even imagined a swimming pool we never had, drained and full of consumerist trash: broken bottles, cans, rusted bicycle wheels, children's toys, planks of wood, rags – all stagnant and rotten. The smell of deterioration and decay.

Then we turned the corner and there it was, our old house – freed from the ice pack of memory – with its magnificent yew tree and long, undulating garden sloping down to a drystone wall and out beyond to fields and meadows where cattle grazed. Katya must have sensed a change in me, since she took my hand. Together we leaned against the gatepost. There was a car, a red sports BMW, on the drive, and windows were open in the kitchen and in an upstairs bedroom.

'Has the house changed much?' she asked.

'My father must have stretched himself to buy it.'

'Let's knock?' Katya said.

'What can we say?'

'What about "hello"?'

'And then?'

'Well, there's always "goodbye".'

She led me by the arm through the gate and enthusiastically up to the door. There was movement in the kitchen. 'Come on, it's too late now,' she said, ringing the bell.

I heard a child's voice. A smart, composed woman in her

mid-thirties opened a door constrained by a security chain. Her evident hostility rendered me immediately uncertain.

Katya spoke. 'Sorry to bother you but we were just passing and wondered' – she hesitated – 'well, my friend here used to live in your house.'

The woman smiled. 'So what?' Her young son appeared, squeezing mischievously between her legs. 'Stay here, Matt,' she said. 'Daddy'll be home soon.' Her quiet voice carried a warning. The twin sparkle of her engagement and wedding rings drew my eye. 'I don't know what I can do, even if you did live here,' she said, looking at me.

'It's true, I did live here once, a long time ago,' I said. 'We were the Winters, were here until 1984.'

She smiled thinly. 'We only bought this last year.'

I felt embarrassed. I didn't know what more to say, or really what I was doing at her door; and I felt something approaching resentment towards Katya – she was culpable for exposing me in this way.

'Sorry to have bothered you,' I said, and the woman withdrew into the house, without so much as saying goodbye. I heard her bolt and double-lock the door from inside. Locked out, all over again.

'Well, she wasn't very friendly,' Katya said, as we made our way down the hill. 'In Russia, if this had happened, we would have been invited in, had coffee and cakes.'

'This is England,' I said. 'I'd react in the same way if strangers came knocking on my door.' I walked sullenly on, ahead of her.

We spent the rest of that increasingly overcast afternoon exploring Poole and Studland by car. Things *were* indeed at once the same yet dislocatingly different. To read the London newspapers, particularly the Sundays, with their prurient celebrity gossip; their febrile investigations into the serial adulteries and undeclared homosexualities of politicians; their alarmist speculations about the impending traumas of the bio-tech revolution and the new genetic century; their fascination with Prozac and other self-styled wonder drugs; their obsession with health, money and sport – reading all this was to find yourself in a radically changed country, no longer gentle or wise. Yet driving around on that ordinary afternoon, past the church where Mum and Rachel sometimes went, past the recreational football parks where Dan used to play, past the golf course where Pa was a weekend member – all this was to find yourself transported back in time, returned to a place you once knew and liked. The shops were a little brighter perhaps, the food more cosmopolitan, the people more obviously fashion- and style-smart, the social groupings more multiracial, the spoken vernacular a little more wised-up and Americanized; but I knew these people, I went to school with them, they were recognizably my people. This, in a way, was appealing, as finding our house in Studland largely unchanged was appealing – the homely tug of continuity.

Over dinner, on the waterfront later that evening, Katya announced that she was returning on Friday to Russia for a short break.

'How long will you be away?' I said.

'Not long, perhaps three to four weeks. It's my mother, I always try to see her at this time of year, before it gets ridiculously cold.'

I was relieved to hear her say that. Perhaps she sensed something of my relief, for she immediately said, 'You know, we met at the wrong time, didn't we, Josh?'

'What d'you mean by that?' I said.

'Well, in our way we're both tainted. You by your father, and me by . . . O God, I don't know by what. I just feel so tired sometimes, so cut off in London.'

I looked up at her with fresh interest. Had she sensed that my feelings for her were already changing. She'd annoyed me up at Studland and I still felt humiliated by what had passed –

the cold indifference of the woman at the door of the house I'd once called home. Any thoughts of a more permanent relationship with Katya, even if she wanted one, which I'm not even sure she did, were fading. And yet her words – so redolent of last things – troubled me. What did she really mean by *tainted*? I leaned across the table and kissed her curious, open mouth. She certainly didn't taste . . . tainted.

That night, back in the bungalow, we made love again. The last person I'd slept with before Katya was Amy, a month before the accident. I remember it was then, as Amy and I lay together in her apartment out at the Beaches, that she'd told me how much she loved Tom, that she'd always loved him, continuously, 'desperately', and wanted me to tell him. I wasn't *that* offended. Amy was more like a sister to me really, with whom I enjoyed the occasional incestuous game. Still, I felt a pang of intense jealousy to hear her speak so passionately about Tom, having just had sex with me. Why doesn't she 'desperately' love me, I self-pityingly thought. Did our sex mean nothing? The truth is, I never told Tom what Amy had told me that night. But I like to think he knew how she felt about him, and I'm pretty sure the feeling was mutual – and that if they'd lived, if I hadn't dragged them out to Walden Pond that afternoon, they would have worked something out together, would have made it in the end.

Katya placed her hand over my mouth to stifle my moans (which were really sobs for Amy) from waking the old couple down the corridor. Even now, much later, I can still feel Katya naked against me, smell her on my hands, taste her saliva in my mouth. If only I'd seen what was hurtling towards me like a runaway truck, I'd have clung to her that night in Dorset, clung to her and never let her go.

Our final journey on Sunday morning, before returning to London, was to the central police station in Poole, a dull, flat-roofed building harassed by a concrete high-rise car park that commanded the skyline like a dinosaur. The duty officer's bored expression remained unchanged when I explained I wanted to discuss my missing father's files. Katya and I were told to wait in a desolate room, where we were brought cups of machine coffee. There was a red-top tabloid on the table, a couple of empty ashtrays. You could feel the sun beating on the flat roof above. Ten minutes passed before we were joined by a tired-looking woman. She was dressed in a police shirt, tie and dark trousers. She was thin and the uniform didn't flatter her.

'I'm Sergeant Fitzpatrick,' she said. Her flaxen hair was pulled into a ponytail and her fair eyebrows were plucked finely into the shape of two floating commas. There was a pale circle of skin on her wedding finger, lighter than the rest of her hand, where perhaps a ring had been removed. Her nails were short and bitten down. She wasn't wearing any make-up.

I explained the circumstances of the disappearance and asked, having shown her my Canadian ID card, if I could read through the case files, if they still existed. She listened with sympathy. Her questions resonated with my own. Was his body ever found? Did he have a reason to disappear? What had the original investigations uncovered? Was he involved in anything illegal? Had there since been any reported sightings of him?

'Sounds a bit like Reggie Perrin to me,' she said, and I smelt the coffee on her breath. She had the kind of West Country brogue I remembered from some of the poorer kids at school. 'If you say his body was never found,' she went on, 'then his files will theoretically be open, if not exactly live. But I doubt they'd be here after all this time. They've probably gone to headquarters in Dorchester.'

'Would I be able to see them there?'

'Twelve years ago you say ... They're probably not even computerized, although some files are being retrospectively updated.'

She gave me the number of another police officer to call on

Monday. 'He'd have a better idea of what you want. We have a skeleton staff here at the best of times.'

I asked if she would forward a letter to him. 'It'll save me going over everything again when I call him.'

She agreed, although her lugubrious expression revealed her diminished enthusiasm. I summarized the case on one side of A4 paper, explaining why I wanted to read my father's file. Then we left for home, pulling out of the station and straight into a traffic jam.

Katya wound down her window, dangling a bare arm against the side of the car. 'Oh, this is terrible,' she said. You could feel the heat of the engine inside the car, the stink of petrol fumes outside.

And then it occurred to me, with all the clarity of the sun emerging from behind a cloud, that the solution to my quest was that there was no solution: other people in all their tortured interiority were essentially other, mysteries ultimately even unto themselves. So demystification had done nothing for me but create greater mystification. Beyond the apparent worst there was a worse suffering. Either that, or I simply get on with my life, as my mother had done with hers, allow his memory to slip gently into the past, merely preserved like a dusty image in an old family photo album.

Even if I did eventually see the police files – the summary of all those inquiries – with their cataloguing of his shambolic, if not entirely worthless, business affairs, if that wasn't too grand a description for what was essentially no more than a speculative portfolio of struggling interests, what would they reveal anyway? I accepted that I was no closer to understanding the riddle of his disappearance, to understanding what had made him run or kill himself. I'd reached a kind of terminus: the point beyond which I could go no further without going backwards, rethinking everything – for example, did my mother have him murdered? In such thoughts, madness surely lay. So, sitting in the car with Katya, I allowed myself to be overwhelmed by a kind of nostalgia for all the hopes I'd nurtured on arrival in London, especially the thin-spun illusion that my father was alive, and someone was destined one day to lead me to him, like a sniffer dog locating a long-buried skier in the snow.

Katya beat her hand against the side of the car, recalling me to the tedium of the road. 'When I come back from Moscow, Josh, it'll be nearly winter.'

'And I'll perhaps be a month away from returning to Canada.'

'What then?' she said.

I didn't answer. All I knew was that I was looking forward to starting work, to starting all over again.

V

As a child Anthony Winter used to go to Upton Park some-times with his father. They would stand together on the Chicken Run, with Anthony balancing on a wooden box to enhance his view of the pitch. He remembers how odd it was watching his father – so reticent at home – lock shoulders with the strangers around him, swaying as he sang 'I'm Forever Blowing Bubbles'. Old Frankie seemed so completely absorbed by it all as he succumbed to the will of the crowd. Yet no matter what the score – win or lose – he would spend the entire return journey to Forest Gate complaining about his team, their faults and frailties. Once back at home, Frankie would revert to order, becoming all remotely locked up inside himself again, inside his capsule of silence. Perhaps it was the tinnitus.

At half-time, Anthony Winter leaves his seat and goes searching for a telephone. He generously tips a steward, who takes him to a small, unheated office behind the stand. Nick Dundee answers the phone. There's no warmth or encourage-ment in his voice. Anthony Winter is immediately concerned. What has he discovered?

'Where've you been? I tried reaching you,' Dundee says.

'I've been digging around.'

'Have you found anything?'

'No. Have you?'

'Yes, I have actually.'

'What have you found out?'

'I'll tell you tonight, when we meet.'

'No, I can't, not tonight. I've got my boy with me.'

'What about now? Can't you leave him for half an hour and come over?'

'No, we're at the football, at West Ham.'

'What's the score there?'

'Nil–nil.'

'Good game?'

'Nope, it's shite.'

'How are you feeling?' Dundee says.

'Not good. You?'

'Like shit, actually. D'you know what? All my eyelashes fell out yesterday.'

'What?'

'Yeah, the whole lot. I woke up and they were lying all over the pillow. The doctor couldn't explain it. He'd never seen anything like it before.'

The crowd's roar indicates the resumption of the game.

'I've got to go,' Anthony says.

'Tomorrow then?' Dundee says.

'I'll come to yours, once my boy's gone.'

'What I've found out, it doesn't look good.'

'Anything I should know now?'

'Well, it looks as if Kingy stitched us up good and proper. There was no order. So what I want to know, Tone, is where's our money?'

On the way back to his seat, Anthony buys a coffee for himself and lemonade for the boy. He swiftly smokes a cigarette and then lights another. People stand up as he squeezes along the row. He is waiting, mumbling something about Anthony having been away longer than expected. It's raining much harder, too, but the boy keeps talking, bafflingly, about snow when there is none.

He wonders about the boy as he hands him his drink: what will become of him? He's so quiet and self-contained, a bit like his grandfather in that sense. Anthony realizes that he's spent so long away that even his own children are becoming strangers to him. That he will never know them now. How does he feel about that? Still, he's pleased the boy supports West Ham. At least Frankie would have approved.

93

He begins thinking about Nick Dundee, about the fake note of support sent to him after the murder.

Dear Nick
Just want to say how much I've enjoyed our time together. I want you to know you can always count on my trust and support. Never let the bastards grind you down.
Tony

He'd known Dundee for less than a year and felt no attachment or loyalty to him. He didn't even like him. When he thinks about Dundee, nothing occurs to him. Dundee is empty, a cipher. He was useful because he had contacts and seemed to know how to make money. Anthony Winter laughs aloud. He knows how to lose it, too. Hearing his chuckle, the boy looks up, asks if everything is all right. 'Course it is,' he says, and pats his son on the back.

Then, many miles away, he sees something crawling from the slime at the bottom of a dark Suffolk pond.

Doors Unopened

My resolution was unchanged when I awoke on Monday morning, the first day of a new month of a new start. No matter how much I loved and respected my father, I was prepared finally to let him go. There was nevertheless one last thing I had to do before that afternoon's induction meeting at Clifford Chance.

Would that I hadn't done it.

What I did was return to Companies House one last time to search on microfiche, with the help of the ever-diligent Welshman, for details of Nick's Bistro in Camden Town. To my surprise, it was listed, along with a second Nick's Bistro in Loughton, Essex; and to my greater surprise, Anthony Winter was listed as one of three co-directors of the Camden operation. My father. The other co-directors were a woman, Jude Slammer, and someone called Nicholas Dundee. There was an asterisk against his name, suggesting, according to the Welshman, that he had other 'more contemporaneous directorships'. The bistro went into receivership in 1984. At which time my father was still listed as a co-director . . . a year *after* he'd disappeared.

My hands were perspiring as the Welshman ran computerized searches for Nicholas Dundee and Jude Slammer. There were no further listings for Slammer, but Dundee was there in the computerized present. He appeared as the sole director of three companies: Sterling Securities, which was listed as a private security firm; Hollywood Videos, a chain of video and home-entertainment stores, with more than twenty-five branches in London and the south-east; and Forest Projects, an 'entertainment and nightclub group'.

I took details of his home phone number and address, which was in High Beach, Essex. On leaving Companies House, I realized I'd left my mobile at the flat and so found a phone box, which smelt of sweat and stale breath. Vice cards of many colours were stuck to the windows of the booth. Every perversion was advertised and provided for: spanking, S&M, 'deep throat oral delights', breast relief, hand relief, fucking, sucking, rimming, buggering. You could meet English roses, African 'black beauties', pre-op transsexuals, new Aussies in town, Taiwanese and Japanese teenagers, Scandinavian 'blondes', rent boys. Although most of the cards were as professionally produced as the very best corporate business offering, there were also several white stickers on which a name (say, Gina), bust size (invariably huge) and phone number had been scribbled slackly in lurid pen. Nothing was left to the imagination. Everything was on display. These cards were a passport to the lower depths of London, a subterranean twilight world of vulgar motivation and degraded aspiration.

I must have read every card in the booth before I heard a coin being rapped on the reinforced glass behind me. I turned irritably. A young black woman was mouthing, 'Fucking get a move on.' Behind her was a young couple. They had multiple piercings, in their ears, noses, lips, eyebrows and cheeks. I wondered what piercings lay beneath the ragged outline of their clothes. I held my hand up contritely to the woman and then punched in Nicholas Dundee's number. The phone rang four times before a message picked up, a woman's voice: 'Please leave your name and number.' Nothing more. I replaced the receiver without saying anything. I stepped out into the road and jumped back quickly as a car screeched past. The driver shouted out at me, 'Wanker!' Funny word 'wanker', not one I ever heard in Canada.

Later that afternoon, having asked Katya if I could borrow her car, I drove out to High Beach, which, according to the road map, was a small hamlet carved out of Epping Forest, somewhere north-east of London. The traffic was slow through Camden Town, with its strips of overlit boutiques, fast-food joints, personal finance centres, banks and bars: the anaesthetized homogeneity of the English high street. I parked and went in search of what had once been Nick's Bistro. It was now a pasta restaurant, squeezed between a bookshop and a building society. I pressed my face up against the glass, peering inside. There were a couple of people at a table, a waiter with his back to me. I tried to imagine what the place must once have been like when my father was a regular, and as I did so the couple at the table mutated into my father and Killer Kellor, the two of them discussing a business project that would never come to fruition. I even saw Killer Kellor open a tin of Ettan, place a pellet on his lip and then discreetly return the tin to his jacket pocket.

Beyond the metropolitan centre the roads were less congested and I drove through an urban landscape of drab housing, high-rise flats and run-down factory units. I passed through Finsbury Park, Tottenham and then further out, picked up the A11 towards Epping Forest. I arrived just after six p.m. in High Beach – a hamlet of about a dozen smart houses, a pub and a golf course. Nicholas Dundee's house was called Forest Lodge and was set back, facing the golf course, behind high security walls and an electronic gate. He'd obviously made money; he had land, space and something to protect. I left the car in the pub car park, and began rehearsing what I would say to him if he were there. 'Hi, Mr Dundee. Just happened to be passing and thought I'd pop in, because you might once have known my father.' Er, not quite.

A security camera monitored me, swivelling as I approached the gates of Forest Lodge. I pressed the buzzer of the intercom. There were two cars parked on the white gravel drive, a Range Rover and a Mercedes sports convertible. There was no way round to the back, and the house seemed to emerge out of the surrounding gloom of the forest. A car pulled up behind me and I wondered if it might be Dundee until the driver swung right into the golf club car-park, scuffing up dust. Two women were standing at the first tee, waiting to begin their round. I thought again of my father, in Belsize Park, stroking balls into a hole that only he could see, his eyes obscured by the peak of the baseball cap pulled low over his brow.

I was preparing to give up when I heard the mechanical creak of a garage door. From a withdrawn range, I watched a man emerge from the shadows, carrying a long rake. He was very tall – perhaps as much as 6 feet 4 inches – and his dark blond thick-layered hair was worn long over the ears. He walked with a slight stoop, as if attempting to disguise his height. Pale and etiolated, his clothes were American college boy casual: Atlantic Braves T-shirt, baggy dark shorts, white socks, deck shoes. His arms were sinewy, long. He was with a little blonde girl and she was dragging a black plastic sack, her hands obscured by extraordinarily battered adult gardening gloves. She and the man, who were both wearing sunglasses, were teasing each other. They seemed to be having fun.

Was this Nicholas Dundee?

I approached the gate and peered through the black-painted bars, hoping he might see me before I called out. 'Hello there,' I said eventually. 'Nicholas Dundee?'

The man froze in mid-movement, like a figure on a vase. He looked towards the gate. The little girl ran ahead of him, bouncing freely towards me across the loose gravel.

'Hold on there, Emma,' he said. 'Let Daddy see first.'

She kept on running. He dropped the rake and jogged after the girl, catching up with her, hooking his hand into hers.

'Hello,' I called out again. 'Is Nicholas Dundee about?'

'Who wants him?' he said. His voice was sure.

'I'd like to talk to him, if he's there.'

He moved closer, so that there was only the thickness of the bars between us. He removed his sunglasses and his eyes were strikingly blue. He had fair sun-bleached eyebrows and his face was worn and distinctly lined, as if he'd spent too long in the sun, or had had an African or Australian childhood. I noticed that the bridge of his nose was slightly flattened on one side, as if broken and reset just out of line. And yet there was something unusual and sensitive about his face, something almost feminine . . . The fine bone structure? He looked a bit like a portrait of a not quite beautiful woman; Picasso's weeping woman even. He was almost attractive, like her, in a maddening, eccentric way. The features were disparate and unimpressive in themselves but somehow they formed a unity of appeal. It was something like that with Nicholas Dundee.

He formed his right hand into a wedge above his eyes, a block against the lowering sun.

'Who are you?' he said.

I told him, pressing my ID to the bars. There was a flicker of something in his gaze – partial recognition.

'I'm Nick Dundee,' he said. 'What d'you want?'

'I want to talk to you about my father, if I can. I think you once knew him.'

'What makes you think that?' His tone had hardened into suspicion. His eyes seemed to be restlessly scanning behind me, as if he were expecting someone else to appear.

'My father's name is Anthony Winter,' I said.

He seemed to sway slightly, a look of panic passing across his face so fleetingly that I wasn't sure it was even there. But he hadn't been expecting that, I was sure. He pulled his arm tightly around the girl and whispered to her, as if protecting her from an ineffable threat.

'This is Emma,' he said. 'My elder daughter. Say hello to the young man, Emma.'

The child giggled shyly, withdrawing behind her father's pale legs.

'So you're Tony Winter's son, are you?'

'Yes, I am.'

'And?'

'Well, I'd like to talk to you about him, if I can.'

He released the gates and they swung open stiffly.

'You're really Tony Winter's son?' he said, beckoning me towards him. He framed my face in his hands, momentarily pressing a little too hard, I thought, against my temples. 'Yes, the resemblance is certainly there,' he said.

And then I realized what was so odd about his face: he didn't have any eyelashes.

The surveillance camera was tracking us as I followed him through the double garage and then out into the large back garden. He had a long, flat, immaculate lawn, a small coffin-shaped swimming pool, not as big as ours in Toronto, and a hard-surface tennis court. On both sides of the garden the forest ran up to high fencing, which formed a tight security ring around the boundary of the property. Lamps and surveil-lance cameras were mounted on the garage roof and at the rear of the house. You could see that he ran a security business. He invited me to sit down at a black metal table. French windows opened from the house on to the splendid patio area. Wind chimes stirred behind us in the early-evening breeze. An extension had been added to the garage. Through the window you could see a snooker table and a bar. There was a barbecue area to my right.

He brought out two bottles of cold beer and sat opposite me, his arms resting on the table. He produced a pack of Marlboro cigarettes and offered me one. Without thinking, I accepted my first cigarette since the accident. He lit the pallid tip and the hot smoke scorched my throat as I inhaled. I breathed in again and this time felt my head spinning, as if I'd risen suddenly from the depths of his pool.

He was watching me questioningly, smiling to himself, as if waiting for me to explain myself further, testing me with long silences, offering not even small talk himself. I felt extraordin-arily uncomfortable.

'Great place you've got here,' I said eventually.

'Thank you.'

He called out, 'Not too close to the water now, Emma.'

'Handy for the golf course, I bet,'

'Yes, but I don't play.' He raised his eyebrows whimsically. I noticed three or four long, curling rogue hairs and I imagined plucking them with tweezers, offering them shape, definition.

'So how's old Tony then?' he said.

The trees rustled and the wind chimes moved. He drew deeply on his cigarette.

I didn't know what to say and found myself reddening as he looked at me, not once blinking. 'You don't know?' I said.

'Know?'

'Well, he disappeared twelve years ago, in November.'

Smoke from his mouth hung in a cloudy barrier between us. I struggled to read the expression in his eyes, which seemed to have turned dull grey. But I was sure that I'd detected surprise there.

'What do you mean he disappeared?' he said.

'There's nothing more to it than that. He just disappeared, in November 1983. No body was found, there was no suicide note. Nothing. He's never been seen or heard of since.'

'Was he in some sort of trouble then?' Nick said.

'Not that we know of.'

We both fell silent. I watched him watching his daughter playing by the pool – the flat, hard gaze of his lashless eyes.

'You worked with my father, didn't you?' I said, a little shakily.

'What makes you think that?'

I told him about my research at Companies House; how my father was listed as a co-director of a wine bar which no one in our family even knew existed.

He dropped his half-finished cigarette on the patio and drew his foot raspingly across the smouldering butt, as if composing himself.

'What really brings you out here, young man? What's your purpose?'

'Like I said, I'm over for a few months from Toronto. I'm kind of trying to find out what happened to my father . . . You knew him. There was some kind of connection between you both, however tenuous. I thought you might be able to help.'

'In what way?'

I shrugged my shoulders and peered down at the table.

'There was a slight connection between us, that's true,' he said. 'But it still seems a bit odd to have his son turning up like this out of nowhere. I'm naturally curious.'

'What happened to Nick's Bistro?' I said.

'It was sold . . . Emma, steady now.' Then, 'I used to have two wine bars, in Camden and locally, down the road in Loughton. The Loughton one did better business. Tony was interested in buying the Camden one from me. I think he wanted to turn it into a fancy restaurant. About ten years too early for something like that, I'm afraid.'

'You're the only person I know who calls him Tony,' I said.

He didn't say anything.

'At Companies House, he's' – I almost said Tony – 'listed as a director of the wine bar. How did that come about?'

'He wasn't exactly a director, not for long anyway. He just put some money in.'

'How much?'

'Can't remember, but it wasn't much. The business was small, struggling. I took it on when it was virtually moribund. He was trying to raise some money to buy me out. Then he just kind of drifted away. Stopped turning up at the wine bar, stopped calling. I assumed he'd got involved in something else. He was like that. It wasn't as if he'd put much money in.'

'Weren't you worried?'

'Why should I have been worried? I hardly knew him.'

'But didn't you try looking for him? Weren't you curious?'

'Joshua, is there something about your father you're not telling me? Something that makes you think I would have wanted to look for him?'

I shook my head. 'Can you remember when you last saw him?' I said.

Now he shook his head, half-smiling to himself.

'Did you know him for long?'

'About a year.'

'How did you meet?'

'Through a friend of a friend, I think.'

'Which friend? Can you remember?'

He shook his head again. 'I'm not being very helpful, am I?'

I accepted his offer of a second cigarette. He called Emma over. She leapt on to his lap and he began teasing her soft blonde curls.

I told him briefly about our family's unsuccessful search for my father; the failure of the police to turn up any leads; and our move to Canada. And all the time he regarded me with an expression which I can describe only as one of sceptical amusement. I'm not sure he believed a word of what I said, but he still heard me out. His skin, I noticed close up, was drawn so tightly across his face as to suggest he'd perhaps had plastic surgery. And those eyes, they were pale and weirdly penetrating.

As I finished the cigarette, he mentioned that his wife would be home soon. I was glad of the hint to leave. We walked together through the garage and out towards the front gates. He seemed to admire them as they creaked open.

'You're in the security business?' I said.

'That's right.' Nothing more offered. 'Let me know if you turn anything up,' he said, then held out his hand.

I passed through the gates and into the consoling warmth of the late-evening sunshine.

'Oh,' he called after me, 'I'm having a little party next week for my wife, Judy. It's her birthday. Why don't you come along? For old times' sake.'

'Is it here?'

'No, on the river.'

'The river?'

'I'm hiring a little boat on the Thames. Let me have your number. I'll get someone to call you.'

He asked Emma to run inside for a pen and paper. We stood there in awkward silence, about ten yards apart, his eyes shrewd, patient and watchful. Despite his charm, I sensed his extreme suspicion, his puzzlement.

'I liked your father a lot, Joshua,' he said, as we both watched Emma emerge out of the darkness of the garage. 'He was a very amusing man, an ideas man. I always thought he was going to make an immense success of his life. Beats me why things turn out as they do.' He paused. 'What's the family view on what really happened to him?'

'Some people think he was murdered,' I said.

'Is that what you think?'

'I don't know what to think any more. I used to think he was still alive, making a new life for himself somewhere else.'

Emma bounded up to her father.

'Jot me down your details,' he said.

I gave him my home and mobile numbers, and also my address.

'Nassau Street, where's that?'

'It's just off Oxford Street. I'm renting a flat there.'

He nodded. 'Very good, you'll be hearing from me.'

Dusk was spreading milkily through the forest as I drove away.

There were four messages on my answering-machine when I arrived back at Nassau Street. The first was from Mum, wondering why she hadn't heard from me. The second was from someone at the law firm, asking where I'd been that afternoon – I'd completely forgotten about the induction meeting! The third, from Inspector Arnold of Dorset police, simply confirmed what I expected: he'd read my note but couldn't offer much help. 'Your father's file is most certainly a manual one, although brief details should be present and archived in the computer system. Unless you have new information on the matter, wait to hear from me.' The fourth caller – the most interesting – spoke without introducing himself but I immediately recognized the calm, monotone delivery of Nick Dundee.

'Pleasure to meet you this evening, Joshua, if unexpected. The party is on Friday week. Venue: the *Taipan* yacht. It'll be moored in South Quay, across from Canary Wharf tower. Hope to see you there around eightish.'

I was impressed. He'd honoured his promise – and so promptly. Replaying the message later, I was undecided as to what was so unusual about his voice, what it was that seemed altogether *artificial*. Despite feeling clumsy in his presence, there was something about him I liked, something attractively circumspect. He seemed to leave much unsaid. And yet he obviously liked my father – he was also a link to the past I'd discovered myself – and he'd received me with courtesy, even if it was a reserved, wary kind of courtesy.

'Joshua, why haven't you been ringing?'

There was annoyance in Mum's voice when I returned her call that evening. No 'Hello' or 'How are you?' – just a series of piqued questions delivered with the rapidity of gunfire. I appeased her by lying about having visited Clifford Chance that afternoon, and reminding her that I started work in a couple of weeks. And yes, I would be home by Christmas. She relaxed when she heard that and began telling me about the life I was missing: that my sister, four years married, was finally pregnant; that my brother had a new job in corporate finance ('You could have his success, Joshua, you're just as bright'). She lost fluency only when I asked her, without any preamble, about the wine bar.

'What wine bar?' she said. 'There wasn't a wine bar. I don't remember your father being involved in anything like that.'

'Are you sure, Mum? Are you sure the police never mentioned anything like that to you when he went missing?'

'He was always involved in something – had a new idea nearly every week – but never a wine bar.'

'D'you remember hearing him ever mention a guy called Nicholas Dundee?'

'Why are you asking me all this, Joshua?'

'Well, I was in Poole the other day. I went to see Dr Kellor.'

'Killer Kellor! Whatever for?'

'He was an old friend of Pa's.'

'My eye he was. Your father couldn't stand him. Used to say he'd never trust a man called Kim.'

'He seemed all right to me. Actually, I rather liked him.'

'He was a terrible doctor ... ' She went on to unfurl an inventory of error: Killer's errors.

I never asked her again about Nicholas Dundee.

Mum had returned from her honeymoon in Sorrento three weeks before I left for London. Her wedding ring, a subtle white-gold band encrusted with a circle of fine diamonds, was less ostentatious than the huge engagement rock Al had bought her while they were on holiday in Cape Town the previous year. I remember her delight when, calling up from South Africa, she'd told me of Al's proposal that morning on top of Table Mountain. How they were looking out at the glassy calm of the Atlantic when he leaned across and whispered his proposal; and how she'd shyly accepted as they were descending in the cable car. 'I threw my arms around him and just said, "Yes, I will. Yes. I will marry you." Then I collapsed into tears. Everyone in the cable car looked at me to see I wasn't faking. Then they applauded. It was a great moment.'

I'd grown to like Al since he and Mum had lived together. He'd enjoyed a profitably ambulatory career as a construction engineer, moving from Paisley to Cologne as a young man, from where every half-decade or so he'd moved on again to another building project in another country: Mexico City, Detroit, Bogota, Montreal. He was in his mid-fifties, twice divorced, when he finally settled in Toronto. He met Mum at a dinner party, not long after his second divorce. From the beginning, they were comfortable together. Everyone said so. I responded to Al's wry, laconic humour and our mock Scots/ English rivalry even if, as my brother once observed, his overly congenial manner and elaborate generosity, his worldliness and traveller's tales, carried a faint air of self-congratulation. There was something in that.

Yet I understood now how their marriage, and Mum's decision to have my father declared legally dead, had stirred something long dormant within me. It was like turning over a neglected stone in the garden to find a thriving micro-world beneath it – something repressed and out of sight. It wasn't exactly that I resented him; more that in the lethally lethargic months that followed the accident, I found myself endlessly absorbed by distant places, other times, by the life we might have led if we'd stayed on: the people never met, the towns not visited, the opportunities missed, the doors unopened down passages we never took, the pleasures unknown. A lost Englishness.

How could you not wonder about all of that?

Did Mum ever love Anthony Winter? I've often asked myself this. As a child, I'd sometimes wake to hear them arguing deep into the night. Her voice was more strident than his and seemed to fill the darkness of my bedroom like a warning. His voice – heard from a distance – seemed to gather momentum, like a train emerging from a long tunnel, softer at first but then becoming an agitated appeal of protest. He always sounded defensive.

I remember once leaving my bed to creep downstairs. They were in the kitchen. I looked at them through a crack in the door. He was sitting at the table, smoking. He looked tired. She leaned against the wall and was shouting at him, banging her fist into her open hand, as she remonstrated with him about his absences. 'You don't care about the kids,' she said. 'You don't care about anything. I would have left you years ago but for them.' Was *them* us? In fact, she did walk out a couple of times, staying with friends, but she was always back within a day or two. She never walked out, though, once Pa started spending so much time in London; that wouldn't have been like her.

And then I began to cry, and they both looked up and saw me there, crouching like a dog by the half-open kitchen door. 'Now look what you've done with your big mouth,' my father said, turning his back on her. But it was Mum who took me back to bed.

So did she love him? The week before I left Toronto for London, Mum and I had lunch in the garden, sitting together under the silver birch tree. She talked that afternoon about Pa's intense physicality as a young man, his passionate curiosity – she'd been intoxicated by his touch, she said. 'In the early days he was exciting to be around. He had loads of energy. I had the feeling – everyone did – that he would do great things. He simply swept me off my feet. How else can I explain what happened, coming to England so soon after meeting him?'

My mother was in her early fifties and she was still an extremely handsome woman: tall, straight-backed and very fit. She worked out regularly at the gym and swam most mornings in the pool. She cooked experimentally, she cycled, went to yoga and had recently begun learning Italian. Despite Al's wealth, she still worked in a local school, having retrained as a high school teacher on our return to Canada. Why should she give that up simply because she'd married again? She'd eschewed plastic surgery, unlike many of our middle-aged male and female neighbours in Rosedale, and her only cosmetic indulgence was to have her teeth occasionally bleached. Although, in one way, it frustrated me to see how she'd revitalized her life in the years since Pa disappeared, refusing to martyr herself to his absence, I was impressed by her all the same. She wasn't a victim. She was a woman at ease with herself.

'D'you feel you still have unfinished business with Pa?' I asked that afternoon over lunch.

She looked up, resetting her spectacles on the bridge of her nose. 'Unfinished business? What do you mean by that, Joshua?'

'Well, wasn't his disappearance the defining point in your life?'

She was pensive for a moment. 'My life has been different since it happened, true, but it wasn't the defining point. No, that was coming back to Canada, which was the best thing we ever did.'

'D'you think you would have returned if it had never happened?'

'No,' she said.

'Would you have regretted not returning?'

'Yes,' she said, and her voice was barely audible above the sound of the nearby water sprinkler.

I finished my glass of white wine and poured another one. She was clearly reluctant to talk about Pa.

'D'you think it was wrong to have had him declared legally dead?' I asked her.

'Could I have half a glass, please?' she said, forestalling her answer.

I poured the wine, watching her watch the sunlight rippling across the surface of the pool.

'I don't think it really matters now, does it? Anyway, I wanted to get married again,' she said.

'Yes, but you could have had him declared dead after seven years – that's the legal requirement . . . presumption of death after seven years of absence and all that. Which would have meant you were granted full probate of his estate sooner.'

'But he didn't have anything, you know that,' she said. 'If he had had, I might have done something about it. Your father was a very poor custodian of his talent.'

'What d'you mean by that?' I said.

'He had a big chance in life. He had a lot of energy, ideas, but no real outlet for that energy. That was part of the problem, I think. He let it all go.'

'In what sense did he let it go?'

'Oh, I don't know, in every sense . . . But, Josh, please, we've been over this a thousand times before.'

So we spoke instead about her own parents, about how much she'd missed them when she moved to England. 'Emigrating was a huge struggle for me at first,' she said. 'Your father took me to live in Forest Gate, for goodness' sake. We had a room in your grandfather Frankie's house. I found Forest Gate awfully depressing. Dark, always damp. It was my idea to move to Dorset. I loved it down there at first – the light, the sea – but moving to the big house in Studland, that was a mistake.' Her voice faded with the echo of a sigh. She peered across the lawn ... the dazzle of the sun on the pool ... scorched white light.

At such moments there was an uneasy intimacy between us. Since the accident Mum and I had rediscovered the art of conversation, and I sometimes chatted to her less as a mother and more as a friend. You could still feel the pressure, though, of what was left unsaid between us, the subjects never fully explored, the wounds left untended.

That night I sat in the garden thinking about my dead maternal grandparents. I'd stayed with them once, in Toronto, while on holiday from England, and they visited us in Dorset for a period after the disappearance. They died three years after our return to Toronto, within a fortnight of each other, their funerals held in the same sad month, a solemn blur of prayer and incense. My grandparents were, like my father, locked out of time now. I could scarcely recall their verbal tics and mannerisms, their famed garrulousness. Who were they, these people whom Mum never stopped mourning? To me, they were nothing more than familiar names, and ones I never thought much about at that. Soon it might seem as if they'd never existed at all, so diminished would my recollection of them be. In time, surely, no one would remember them, the records of their lives being filed away, ignored and unread, like the medical records of so many ghost patients.

*

A week before Nicholas Dundee's party on the Thames and on the eve of Katya's return to Moscow, she and I went out for dinner at an Italian restaurant in Covent Garden. We talked about the time before Katya met me, the life she'd led. And I felt a sad jealousy about those years when she used be so young. She'd first arrived in London in 1989 to study English. In Moscow, she'd lived with her mother in a four-room flat in a 'Brezhnev-era tower block', a short walk from Malaya Nikitskaya Street, where 'Pushkin married his teenage bride, Natalia Goncharova, in the white church named after the Great Ascension'. Her mother's flat, she said, was 'in such bad condition that it was impossible to receive anyone there' – and nowadays her mother was debilitatingly poor, too sick and old to work. 'Support from social services was better in the Soviet times,' Katya said. So it was up to her 'to provide for the family', which was easier for her than for most Russians since, working for the BBC, she had the luxury of a Western salary.

When I commented flirtatiously on her remarkable eyes, she laughed and told me a story about how, back in Moscow last Christmas, she'd been travelling home late on the metro on an unseasonably mild night ('two degrees warm, even rainy'). An old man had approached her. 'He was a little man, like a gnome, with a long white beard and a pointed hat. He was looking at me, and I thought, OK, you can look at me, it's nothing. Then he came over and sat near me on the train. He said, "Do you have green eyes?" "Yes," I said. And he said, "Excellent! I decided in my youth that if I ever met a girl with green eyes then everything would be all right in my life." He got out a bottle of cognac and I shared some of it with him on the train. Can you imagine it? It's a very Russian scene. When he got off the train, he said, "Right, I'm off to sign a very important contract now." He asked for my phone number . . . Did you see that?' Katya said, interrupting herself.

'See what?' I said, following her gaze.

'At the window, a man was watching us.'

'Watching us, are you sure?'

'Yes, definitely. He withdrew as soon as he saw me looking back at him.'

'What did he look like?'

'I could hardly see him, but I think he had long hair.'

'It's nothing,' I said. 'People must look in from outside all the time.'

'But he seemed somehow different, more threatening.'

Katya Lokteva was twenty-eight – 'I was born at eleven o'clock on 6 January, one hour before Jesus. That's going by the Orthodox calendar, by the way.' Her family name, she said, had once been Loktenstam. 'But after her divorce, my mother thought it sounded too Jewish, which is sad.' She proudly described herself as having 'mixed nationality' – 'I have four nationalities in me: Russian, Jewish, Kazak, Ukrainian.' So that probably accounted for her exotic difference: the rich pout of her lips, the slightly Oriental shape of her eyes, the glassy gaze, the dark hair – the brilliant effect of miscegenation, of the merging of the former Soviet identities.

Katya had written poetry as an adolescent, had had several poems published in Ukrainian and Lithuanian newspapers, but she hadn't written anything since, returning home from school one afternoon, her mother told her that two KGB officers had visited the flat. They hadn't threatened her mother; they simply wanted to 'inform' her that they were aware her daughter wrote poetry and that her work was known to them. It was a characteristic Soviet threat, terrifying in its unspoken implications and veiled menace.

I asked about her father, the graphic artist. She had, she said, a difficult relationship with him. 'He's a cold man.' He had 'mixed sexuality', and left her mother when Katya was sixteen. But her childhood had been mostly happy, although she fractured her spine when she was eight, in a gymnastics accident at school, and had to spend two years studying at home. When she returned to school, there were times when her back ached so intensely, when her discomfort was so acute, that she had to

112

spend entire lessons standing up at her desk – the loneliest girl in the class. 'This is why I must look after my mother now. She was amazing to me back then, when I couldn't go to school. She cared for us when we really didn't have anything. She was our hero.'

By this time, we were on our way home, holding hands as we turned into Nassau Street. 'Look at that,' I said, pointing at a car, a metallic-blue Ford XR2, parked on double yellow lines at the top of our road. 'The poor bastard's been clamped.'

The car had brake lights mounted in the rear window and a sticker on the glass. 'The Repton,' it said.

'Serves him right for driving a car in the first place,' Katya said. 'If only there were no cars, the world would be a much better and cleaner place.'

'But you drive a car,' I said.

'Yes, but I'm a big hypocrite.'

Back in my flat, having shared a bottle of white wine, I asked her to lie with me on the bed. She came over, kicked off her shoes and curled up alongside me. I began to wrestle with her, pinning her down and pressing her head into the pillows. I could smell the wine on her breath, feel the excited murmur of her heart. With my free hand I reached out to touch her breasts, but she immediately seemed to recoil, as she had done that night outside the Savoy. I asked her to trust me. Freeing herself from my grasp, she responded by resting her left hand on my lips, her fingers soft as feathers. Her skirt had lifted and twisted. I began stroking the warm flesh of her thighs and arms, and then her feet. I stroked her pale face.

'I'm the clamping man,' she said, in a sing-song voice, and grabbed my leg fiercely.

We lay there, looking at each other, saying nothing in the blurred blue light. At that moment, I wanted to kiss her so keenly that I felt short of breath, as if my lungs had deflated like two balloons. But her eyes were watchful, ever alert, and I began slowly to feel overwhelmed by the mystery of her, by her imperious, sovereign self. I felt strongly, too, that there was something essential to herself that she was holding back.

She looked at me in the dim light of the room and smiled. When she spoke next, her words were baffling. 'Andrey Tarkovsky, the film director, said something once that I've never forgotten,' she said. 'He said that he didn't understand the word friendship. "I love a person or I don't love a person. There's nothing in between." D'you understand what he meant by that?' Before I could say that I didn't, she'd slipped away and gone without even saying goodbye. I heard my door open and swing shut. The silence in the room swelled to fill the abruptness of her departure.

Later I was falling asleep when the phone rang. It was Katya, despite her being just down the hallway. She seemed agitated. I scarcely spoke at all, allowing the long roll of her monologue to reach its natural end. She was talking of her hopes, of my 'joining her stream of life' – in Moscow, in London – of what she hoped to do on her return to Moscow. 'I want to sell my flat and buy two new smaller flats, one for my mother and one for me to rent out.'

She continued on like that until, in my alcohol-fatigued state, I could listen no more. But before I let the phone slip from my grasp, I said, 'Why did you leave tonight before I could kiss you? Don't you want to kiss me any more?'

On the edge of sleep, I imagined a red phone box falling, as if into a huge bottomless canyon. And I was trapped inside it. I beat against the glass with my hands, like someone trapped in a car under water. The air was black and feculent around me. I sat up terrified – of what exactly? I had nothing to fear and yet I felt fear; and there was an unfamiliar name on my lips which I have long since forgotten.

A letter and a set of car keys were waiting for me on the mat the next morning. I knew immediately from the erratic handwriting that the letter was from Katya – her characters had the lovely curled decorative shape of the Cyrillic alphabet. I impatiently tore open the stampless envelope, on the back of which she'd scribbled a picture of a figure in a hat. Underneath she'd written, 'That's me in a big man's hat.'

Dear Mr Winter!
Is trust important for you? After I came back to my room last night I began thinking about trust – I have been too open with you about myself. When I rang you, I couldn't stop myself from talking about everything. Then you weren't listening any more, I knew. I began to think of one of my favourite phrases from Tolstoy: 'Lovers are always trusting.'

That's true, I think. For me trust is a kind of love. Because without trust you cannot create anything, and without love you will never leave anything good behind you.

You know, I used to go late sometimes at night by the Moscow metro. I used to study the lovers in the carriages, because everything is written on their faces and hands. To see if they trusted each other, or not. To see if their love was for real. I could always tell if there was boredom or nothing at all between them. But I mustn't – cannot – go on like this. I've talked to you so much inside my head since last night that, when I tried to write this letter, it had become too difficult for me to speak or even think in Russian. And now, today, I need my Russian as I'm going home. I'll write to you. And call if I can.

PS I was sitting in the Tretyakov Gallery once and this man came up to me. He said, 'Your lips are very sexy. I would like to kiss you.' Then he said, 'But there's too much lipstick on them.'
PPS He didn't ask me if I wanted to kiss him.

I'm a hooligan.
Bye,
Katya

PPPS Use my car while I'm away, if you want.

I read her letter twice, at once baffled and moved by its

honesty. The accident of our sharing the same landing had led to an attachment of sorts being formed between us. I had no idea where it might lead, or if I wanted it to lead anywhere. Still, I was happy for now to go along for the ride.

There was no reply when I knocked on Katya's door later that morning – a forlorn gesture, since I knew that she'd long since gone.

'She's gone,' Mrs Green confirmed, appearing so promptly on the landing that I suspected she'd been watching through her spy-hole.

'What, away with the ramblers again?' I said.

'No, she's gone home to Russia, where they wear them big fur hats.'

I could hear her caged birds in the background.

'Did you see her off then?' I said.

'You're too late for her,' Mrs Green said, laughing.

'Yep, too late,' I said. 'Too late.'

'I don't know why she's going to Russia,' Mrs Green went on, '' 'cause it's much cheaper in America.'

'Cheaper in America?'

'I saw a programme about it last night.'

'You're right, it *is* cheaper in America. So, Mrs Green, are you on your way to America then?'

'Don't be stupid! I can't afford it.'

There was a blast of manic laughter as she closed the door.

VI

'See you next weekend,' Anthony Winter says to his wife, leaning over to kiss her cold lips. He feels her shiver as he rests his hand on her arm, the roughness of her coat between them. Her face is pale, strained. He notices she's bleached the fine hair on her upper lip, and that her mascara has carelessly smudged. He wonders at her pallor and obvious tiredness, at how much she's aged in the past year. He messes up the boy's hair, smiles as he clambers in beside his mother.

'Thanks again for the clubs, Pa,' he says. 'They're great.'

'We'll get a game in soon enough. Remember, keep your head down, like this' – Anthony sinks an imaginary twenty-yard putt with an extravagant flourish, lifting his right hand to acknowledge the crowd.

The doors slam shut. He sees his wife looking at him in the rear-view mirror. She smiles sadly as their eyes meet. The car pulls away. He smells the exhaust fumes in the damp air. The pavements are drying out. As he follows the departing car with his eyes, he notices a man standing a short distance away at the corner of Belsize Avenue, clutching an unrolled umbrella. He's dressed in a black Crombie coat and a scarf, and has dirty-blond hair. He does nothing, but there's little to suggest impatience in his manner. Or boredom.

The car reaches the end of the tree-shadowed road and turns right down the hill, disappearing from view as it speeds towards the West End and then on to faster roads and down towards the watery foot of England. He knows the route well, pictures the familiar landmarks, the buildings and parks and shops and cars. He sees Harrods lit up at night, a dazzling luminosity. He looks over at the man in the Crombie, who flatly returns his stare. There's something about him; he seems to be doing something peculiar even in his nothingness, suggesting purpose in stasis.

He climbs the stairs to his flat, pushes heavily against the door and goes inside. Everything seems such an effort. The flat feels too warm, overheated. He immediately goes to the window; the man is still there, waiting. For him? He goes into the bedroom, reads a train timetable and then begins hurriedly loading possessions into a suitcase, glancing repeatedly at the clock. He loads shirts, T-shirts, jumpers, trousers, one jacket, underwear, socks and handkerchiefs into the case. He opens a drawer and begins searching through files, papers and cuttings until he finds a folder of colour and black-and-white photographs. He tosses these into the case, along with his shaving gear, his passport and Dundee's flick-knife. He goes into the bathroom, removes the rug and lifts up the floorboards, where there is the briefcase in which he has his share from the sting. He carries the briefcase into the bedroom, then returns to the window, picks up the phone and orders a cab to meet him at the intersection of Adelaide and Eton roads in ten minutes. The man is still down there, standing on the corner of Belsize Avenue. He wonders about his own unease, the slow accumulation of guilt that he's beginning to feel.

Moving into the bathroom, he turns on the taps, removes his watch and splashes water on his face. When he looks up from the basin, water draining out, he notices a patch of damp in the corner of the room above the bath. He remembers similar patches of damp in his father's house in Forest Gate, and how sometimes these gave off an unmistakable odour, like stale cigarettes.

He puts on his leather jacket, moves into the kitchen, drinks some water and drags the cases across the room. Then he leaves his flat, double-locking the heavy white door behind him for the last time. Instead of taking the stairs, he crosses the landing and goes down the spiral fire escape at the rear of the building. The bulk of the suitcase slows his progress. He struggles to the end of the communal garden and then cuts along the narrow, moss-covered path which leads behind the gardens and down to Eton Avenue. He makes sure no one has followed. When he glances at his watch he encounters only the hairy thickness of his wrist. He has forgotten his watch; but it's too late to return for that, too late for most things.

The taxi is already waiting.

Future Shock

I couldn't remember much about the old docks. When we left England the transformation of what became Docklands had only just begun. In time, the arrival of a nexus of new roads, light railway networks, riverboats, skyscrapers and corporate money was to transform one of the most decayed areas of London into a thriving, self-styled enterprise zone, an island of concrete and steel dropped as if from an alien spaceship into the heart of an embattled community. Many of the old families of Limehouse, Poplar and the Isle of Dogs were still there, clustered in third-rate tenements, onlookers to a transformation in their neighbourhood that had never sought to include them. And what a transformation. Since my return I'd seen the blue blink – like the lights of a low-flying aircraft at night – of the cloud-grazing Canary Wharf tower from all over London but had never bothered to make the journey out east. But that day, as I wandered amid the memory-erasing architecture, I was impressed by the scale of the development, the ambition that must have driven it. The cataclysmic desire for change.

I left Katya's car in a cavernous underground car park. It looked out of place among the Mercs, BMWs, Porsches, Jags and Mazda sports ... the wheels of the money men. I took the elevator up to the ground floor and walked through the air-conditioned marble-paved malls of Canada Square, with their designer boutiques and cosmopolitan eateries. As I was early, I stopped for a skimmed-milk latte and bought a packet of cigarettes, although smoking was forbidden inside the complex. I sat at a table and re-read the letter that had arrived that morning, from Inspector Arnold of Dorset police.

Dear Mr Winter

Apologies for the delay in answering your questions, due to night shifts and resource allocation. Anthony Winter went missing in November 1983 and his body was never found. We received a missing person's report from the next of kin, his wife, in the same month. In view of the fact that your father left no suicide note and appeared to have no severe mental or serious financial problems, he was categorized a 'low risk' case. The files show that we made inquiries to family members, and also to friends, to establish that there were no other facts not known to the family. You asked about a wine bar, but our researches show no record of his having any involvement in a wine bar. His bank details were checked to see if there had been any unusual activity on his accounts, or any attempt to withdraw money after he went missing. Because those inquiries failed to give greater cause for concern, he remained 'low risk'. Police forces concentrate their searches for missing people when foul play is suspected. Information about him was circulated in the force area in which he disappeared and in other force areas. These included north-west London, where he spent some time. If a missing person is particularly wealthy, then his financial assets could be frozen by the next of kin, pending the reappearance of that missing person. As Anthony Winter appeared not to be, this did not happen.

The point you raised about when a missing person can be declared 'legally dead' is not straightforward. I believe you are right that in certain circumstances a person can be declared 'legally dead' after an absence of seven years, which isn't what happened in the case of Anthony Winter. This would depend on the circumstances surrounding the person's disappearance. For example, if the individual had been lost in a storm while at sea, then the balance of probabilities would suggest that he is dead. Anthony Winter's 'disappearance' was not that clear cut and suicide was not ruled out.

I'm afraid that we are unable to show you the files relating to Anthony Winter. Of course, an officer would talk to you about the case if you had any more questions. But if you have no new information to give, the report will remain filed. You might like to consider seeking the help of the Salvation Army, who have an excellent record in tracing people who have been missing for long periods of time. It is also worthy of note that computerized records and privileged information are subject of the Data Protection Act, introduced in 1984. So even those who are missing have their rights of privacy.

I hope this information is of some assistance.

So that was that. Low risk. Low priority. Gone.

Canada Square was aptly named. It had the same anodyne, rinsed, clinical feel as the underground walkways of downtown Toronto, the same expensively suited young men and women, the same clusters of smart restaurants and shops, the same murmur of air-conditioning and fetishization of security – cameras, surveillance equipment, uniformed guards.

The *Taipan* was moored in South Quay, in the shadow of the 800-foot tower. I walked along smooth concrete paths, surrounded by artificial pools of coloured water, and then took a footbridge across West India Quay. On the horizon a driverless train was threading its way towards the Isle of Dogs, on track elevated above the jetty on concrete stilts. And out there somewhere beyond the horizon was the unfathomable Thames.

Nick's 'little boat' was anything but. It had a brilliant white shimmer, three decks and seemed as long as a jumbo jet. There were several smartly dressed people on the sun deck; their voices carried towards me on the chill breeze. Freezing into immobility, I looked across the waterway at the old warehouses that were being reclaimed as 'riverside apartments', and out towards the London Arena, as vast and forbidding as an aircraft hangar. I couldn't go through with any this. I had no right to be there, underdressed as I was in my crumpled linen jacket, open-necked button-down shirt and chinos.

Then I saw Nick's daughter, Emma, skipping across the sun deck. She was waving to me. Her friendliness was consoling, like unexpectedly meeting an old friend in a foreign city. Boarding the *Taipan*, I was greeted by a young American who introduced herself as the chief stewardess. She led me along the main deck and into the bar, where I accepted a glass of champagne from a nervously smiling waitress. The stewardess then turned her attention to the next arrival, a tall, imperious, pinstriped figure, his greying hair parted on one side and greased back immaculately, like an old-style matinée idol's.

'Have we met before?' he asked me.

'I don't think so.'

'Do you work for Nicholas?' he said.

'No, I don't.'

'So what's your line then?'

'I'm sort of between jobs, at the moment.'

'You mean unemployed?

Before I could explain further he'd moved on, having seen someone across the room he seemed eager to congratulate. I remained leaning against the bar, where I accepted another champagne, and drank it more slowly, my confidence beginning to return.

I introduced myself to an attractive older woman. Her dark evening dress was worn revealingly low – her supported breasts bulged. When she drew on her cigarette, her neck seemed to crease like a tortoise's. She released hurried curls of smoke through painted lips.

'That's a lovely dress,' I said, offering her my hand. She left it dangling.

'It's a Hervé Léger,' she said.

'Didn't he write the Tintin books?' I said.

She fluttered her eyelashes.

'Nice to meet you,' I called after her.

I felt a tap on my shoulder. The man was tall, thin-faced and dressed in a white tuxedo. His thinning hair was pulled back into a ponytail. I saw immediately that he had scar tissue around his eye sockets. 'Mr Dundee wants to see you,' he said, 'up in the office.'

I followed him in silence across the octagonal bar, with its glazed wooden floor, through the thickly carpeted lounge – where golden seahorses and an ornate sword were suspended from antique mirrors – past a door which opened on to a twin-berth cabin, where I glimpsed teak carvings of Oriental figures and dragons, and then along a narrow corridor to the small office. But there was no sign of Nick Dundee.

'I'd better find him,' he said.

I waited alone in the office, distracted by my own reflection in the blank screen of a laptop computer. There was a printer and fax machine, and at the curved end of the desk a television and satellite phone link were mounted on a wooden cabinet.

After a short interval, Nick Dundee appeared. 'Terribly pleased you could come,' he said. He leaned in very close to me, and his face had an eerie, compressed glow in the soft sliding light of the cabin, as if he were wearing make-up. He'd had his hair cut, although the style was unchanged: longish layers worn over the ears. I looked for the eyelashes that weren't there.

'It's a fabulous boat,' I said, feeling tongue-tied and bashful.

'Perfect for a party, don't you think?' he said.

I waited as usual for him to offer more conversation.

'Thanks for coming up,' he said at length. 'Wanted to see you were OK. Saw you arrive but then you got chatting to old Henry.'

'You mean the big guy with the hair and suit?'

'Yes, Henry Lewis-Lloyd, our local MP for Epping Forest. Awfully nice chap. Legal background, I think, very smart. Tipped for high office one day.' He paused. 'You can sit down if you want.'

But I preferred to stand.

'So,' he said, after another interval of silence, 'what have you been doing with yourself in London?'

'I'm supposed to be starting work on Monday, with a law firm, but I'm not really sure I want to.'

'Been thinking about old Tony,' he said, rebooting the laptop computer. 'Keen to know if you had any luck digging anything up on him. Lovely to think you'll find him.'

'You'll be among the first to know if I do.'

'Catch up later then,' he said, and his hands appeared to tremble as they were poised like a crab over the keyboard.

'Oh, Mr Dundee –'

'Nick,' he interrupted, 'and yes, what is it?'

As I looked at him, I could feel myself blushing.

'Go on, Joshua. What is it?' he said.

'Well, I was just wondering, did the police ever contact you?'

'The police? Whatever for?'

'I assume they spoke to everyone who'd known my father, after he vanished.'

'Oh, right, I see what you mean. Don't think they ever did, no. If they had, I would have known what had happened to him, wouldn't I? That he disappeared. And your family would certainly have known about the wine bar years ago. But I might be wrong. Close the door when you go, Joshua, please.'

I walked back to the party, listening to the sterile rustle of muzak, the *Taipan* rocking gently on the water.

I accepted another champagne, and a cheese canapé. Then, seeking fresh air, I followed a spiral staircase up to what I assumed was the sun deck, but found myself instead in something called the Galactic Skylounge. There were white-leather sofas too pristine to sit on, elaborate ice sculptures and a dark fibre-optic ceiling brightened by stars. Through the darkened windows you could see the lights of Canary Wharf tower, and the human shapes moving behind the glass.

'Look, Mummy, there's that man again.'

It was Emma, and she was with a younger girl and a tall,

slim, attractive woman in her mid-thirties – her sister and mother, I presumed. They were accompanied by one of the crew.

'I'm Joshua Winter,' I said. 'You must be Judy.'

'Nick said you were coming,' she said.

'Yes, I've just seen him.'

'Remind me,' she said, 'what's the link between you both again?'

'Your husband used to know my father back in the eighties.'

'What's his name?'

'My father? Anthony Winter.'

'I've never heard Nick mention him.'

'It was a long time ago. They weren't close.'

Judy seemed cool, smilingly impersonal. Her loosely permed hair spilled across the back of her black sequinned dress. She introduced me to her second daughter, Chloe, who, like her mother, was much darker in complexion than Nick, with brown eyes and a light natural tan.

'It's a fabulous setting,' I said.

'I'm told this yacht used to belong to the Amir of Bahrain,' Judy said, introducing me to First Officer Malcolm Malkin.

'Yes, it used to be the royal yacht,' he said, a faint antipodean lilt in his voice.

Judy asked if I'd seen the dining room. 'No! Oh, you must. There are these amazing Buddhas down there.'

'I'll take you down if you want, sir?' First Officer Malkin said.

I followed him down to the lower depths of the yacht, even though I had no wish to see these Buddhas, no matter how 'amazing' they were, where a banquet was laid out in the dining lounge.

'The Buddhas are hand-carved antiques,' he said. 'I like the way they sit watching over diners with haughty disapproval.' He stroked the head of one of the Buddhas with the delicacy of a mother removing a speck of dust from a baby's eye. All this Buddha-fancying, I didn't get it.

'How much would a thing like this cost to hire?' I said.

'The yacht? You can charter it for about eighty thousand dollars a week.'

'Is that how long Nick Dundee's got it for?'

'No, he's got it just a couple of days. Tomorrow we're taking him and some friends to the Azores. He'll fly back from there and we'll go on to Florida.'

We were interrupted by the guy with the ponytail. He looked at me pointedly and then at First Officer Malkin. 'How's it going, Captain?' he said. 'Can I send them in?'

'Give us five minutes, please.'

'Who was that?' I said, when he'd gone.

'He works for Mr Dundee. I really hate the way he keeps calling me captain.'

Everyone began filing through – everyone except Dundee. Soon afterwards he appeared from the staff quarters. He'd changed and was now wearing a superbly cut lounge suit, white shirt and navy polka-dot tie. He had a handkerchief, made from the same silk as the tie, peeking from his jacket pocket. He was introduced by another member of the crew, who commanded our attention by tapping a knife against a glass – instant respectful silence.

'Thank you, Captain Maund,' Nick said. 'If you can bear to pause a moment before we begin, despite these lovely smells, I just quickly want to say a few words.'

I had the impression he knew exactly what he wanted to say, and how to say it.

'Of course, this is a very special evening for me. Not only is it Judy's birthday, it's our tenth wedding anniversary, as I'm sure you know.' He paused to accept applause.

'What can I say about Judy? About a woman so devoted to shopping that in one breath she tells me she doesn't have enough clothes and in the next that she needs a new wardrobe?'

Gentle laughter.

'An old friend once warned me that before marriage a man yearns for the one he loves but after the wedding the "y" disappears from yearn. The same friend also posed this question: "If a married man is out walking alone in a forest, is he still wrong?" '

This time, politely baffled laughter.

'But seriously, everyone, I'm delighted so many of you who have shared these past years with us are able to be here tonight.'

I felt as if he were addressing me and I half-prepared myself to be introduced as the son of an absent friend.

'Judy has been with me from the start, before everything took off really. She's frequently played steady Judy to my stumbling Mr Punch. She was there in the bad times, she's been here in the good. A husband can't ask for any more than that. She's the rock on which everything is built. Patient, tolerant and above all a wonderful mother . . . So, on this special night, could I ask you all please to raise your glasses to Judy, Emma and Chloe.'

His sugary words were returned to him. We broke spontaneously into a chorus of 'Happy Birthday', and then Nick and Judy were acclaimed 'Jolly good fellows'.

At last, sentimentalities over, the party began.

I took my plate and wandered through to the lounge, where I was introduced by First Officer Malkin to a Chinese guy called Geoff Lee and to his diminutive, nodding wife, Wai. Geoff Lee was small, warily crouched, with tinted spectacles and a thin strip of moustache. The skin between his eyes, where his eyebrows touched like two sides of a bridge, was as dry and patchy as parchment – eczema, perhaps. He and his wife were drinking sherry.

'Do you work for Nicholas?' he asked me.

'No. He's an old friend of my father's.'

'You're a father?'

'No. He's a friend of Anthony Winter, my fa–'

'You are?'

'His son, Joshua.'

'Nicholas's son? No, it can't be. He doesn't have a son.'

'No, not his son. Anthony Winter's son.'

'This Anthony Winter, he's here today?'

'No, he's away.'

It amused me to think of him as alive and I decided to stay with the notion.

When Geoff Lee heard I was from Canada, a summer visitor to London, he said, 'I'm a visitor to these islands as well.' Then he offered his views on travel and migration, describing what he called his own 'inner exile'. He'd left Hong Kong at the end of 1989. He'd worked for the Hongkong and Shanghai Bank, specializing in export markets, but, fearful of what might happen once Hong Kong was returned to China, he negotiated a transfer to London. To him, the massacres in Tiananmen Square were disturbing portents of what lay ahead.

'So how come you know Nicholas?' I asked him, responding to his congeniality.

'He's my neighbour.'

'Over at High Beach?'

'Yes, that's right. You know it there?'

'I've been that way once or twice. Nice little golf course there.'

'I play every week.'

'What's your handicap?'

'Twelve. Do you play, John?'

'Joshua. No, I don't play. Hoped to once, though. Even had some clubs.'

'It's never too late to start.'

Geoff Lee liked London, he said, liked its diversity and heterogeneity, but he still missed Hong Kong, the people and places he'd left behind. Some of his business associates, on the Chinese mainland, had disappeared, he said, after the Tiananmen massacres, their bodies never found, their lives unhonoured.

We were joined by Henry Lewis-Lloyd. He seemed to know the Lees. 'Geoffrey,' he said, greeting him extravagantly. 'Long time no see. Keeping yourself well?'

I was awkwardly on the margins of their conversation before

Wai Lee introduced me. 'Henry, this young man is a friend of Nicholas's.'

'Lewis-Lloyd,' he said, offering me his right hand. He turned away. 'Anyway, Geoffrey, tell me, how's business really going?'

Wai Lee smiled regretfully as she and her husband were guided towards the bar by the intolerably tall Lewis-Lloyd.

It was then that I was approached by a guy whose hair was worn in crisp, tight dreadlocks, as intricate as a wasp's nest. He was significantly shorter than me and smiled jauntily.

'Sorry to bother you, mate,' he said, 'but I couldn't help overhearing . . . Did you say you were the son of Anthony Winter?'

I looked at him.

'What's the matter?' he said. 'Did I say something wrong?'

'No, it's just . . . Why d'you ask?'

'I was wondering if he's the Tony Winter I used to know.'

I was curious. 'He might be. Go on.'

'Well, I used to know a bloke called Tony Winter back in the early eighties.'

'Are you friend of Nicholas Dundee's?'

He nodded.

'My father is too. Or was. They've not seen each other for years.'

'He must be the same one then,' he said. 'Is your father here tonight?'

I shook my head, some kind of sixth sense preventing me from revealing the truth about him.

'So how's your old man doing now?' He handed me his card. *Justin Bliss, Operations Manager, Hollywood Video, Forest Road, Walthamstow.* 'It's years since I've seen him.'

'How many years?'

'How long's a piece of string, mate? Twelve, thirteen.'

'Were you friends?'

'Not exactly, no. He hung around a wine bar I used to go to.'

'Nick's Bistro, in Camden Town?'

'Yeah, that's it. Did you know it then?'

'Went in once or twice when I was a kid.'

'A right dump.'

'It was all right.'

'No, it was a complete dump. So what's your old man doing now?'

'This and that,' I said.

He seemed surprised to hear me speak of him as an active presence in my life, operating in real time. He asked why I was at the party.

'Because of my father.'

'How come? I didn't know him and Nick were still in touch.' He broke off, looking towards the nearest window. 'What's going on out there?'

From outside came the wail of police sirens and an urgent voice amplified as if through a loudhailer. Something seemed to be seriously wrong. The sirens intensified and there was the intimidating thwack-thwack-thwack of a helicopter overhead. I looked through one of the portholes. A searchlight was shining down from the low-hovering helicopter.

Captain Maund appeared at the top of the stairs, distressed. 'I'm afraid we're being asked to leave the *Taipan*. There's been a security alert over at Canary Wharf. Could everyone please make their way to the aft deck lounge. But please, there's no need to panic.'

A gasp rippled through the lounge like a Mexican wave. And people were not so much panicking as *panicked*, jostling for space as they converged on the main deck from different parts of the boat. I saw one woman stumble in her long evening dress and heels, her ankle bending over like a wind-bruised flower. From behind me, emerging forcefully from a ruck of dark suits, was Henry Lewis-Lloyd.

'Make way,' he shouted, 'I'm coming through.' He barged his way to the front of the deck and began supervising operations, waving his arms like a tick-tack man on a racecourse. 'Women and children first,' he called out.

131

'He thinks he's on the *Titanic*,' someone said.

Two policemen were standing on the quayside, directing us away from Canary Wharf and towards Marsh Wall. From the helicopter a metallic voice rasped, 'Evacuate, evacuate the area immediately.'

A disturbed calm settled on the yacht as we filed down the ramp to the quayside, where First Officer Malkin waited, helping us on to the pavement. And then, from a distance, it happened: a big boom of an explosion, like the sound of slow-breaking thunder. The lights in the yacht flickered. There were screams and panic and children's tears. Sirens shrieked. People were running across the concourse, away from the tower, as if fleeing a fire. There was much pushing behind me on the ramp and several people went over, including little Emma. I stooped to pick her up but Nick, brushing my arm away, reached her first, regarding me as if with hatred, as if I'd attacked her. His lashless eyes were rimmed red.

The chopper swooped down low, scuffing up dust from the pavement. I looked over at the tower and braced myself for another explosion, for the heart of that material temple of glass and steel to be blown out from within, a monstrous inversion.

VII

A Sunday afternoon and the station isn't crowded. Anthony Winter's hurried flight from Belsize Park has left him fatigued and irritable, and he attempts to disguise the despondency in his voice as he orders coffee. The waitress peers at him strangely, as if he were famous, and he wonders to himself how she would look dead. Would she, for instance, look as casually contented as Oliver King? Death was awesome. Incomprehensible.

Anthony Winter begins drumming the tips of his fingers on the table, rattles a spoon against his wedding ring. He isn't sure how long he will be away, or quite where he's going. All he knows is that he can't continue in his present life. The train is more than thirty minutes away from departure, so he lights another cigarette, and meditates on what has happened, the slow, sickening sequence of events. I'm not guilty, he says to himself, I'm really not.

'What?' the waitress says, glancing over from a table she's cleaning. He stubs out his cigarette, embarrassed to have spoken aloud. She looks at him, he thinks, suspiciously, before she loads up plates and cups on to a plastic tray.

He takes a pen, his diary and an envelope from his jacket pocket. He removes a letter from the envelope.

Nicholas Dundee
Flat 4b, Lordship Park
Stoke Newington
London N16

Nick
I've been thinking: what happened was way out of order.
You were out of order. I can't believe the mess you've landed us in. I'm going away for a bit and my advice to you is do the

same. Keep quiet and it might blow over. Silence is your best, perhaps your only, chance. He won't be missed, not immediately. He's got no one in his life. And there's nothing I can think of to link him to us. If you're thinking of coming after me, don't. I've taken out some 'insurance'!!
Keep your chin up.

An old friend

He crosses the station and approaches a uniformed attendant, who leads him to a safe-deposit box. Surveying the concourse, he places the flick-knife, a handwritten copy of the letter and a rough diagram of the woods at Stratford St Andrew he sketched the night before inside. He will consider what more to do on the train out of London, because, he knows, Dundee will come after him, won't let any of this rest. Perhaps he should make his threat more explicit: call Dundee and warn him that he may go to the police.

The train isn't in. So he buys a newspaper, another packet of cigarettes and then makes his way to Platform 6. He can feel himself settling for the first time that day as he idly flicks through the black-and-white pages, ink coming off on his hands – swathes of bad news. He smiles to himself and kicks out at the cases at his feet. He looks up at a skylight and out through the roof into the cloudy sun-dulled smudges of sky. How quickly the light fades at this time of year. Then he hears rapid footsteps approaching behind him and feels, before he can move, the pressure of a firm hand on his back. Oh, no, he thinks, so soon.

Unheard Melodies

One person, I discovered the next morning, had been killed in the explosion, an unemployed musician who sold newspapers from a stand in South Quay, where the bomb went off. A scratchy recording of one of his songs, an acoustic lament, was played on a local news bulletin. It wasn't much good. Several office blocks were also destroyed, and windows from many of the nearby council-owned high-rises were blown out. The photograph in the paper revealed a scene of apocalyptic devastation. It was a wonder that there weren't more casualties.

I wasn't able to collect the car until Sunday morning. There was an anxious police presence at Canary Wharf, controlling the routes in and out of that sepulchral complex, when I finally arrived there. Eventually I passed through the various check-points and left via the Isle of Dogs. On the side of a shop, in yellow paint, someone had written: 'The Isle of Dogs was left barking last night. Victory to the IRA.'

On Monday morning, when I should have been starting work at Clifford Chance, I went in search of Justin Bliss. He'd tantalized me. I wanted to know more about him and his relationship with my father, and that naturally took precedence over any routine return to full-time employment. So I took the tube out to Walthamstow, to the headquarters of Hollywood Videos, in the scrublands o the north-east London/Essex borders – a suburban sprawl of low-rise, inter-war excrescences; of tatty shops and narrow roads in a state of emergency repair; of desolate pubs flying the flag of St George; of small cafés which smelt of deep-fried animal fat; of men idling their way through the banal jobless hours of mid-morning.

It was noon by the time I arrived at the depot, on the Forest Road. There were two warehouse-sized buildings, several smaller outbuildings, a strip of offices and several vans and trucks parked in the yard. I was shown into a clean, warm prefab. A young woman introduced herself as Justin Bliss's assistant. She sat at a desk, her papers and notes stacked in ordered piles in front of her. A television was on in the corner. 'You can wait for him in there, if you like,' she said. 'He should've been back ages ago.'

I went through into the office, which smelt faintly of fresh coffee and cologne. I sat opposite Justin's empty desk on an uncomfortable, hard-backed chair. There was a framed photograph on the desk of a pale, dark-haired woman. Dressed casually in a white sweater and jeans, she was holding a baby boy – their child? On the wall above Justin's chair were posters of an aged Nelson Mandela and, bizarrely, Prime Minister John Major, dressed in cricket whites and pads. The glass windows of the prefab shuddered whenever a vehicle pulled into the yard.

I waited in the office for more than half an hour, listening to the young woman on the phone. She used one voice for business calls, another more relaxed tone for friends. She spoke to me only to repeat that 'he should've been here by now', before returning her gaze to the television, which she monitored with desultory interest. In the end, deeply bored, I left a message for Justin to ring me.

It was early evening when I finally arrived back at Nassau Street. Mrs Green was banging a dusty mat against the wall. 'It's all go for some,' she called out, chuckling away to herself. As usual, her silver hair hung thickly around her face, framing its manic animation.

'Some of them don't know what to do with themselves, do they?'

Her door was open, her pram was parked in the hallway and coming from deep within the flat was the bitter, plangent music of her unhappy birds.

'Hello, Mrs Green,' I said.

'He's been hanging around for you today.'

I stopped. 'Who has, Mrs Green? Your son?'

'No, he's indoors.' She pointed behind her. 'This other one, with the car.'

'Oh, right, him,' I said, closing my door on her laughter. I had no idea what she was talking about, nor did I want to know.

There were two letters and a phone message waiting for me. Justin Bliss's assistant had called, leaving a number. I rang it but the same voice answered, a recorded message: the office had closed for the day. Frustrated, I rang my uncle in Manchester but another voice message picked up. I spoke a few hesitant words.

The first letter, from Mum, was short, simply wishing me luck in the job I hadn't started. The second was from Katya.

Dear Mr Winter!
It's very cold here in Moscow now, we've already had our first snow. I waited up last night, when I heard the forecast. The first big snows are always the most special – how everything becomes white and clean and silent. But I fell asleep too soon. When I awoke I knew the snow had arrived and was deep by the glare against my curtains, and how muffled were the cars.

You know your existence there (anywhere) in London brings me a kind of aching feeling. I don't know why. But I'll not load all these thoughts on to you. I know you see life in a different way from most people, maybe in the same way as me. That's enough for you to know, isn't it, maverick person? I didn't really want to tell you about my life in Russia, but you kept asking me questions. I don't know if I'm ready to let you come too close to me. Because I'm always reminded of what I might lose, and because I don't really have the answers to your questions, to any questions.

137

I'm eager for news from London, and from you.
Bye,
K

PS Good luck with the job.

I'd thought a lot about Katya since she'd gone and felt genuinely ambivalent about her. When I was with her I often felt that I was falling in love with her, but when she was absent her melodramas – her trust in trust – and willed emotionalism, of which this letter seemed simply the latest example, well, it all seemed too much. And what future could we possibly have with my returning so soon to Toronto?

When Katya and I were in bed together I'd cynically whispered all the things I guessed she wanted to hear – the promises and encouragements – and yet after our calm consummation the excitement had faded. Why that was so I didn't know, nor knew why heard melodies seemed always to be sweeter than those unheard, why happiness seemed too often to be located in the search for love, rather than in its realization; in the dream of desire, not in its fulfilment. More seriously, Katya and I were too unalike. I couldn't share her radical enthusiasm for culture, literature and poetry. And how out of place she'd have seemed at Nick Dundee's party, how unlike the controlled, rational Judy, whom Nick so impressively cared for. So I decided not to reply to Katya's letter, or call her. Better to let it all go, let her fade away like a warm memory of a brief, intense holiday romance.

The evening was dragging. I didn't know what to do with myself, racked as I was by lingering feelings of incompleteness. I was feeling guilty about everything: about Katya, about not having taken up the job in the City, about deceiving my mother. Boredom, frustration, drift and more boredom . . . Nothing was happening.

It was getting dark by the time I went out.

This was what I encountered on my way to Covent Garden.

Rap music pouring from the open window of a car. Light from a television flickering in an empty room. Two men speaking a language I didn't understand. A woman humming behind a shuttered window. An old tramp asking me the time. A red car lightly colliding with a parked car as the driver manoeuvred into a tight space. A battered pigeon fluttering and landing in front of me – I wanted to kick it. A young child holding a baby doll in her hand. A black woman blowing a kiss at a friend before entering a bar. A stuttering, air-polluting, red double-decker – I thought of my grandfather Frankie. And then, on the corner of Tottenham Court Road, there was an old woman, crouching over a mini-organ. An extension lead ran from the organ and climbed the wall behind her like ivy, before threading through a partially opened window. I recognized the tune the organ was playing to itself – an engine of self-delight – and I dropped coins of pity into her wooden box.

I ended up in a pub on Endell Street, attracted in by the boisterousness of so many drinkers. I drank three quick pints of cold gassy lager. The pub was crowded. An international football match was on, and although I had scant interest in it, the atmosphere swept me along like a rush-hour crowd, and soon I was pulling for the team in white. The pub had a torpid blokey odour: too many perspiring bodies crowded too closely together. Because I'd eaten nothing much all day, the effect of the alcohol was immediate.

When the match ended and the pub began emptying, I stayed on to drink vodka and tonics. Across the bar, I was aware of a solitary woman's gaze, but when I attempted to flirt with her she looked away. So I watched a news bulletin instead on the big screen. A young boy called Colin Hughes had gone missing from an estate in Hackney. His was the latest in a series of disappearances of young boys in north and north-east London. There was discussion about a paedophile gang. I watched the blanched faces of the boy's parents, flanked on either side by female cops, as they stumbled through a press conference, their mannerisms as stilted as actors working from an unfamiliar script.

The next time I looked across the bar, the woman had gone.

Outside the air was still unnaturally humid and threatened rain. Moving along the streets, I felt dulled, hollowed out. The air was alive with young voices and music, but I didn't feel part of that constituency. I then went up Charing Cross Road, pausing to light a cigarette by Centre Point, and turned into Oxford Street, past the blaze of light from the Virgin Megastore, the hectic McDonald's, the guy selling sweet-smelling chestnuts on the corner – the homeless huddling hopefully around his cart – past the foreign students gathered outside the language schools. I walked with purpose until I reached the crossroads by Oxford Circus tube station, and still I had energy to squander.

I made a left into Regent's Street, just as a red double-decker bus almost mounted the kerb, the driver's eyes emerging threateningly through an exhaust haze. I swerved as if to avoid the bus – and then something made me halt there and then, and it was more than the realization that I might so easily have been killed if the driver had really lost control. There was someone coming towards me through the crowds, someone I recognized: a bespectacled grey-haired man in late middle age. He was holding hands with a much younger woman, and they seemed to be in a curiously heightened state. They were rushing. Once they had passed, I understood more clearly what my rapid eye had merely suggested. That, for a start, I knew this man. He was my father. But he and the woman were already slipping away from me, and yet they'd been close enough for me to have seen the perspiration on her high forehead, and in the fleshy furrows between her top lip and nose. Maybe I'd even smelt ghost traces of alcohol on her breath (or was that another memory confusingly crowding in?).

Because I did not want to turn away from him, I went after them, calling out, but my voice had dried into a rasp of incoherence; and so already they were part of a dense fast-flow of bodies (people were massing outside the station, hustling for space on the stairway). Perhaps frenzied now, I set off after them, as you would, saw them crossing Oxford Street, agile enough to beat the red-turning lights. I watched from the other side, trapped on the wrong side . . . They were hailing a cab. The lights changed and I was free. For a moment, I was sure that my father had recognized me, for he was waving in my direction. I waved back, but he seemed to be not so much looking at me as through me. I turned again to see a cab pull up, heard the squeal of its brakes. They climbed in. Before the cab pulled away, I was there alongside it, rapping on the window. I looked at the driver, at the young woman, then at my father. But he *wasn't* my father. I saw that clearly now. There were certain resemblances: he had the same shaped face, the same receding curls, and they were roughly the same height, build and age. Not him at all.

'What is it?' the driver said, but I didn't say anything.

The black cab pulled away. I was losing them for a second time, following the car with my eyes as it vanished from view, slowly, eternally, vanished from view, carrying them away with it. For good.

I felt ashamed by my gauche behaviour and did a tired boxer's stagger until I found support against a shop window – and it was only then that I realized I'd been holding my breath. Resting against the glass, I looked at the bright shop frontages of Oxford Street, at the glare and the hard sell of commerce. I doubted everything: that I'd even seen a man who resembled my father. I'd invented that couple as they'd moved towards me along make-believe streets, in an unknown city. That man and woman – my 'father' and his girl – were fakes, no more than sentimental chimeras. And yet for that fleeting moment after the bus had nearly mounted the kerb, I'd seen him: older, yes; greyer, certainly; heavier and bespectacled, yes. But indisputably, unmistakably Anthony Winter as he might have looked if he were alive today. In that moment, before I'd looked into the taxi, I'd felt the weightlessness of liberation.

But now – nothing but a disappearing world . . . footsteps in the sand.

Then: my mobile!

'Joshua Winter?'

'Yep.'

'It's Justin Bliss here. You was at my office this afternoon.'

'Thanks for calling,' I said.

'You all right, mate? You sound out of breath.'

'I've been running.'

'Not from the police, I hope.'

'No, nothing like that,' I said, my head clearing a little. 'Justin, I'd like to meet up if possible, have a chat about a few things. You know, after our meeting on the boat.'

'Yeah, it all went a bit pear-shaped that night, didn't it?'

'So can we meet up?'

'Yeah, sure.'

'I wouldn't mind asking you a bit more about my father.'

'I didn't know him that well, like I said.'

'It doesn't matter.'

'What are you doing on Friday night?' he said.

'Nothing, I don't think. Why?'

'I'm going to Nite Flite's.'

'What's that?'

'It's a club. If you don't know it, you should.'

'All right, I'll be there.'

I took the address of Nite Flite, in Finsbury Park.

Finsbury Park in early autumn, and the weather was, at last, changing, with the temperatures falling more comfortably for that time of year into the mid-sixties. Yet in recent weeks the unseasonal extremity of the weather had seemed to find an echo in the extremity of life around me, and Finsbury Park, at night, was an edgy, brutal place. You felt a kind of madness in the air.

I arrived at Nite Flite shortly before midnight, but the club was only just stirring from the long daydream of the daylight hours. To enter, I passed down a corridor at the end of which were doormen dressed incongruously in wing-collared shirts, bow ties and rugged leather jackets. I passed through an airport-style metal detector and was then frisked. I thought about turning back, until I glimpsed the dance floor and the girls leaning against the mirrored walls. I exchanged a £20 entrance fee for £3 worth of gambling chips, all as intricately patterned as a dartboard.

I went straight downstairs to the gaming room, where I had a swift, relaxing double Scotch. There were twelve tables for playing roulette, blackjack and stud poker. Men of all nationalities were huddled around the green-baize tables, supervised by women in velvet evening dresses, split at the side, and by young guys in lounge suits. The gaming room was luxurious: mahogany panelling, thick carpets, crystal chandeliers and an ornate grandfather clock in one corner. The lighting was soft. I approached a blackjack table and put down one chip. The woman evaluated my contribution with ill-disguised contempt. I followed her restless gaze across the room, where another woman, dressed more formally, seemed already to be on her way over.

'I'm afraid, sir,' she said, 'the minimum stake on the table is fifteen pounds.'

'Are you the manager?' I asked her.

'On this shift, I am, yes.'

'It's crazy money, isn't it, fifteen pounds a hand?'

'Not for some.' She seemed eager to be off and away.

I found a roulette table that had no minimum stake and put my three chips on number 6. The woman spun the wheel. The ball rattled and bounced, jumping more slowly as the wheel reached the end of its spiral. Number 23 came up. I bought some more chips and had another couple of luckless spins on the roulette table.

Then across the room I saw Justin Bliss playing blackjack. I approached him just as he was being dealt his cards. I watched him discreetly raise his hand to signify his intention: another card. He received a seven, chuckled, and then collected his winning chips. The girl dealing the cards was unmoved; she seemed aloof, disdainful.

'You've brought me luck, mate,' Justin said.

He suggested we went upstairs to the lounge bar, which turned out to be modelled on a nineteenth-century gentleman's club, with its sofas and cushions, its open fireplace and vases of dried flowers, its mirrors and ceiling-high shelves of hardback books. The room had an air-conditioned chill. We sat at the bar, opposite a glass cabinet of malt whiskies, brandies and vintage ports. At regular intervals, a woman appeared from one of the private gaming rooms to place a whispered order for drinks. Soon afterwards one of the barmen hurried across the lounge, carrying a bottle of champagne thrust into an ice bucket. He would always disappear into one of the private gaming rooms. There was a peculiar atmosphere about the club – everyone seemed to be behaving as if they were members of a secret society – but I couldn't work out quite what was so curious about the place, except to note how few, if any, of the provocatively dressed girls seemed to have male partners.

As Justin paid for our drinks, he began, unprompted, complaining about his relationship with his wife. He approached the subject obliquely, by first asking if I was married. 'Let me tell you one thing, mate,' he said, 'the problems always start once you have kids. All the love goes from you to the kid. That can't be right, can it? Don't get me wrong, I'm not saying that a kid shouldn't be loved. He should, he should. But at the expense of the husband? That ain't right. If I had my time again, I wouldn't get married. I'm speaking as someone who's been up the aisle twice. I'd get myself a little flat and a nice little sports car – magic, no ties. I'd leave my wife tomorrow, if I could, but I can't stand the thought of some other geezer bringing up my little boy. I couldn't handle it. They'd have to put me inside, because I know I'd go berserk about it.'

As he spoke, I saw my parents arguing in the kitchen all

those years ago, heard my mother saying she would have left if it hadn't been for us.

I wanted to draw Justin away from the subject of himself, so asked him about Dundee.

'Nick's all right,' he said. 'He's got much harder to know the older he's got. I can't say we're close any more. I respect the way he's worked hard, built up his business empire. He's mentally a very tough guy. In the early days, the business was in trouble, no one expected it to last. He was bleeding from the back, so many knives were out for him. I reckon he's mended well.'

'His daughters seem nice,' I said. 'How children turn out is often a good test of the parents.'

'Yeah, he dotes on them little girls. Sends them to private school. I like that. I want some of that for my boy one day. I want the best for him, mate, I really do. Nick's girls get the best – singing lessons, riding lessons, a bit of sport. They play musical instruments. They speak nicely.'

'Have you worked for him long?'

'Off and on since the early eighties. Fuck of a long time actually. I met him when I first came out the army and was struggling. Slipping a few rungs down the social ladder, I was. He's changed a lot since then. Used to be a right hard bastard, always getting into scraps. That conk of his, it must have been rebuilt half a dozen times.'

'He seems quite gentle to me,' I said.

'He's mellowed, believe me he has.'

As we were chatting, my attention was engaged by a glimpse of someone in one of the mirrored drinks cabinets, a crop-haired man I thought I recognized. I turned to see him leaving the room.

'That's weird,' I said.

'What's that?'

'I thought I recognized someone.'

'Who's that then?' Justin said, turning round to look.

'He's gone now. I only saw him in reflection but I'm pretty sure I knew him.'

'Probably a lookalike. They say everyone's got a double.'

'Maybe,' I said, distinctly puzzled.

We talked about the wine bar in Camden, and slowly I spun the conversation on to my father.

'You know he was considering buying Nick's Bistro,' I said.

'Who was?'

'My dad. He wanted to turn it into a classy restaurant.'

'Dunno why. It was shite.'

'D'you remember much about my father?'

'Didn't see much of him, but from what I remember he was a nice enough bloke. A bit of a lad. Did impressions, didn't he? Saying that, I can't remember who he did.'

I thought I'd find out how much he knew, so I said, 'John Wayne?'

'Yeah, he did him, that's right. "*Get off your horse, you dirty rat.*" Yeah, that was one of his best.'

I hoped my father's John Wayne was more convincing than that, even if I couldn't remember my father's repertoire including the old bow-legged cowboy. I'd simply chosen his name at random, as one does a roulette number.

'When did you last see him?'

'Your old man?'

I nodded.

'Can't remember.'

'How close was he to Nick?'

'I dunno.'

'Would you say that they were friends?'

'I can't. It was too long ago.'

'Did you ever go out with my father, just the two of you?'

He shook his head.

'But you remember him, don't you?'

'Of course, yeah.' Justin shifted awkwardly in his soft-topped seat, as if he were feeling suddenly extraordinarily uncomfortable. Something wasn't quite right, I knew, but what?

'Can you remember what my dad looked like back then?' I said.

146

'What's this, mate, *Question Time*? Look, like I said, the bloke wasn't my best mate. I hardly knew him.'

'But you brought him up, on the boat, not me.'

'Yeah, but I don't know what you want me to say. He was a good-looking geezer.'

'Fairish hair, like me?'

'Yeah, that's it, like you. A good-looking geezer like you. Satisfied?'

I knew then that he was lying. No one who'd met my father could ever possibly forget his flamboyant dark curls.

Justin said, 'You haven't told me what your old man's doing now anyway, have you? Is he in some sort of trouble? Is that why you're so concerned about him?'

Now it was my turn to lie. 'He's doing fine.' I could tell he didn't believe me.

'What's his line then?'

'Property. Buying and selling.'

'I bet he's doing all right at that,' he said, his eyes searching the room.

I nodded.

'Good luck to him.'

I was becoming intensely suspicious of Justin, and by the time we moved through on to the dance floor I was convinced that he'd never met my father, or perhaps was confusing him with someone else. Whichever, he seemed genuinely ignorant of the truth of his disappearance, and I felt inclined to leave it that way, in the hope of teasing something more from him later.

A small stage was overlooked by a ring of elevated glass tables. We sat up at the bar, drinking shorts, and watched a young dancer energetically performing her clinical, choreographed routine with all the enviable suppleness of a gymnast. Between perfunctory somersaults, doing the splits and one backflip, she began to remove her clothes. Soon she was wearing nothing but a black-leather thong. The techno was hectic, harsh. Her tanned buttocks were worked and muscular, but there were very few punters there to appreciate her hard work. We were outnumbered, at least two to one, by waiters and lip-glossed women. At the end of her routine, she smiled professionally and was gone, replaced by a thick blast of dry ice.

Justin had returned to the subject of his wife. 'We don't even share the same bed now,' he said. 'She really doesn't want to know. I've got this new motor – a Cherokee Jeep – and you know what? She won't even get into it, let alone drive it. She has no ambition. Don't really want to see me get on. "I'm happy being ordinary, Just" – she calls me Just – she tells me. "I don't want to live in a big house or nothing like that." Another thing, mate, earlier this year we went on holiday to Tenerife. We met this other couple, as you do, got chatting to them. Their boy got on well with my boy and the two women got on all right. Now they've asked us if we wanna come to Gran Canaria next month. But she won't come with me. Who the fuck would turn down a holiday to Gran Canaria?'

'Especially at this time of year,' I said, feigning interest, 'when everything here is so dark and miserable.'

'Yeah, you're right about that. I'm gonna take my old man with me. He's got Parkinson's, the poor sod. That's a terrible disease, mate, absolutely sinks you. My old man looks like a walnut now. He's got the fucking shakes, too.'

I was beginning to feel claustrophobic, caged by the relentlessness of his bluster. 'Justin, I'm going to get some air,' I said. 'I'm feeling a bit drunk.'

'All right, mate, no dramas.'

Yet I found my way quickly blocked by a dark-haired woman, dressed forbiddingly in a long red backless dress. She had thick hair – big hair – and a synthetic black mole on her cheek. I glanced down at her six-inch stiletto heels, the points of which were sharp enough to pierce a man's heart. The huge red pillows of her lips were, clearly, collagen-enhanced. She was swinging her bag between her legs like a pendulum. Oh, no, I understood everything now, knew what was coming next.

'Would you like me to come with you?' she said, in heavily accented English.

'Come with *you*, where?'

I felt more enervated than excited by her offer. In truth, I felt frightened – by Justin, by her, by everything about that club.

'I'm afraid I'm meeting someone for a drink,' I said.

'Afterwards then?'

'No, I can't.'

She puffed contemptuous, peppermint-freshened breath into my face.

Justin was still at the bar, talking to a woman himself, one arm draped protectively around her shoulders. I moved towards the front door, but was stopped again, this time by a younger, less severe-seeming woman. Her blouse was pulled tightly across her shoulders and buttoned loosely at the swell of her cleavage. Did I want to dance? She had an East European accent.

There was something appealingly vulnerable about her and so I allowed her to lead me across the dance floor, where we began moving stiffly among the more intimately embracing couples, beneath a mirrored ceiling. An old Lionel Richie track I half-remembered from adolescence was playing, and I found myself inexplicably moved by the mawkish lyrics. I rested my head on her chest and she gently stroked my hair. I wrapped my arm around her waist, drawing her more tightly towards me. I felt her G-string through her skirt, knew that she wasn't wearing a bra.

I asked her what she did.

'What do you think I do?'

I shook my head.

She laughed. 'I'm a working girl.'

'You mean you're a prostitute?'

'Don't say that. It sounds horrible.'

We continued dancing.

'It's not so easy, you know, to earn money in Ukraine,' she said after an interval. 'My work helps me in the real life.'

'What do you do in real life?'

'I'm a law student. That's why I'm in London.'

'I work as a lawyer myself, in Canada,' I said, conscious that I was slightly slurring my words.

'So you're here in London as a tourist?' she said.

I nodded.

'Are you in a hotel?'

'Yes.'

'Well, tonight, I'm three hundred dollars for you.'

There was a break in the music. We separated.

'Where are you going?' she called after me.

Where am I going? If only I knew.

Justin, alone now, greeted me with a wink and a lascivious grin. 'Enjoying yourself?'

'This place is full of prostitutes,' I said.

'Yeah, they get in free.' He'd bought me another drink, this time a vodka cocktail.

'Haven't the cops ever busted it?'

'Not that I know of. Anyway, these girls aren't soliciting. They're just here. It's above board. It ain't a brothel or a sleazy strip-joint.'

'The girls, they're mostly foreigners, aren't they?'

'The East Europeans are best. In the old days, when you thought of Eastern Bloc women, what did you think of? You thought of shot-putters and babushkas. The quality of the women behind the Iron Curtain was the best-kept secret of the Cold War, if you ask me.'

Katya's image appeared luminously before me, like a hologram projected on to a blank screen, and I felt a squeak of remorse at how I'd allowed the ties binding us to slacken since her return to Moscow, how I'd never responded to her letters.

'Have you ever been with one of the girls here?' I asked Justin.

'I'd never pay for it, mate, never. Got more self-respect than to do that. I come here really to window-shop and have a few drinks with the boys. But I like a goer. There's this place we go to every Friday night – a real fucking cattlemarket. Some of the women are young, in their early twenties, others are married. The married ones are the easiest pick-ups – no strings attached. Check into a local Moat House – forty or fifty quid a night – a quick one-two, shower and then home before two. If I'm too late for a room we forget it. It's a bit insulting, isn't it, for a woman to do it in the car? And I'm past doing the old knee-trembler bit against a wall. I don't know how I keep doing it, keep picking the birds up, mate, apart from being a right handsome bastard.'

'Does your wife know about any of this?'

'She's never let on if she does.' Then, completely unexpectedly, he asked if I wanted a job.

'A job?'

'Yeah. What are you doing for money at the moment?'

'I'm all right. I was due to do a placement at a law firm, but that's kind of fallen through.'

'What d'you mean, kind of?'

'I just didn't take it.'

'So how about it? I need some urgent help at the depot. Only light driving work, cash in hand, for a couple of weeks. Fancy it?'

'I'll think about it,' I said. 'But honestly, I'm not desperate for work.'

'What are you, one of them pampered rich kids who doesn't have to work – a trustafarian?'

'A what?'

'A trustafarian – a trust fund kid.'

I felt extraordinarily tired, flattened by him. 'I think I'll go now, Justin.'

'You had enough already? This place doesn't get going for another hour.'

I told him I'd had enough.

'Call me at the depot if you're interested. I could use the help.'

*

On my way out, I saw the Ukrainian I'd danced with. She was playing on the slot machines, watched over proprietorially by a turbaned Sikh. He was stroking her bare shoulders – she'd removed her flimsy top – and she was furiously feeding coins, his, no doubt, into the insatiable slots. I smiled at her but she seemed already to have forgotten me. I was invisible to her. The last thing I saw as I left the club was the Sikh's metal hook, where his left hand should have been, impatiently tapping the top of the machine.

The night had cooled. Autumn, you hoped, was at last freeing itself from the cloying clutches of an unnatural summer. The streets were quiet, eerily becalmed. The moon sulked behind a ragged knot of cloud. At such times, I felt the beauty and deep peace of the inner-city streets, the difference that emptiness makes to them. I began searching for a minicab.

I'd not been walking long when I heard footsteps. I turned but there were only lonely shadows behind me. Soon after I heard footsteps again; this time I saw three men, silent and sober. I began to walk more quickly in an attempt to convince myself that they weren't following, but their pace quickened in line with mine. I searched the surrounding roads again for a minicab. Nothing. They were still behind me, neither retreating nor showing any inclination to overtake. I crossed the road and looped back towards Nite Flite. When they followed across the road, I began to move more quickly, turning into a side street flanked on either side by three-storey brick-built terraces. The men followed. I made a right and then a left. Before me, in the distance, I saw the chalky art deco frontage of the Arsenal football stadium. I looked back and there they were, still coming. I lacked the necessary confidence and will to outpace them, so I opened the gate of the nearest house, ran up to it and rapped speculatively on the door. They quickly followed, and this time I turned to confront them. As I went down, taking hits and blows to my stomach and head, a window opened in the house above, a woman's voice shouted out. With fiendish application the men lingered, leading me to the edge of an abyss before pushing me over. Falling, I heard only the pitiful sound of my own voice – and their wild laughter.

The boots came in. Again, looking up, I thought I recognized the man with the crop I'd glimpsed in mirrored reflection at Nite Flite.

I opened my eyes, without any idea where I was or how long I'd been there. For sure, I was in a child's bedroom – there was an empty cot under the window, the walls were decorated with pictures of brightly coloured farmyard animals. The curtains opened on to the blue darkness of sombre city streets. I heard someone moving about in another room, and then I remembered, and the returning pain gripped my arms and legs, and I saw my left hand was wrapped in a crêpe bandage. I stood up without too much difficulty, the back of my head slightly tender and swollen. I turned on the light and saw in a mirror that the skin around my left eye was bruised. There was a large zigzag-shaped graze on my forehead, visible through my fringe. From the window you could see how the dusty trees had wilted in the heat, how yellowed and patchy the grass had become. Everything seemed oppressed by the weeks of hard heat. A car passed by below, its path lit by a pale wash of light. I felt on the edge of nowhere. I felt, too, extraordinarily dehydrated. Then a young woman came into the room.

'You're awake,' she said. 'How are you feeling?'

'A bit sore. But who are you?'

'I'm Jackie.'

'I'm Josh.'

I asked her the time, what I was doing there.

'It's nearly six. You've been asleep for a few hours. What were you involved in out there? They were kicking the shit out of you.'

'I can't remember much about it. I'd been at a nightclub, had a few drinks, was looking for a cab and then the next thing they were following me.'

'What club were you at?'

'A place called Nite Flite.'

She nodded.

'Maybe they saw me come out, thought I was carrying a lot of cash.'

'Did they take anything from you?'

My newish wallet was still in my back pocket. To have lost this one too would have been more than careless. 'No, my money's there,' I said, opening the wallet.

'Are you American?' she said, the first person ever to ask me that.

'No, I'm not, but I've lived in Toronto.'

She nodded again, her curiosity satisfied. 'You woke me up,' she said, 'smashing on the door like that. When I looked out they ran. Eric, the bloke who lives downstairs, is away, so I didn't know whether to call the police, go down, call an ambulance or what. In the end, I went down. You were conscious but were pleading for help. I was a bit scared, but then I saw you lying on the step, in pain . . . '

'Why didn't you call the police?'

'I was going to.'

'What made you take me in?'

'I don't know. But you were in no state to help yourself. I could smell the drink on you.'

'But I might have been dangerous.'

'Yeah, you might have been.'

'I still might.'

'Well, if you are, you can go now.'

I smiled.

'Do you want something to eat?' she said.

'D'you mind if I lie down for a bit? I'm still feeling a bit groggy.'

I woke again at around nine and went to find Jackie.

She was pale, short and plumpish but had a young, gentle face. Her make-up had a freshness to it, as if recently applied, and her jeans were tight, exaggerating the swell of her broad

154

hips. Her feet were bare and the red varnish on her thickened toes was chipped; her teeth were slightly crooked and discoloured when she smiled. But after the cool perfectionism of North American orthodonture her imperfections seemed attractively real. About right.

Along the corridor, I'd passed a door through which I saw an unmade double bed tucked into an alcove, the open doors of a wardrobe, a table cluttered up with make-up and hairspray, a chest of drawers. Jackie's sitting room was large, sparsely furnished and cheerless. It didn't feel like someone's home. There was a powerful air of neglect about it – the walls were patchy and required painting, the curtains were yellowy and stained like a heavy smoker's fingers. There were magazines and a mug of either cold tea or coffee on the table. The television was on: twenty-four-hour-a-day satellite news. The window was open and the curtains billowed faintly in the cooling breeze.

'Sssh,' Jackie said, lighting a cigarette, 'she's still asleep.'

It was then that I noticed a baby lying in a pram. She had fine dark hair and impossibly fragile hands.

'How old is she?' I whispered.

'Twelve weeks. I'm just gonna take her through. I don't like smoking around her.'

I wondered about the father of the child, where he might be.

'You did this?' I asked, holding up my hand on her return. The slow seep of blood was beginning to darken the crêpe.

'Does it still hurt?'

'Not really.'

She squirted oily green liquid into the sink, then began loading it up with soiled cereal bowls, milk-stained saucepans, cups, mugs, glasses and used cutlery. She did this apologetically, as if embarrassed or awaiting my disapproval. She turned on the hot tap. Water gushed and swirled, and a bowl of foamy bubbles formed like a soft-sculpted cloud. She then filled the kettle and, once it had boiled, poured the steaming water into a plastic bowl. She sprinkled salt and disinfectant in before adding cold water, monitoring the temperature with the tip of her elbow. 'Should be OK now.' She guided my hand into the water, picking at the bandage with a sharp knife, exposing the deep cut in the fleshy webbing between my forefinger and thumb. Steristrips peeled away in the water, floating to the surface like dead sticklebacks, and there was purple swelling on my knuckles. She used a dishcloth to clean the wound, plugged the flow of blood with more steristrips, and then wrapped my hand again in another crêpe bandage, as rough as stubble against my skin.

She never once looked at me as she did all this, never attempted to explain herself. There was something warm and gentle about her that inspired trust. I had no idea what her life was like inside those rooms, but sensed the difficulty of her circumstances. Later, as we stood at either end of the kitchen, she watched me quizzically, as if she herself was wondering, as I was, how exactly I'd come to be in the flat, and when I would leave. The motivelessness of the attack had left me numb.

'I think I'd better be going,' I said.

She seemed disappointed. 'Are you going to the police?'

I pictured a green-baize gaming table, bright lights, leering faces and then heavy boots going in. 'I'm going,' I said again.

'Let me at least make you a cup of tea before you go.'

She did that, and I ended up staying for the rest of the afternoon and strangely on into the evening. I was grateful for the interlude from my recent routine; and she seemed glad of the company, the conversations we had.

Jackie was reluctant, at first, to give much away about herself. She was, at all times, quiet and wary. When I asked about the father of her daughter, she said she knew who he was but hadn't seen or spoken to him for five months. 'He doesn't even know he's a father,' she said.

She told me more about him: that he'd worked as a motorcycle courier before leaving, that they'd been together for ten months. The relationship had ended when she came home one afternoon to discover him, in their flat, with the teenage daughter of a Jamaican couple who lived across the road.

'They weren't exactly doing it but I could tell they had been. The girl – Donna – was sitting on the chair where you are now, wearing only a T-shirt. It was too small to cover her up properly. She kept trying to pull it down over herself. I suppose it was quite funny really.'

'What did you say to them?'

'I told them both to fuck off.'

Jackie explained how isolated she'd become since the baby's birth. She had had the assistance of a midwife and her sister, who lived locally, came to see her initially; but mostly she was alone, leaving the flat only to draw benefit and do the shopping. She hadn't had a 'proper job' for three years. Once she'd hoped to be a physiotherapist, but she had ended up training to be a hairdresser instead (she never completed her apprenticeship). After that her working life had passed by in a blurred stream of casual contracts, in shops and offices, as a cleaner, and in several pubs and bars. Not much progress.

The phone rang only once for her while I was there, but she never bothered to answer it, allowing her voice message, underscored by jangly pop music, to pick up. The caller was deterred from speaking.

'The trouble is', Jackie said, 'my phone's only wired for incoming calls.'

'So why didn't you pick it up then?'

'Because no one I want to talk to ever calls.'

From there the rest of the day passed in a collage of fragmented episodes: shouts and sirens from the street, police on horseback outside patrolling the fans on their way to Highbury, the whoosh of the crowd itself from inside the stadium. We never read a newspaper or listened to the radio. We were intimate but ours was a reserved, wary kind of intimacy – the comfort of strangers. Because of my bandage, I asked Jackie, without really considering how she might respond, to wash my hair. I knelt in front of the bath as she crouched over me, massaging shampoo into my still tender scalp, running her fingers gently across the painful bump on the back of my head. She was wearing a skirt and I felt the loose flesh of her bare thighs against my arms as she stretched to rinse away the shampoo, her warm breath on the back of my neck. Her touch was sure. She worked conditioner into my hair and combed it through.

Once she'd rinsed away the conditioner, she lit a cigarette, balancing the thin white filter between her lips as she briskly dried my hair. I sat on the lavatory seat and looked up at her, the smoke escaping from the side of her mouth. Her mascara had dribbled across her cheek. I leaned over to wipe her face, using the wetness of the towel to remove the smeared patterns from beneath her eyes. We stared at each other. The bathroom was hot and steamy. There were dark patches on the carpet where water had splashed. Her face was a mirror reflecting my own frustrated desires.

We were interrupted by my mobile phone.

It was Justin Bliss. He wanted to know if I could start work on Monday.

Why was he so keen to have me?

He asked if I had a driver's licence (yes, an international one); if I fancied the job (I wasn't sure); if I fancied a bit of 'spare change' (I wasn't bothered). I told him nothing about the attack but agreed, more out of boredom in the end, to do five days' work for him, starting on Monday, at six a.m. The money, I suppose, would be useful, what with my non-showing at Clifford Chance (although there was always Al to call on). And more, Justin Bliss was, like Nick Dundee before him, a link to my father, however tenuous, and I owed it to myself – to all of us – to see where our association might lead.

We were out of it for much of that evening – doped, dazed – but never so completely that Jackie lost awareness of the child, whom she would feed or slip down the corridor to see at regular intervals. And the longer I spent with her, the more I liked her and the less I wished to leave: with Jackie, I had a double identity and could start again; there was no extra baggage, no struggle, no search, no vanished father. I told her that I worked as a lawyer, that I was engaged to be married, and that I lived out at High Beach in Essex. I never gave her any cause to doubt me.

After a take-away, we shared another joint, played CDs and watched videos in a darkened room, the child sleeping silently somewhere down the corridor.

'No tears, no pain, no broken heart,' Jackie sang, along with the song. As it was getting late, Jackie asked if I wanted to stay, explaining that the sofa folded down into a bed. Without thinking much about it, I accepted her invitation, wondering what it might lead to, where it would end.

She never heard me come into her room. I only realized she was awake when I lifted the duvet and she turned, opening her eyes – her blonde hair partly obscuring her face. The curtains were half open and light from a street lamp beat like a bird against the glass. Jackie gasped as I climbed into bed with her, and I expected her to roll over to create some space for me. She was wearing a long T-shirt and smelt faintly of alcohol. I wondered what time it was – the streets were quiet. I was wearing boxer-shorts and a T-shirt.

'I'm cold, Jackie,' I said.

Before I could pull her towards me, wrapping my arms around her, Jackie had answered. 'No, Joshua, please, not this. That wasn't why I wanted you to stay.'

I felt feeble, surprised. 'I promise not to do anything, Jackie, I'm just feeling . . . '

This time she moved to create some space for me and I climbed in.

She rolled over so that her back was to me and I pulled her into an embrace, momentarily feeling, as she turned, her breasts. She breathed through her mouth: the rhythm was sluggish. She shifted slightly in my arms. I felt her muscles tighten, then relax. In the blue light of the room, I could tell she was falling asleep. I nudged her gently without rousing her. She was absolutely lost to me.

I listened to the sleeping woman as she shifted position beside me, the wheezy ache of her lungs, the seep of her breath, her unquiet gut. Her T-shirt had lifted, and I felt the wiry snag of her pubes against my perspiring legs. Her breasts were soft against me now. I was caged in her sleeping embrace. The radiator clicked and from somewhere down the corridor I thought I heard the baby stir.

Jackie didn't even move when, ten minutes later, I slipped out of the room and returned to my sofabed.

The next morning we ate breakfast together. Jackie said nothing about my appearance in her room, about her gentle rejection of me. The baby lay on the sofa as Jackie changed her nappy, gurgling and kicking her legs in the air like an upturned tortoise. Jackie sprinkled powder across her daughter's bottom. Then, carrying the baby in her arms, she walked downstairs with me. She opened the main door, pointing out where she'd found me, and I stepped cautiously, as if over my own prostrate body, into the damp fogginess of the morning.

I took several faltering steps before returning to Jackie, strangely reluctant to leave her there. She and the baby felt small and compact in my arms. We kissed for the first time on the mouth.

'Your poor eye,' she said, wiping her moist lipstick from my face. 'You better take care of yourself now.'

I reached out to touch her lips again, her lipstick leaving an imprint on my fingers, a gorgeous red flower of parting. I wiped the lipstick from my fingers and transferred it on to my lips.

She smiled.

As we prepared to part, outside her flat, she turned to me. 'D'you think I should get married?' she said.

Her question had come from nowhere.

'Well,' I said, 'if you love your boyfriend, why not? But I thought you said you hadn't seen him for five months.'

'That's true.'

'So, d'you love him or not?'

'I think he's a complete arsehole.'

With that she was gone, leaving behind nothing but the faint memory of her ironic laughter – and the sound of her baby's distant tears.

VIII

Anthony Winter turns to encounter a young pretty woman standing on the platform. She's wearing a hat, and her face is in slight shadow. 'You dropped this,' she says, 'by the cigarette stand.' She holds his wallet in her gloved hand. He can hear the train pulling in behind him. 'Thanks,' he says. She smiles beneath the brim of her hat as she passes him the wallet. The creased brown leather feels warm. She hesitates, and he wonders if she's waiting for something. 'Oh, here, take this.' He opens the wallet, tries to slip a fiver between her fingers. 'No,' she says, 'really, no. That's not necessary.' He fumbles and drops the letter addressed to Dundee. Their heads almost collide as they both crouch simultaneously to retrieve it. 'Ooops,' she says. He laughs, although he's worried that she's read the name on the envelope, if that matters.

They board the train together.

'Where are you heading?' she says.

'I don't know.'

'You don't know?'

'Somewhere down south,' he says. 'What about you?'

He thinks about her as he sits alone in the smoking carriage: her honesty and easy warmth, her natural smile. There's something propitious in her act, something *willed*, he knows it. He regrets not asking her to sit with him. As the train hurtles south he feels the darkness lifting. He feels lucky. Was life beginning at last?

Then, finishing his third cigarette, he goes searching for the woman. He passes through three carriages before he sees her, the hat and her bag on the table. The curls of her dark red hair tumble thickly, attractively. He sits down in the seat opposite her.

'Hello again,' he says.

She looks up from her book, seemingly pleased to see him. 'Had enough of the smokers?'

'Yes,' he says. 'I've been meaning to give up for ages.'

'I never asked your name?'

'I'm Greg,' he says, with enormous confidence, and holds out his hand. He likes the name, feels it suits him.

On arriving in Plymouth, he takes a cab to the town centre. He checks into a small family-run hotel, requesting and receiving a room with a sea view. From his window the sky seems to merge with the sea in a long dull-grey perspective of nothingness. It has been raining. He notices the puddles on the pavements, the seabirds on the pale, bleached winter beach.

That evening he walks around the unknown town, no longer even desultorily looking for a woman. The streets are damp and empty. There's no starlight. He looks at his unfamiliar reflection in a shop window. He's stopped resisting, he feels it. He looks at his new hands, touches his own hard, cold face. When he looks into himself, what does he encounter? Was he anything more than a bundle of random sensations? Back in his room, he rings the woman from the train at her home but there's no reply. He imagines the phone ringing in her house, the lonely, empty echo of its tone. Another time, perhaps: he's glad she gave him her number.

The next morning he will take the first ferry out to Santander.

He sleeps easier that night.

Fade to Grey

'What's happened to you?' Justin said, when I arrived at the depot half an hour late on Monday morning.

'I walked into a door,' I said, looking at myself in the glass, at the heavy purple bruising around my eye, the scab on my forehead, the swelling on my cheek the colour and texture of an exploded plum. I'd never looked this bad, even when I played rugby and boxed occasionally at university. I'd always prided myself on having physical courage, on being a bit hard, in the argot, prepared to take a knock or two in a ruck and maul. Perhaps if I hadn't drunk so much I would have made more of an effort to defend myself on Friday night, not succumbed so easily. 'I was jumped leaving that bloody nightclub of yours,' I said.

'What happened?'

I explained exactly what had happened, including my stay at Jackie's.

'Did you go to the police?'

'Not until Sunday afternoon. There wasn't much they could do. In fact, they didn't seem interested, not once I told them nothing was stolen. All they kept asking was why I hadn't reported the incident earlier.'

'Why hadn't you?'

'I told you, I was at this Jackie's.'

'You horny bastard.'

'No, it wasn't like that.'

He chuckled dismissively.

'It *wasn't*.'

Justin poured two cups of coffee. He sat at his desk beneath the posters of Mandela and Major, idly rearranging his papers. Outside the early-morning darkness was lifting and there was a mournful flicker of a desk lamp through the window of one of the outbuildings. Since our meeting at Nite Flite, he'd had several blond hair-extensions woven into his fringe, and he was wearing Oakley shades, a blazer, a blue-and-white-striped shirt, and black jeans. When he removed his Oakleys, he looked tired and unshaven, and his eyes were streaming, as if he had a cold.

'I was reading this report.' He reached for a copy of the newspaper on his desk. 'Another kid's been found murdered in north London. Third in three months. I don't know what's happening – kids being snatched, your attack.'

'I heard about that kid on the news,' I said.

'Word is his knob was cut off and shoved in his mouth. What kind of fucking freak does that to a kid?'

'We had a similar case last year involving a snuff-movie gang in Canada. They kidnapped a boy off the street and used him as a sex slave before killing him.'

He looked up from the paper. 'Canada? D'you know it then?'

I'd forgotten I hadn't ever told him about my other life in Toronto. 'I've been there a few times, to visit friends.'

'Snuff movies,' Justin said, 'I hate that kind of shite. In the very early days someone approached us about doing a bit of porn out of here . . . Nothing too sick. Standard stuff from the States and Europe. Real fucking and sucking, the kind of stuff that goes on in most bedrooms up and down the country – except mine – but what you can't pick up in Soho because of our poxy censorship laws. Nick didn't want to know – the porn game is totally criminalized at the top. There's big money to be made, but to make it you tread on people's toes. Not very nice people.' He paused to resettle his Oakleys on his small straight nose. 'Are you interested in it?'

'What, in porn? Never given it much thought really.'

'Your old man liked a bit.'

'My dad?'

'Yeah, always had a few tapes to push.'

'What kind of tapes?'

'Don't get me wrong, nothing heavy, but he was as slippery as the next man.'

'Are you sure my father sold porn videos?' I said.

'He was the kind of bloke who could sell you anything, if you gave him enough time to find it.'

I asked Justin how long he thought my father was pushing videos, but he cut me short. 'I'm running late, mate. Can't stand around gassing all day. Maybe you should ask him yourself. He might even show you some tapes, if you're that interested.' He then explained what he wanted of me, and it seemed simple enough. I was to drive out to branches of Hollywoods in Harlow, Ware, Bishop's Stortford and Cambridge. I was to deliver boxes of new video releases and collect returns – videos which had once been so resonant with promise but were now as neglected and tarnished as an old Christmas tree.

I set off from the depot, under a gently glowing morning sky, as confused as I'd ever been as to exactly what to believe about my father. My restlessness seemed endless.

My journey began badly when I became lost in Harlow new town's labyrinthine network of one-way systems and round-abouts, so lost in fact that I was forced to stop to ask a bicycling copper I saw waiting to cross the road for directions. Which almost caused an accident – I touched my brakes too abruptly when I saw him, forcing the two cars behind mine to pull up in a squeal of scorched tyre rubber. The copper, observing what had happened, warned me against dangerous driving and sent me on my way suitably chastened.

There was also something slightly troubling. I'd been vaguely aware that one of the cars which had pulled up behind me – a metallic-blue Ford XR2 – had been on my tail ever since I'd joined the motorway at Walthamstow. I was sure, too, it wasn't the first time I'd seen that particular car.

Hollywoods in Harlow, when I eventually found it, was situated opposite a derelict bus station. Bright and garish, it

166

had red carpets, yellow shelving and a large TV screen above the counter. The store stank of stale cigarettes. An American movie was showing on the screen but no one seemed to be watching it. The counter staff – all apparently teenagers – wore identical green polo shirts, a generic Hollywoods logo on the breast pocket of each.

'Can you drive with your eye bruised like that?' one of them asked me.

From there I went to Ware and to Bishop's Stortford, where I delivered more boxes of videos to identikit shops, and collected boxes of unpopular videos from more teenagers all dressed in those vulgar green polo shirts. I then drove to Cambridge, still watching out for the Ford XR2 en route. Having delivered the relevant videos, I parked near the town centre and explored the city in the fading light. A dirty cold wind blew across Market Square and seemed definitively to presage the onset of that delayed autumn. I bought something to eat, crossed the soupy, wind-rippled river and stopped for a drink in a darkened, low-beamed pub, opposite one of the colleges, Magdalene. I bought a bottle of Molson Dry and sat up at the bar.

The pub had a melancholy late-afternoon emptiness. There were a couple of businessmen in tight suits at one corner table, a huddle of student types at another and a boy who looked about sixteen messing around on the slots. I'd been there for about fifteen minutes when a young guy wearing a reversed baseball cap came in. He sat at the opposite end of the bar from me and ordered a pint. He never once lifted his head in my direction, but there was something about him I didn't like, didn't quite trust. As I watched him, the shadows seemed to deepen further in the room.

'Live all you can, Josh – it's a mistake not to.' Squandering time in a Cambridge pub, I thought of what Mum had said as we'd waited together in the departures lounge of Toronto airport, her eyes, like Justin's that morning, hidden behind dark, emotions-evading glasses; and thinking of her, I couldn't help but remember my father, too, and what he'd done to her.

Had I really learned anything about him since being in England? For most of my adult life he'd served as a kind of invisible cheerleader for me, offering, even in his absence, leadership, guidance and a form of inspiration. Now I no longer knew what to think about him; all I knew was that I'd never really known or understood him. I didn't know what I thought about his selling porno videos. Still, a picture of him was beginning to emerge and I didn't really like it: of a man on the edge, hanging around seedy bars and clubs, so committed to making an unconventional living, to the entrepreneurial life, to living intensely and on his own terms, that, at some stage, he must have lost sight of the need for ethical restraint in his life; must have lost sight of what really mattered about having a family. From selling houses to selling free newspapers to selling porno videos to . . . To what? To disappearing? When I compared my father to Nicholas Dundee, for all his pale-faced inscrutability, what did I feel? Which of them offered the better example? Perhaps that question could only be answered by my posing another one in return: which of them was still around, still committed to his family, to working hard and bringing up his children properly?

Answer: Dundee.

Later, as I returned to the van, I saw the youth from the pub again, this time in Market Square. What was he doing there? He had to be following me. My suspicion was confirmed when, aware of my eyes on him, he turned abruptly down a side street, hurrying out of sight. I rushed across the square in time to see him going into McDonald's. I immediately followed him inside. He was standing in the queue, which I joined directly behind him, making him aware of my presence by tapping him firmly on the shoulder.

'D'you want something?' I said.

'Pardon me.' He sounded foreign.

'D'you want something?'

'Sorry, I don't understand.'

He was frightened by my bruised face, I could tell that.

'You were in the pub, by the river just now. I saw you.'

He nodded. 'Did I do something wrong?'

I didn't know what to say.

'Did I do something wrong?' he said again.

I realized I was making a fool of myself. He was genuine, little more than a harmless kid, and yet I'd found him threatening. What was happening to me? The paranoia about the car and now this – I'd obviously not recovered from the aftershock of the attack, its sudden brutality. 'I'm sorry,' I said, 'it's a mistake. Please forgive me.'

I could hear people whispering as I hurried out.

By the time I returned to the depot Justin had gone for the day. His assistant dropped me off at the station on her way home.

The next morning I worked mainly in the warehouse, helping to log and prepare orders for distribution. On the third day, however, I was out on the road again, this time being sent to Romford, Benfleet, Braintree and Southend. I enjoyed the loneliness of being a driver during those soft autumn days – the early starts, the long stretches of open road and the crepuscular light at that time in the morning. Most of all, I enjoyed being free from the pressure cooker of the city, away from the intolerable pace, the noise and bluster of it all.

What was most shocking to me as I drove, though, was how little wilderness there seemed to be left in England; after the glorious open spaces of Ontario, how controlled everything seemed, artificial, hemmed in and stripped of risk. The call of the wild. And yet, the first part of that week on the van, working for Justin, despite my moments of heightened anxiety, seemed like the most peaceful of my English journey, even if the second half of the week signalled, in effect, the beginning of the end.

*

Late on Wednesday afternoon, when I returned from South-end, Justin told me Nick Dundee had returned from the Azores.

'How is he?' I said.

'He seemed fine. He was delighted when I told him you was working for me.'

I was curious to talk to Nick. In his absence, I'd often wondered about him. I wanted to know what he thought about Justin's claim to have known my father, about all that Justin had revealed. So I rang Nick on my mobile.

Judy answered, putting me straight through.

'Joshua, how are you?'

'Did you have a good holiday?' I said.

'Yes, we did. Thanks. Terrific, especially after what happened at the party, the bomb and everything. The Azores, if you've never been ... No, well, they're quite something. Wasn't too hot there, either, after the weather we've been having. Nice to see it's cooling down now, more in line with what you'd expect at this time of year.'

'Did you know a man was killed by that bomb?' I said.

'I heard. Thanks, by the way, for trying to help Emma.'

'That's all right,' I said. 'You know I've been doing a bit of work for Justin?'

'Yes, so I understand,' he said. 'What happened to the law?'

'I ducked out in the end.'

'There's always another time, I suppose.'

'I'm actually here now, at Forest Road. Was hoping to come over to see you.'

'Why's that then?'

'Can't really say at the moment' – Justin was sat behind me, watching the sports channel – 'it's a bit tricky.'

'Under pressure to talk?'

'Sort of.'

'Well, what d'you want to ask me about?'

'I'd rather see you.'

'See me?'

'If it's not too much trouble.'

'No, no, course not. Why don't you come round tomorrow afternoon.'

'I'm working tomorrow afternoon.'

'Afterwards, when you've finished.'

'Is five-ish OK?'

That night I was awoken by the sound of my own screams. I turned on the light and drank some water. Lurid images of being pursued through the deserted night-time streets played themselves over and again. As I lay there, I thought about phoning Jackie, tormented as I was by vague physical desires, but realized I didn't have her number. I pictured her alone in the flat, her phone wired up only for incoming calls, waiting to hear from someone who cared. I'd missed her, in a curious way.

I crossed the room, opened the curtains and looked out on to the wet streets. I felt the swelling on the back of my head, the tenderness around my eye. At least I'd been able to remove the bandage from my hand.

Fine rain was falling, visible in the dim glow of the street lamps outside. And beyond that, on the distant horizon, the city seemed to collapse impalpably into greyness, an unknowable sprawl.

I arrived at Nick's shortly after five the next day. The leaves in Epping Forest were changing colour; in places they'd already fallen and been blown into irregular piles along the side of the road. The gates of Forest Lodge were open: a kind of welcome mat. I drove across the gravel in a Hollywoods van, and stopped outside the front door. Nick was waiting there, as if having spookily emerged from the trees themselves.

'Very good,' he said. 'Nice to see our vehicles getting some use.'

'You look well,' I said.

'We all enjoyed the break, thank you. But look at you, what's been happening? You look as if you've been in the wars.'

'I had some trouble outside a nightclub.'

'What kind of trouble?'

'I got beaten up.'

'Not outside one of my clubs, I hope,' he said, allowing me to pass ahead of him into the house, through the open front door.

'No, it was a place called Nite Flite in Finsbury Park.'

He raised his eyebrows nonchalantly, smiling to himself. For some reason I was feeling extraordinarily uncomfortable in his presence today, as if I was unwittingly the butt of an elaborate joke, or part of a macabre conspiracy.

He led me into the airy hallway, with its bare wooden floors and the high white sheen of the walls and ceiling. There were several open doors leading off into rooms I regretted I'd never enter. These, from what I glimpsed of them, were a mix of contrasting bold colours balanced with touches of softer shades – slate grey, lavender, chartreuse and pale blue.

'Interesting colour combinations,' I said.

'Yes, that's Judy. She's the one who's into interior design. Loves the Designers Guild stuff.'

Nick waved me through into his immaculately ordered study. The carpet felt new and stiff underfoot. In the corner, next to the window, there was a tall bookcase, stocked with shiny pristine hardbacks, which seemed more ornamental than read. There was a silent computer on the desk. We sat at right angles to each other, in two soft chairs. On a table beside me there was a vase from which exotic flowers were blooming like fists. I was waiting for him to speak when there was a gentle rap on the door. Judy came in.

'Hello, Joshua,' she said.

She was a slim, fine-boned woman and she appeared more relaxed than she had on the *Taipan*. Her clothes looked suitably bespoke and flamboyant: a whirl of loose materials. She asked if we wanted some tea.

'Earl Grey, Assam, Darjeeling or Afternoon?'

'Joshua?' Nick said, deflecting her question.

'I don't mind.'

'Earl Grey, please, darling.'

'Would you like some cakes?' Judy said.

'I don't think so,' he said, 'unless – '

'No, I'm all right, thank you anyway,' I said as Judy left.

Nick then turned to me. His skin was red rather than tanned and his ears were peeling. 'I expect you've come about your father?' he said.

I blushed and he courteously averted his gaze, crossing one long leg over the other.

'Not exactly,' I said, composing myself.

He waited, his lashless eyes never leaving my face.

'As you know, I've been doing a bit of work for Justin – we met at your party, on the *Taipan*. He remembers my dad as well.'

Nick tugged at his blond eyebrows. 'Yes, he told me. From the wine bar.'

There was another gentle rap on the door. Judy re-entered. 'I'm just going to pick up the girls, darling,' she said.

Nick nodded. He poured the pale, hot liquid through a strainer, added some milk. I looked on with something approaching regret as he served the tea in fragile Wedgwood cups. So much about him impressed me: his calm, thoughtful manner, his elegant home, the obvious love he felt for his wife and the girls, his patience with my questions. He'd made his life work; he'd created a sense of harmony and order out there on the edges of Epping Forest, whereas my father had left behind only chaos and disorder. I envied Nick the family life he had, the success he'd achieved. His was an example of how a life could go absolutely right – and at that moment, if I were honest, I wished that he were my father.

'What is it, Joshua?' Nick said eventually, continuing as if I hadn't mentioned Justin. 'You don't seem quite yourself today. What's troubling you?'

'You're right, Nick' – he smiled to hear me use his name so familiarly – 'I do feel confused.'

'No news on old Tony then?'

'Nothing. I've hit a wall. There's nothing else I can think of doing.'

'Have you been back to the police?'

'The file's technically open, but they're not really interested. Why should they be after all this time? I've got nothing new to tell them.'

'I don't know what to suggest,' he said, rattling his cup in the saucer.

'There's just one thing troubling me.' I hesitated.

'What is it, Joshua?' he said, and I felt the heat of his gaze on me. Then I began: 'You know Justin says he knew my father, well, when I asked him about dad he didn't really convince me that they'd met. He didn't, for a start, seem to remember what he looked like, didn't really seem to know anything about him at all.'

'It was a long time ago. I'm not sure how well Justin did know your father. Not very well, I suspect. I never saw them together. But if he says he met him, then I'm sure he did. Why would he lie? They both used to go to the wine bar, after all.'

'But he even got the colour of his hair wrong!'

His cheeks swelled like a trumpeter's.

'There's one more thing,' I said. 'Nick, did my father ever try to sell you a pornographic video?'

'No,' he said, without the slightest hesitation, although his eyes did leave my face for the first time.

'Did he ever talk to you about porn,' I went on, 'boast he could get you movies and other stuff?'

He leaned towards me, resting his hand on my knee. 'No, I don't believe he did,' he said. 'Why are you asking me this, Joshua? What have you discovered?'

I shook my head.

'Are you sure it's nothing? Or is it that you've discovered something unpleasant about your father, something you didn't expect?'

I looked at him speechlessly and then out at the mournful gloom of the forest, the centuries of secrets it concealed.

'Josh,' Nick said – the first time he'd called me Josh – 'before you came over this afternoon, I was going through some old papers to see if I could turn anything up on old Tony. Found this.'

He handed me an undated note in my father's hand. That handwriting: I felt destroyed every time I saw it.

Dear Nick
Just want to say how much I've enjoyed our time together. I want you to know you can always count on my trust and support. Never let the bastards grind you down.
Tony

So he did call himself Tony: something else he kept from us. 'Who are the bastards?' I asked, returning the note.

'Been thinking about that myself. No doubt some local council jobsworth who was interfering with the wine bar.'

'What d'you think happened to my father, Nick? D'you think he killed himself? The whole thing's beginning to drive me slowly mad.'

For the first time, he seemed disturbed by the directness of one of my questions. He rose from his chair and turned towards the window, so that I addressed only his broad back. 'I wish I knew,' he said, stooping slightly, 'you don't know how much I wish I knew. Ever since you turned up here, I've not been able to get old Tony out my mind. People are deep, Josh. You never know what their real motivations are. I, for instance, could be a completely different person from who Judy and the girls think I am. Could be leading a double life for all they know. I'm not, of course, but I could be. That's the trick of it. Sometimes I think it's the unknown part of life that's the most pleasurable – the part that takes place inside your head, away from other people, in the private spaces of thought and sleep and daydream.' He spoke without once turning to look at me.

From somewhere deep inside the house a clock chimed. I didn't know what to say next. His flow of words had evaporated into stern silence.

'I'm sorry about all this, Nick. You've probably got enough on your plate without worrying about me as well.'

'No, it's really no worry,' he said, turning. 'I just wish there was something I could do. Finding that note, it sort of brought him back to life.' His voice trailed away.

It was getting late and the last of the light was being swallowed up by the maw of the forest. I watched the spectral trees, the way they swayed in the enveloping darkness, seemingly pushing up against the boundary of Forest Lodge, as if they were on the move, seeking to reclaim lost territory. Nick turned again to peer out at the leafy shadows behind him, his expression becoming momentarily lost and reflective.

'How the nights are drawing in,' he said. And then: 'I'd offer you a cigarette, but Judy doesn't really approve, not in the house.'

'It doesn't matter,' I said. 'I'd better be going anyway.'

As Nick showed me out to the van, Judy's car swung into the drive. The faces of the girls, belted into the back seat, were alert through the glass. They waved at their father and he waved back, chuckling to himself

'I love those girls,' he said. 'One day, Josh, when you're a father, you'll know what it feels like. Changes everything. Feel you'd do anything to protect them. If your father walked out on all this, if he' – he swept his hand expansively in the direction of the house – 'there must have been something desperately wrong in his life, that's all I know.'

Chloe and Emma leapt out of the car and began running towards Nick, who was moving quickly to meet them. They were dressed in smart white tennis outfits, their softly tanned faces showing the flush of recent exertion. Emma reached her father first and he swept her up into his arms, while Chloe grabbed his legs. He was a strange man: charming, likeable in his way, but utterly unreachable. There was so much I wanted to know about him, so much that intrigued me; but I sensed now that we would never become friends, just as I was beginning to relax in his presence. To him I was a minor inconvenience, a poor kid who couldn't shake himself free of the baggage of the past, nothing more than that.

Nick kissed the top of Emma's head, then looked up at me, mouthing, 'I'll call you.'

I nodded at Judy and climbed into the van. The gates closed creakingly behind me as I drove out into the surrounding shade of the forest, feeling curiously estranged from a landscape that had until recently pulsed with the promise of imminent discovery.

I'd been supposed to keep the van overnight but didn't feel much like working for Justin any more. I felt in some important way deceived by him, cheated. If he'd known my father, it wasn't in the way he'd first led me to believe. His initial introduction on the *Taipan* was probably all part of his bravado, his laddish, swaggering routine. Perhaps he'd met my father once or twice at the wine bar, like he said, but no more than that; perhaps Nick had spoken about him and Justin was keen to ingratiate himself further with the boss, by claiming to have met the man whose son was coming to Judy's party. Whatever, he had nothing new to tell me beyond some unverifiable garbage about porno videos. All this talk of pornography and smart deals ... He'd held a gold chain in front of a beggar then snatched it away. His stories about my father were fictions, I was sure, no more accurate representations of him than my own flimsy, often contradictory memories.

The lights were on in the warehouse as I pulled into the Forest Road depot. And there, wretchedly, I saw it again, no doubt about it this time. Parked alongside a Hollywoods truck, in the corner of the yard, was the metallic-blue Ford XR2, with brake lights mounted in the rear window. The same car I'd seen before on the road to Harlow, and, of course, it came back to me at last, clamped outside Nassau Street when Katya and I had returned from the restaurant the night before she left for Moscow.

A warning went off inside my head, like a distress flare. I parked the van and approached the car, pressing my hands on the warm bonnet. I checked the rear window of the car – the 'Repton' sticker I'd seen that night in Nassau Street at once confirmed everything and nothing. I peered into the drab interior of the car and then over at Justin's darkened office. There had to be a connection between him and the car. I went over to the prefab and knocked on the office door. No reply. I moved across to the window and rapped on that, too. Then I went through into the hot, dusty interior of the warehouse – where I was almost blown backwards by the disco thump of engines, the rattle of machinery. There were several young men loading boxes on to a conveyor belt, an air of bewildered detachment about them, as if they were at once there and dreamily elsewhere, unengaged by their work. I asked one of them about the car.

'What car?' he said, plucking two soft yellow plugs out of each of his ears.

I repeated my question.

'What car?' he said again.

'The blue Ford outside.'

'Ask him down there. He might know.'

I moved deeper into the warehouse in search of 'him', who turned out to be a middle-aged man, also working with earplugs.

'Sorry to bother you,' I said, shouting above the roar of machinery, 'but d'you know whose XR2 that is out there?'

'I didn't know there was an XR2 out there,' he said, moving to the window.

The first guy had joined us. I asked them both if they knew of anyone at the depot who drove such a car, or whether they'd seen it before. They hadn't.

'Is Justin Bliss around?' I said.

'Haven't seen him all day.'

I thanked them and returned to the van, where I sat in the cab, waiting for the driver of the XR2 to return. After about an hour, when he still hadn't appeared, I took the registration of the car and then left for the tube station.

There were three messages on my return.

First, 'Mr Winter, it's Karen from Clifford Chance. Having not heard from you for a while, we know you're not interested in your placement with us. Perhaps you could inform your mother of this. She seems to be under the impression that you started work here. Thank you.'

Second, from Justin: 'It's me. I'm not in tomorrow – having to fuck off somewhere at short notice – but catch up over the weekend. There's another week for you if you're up for it.'

Finally, from Katya. I deleted that one as soon as I heard her voice – a voice that I heard again, much later, in the shifting, restless, sleepless hours of early morning.

I rang Binoo John.

'Is everything all right with the flat, Mr Winter? And what news, sir, what news?'

'Yes, everything's fine at Nassau Street. I've been pretty busy with that new job at the solicitor's.'

'Clifford Chance?' he said.

'Yes, Clifford Chance. You remembered. It's going fairly well.'

'Been busy myself. Started going to gym, working with personal trainer, on bike, on rowing machine, on bench press. One mustn't boast, but I think it's helping my asthma – and my morale.'

'Mr John,' I said, 'I wonder if you could do me a huge favour?'

'Depends what it is, my friend.'

'I recall you once mentioned your brother worked for the DVLC in Swansea?'

'Yes, yes.'

'Is he still there?'

'Yes, he is. Why?'

179

'Well, this is going to sound a bit weird, but d'you think he could track down the owner of a vehicle for me. I've got the number plate.'

'I don't like to bother him, not with things like that. Could be sacking offence for him – he has wife and family now.'

'I know it's a lot to ask, but I'm desperate.'

'Is it to do with your father?'

I said it was, and he asked what I'd discovered.

'I'm close to finding him, I think. This number plate, it could hold the key.'

'Let me think about it.' He took down the registration.

'I'm after the owner of the vehicle, his name and address. If you can get hold of them for me I'll be forever in your debt.'

There was a brief pause, a hiss of static on the line.

'You already are, Mr Winter.'

'What?'

'In my debt. I've just looked you up on computer. Your rent is overdue.'

'I'll write a cheque immediately.'

He was chuckling as the phone went down.

On Saturday afternoon, with nothing better to do and not having heard back from Binoo John, I found myself, against my better judgement, returning to Belsize Park. It was the first time I'd been back in more than a month and I was struck, observing how the weather had changed and how far away seemed the unrelenting sunshine of my early days in the city, by how little progress I'd made, how aimless my life had become. Even the streets around me smelt stale and mouldy, even the air seemed dull. I thought back to my second night in London when, bathing in the lights of Piccadilly, I'd longed for time to stand still. Now it couldn't pass fast enough.

I bought a sandwich and a beer and sat inside a café, watching the entrance of the tube station, for whom or what I didn't know. On leaving the café, I wandered down Belsize Avenue,

lingered fleetingly outside the flat and then, following the perimeter fence of Primrose Hill Park, crossed Prince Albert Road
into Regent's Park. I went west along the outer circle, the curve
of the boating lake running parallel with Regent's Park Road. I
sat on a bench, at a convenient distance from the water, and
watched the young children feeding the ducks. The soil was
still hard and patchy underfoot but the grass had a rich green
lustre.

The tourists who claimed the park as their own ambled by
the lake, watched over by the imposing white terraces across
the road, the gleaming fortresses of the rich. The water was
opaque. Traffic passed routinely on the road.

As I sat there, I thought seriously for the first time about
returning to Toronto. Things hadn't worked out as I'd hoped in
London; and yet to return so soon before Christmas would be a
kind of defeat, the end of all possible adventure. I had to hang
in there, lift myself out of impassivity and indolence, and in so
doing locate an engine of change in my life. Wearily, I closed
my eyes, thinking again of Jackie and of her baby alone in that
grey flat – and all the time I was asking myself if I'd been wrong
to forfeit the chance of reviving my career as a lawyer. The
woman from Clifford Chance was right: I ought to call home.

Then I became aware of a group of people gathering at the
water's edge, clearly agitated about something. I went down to
see what was happening. What looked like a pelican was
thrashing in the shallows. At first, I couldn't understand what
the problem was, until I saw a duck – or possibly something
smaller – had become somehow trapped inside the pelican's
distensible pouch. You could see the thick shape of the bird
writhing like a child tied up in a sack. The pelican seemed
traumatized and was shaking its head, attempting to vomit its
living load. The two birds were locked in a mortal struggle,
working antagonistically towards death. Several onlookers
shouted out in different languages but no one intervened. At
once, we were compelled and repelled by what we saw: two
dying birds.

By this time, the ribbed skin of the pelican's pouch had crumpled like rice paper and was beginning to tear. Inside, the duck was scarcely moving. A swan paddled past, lowering its arrow-pointed head below the water. A young couple in a rowing boat dropped oars and watched.

'Why doesn't someone do something?' a female voice said.

I looked round and recognized her immediately. It was the blonde woman from my father's flat. I'd not heard her speak before, beyond the odd sentence or two in the restaurant basement, and I was surprised at how unremarkable was her low-toned voice, with its flattened vowels (how did I expect her to speak, anyway ... like a pampered princess?). It occurred to me that our roles had been reversed and this time perhaps she'd followed me. But no. She dropped her bag, kicked off her shoes and, lifting her long skirt, prepared to wade out into the water.

As she went a Japanese guy filmed her on his camcorder, mumbling an unfathomable commentary. A man announced that he'd called the RSPB on his mobile. A woman said her husband was searching for a park warden. The young woman didn't seem to hear any of this as she went in aid of the pelican; but, watching her approach, the frightened bird panicked and opened its wings, smacking them against the water. The woman slipped, losing her footing. Then the pelican lifted itself out of the water and began flying low across the lake, carrying its load with it, like a storybook stork with a baby.

She stumbled towards us, the outline of her dark bra showing through her damp white sweater. Her nipples were erect. As she stepped on to the grass, she accepted an offer of assistance and was helped over to a bench, where she rubbed herself down with someone's scarf.

'Why were we just watching?' she said. 'The poor thing, it was choking.'

People were drifting away now in the direction of the zoo, from whose aviary I wondered if the pelican had escaped.

Then I noticed her bag lying, apparently forgotten, on the grass. I approached, stooping low to collect it in one smooth, swift movement. Then I was off and away, hurrying across the park. Before leaving altogether, I looked back at the bench, where she was obscured behind a close huddle of women.

That evening, as I lay in the cool privacy of my flat, I opened the bag belonging to Jessica White, for that was her name, emptying its contents on the bed. There were a Filofax containing telephone numbers and addresses, car and house keys, prescription sunglasses, an asthma inhaler, picture postcards bought recently from the National Portrait Gallery (I found receipts in her purse), a lighter but no cigarettes, contact lens solution, a make-up bag, a hairbrush, elastic bands, a mobile phone, a packet of tissues, nail clippers, lip gloss and a corporate card for something called Ambassadors.

I inspected the card:

Ambassadors

Escorts

So Stunning, Very Friendly and Patient

London's No. 1 Escort Agency

Jessica White, an escort? The very idea seemed absurd. I'd seen her during happier times, on the street with her presumed boyfriend; I'd followed her, confronted her even in the air-conditioned basement of a restaurant. And all through that time of watching her I'd wanted nothing more but to see inside her place, to see how much it had changed and what she'd done to transform the dreary wastes among which my father had lived. True, I'd seen her with different men, but she'd always seemed at ease, as I had been back then, flushed with the optimism of first arrival, in those early weeks in the city. I'd always thought Jessica moved as one with purpose in her life, a sense of direction and a place of her own to live. The world of Nite Flite wasn't – couldn't – also be her world. If so, then everything I'd believed to be true in the world was false.

I lit a cigarette, smoked it quickly. Lit another. I was beginning to enjoy the old habit, savouring the smell of a cigarette when first lit, the thick texture of the smoke inside my mouth, the slight scorching sensation at the back of my throat, the tingling in my nose as I breathed out.

There were personal numbers in her Filofax – people I considered calling up. Inside her purse there were bank, credit, store loyalty and gym membership cards. An Equity card, too (did this make her an actress?). She had £35 in her purse which I pocketed, numerous receipts and a photograph which appeared to have been taken at a restaurant or a dinner party. Jessica, in evening dress, was with a young Indian man. They were smiling warmly, their heads not quite touching. How beautiful she looked in the picture, and near and young. And the way she'd run into the water today ... her anger at our vulgar curiosity.

I rang the number on the card. A woman speaking with a possibly Hispanic accent answered. 'Ambassadors,' she said.

I asked to book an appointment.

'Have you used us before?'

'No.'

'Where did you hear about us?'

'From a friend.'

'What sort of girl are you looking for?'

'My friend visited a girl he recommended. I think she was called Jessica, in Belsize Avenue.'

The phone went dead.

Binoo John called early on Monday morning. He'd spoken to his brother and had the information I wanted. Or what I then thought I wanted.

'My brother was reluctant to give me information but I explained your circumstances,' he said. 'He was moved by your plight.'

I thanked Binoo and suggested we met for a drink.

'Call me, please,' he said. 'We must get it on. Until then, until.'

I rang the depot in Forest Road. 'Is Justin there?'

'No, he's away.'

'He was away on Friday as well, wasn't he?'

'Who's that?'

'It's Joshua Winter. I did some work for him last week. D'you know when he's coming back?'

He didn't. 'I thought he'd be back today,' he said.

'Can you tell him I called?'

The owner of the car, according to Binoo John, was Gary Dance. He lived at 12 Port Poole Lane, King's Cross, London. So later that afternoon I set out for King's Cross, for the old, familiar territory that had seemed so hostile during my early days in the city. King's Cross had an atmosphere entirely its own, engaging and repugnant in about equal measure. In daylight hours I remember how it could (almost) seem like any other teeming suburb, were it not for the prevailing squalor, the stench of failure that hung like bad news above the dropouts who gathered around the train station: to beg, to drink. You couldn't ignore the downbeats and runaways – and the cops who patrolled them. You couldn't ignore the panic in the eyes of the guys begging for change as they sat in doorways, or stuck their crooked noses into bins, sniffing like dogs. You couldn't ignore them even as you stepped over them, hearing their plaintive pleas, their beggars' grumbles.

With nightfall the streets around King's Cross Station usually changed into something more urgent, sinister and extreme. The air was sweaty with the whoop of sirens and agitated voices. You sensed something might go off at any moment – and it usually did: a street fight, a stutter of car horns. The hookers were out as usual, but most of them seemed frail and emaciated, in bad shape. They scarcely bothered to smile as you passed them. There was no sales pitch or patter. No real lusty banter.

I was uncertain as to my exact motivation for tracking down Gary Dance, although I had the vague idea – half confirmed when I saw the car parked at the depot – that he might have been following me, and that Justin Bliss or perhaps, more improbably, Nick Dundee was somehow implicated; that my appearance in their lives had worried them. What was really baffling, though, was the reason anyone had for following me. I wasn't important. I'd kept my head down since arriving in London. I'd done nothing wrong, made no enemies. Yet, since being attacked after leaving Nite Flite, I'd felt uneasy, as if I were being continually watched. I had lost my faith in the city.

I found Port Poole Lane easily enough on an A–Z but it nevertheless took some time to find the neighbourhood. Arriving at King's Cross Station, I'd felt extraordinarily exposed, as if returning to a place of greater danger. Darkness had fallen. From the station, I descended into an underpass. Wires from busted light fittings hung down from the ceiling like vines. There was the smell of piss in the air. I emerged into the backlands somewhere beyond the station. There were scrawny teenagers out on the street, messing around in the dusk. Several of them were wearing football shirts – numbers and sponsors' and players' names stitched on the back and front. The street lamps were on and the boys were paddling in all the gathered moments of light. There were no green spaces anywhere, and in the background I could see the glowering outline of two gasometers, like giant sentries keeping watch over the suburb.

There was a special kind of desolation about those backlands; there the streets seemed to merge into one continuous inner-urban concrete landscape, and I couldn't ignore the stink of poverty. Nor the undercurrent of menace, even though those were only kids over there and this was London.

I passed a trailer selling drinks and snacks. I paused to buy coffee, served scaldingly in a polystyrene cup by an old white-haired man. One of the side windows of his trailer was cracked

and patched up with black tape. On a strip of nearby waste-
land a tall, gangly youth and two shorter boys were kicking a
ball around; the youth wasn't wearing a shirt despite the harsh
chill. I noticed a crumpled jacket and a couple of T-shirts were
being used as goalposts. I made a left into Port Poole Lane,
where I stumbled on a burnt-out car, a shell of blackened
metal and shrunken springs. The surrounding estate, though,
wasn't as desolate as expected. Many of the houses had
been bought from the local authority and duly customized,
with flagstone steps, splashes of pebbledash, neat brick-
work, creosoted gates, coloured door panels, porches – the
cheap, vulgar attractions of private property, as I sneeringly
saw it.

Once I'd found Gary Dance's house, I circled the block twice,
ensuring that I was alone. Then I searched the surrounding
streets for the metallic-blue Ford XR2. Nothing. I withdrew
across the road, keeping watch from an anxious distance on the
sturdy white-painted front door of what I assumed to be
Dance's end-of-terrace house. It was completely dark and getting colder all the time. There were lights on in the house, both
upstairs and down. I waited for about forty minutes, but there
was no movement either in or out of the property. I was
beginning to despair (and freeze) when I saw the three boys
who'd earlier been playing football by the coffee trailer. I
called out to them, addressing the tallest of the three. He was
thin, awkward, but looked like a street-hardened, canny
scrapper.

'All right, lads?' I said.

They paused.

'D'you want to earn yourself some quick money?' I
flourished a tenner from my wallet. The tallest youth bounced
the football twice on the cold flat pavement, unimpressed.

'Who the fuck are you?' asked one of the smaller boys,
ginger-haired with a hooped earring.

'I'm a police officer,' I said.

'What happened to your eye?' the third boy asked.

'Don't worry about that,' I said. 'D'you want to earn some money or not? Here, you can have a tenner each.'

'Come on, I'm going,' the tall youth said, and the others obediently followed.

'Listen,' I said, 'I'm serious. You can have twenty quid each. All I want you to do is knock on that door over there and offer to wash someone's car.'

The tall youth stopped, turned. 'At this time of night? Are you mad?'

'As I said, I'm a police officer. You'll do yourselves a huge favour helping me.'

'I don't wanna help no coppers,' the ginger boy said. 'My dad says you're filth.'

'Does he now? Whatever. Twenty-five quid each – my final offer. Take it or leave it.'

The tall youth said, 'You're on.'

I gave them the money and explained what I wanted. Then I crouched behind a van at an oblique angle from the house and watched the boys in their easy approach. The taller youth rang the bell twice. A shadow fell across him as the door opened. The boys spoke to a man, who ... My God, even from that distance I recognized him. I felt as if a blindfold had been removed. What had stopped me from seeing the link before? For I knew this man, I'd seen him when his hair was worn longer in a ponytail on the *Taipan* and then again, this time his hair cropped short, in mirrored reflection at Nite Flite. I suspected, too, that he'd been among my pursuers through the empty night-time streets of Finsbury Park. Was this Gary Dance, the driver of the Ford XR2?

I was disturbed to consider what I might be caught up in. The idea that there was someone out there now, watching me in the darkness of the surrounding streets, invisible, seeing everything, silently waiting for his opportunity to move – it seemed preposterous.

The door closed and the boys skipped towards me, delighted. As they reached the nearside of the van, I urged them to keep going, not to look back, addressing them in a troubled whisper.

'He didn't want his car cleaning,' the ginger boy said, and the other two giggled; but they didn't look back, as instructed.

I watched them merge into the powdery darkness.

Back in my flat, feeling as vulnerable and isolated as I'd ever felt in the city, I rang Ambassadors a second time. Once again, a woman put the phone down when I asked about Jessica White.

Much later, on waking from a dream, I called Justin Bliss on his mobile, but his answering service picked up. Much later still, the phone rang in my flat, but when I answered it there was only silence, and then the click of a receiver going down.

I'd been waiting outside Jessica White's flat for half an hour, daydreaming about her life as an escort and the prospect of my being alone inside the flat with her, before an opportunity arose to slip into the building behind a returning resident. I had no idea if she was in or not. I walked up the neat, unremarkable staircase to the third floor, carrying her Prada bag. I rang the bell. As I did so, I saw again the clutter of my father's bedroom, his open drawers, scattered papers, suitcases and the unmade bed – the melancholy of his impending departure. A light was switched on and she opened the door.

'Jessica White?'

She frowned.

'Sergeant Winter, from Holborn police.' I flashed the fake warrant card I'd made from my Canadian ID that afternoon, withdrawing it before she had the opportunity to study the hurried workmanship. 'Your bag was handed into the station this afternoon by a member of the public.'

She accepted the bag from me. 'I never thought I'd see it again.'

'Well, this kind of thing can restore your faith in human nature.'

'Yes, it can rather,' she said.

'D'you want to check there's nothing missing.'

'You should have called,' she said, 'I would have come to get it, saved you a trip.'

'I was passing this way anyway.'

I thought then that she looked at me with suspicion, perhaps half recognizing me from that night in the basement, or perhaps wondering why I was out of uniform.

'Have we met before?' she asked. 'You seem awfully familiar.'

I chuckled, enjoying the deception. 'Not unless I've ever arrested you, love.'

She smiled. 'I'm just going out, otherwise I'd make you a cup of coffee.'

'That won't be necessary,' I said. 'But if you could just check everything's there . . . '

'Sure, come in a minute.'

I stepped into my father's old flat. The hallway smelt of some kind of incense. The walls were painted pale peach; the doors and floorboards were stripped, as they seemed to be everywhere nowadays. The kitchen door was closed. She seemed smaller, less forbiddingly confident and metropolitan than I'd previously thought. I liked her easy, relaxed informality.

She led me past the closed door of Pa's old bedroom and into the sitting room. The cool minimalism of my daydreams was nowhere; instead there were dustsheets spread across the floor and furniture, an aluminium stepladder in the middle of the room, pots of paint, flaps of ragged wallpaper, strips of newspaper, old towels and cloths, the smell of white spirit.

'Sorry about the mess,' she said. 'I'm decorating.'

No 'we're', no mention of another person. She sat at the table and inspected the contents of the bag. As she did this I looked round the room: my father had left no decorative signature, nothing to suggest he'd ever lived there. I noticed a drum kit in the corner and asked if she played.

'Sometimes,' she said, looking up.

'Are you in a band then?'

'Used to be.' Her northern accent was becoming more apparent, like a high-pitched sound that becomes truly irritating only once it's brought to your attention – and then you can't escape it. She emptied the contents of the bag on the table. I'd returned everything, even the cash, except for the Ambassadors card, the rough texture of which I was at that moment feeling in my pocket.

As I watched her I imagined having sex with her, the two of us sprawled out together on top of the table, her legs splayed as she lay beneath me, and that familiar look of haughty boredom on her face. It was a strange, oddly distressing experience to imagine myself fucking her. I could see sweat on my back forming in the red ridges of my scars, Jessica passionlessly unengaged beneath me. I looked at her again, but it wasn't Jessica White I saw sat at the table, it was my father, and he was studying the football fixtures in the paper, as he'd done all those years ago, and it was as if I was at once inside my body yet radically estranged from it, subject and object at the same time, as if I was having a kind of out-of-body experience. As I prepared myself to speak to him, he began to melt in front of my eyes, like a cartoon snowman exposed to intense heat.

'Well, everything seems to be there . . . Sergeant, what's the matter?' Jessica's voice recalled me to the shock of myself. 'What's the matter?' she repeated. 'Are you all right?' She was no longer naked on the table but stood there in front of me, causally trusting in her jeans and sweater. An ordinary girl. 'Everything seems to be there,' she said.

'Excellent.'

'Are you all right?' she said again. 'You seem to have gone terribly pale.'

On the way to the door, I asked her if she was an actress.

'Sort of – but how d'you know that?'

'The Equity card. I saw it when checking your bag at the station.'

'Oh, right.'

'Have you been on television?' I said.

'A few times, but nothing major.'

'When are you next on?'

'I don't know. I'm waiting to hear about something.'

'What are you working on at the moment?'

'You wouldn't want to know.'

'Go on, try me.'

'Well, tomorrow I'm booked to dress up as a chipmunk at some rich kid's birthday party.'

'A what?'

'A bloody chipmunk.' She laughed.

I stood in the doorway, disgusted at having tricked my way into her flat. 'D'you want to meet for a drink some time?' I said.

'I can't. I'm going to Australia next week.'

'When you come back?'

'I don't know if I'm coming back. But thanks for asking, and thanks for returning the bag. I never thought I'd see it again.' She smiled, her blue eyes fading to grey.

I knew for sure, as I walked down those stairs and out of that block, that I would never see her again. Nor ever see inside the flat again. And I knew, too, that I was finally beginning to learn to live without the possibility of delight; that, in a powerful sense, the illusion of wisdom began in disillusionment, in stripping away the false codes by which we lived, the lies we tell ourselves, the painful truths we evade.

So was Jessica White an escort girl or an actress? Either way, it no longer seemed to matter.

IX

The two men have little difficulty entering Anthony Winter's flat. The signs of his rapid departure are everywhere apparent: in the open, ransacked drawers; in the chaotic dishevelment of the wardrobe; in the clothes scattered on the bed; and in the displaced rug and floorboards in the bathroom. Nick Dundee and Justin Bliss are both wearing plastic gloves. They search the flat with extreme patience, especially the bedroom. Dundee, a strip of plaster across the bridge of his nose, seems to know exactly what he's looking for: but he doesn't find it. Before leaving, they replace everything meticulously so that the flat's unrecognizable from how they found it. It is ordered and tidy. At peace.

The phone rings as they're on their way out. They pause as the machine intercepts. They hear his voice, then a woman's stripped of any warmth. 'Anthony, it's me. I thought you'd be in. Josh seems to have enjoyed the weekend with you after all. Hasn't stopped talking about you.' There's a pause. 'I'll be in bed by ten-thirty, so don't call after that.'

The two men look at each other but neither speaks. Justin surveys a selection of bills and envelopes on a table: all addressed to an Anthony Winter, not someone he knows or has ever met.

The door of the flat shuts and they leave conventionally via the stairs. They walk along Belsize Avenue, in the direction the boy and his mother had driven less than forty-eight hours earlier. They turn left, cross the road to where they've parked in a street adjacent to the station. They pull away into the cold, wind-bitter afternoon. As he drives, Dundee realizes how much he regrets not having killed Winter when he had the chance. He knows that, one day, the man will return, that his absence is unlikely to be suicide. The thought disturbs him.

Justin Bliss senses something unusual in Dundee's silence. He seems like an entirely different person today. Justin can feel his fury; but he has no idea what's been happening. He glances at Dundee in profile. That strip of plaster looks ridiculous, and whatever happened to his eyelashes?

Dundee, clutching the wheel, peers unblinkingly into the slow grey fade of afternoon. His fingers are wrapped so tightly around the leather-encased steering wheel that his knuckles are turning bone white, hard.

The Hunting

On returning from Jessica Whites's I called my mother. Al's voice message picked up. I spoke stiltedly, explaining how the job at Clifford Chance had turned out to be a disappointment and that, having left it, I hoped to return to Toronto earlier than expected, as early as a week today. London hadn't delivered what I'd wanted, I told them, and I was missing Toronto more than I ever imagined. Which was almost true. 'I'd be home sooner, but I want to see Uncle David in Manchester this weekend.'

Then I rang David Winter. He was delighted to hear from me, if perplexed by my long silence and failure to acknowledge his previous letter. 'I was beginning to doubt that you would ever come.' Still, he was happy for me to visit that weekend, and suggested I arrived on Saturday morning. 'I've got a function on Friday night I can't get out of; but you could always come on Thursday.'

'No, Saturday's fine. I'm really looking forward to seeing you.'

'How have you been getting on down there?'

'Terrific,' I said. 'I just love it so much in London.'

Before climbing into the bath, I called Justin Bliss. I reached him on his mobile, a palpable surprise in his voice. He asked why I'd 'absented' myself from work at the end of last week and what I'd been doing. I invented a trip to Manchester. 'But then you'd already know, wouldn't you?'

'What do you mean by that?' he said.

'Justin, we've got to meet.'

'Why the sudden urgency?'

'I've discovered something unbelievable about Nick

Dundee.' I was unable to think of another way of arousing his curiosity.

'What have you found out?' he said.

'It'll have to wait till tomorrow.'

'Look, mate, I'm busy. I haven't got time to fuck around. If it's really important, why not tell me now?'

'Believe me, Justin, we've got to meet.'

'D'you wanna come to the office?'

I didn't trust him. 'Can you get up here?'

'You mean, up west?'

'Yeah.'

'Maybe tomorrow afternoon. I'm in Hammersmith in the morning anyway.'

I gave him the address of Princes Cappuccino and we agreed a time to meet.

'This better be good, otherwise –'

'What?' I said.

'What the fuck's got into you, Joshua?'

'Any problems, I'll be on my mobile,' I said.

I lay there in the hot bath, thinking of Jessica White, of how sated I felt now that I'd discovered something about her life, finally seen inside the flat. I accepted now that I'd imagined her out there on the streets earlier in the summer, had made of her something abstract like a piece of music, seemingly destined for ever to remain out of reach, like my father, with whom she was so contingently bound up through having lived in his old flat: the golden girl high up in her metropolitan eyrie. For all her supposed haughtiness and studied distance, she seemed, from our meeting at least, as much of a stranger in the city as I was, a vulnerable, aspirant actress embarked on her own complicated mission of self-invention. Let her be.

I was interrupted by the phone. I hopped out of the bath, draping a towel around my shoulders – an old post-accident ritual to which I remained attached – and reached the phone just before the machine picked up. I'd left a trail of damp footprints behind me, like impressions in the snow.

'Joshua Winter?'

'Yes.'

'Hold the line for Nicholas Dundee.'

I waited, shivering slightly.

'Are you still there?' the voice said.

'Yes.'

'I'm putting Nicholas Dundee through.'

'Hello, Joshua.'

'Nick, hi. I've just jumped out of the bath.'

'Oh, if it isn't convenient?'

'No, it's great to hear from you.'

'I just wondered if everything was all right,' he said.

'Yes. Why shouldn't it be?'

'You seemed, well, rather distressed the other day when you came round.'

'Oh, sorry. I was just feeling a bit low.'

'You'd tell me if you needed anything, wouldn't you?'

'Yes, of course.'

'I hear you've stopped working for Justin.'

'Yes, I have.'

'Any particular reason?'

'None, really. It's just that I'm going away to see my father's brother.'

'I'd forgotten old Tony had a brother. Where does he live?'

'In Cornwall,' I said, increasingly distrustful of him.

'Has he been helping you with your search?'

'Not really, no.'

'No luck then?'

'No, no luck. As I said to you last week, I've sort of given up the ghost on that one. I'm thinking of returning to Canada.'

He fell momentarily silent. 'You'll let me know before you go back, won't you?'

'Oh, Nick,' I said.

'What is it?'

'I don't know how to put this, but . . .' I was about to mention Gary Dance when my own internal brakes of suspicion halted me. It was, surely, more than a coincidence that Nick had called so soon after I'd spoken to Justin Bliss about him. 'No, nothing, it's all right,' I said.

'Are you sure it's all right?'

I chuckled. 'I'm just going to jump back in that bath.'

'Very good. I'll be in touch,' he said.

It was raining heavily when I set off to meet Justin Bliss at Princes Cappuccino bar. I'd not been back there since those early weeks in the city and I moved through the surrounding streets as if wading through thick mud; my feet dragged uncertainly and everything seemed an interminable struggle. I half expected at any moment to see Gary Dance or one of his boys huddled beneath an umbrella, following in my footsteps. And still the rain came down, blackly drenching everything. Cars, their lights already on in the afternoon gloom, were bumper to bumper, and the diesel fumes, from the restless buses and cabs, hung pregnant with threat in the air.

From where I was standing, I had an uninterrupted view into Princes. Justin wasn't there. The layout inside the café was unchanged from my last visit, and only three of the seven mirror-side tables were occupied. At the first window table, there was a young black guy and a white girl, student types – they had wet hair, seemed at ease, and there was nothing menacing about them. At the next table, a motorcycle dispatch rider was dressed in a one-piece leather biker's suit, his helmet placed proprietorially on the table, the visor opening into the black hole of his absent face. I was less sure about him. At the third table, three middle-aged women smoked, drank tea or coffee, and ate sandwiches. They seemed entirely benign.

Despite the protection of an umbrella, I could feel the rain seeping through my jacket, jumper and shirt, feel it against my skin. The drenching chill, the dark-coated figures hurrying past on the street, the gridlocked traffic, the wounded rhino's roar of a stationary ambulance, the threat I saw in every half-turned face – there was a quality of phantasmagoria about what I was seeing. And then Justin arrived in a cab, coatless as he climbed out into the rain, a folded umbrella held in one hand like a dandy's cane. He hesitated at the door of Princes, as if surprised not to find me inside, but still went in. The young students were leaving and he slipped into their window seat, a seamless transition, brushing splashes of rain from his sweater. I waited, observing, evaluating, and then made my way over.

'Hello, mate,' Lilo said, when I stepped out of the rain. I was touched by his friendliness. I hadn't expected him to remember me.

'Hey, Lilo, what's up?'

'Where've you been hiding yourself?' he said.

'That's what I want to know,' Justin said, rising to receive me. 'I didn't think you was coming.'

'I'm sorry I'm late,' I said, warily assessing the dispatch rider, still doubtful of his presence there.

'No dramas. I've only just arrived myself. Took ages to get here by cab. The fucking weather's snarled up all the roads.'

'I walked,' I said.

'I can see that.'

'D'you want a drink?'

'I've got some coffee coming.'

'I'll have a white coffee, please, Lilo,' I said.

'Hot or cold milk?'

'Hot.'

'Got that?' Lilo said, passing the baton of responsibility to his brother, Rob, who'd just arrived up from the basement. He nodded with recognition when he saw me, but there was no beginning of a smile. He was wearing an Inter Milan shirt and jeans, his dark gelled hair parted thickly in the middle.

I sat opposite Justin. His back was against the window. Lilo

arrived with our coffees, and we bantered playfully about
what I'd been doing. Working, I said, travelling a bit, enjoying
the sun. As for him, he'd spent three weeks in Sicily, staying
with his uncle's family.

'So what's this all about?' Justin asked me, once Lilo had
returned to the counter.

There was no profit in evasion. 'Does the name Gary Dance
mean anything to you?' I said immediately.

He pondered, then shook his head, his expression as fixed
and unaltered as statuary.

'Are you sure?'

'Totally. Why?'

'I'm looking for him. I'm pretty sure he works for Nick
Dundee, in some capacity.'

'A lot of people work for Nick.'

'Are you really sure you don't know the name?'

'I honestly can't say the name's familiar.'

This time, I almost believed him.

'He was on the *Taipan* the night of the party.'

'Who was?'

'This Gary Dance. Can you recall meeting anyone by that
name at any of Nick's other parties?'

'Can't say I've been to many of his parties.'

'You were on the *Taipan*!'

'Yeah, but I don't know why he invited me. I might have
known him a long time, but I couldn't call him a friend.'

'What could you call him?'

'A fucking cunt.'

His self-amused laughter was so loud that Rob glanced over
at us.

'This guy – Gary Dance – he wore his hair in a ponytail that
night on the *Taipan*, but he's recently had a crop. He's tall, wiry,
a bit hard-looking.'

'Why are you so interested in him?'

'I think he's been following me.'

'Whatever makes you think that?'

I monitored his response.

'Well, don't look at me, I don't know.'

The sound of a car pulling up outside distracted me, the passenger door opening and closing with a dull thump. I anxiously surveyed the figures emerging from the car. Justin sipped his coffee, watching me watching the streets. In the bare light of the café his complexion had the brittle, ashen hue of the overworked, the sleepless. I glanced in the mirror and saw Rob looking over at me, the rich, glamorous shimmer of his Inter shirt. The dispatch rider was getting up to leave, his boots reverberating heavily on the floor as he prepared himself for the weather. Soon the women were leaving, too, and Justin and I found ourselves alone in the café, aware of the driving rain outside, the sound of tyres swooshing through puddles. Unprompted, Lilo returned to the table with two more hot milky coffees.

I looked out at the rain-smeared streets and there, standing across the road, were two men, their faces indistinguishable behind wide-brimmed golf umbrellas, and they appeared to be looking over at the café. They seemed to be doing nothing but waiting. For whom? A car drove past, splashing them with dirty water, and I turned back to Justin.

'Dundee told me', I began again, 'that you never really knew my father, that he'd never once seen the two of you together. He's right, isn't he, you never met him?'

'Nick said that?' Justin seemed incredulous. 'Why did he tell you that?'

'What's going on, Justin? What am I caught up in here?'

He dropped his head.

'I've never told you what really happened to my father, have I?' I said. 'But I guess you already know.'

He looked up. 'Know what?'

'He disappeared twelve years ago, around the time you said you knew him. No one's seen him since.'

'But you said he was working in property!'

'I lied. All I know for sure is that my father disappears and then twelve years later you approach me at a party – all enthusiastic like – and claim to be his old mucker. How am I supposed to take that?'

I could feel the frustration of so many idle, rootless weeks mounting and there were tears I could no longer contain. I wiped my eyes against the back of my hand. The water collected there burnt my skin like molten lead.

'This is really getting to you, isn't it?' he said.

I looked at him through a mist of self-hatred.

'OK, I'll be honest with you. All the stuff on the boat, the welcome I gave you – that was Nick's doing. He wanted you to feel comfortable.'

'Nick's doing? What d'you mean?'

'He's got something strange about your old man. He wanted me to keep an eye on you, be a bit friendly, offer you work. That's why he invited me to the party – to meet you. He was keen to know what you were getting up to in London, if you mentioned your old man at all. That's all.' He looked into my eyes.

'That's all!'

'Honest, it was nothing more sinister than that. And you're right, I never met your old man. Saying so was just a way of getting close to you. Then what I couldn't understand was why you never told me what you told Nick about your father: that he went missing. It made me think you might have been hiding something – the real truth.'

'And Gary Dance?' I said.

'All right, I do know him, he works for Nick.'

'Is he a mate of yours?'

He shook his head. 'I guess he was keeping an eye on you, like I was. No dramas really.'

No dramas.

The noise in my ears had become intolerable; I felt deranged by rage, as if my head might explode.

'You're a lying cunt, Bliss,' I said, shouting at him.

It was too late. Before I could stop myself I'd grabbed his

sweater and driven my fist into his face. There was splintering bone and his nose ruptured like a soft tomato, leaking blood and snot over the table. My coffee had spilled across the Formica and it merged with Justin's blood. Both Lilo and the usually morose Rob were aroused into agitation, but I was already running out of there into the torrential rain, my umbrella lying forgotten on the chair.

I'd not progressed far when I turned to see Justin coming after me, scattering people from his path as if they were pigeons. Even in the darkness, I could see the patches of blood on his sweater. I crossed the road, weaving through the stationary cars, but it was hard to move quickly on such slippery surfaces, and so, imitating Justin, I also began pushing people out of the way. I crossed Soho Square, made a right, then a rapid left, hurrying past restaurants, newsagents, bars, dark-windowed sex shops. I was pulling away from Justin when I realized how near I was to Binoo John's office. I made another right, this time putting more distance between Justin and myself.

'Hey, hey, steady,' Binoo John said, looking up from his desk.

'Binoo, I need you to hide me,' I said.

He removed his spectacles and ran plump fingers through flat, oily hair. He was extravagantly annoyed. 'Where do you think I can hide you in here? This isn't a TARDIS.'

'Anywhere, I don't care, just hide me.'

'I know you, Mr Winter, but your face!'

'Don't worry about my face.'

Through the window I saw Justin turning the corner. He stopped, approached a woman sitting in the window of a basement sex cinema.

'He's out there now,' I said, ducking beneath the line of the window.

'Who's out there?' Binoo John was crossing the room. 'Oh, right, I think your man's coming this way.' There was excitement in his voice and he seemed to be delighting in the intrigue. 'In there, quickly,' he said, pointing towards a small door in the corner of the room.

The cupboard-sized room was cramped, dark and airless, no larger really than one of Mum's walk-in wardrobes. A battered trilby hung on the back of the door, its intricate folds and creases, its greasy patches, signs of hardened use, signatures of its success over many years. And again, tantalizingly, I found myself lost on that breezy morning more than a decade ago, when my father and I had climbed together to the summit of Primrose Hill, and looked out over the expectant city.

The door opened, the sound of a bell. I felt squashed as if inside a shell, unable and unwilling to move. I felt my under-exercised hamstrings tightening as I crouched there, poised to snap like frayed elastic.

'Can I help you, sir?'

'I'm looking for someone.' It was Justin.

'If it's my assistant, he's away today.'

'Look, Paki, cut the crap. Have you had someone in here in the last few minutes or not?'

'I object to your language, even if you are in discomfort. I'm nobody's *Paki*.'

In the silence, I imagined Justin inspecting the dampness on the floor and then waited for him to cross the office to where I was hiding. But no – the sound of the bell again and then the sullen thwack of the door being slammed. I impatiently expected to hear Binoo John's reassurance that he'd gone and through the long anguish of waiting I heard distant voices, other lives, from outside on the street, and the whisper of the rain.

'All right in there?' Binoo John said eventually. 'He's talking to the girl again. Now he's moving away, but he keeps looking over. Hold on, he's coming back. No, he's going now but don't move.'

Move? If only I had the space to move.

'I'll put the kettle on,' Binoo said. 'How many?'

I knew what he meant this time.

'If it's tea bags,' I called out, 'just one, please.'

'Are you sure?'

'I'm perfectly sure.'

At length, the kettle began to whistle.

'You gave me terribly big surprise running in here like that, but not half as big as when I saw his face. Did you do that?'

He opened the door of the cupboard and I squinted up at him, nodding in answer to his question. He was perspiring; there were damp patches visible beneath each arm as he reached up for two mugs from the cluttered shelves.

'On God's earth, what are you involved in? He was in a terrible state, and your own face!' His fringe had fallen across his pale forehead and he brushed it away.

'Thanks for your help,' I said, resting my hand on his ample shoulder.

'This business you're mixed up in, nothing to do with DVLC number, I hope?'

'No, nothing to do with that.'

'Your father?'

'No, not him, either. Let's just call it a little local difficulty. He's someone I used to work for.'

'Owe him money?'

'Something like that.'

'His face?' Binoo wiped his hands across the front of his shirt.

'I hit him.'

'You hit him?'

Binoo told me he was a resolute 'pacifist', that he despised violence of any kind.

'I'd better be off,' I said.

'But your tea?'

'Just drop my bag into your cup – make it a real Anthony Burgess.'

205

He smiled. 'And our drink?'

'Soon,' I said. 'I'll ring you.'

'I'm away next week,' he said.

'The week after then,' I said, although I knew that by then I wouldn't even be in the country.

'One more thing, Mr Winter, when you were in there I checked your account. Your rent is even more overdue now.'

I offered to send him a cheque.

'I thought you said that last time.'

'You're right.' I opened my wallet. 'Here, take this.' I offered him what I had: £140 in notes. 'I'll put a cheque in the post for the rest tomorrow.'

He opened the back door for me. 'You better go this way,' he said. Then, handing me an umbrella, 'Take this.'

'Are you sure?'

'I can always borrow Mr Colin's.'

I thanked him one more time, perhaps for the last time.

'Take care, Mr Winter, take care now,' he called after me, his hand raised in that familiar formal gesture of farewell.

Justin knew where I lived, so I checked into a small hotel in Bloomsbury, paying £80 for a room as claustrophobic as Binoo John's cupboard – a disgusting, cramped hole. There was scarcely enough space to move. The bedroom led into a small bathroom, where a trapped cranefly spun in unhappy loops, whining like a light aircraft. There was no double-glazing or air-conditioning; the radiator was intensely hot and whenever a vehicle passed by everything shook – the wardrobe, the dressing table, my head. I felt like young Alice, a dispossessed giant stumbling around in a shrunken world.

And what of Nicholas Dundee?

Justin had hinted at a possible dispute between him and my father, had said that Dundee had wanted me befriended and watched. What lay behind such subterfuge? In person, Dundee was believable, convincingly charming. Then there were Judy, the girls, the grandeur of Forest Lodge. How could there be darkness in that life?

It had passed nine o'clock by the time I arrived at Port Poole Lane, having bought a torch from a garage en route. There were no lights on in Gary Dance's house and I felt a powerful sense of futility as I stood on his doorstep, pressing the bell, hunched under Binoo John's umbrella. There was no answer. I cut along a wet, unlit alleyway which expired dimly into garages at the rear of the house. There was a light wind and the rain clouds had smothered any starlight. I climbed the fence, my feet slipping on saturated wooden rungs, and dropped awkwardly into the small, paved backyard. Within five paces I was rapping gently on the rear window. I could hear the television in an adjacent house, see the blue flicker of its light. Behind me there was a bank of high-rise flats. I shone my torch into the house.

Two doors led out of the kitchen, one into a long rectangular sitting room. There was a cat flap at the bottom of the door and a bowl with some gristly meat in it on the kitchen floor. There were some mugs and plates and a milk carton on the table, clutter in the sink. I moved sideways to shine the beam through the open Venetian blinds and into the sitting room. It dipped before settling like a moth on the mantelpiece above an open fireplace – there were trinkets and trophies, framed photographs. I followed the torch to a table beneath the line of the window-ledge. There were papers and more photographs scattered across the table, an empty ashtray and a vase of fresh flowers. I tilted my head to inspect the photographs more closely, and there, shockingly, emerging out of the shadows cast by the blinds, were several photographs of me.

There were photographs of me on the table.

Without even considering the possibility that the house might be alarmed, I used the torch to punch a hole in the glass door, slipped my arm through, turned the handle and scrambled in. The heating was on. That smell . . . I was reminded of returning home to Dorset after one of our long summer holidays; the hot, dead air had that kind of stultifying effect. Without turning on any lights, I went through to the sitting room, and shone the torch on the walls, the table, the curtains. I went over to the table, on which the photographs were assembled as casually as holiday snaps. A kind of pictorial narrative of my recent life was there laid out: me arriving for the first time at Forest Lodge – which must have been taken by a security camera; leaving a London restaurant with Katya; on the quayside at Canary Wharf; arriving at Nite Flite. I was utterly baffled to find those images of myself, with the ghostly figures of unknown people occupying the unacknowledged margins of the photographs, unknown people to whom I was strangely connected but who would remain for ever out of reach.

I turned over each of the photographs. Only one – my arrival at Forest Lodge – had something written on the back: 'J. Winter arriving at mine for the first time'. As I read this, a series of snatched images replayed themselves, half-sightings really, of a flickering, spectral presence glimpsed, like a midnight intruder, from the corner of my eye: on the *Taipan*, in the lounge bar at Nite Flite, on the streets of Finsbury Park and out on the roads of the north-eastern suburbs. And by others, too: I recalled the ignored warnings of Mrs Green, for instance.

I moved across to a corner cabinet, opened the drawers and began searching for something revealing about Gary Dance – letters, diaries, address books. Behind me there was a pine dresser, but its drawers yielded nothing other than the usual household ephemera. I went upstairs and felt my way along the narrow corridor into the bathroom, where I splashed cold water on my face, stalling fatigue. Leaving the bathroom, I saw a computer and some papers spread out on a desk in another room. I went through and switched it on. He wasn't on-line. I turned on a desk lamp and began searching through the papers neatly piled in front of his keyboard – bills, faded back copies of *Boxing News*, bank statements (he was overdrawn by several hundred pounds), a short typed letter from someone called Jenny, travel brochures, a computer manual, an article on Sri Lanka torn from a newspaper. Near the bottom of the pile I found a postcard, neatly handwritten, from Nick Dundee. The computer hummed and vibrated. Beneath the formally printed business heading, Forest Projects, he had written:

RE: Winter
Gary, I understand he was turned over outside Nite Flite, Why? If I wanted him roughed up, I'd have said so. My gut feeling is that he's probably harmless. But I'm curious about him – still uneasy about what he's doing. Pls advise immediately what went wrong. And keep your mobile switched on at all times. We've had difficulty locating you. N.D.

Then I heard the front door being opened. I switched off the torch. In the long silence, I was convinced I'd been followed from the station, that my alien presence in that neighbourhood had been observed and acted upon. Then I began to wonder if I'd imagined the noises downstairs, but when the lights came on in the hallway I knew I had better be prepared to talk my way out of this one. Leaving the computer on, I edged out of the room and along the corridor. At the top of the stairs, I looked down and saw Gary Dance on his way up towards me.

There's a flash of recognition. 'You!' he says, taking the narrow stairs two at a time. I don't know where to turn or quite what to expect, so I throw the torch at him and it hits him directly in the chest. Then he's at the top of the stairs and he's on me, forcing me back as he clasps my head in huge hands and attempts to slam it repeatedly against the wall. I can hear the torch bouncing down the stairs. There's a colossal clatter before it stops. He's offered me no chance to explain myself. His lips are parted like a feeding fish. His breath smells, soured by beery belches, and I can feel myself weakening as I struggle with him. His hands are closing around my windpipe . . . Then, from the street, there comes the wail of a car alarm which goes on and on and on, and I can see something approaching normality returning to his eyes, as if he realizes what he's doing. I seize on his loss of concentration and, as if in slow motion, propel him backwards, watching as he flounders, then topples. One big push and he's gone. Falling. He's falling down the long, wooden staircase. Tumbling backwards, his head loose and bouncing as if severed from his body, as if he were as feebly flimsy as a scarecrow. And there's nothing I can do about it. He comes to rest, like the torch before him, clatteringly. He doesn't rise quickly. He doesn't rise at all.

I wait there, feeling myself sliding lugubriously into inertia. I can hear voices and something more: a high-pitched ringing in my ears, like the dreaded onset of tinnitus. Outside the street is silent, the car alarm curtailed. From inside the house, similarly, nothing moves. He is still. I stare down at him and his body seems gigantic, as if glimpsed in a hallucination, and it's like I'm simultaneously looking at myself from the outside, as I did in Jessica's flat, as if I'm locked helplessly into the trajectory of a drugs trip – fragmentary, allusive. The cell walls of my identity are, I know, beginning to break down.

Then, from my pocket, the sound of my cell phone.

'Josh, is it *really* you?'

As soon as I heard Katya's voice, horrified at how removed from her world I'd become, I hurled the phone downstairs. It shattered on impact, showering the prostrate body with shards of black plastic, a macabre confetti.

I went down to look at Gary Dance. I lifted his wrist, feeling for a pulse. Nothing. I placed three fingers on either side of his Adam's apple. Nothing. He was dead. I think his neck was broken. His hands were still warm yet his open eyes were as drained of colour as a washed-out winter sky. I closed the lids over them. There were wet patches at the front of his trousers, where he'd pissed himself. I felt his hands again, pinching his fingers. I'd killed him – and I felt myself shivering at the realization. Why had this happened? Why had he followed me? I knew the answer to that now, had always known it really: Nick, not Justin, was in control. For whatever reason, he must have seen my return to London as a threat to everything he'd achieved in his life, must have feared me as an agent of destabilization and danger. The only rational explanation for this was that his fear was, in some strange way, attached like a rope to my father's disappearance. So could it be that he murdered Anthony Winter – or had him murdered?

I climbed the stairs, took a wet flannel from the bathroom and began wiping the banisters, trying to wash my prints away like so much juvenile graffiti – all rather pointless, since my prints must have been everywhere. I noticed Dance's cell phone lying by his body, at the bottom of the stairs, and regretted the impulsive destruction of my own. So I slipped it into my pocket, knowing how useful it might become.

As I left the house it occurred to me that everyone I'd met in London, apparently so casually, might actually have been put in my way by the ubiquitous Nicholas Dundee.

*

From the darkness of the streets came the rush of heavy rain, like a wave breaking on a stormy beach. The sea was something I'd always associated with my father and with that last year in Poole. By that time, he was seldom coming home at all, and on the rare occasions that he did, he was invariably preoccupied; like a man with a guilty secret. Yet those days on which he declared himself free had a thrilling lustre, as if the rest of our lives were merely preparation for those few brief, intense moments. I recall vividly, during the school summer holidays, being unable to sleep on those Friday nights before he was expected home. I used to set my radio-alarm for six a.m. and, after being abruptly woken, I'd pull back the curtains, hoping to find a clear bright day – and the feelings of hopelessness if it was wet and of exhilaration if it was warm and dry! My father preferred the sun, you see.

Even now, walking back to the hotel in the relentless rain, I could see him on the beach, gesturing wildly in baggy black trunks, the great hairy bulk of his upper body waveringly supported by thin legs as he prepared to dive into a breaking wave; could hear, too, his exclamations as the cold took his breath away . . . see the damp patches of hair gathering like matted reeds across his chest as he climbed above the lapping water.

The sweetest days were the warmest days, when we played rounders and cricket on the beach under wide blue skies and skimmed stones across the surf. Pa had something wrong with his shoulder back then, which meant that, when I challenged him to throw out to sea, he bowled his stones like a cricket ball: that was the only game I could ever beat him at. He could swim, though, and he did, drifting out so far on the Lilo that he was sometimes unable to hear our increasingly despairing attempts to recall him to play. He'd stay out there for what seemed like hours; Mum was always complaining of his reluctance to prepare the picnic. I really couldn't share her disapproval, though, her suppressed rages. He could have spent all day out there on that Lilo, so long as he was with us, so long as he cared.

Once we'd packed up in the evening, Pa would sometimes carry me across the beach to the car – because I hated sand getting between my toes, hated wearing girly flip-flops. Once home and if the weather was fine, we'd gather in the garden for a barbecue, sometimes with our neighbours from up and down the hill. Pa liked to wear a floppy white cricket sun hat and a blue-and-white-striped butcher's apron as he cooked chicken wings, steaks, lamb cutlets and sausages over the open flame, singing half-remembered Cockney ditties, and talking about London, always about London: his city, his home. Meanwhile, Mum and Rachel prepared the salad bowl, while Dan and I set the table and messed around on the hammock, sometimes watched by horses from the fields at the bottom of the garden. We worked as a team. We seemed like a family. Those evenings in the garden, for all their relaxed calm, were nevertheless shadowed, I can see that now, by an impending sense of an ending – for all the time the number of his visits was shrinking inexorably, eventually reaching a vanishing point of none when he disappeared.

Since returning to England, I've repeatedly told myself that I wouldn't want those days back again, that he was a gaudy gangster, a crook, a quitter, a fraud, a walk-out, a failure. Yet what did I really have to complain of? There was no modish sexual abuse in my life, no midnight wanderings from priapic uncles, furtive walks or fetid gropings. Nor were there any brutalities or buggerings at school. No sequence of strange men in my mother's bed, no food shortages or health scares, no religious exaltations, hysterias or madnesses. Nothing unnatural in our lives, except that one strange central event: the disappearance of Anthony Winter, from which all else continued to flow, like an ancient curse. Even the pointless death of Gary Dance.

X

The body lies undisturbed beneath the stagnant water. As the weeks, months and years pass, its flesh festers and peels away; it rots. Creatures gather at first, to feast and defecate. His brains deteriorate, his lungs and heart. Bacteria and micro-organisms flourish. A small rat swims in through his mouth and squeezes out again through one of the decayed eye sockets. His shoes and his jeans decompose. His hair falls out.

The seasons come and go. Mosquitoes and dragonflies hover. Leaves and branches are blown or carried into the water. A tyre is thrown in and later an old bike. Some bottles. A couple have a picnic by the side of the pond and children play there. A punctured football is thrown in, a stringless tennis racquet and a book by Jim Crace. A school party takes samples of the water away with them to analyse back in class. A boy searches for frogs and toads among the reeds. A couple make love in the shadows of the trees. An old man, out walking his dog, pisses into the water; later, another man craps into it. Snow melts into it, and frost. There are storms and droughts, the beginnings of spring. One very hot summer. The nearby fields are ploughed. A tree is blown down in a storm and falls across it, creating a bridge. A dog swims in the water. A fox drinks from it. White water lilies grow there. A dead rabbit is thrown into the water and later some shredded documents. There is no snow one winter. A section of a newspaper is tossed in and later some sandwiches. A wasp floats on the surface. Spiders crawl.

In time, Oliver King becomes a skeleton.

Love Like Blood

I arrived back at the hotel, drenched by rain and sweat. Fever was wrapping itself around me like a spider's thread and I was, at once, shivering and perspiring, soaked through, scared, angry – and ridiculously locked into a situation of my own making. And all the time I was conscious of the hard reality of what had just happened: the photos, his body. I sat on the bed, in the overlit hotel room, staring for hours at the television, its white noise my constant companion through that long sleepless night, but also a cherished link to a more rational world beyond that insulated room.

Later, still unable to sleep, I opened the curtains on to darkness outside. The low winds, the incessant rain and the stink of the unnatural were behind me now, yet the city streets seemed somehow alien and menacingly quiet. The chief sounds, apart from the television, were the rattle and creak of the hotel's generator. Turning away from the window, I was stung by a glimpse, in the full-length mirror, of my own diminished athleticism. I wasn't prepared for that, for the irregular scars I saw running diagonally across my back, for a former rugby player's body shrivelling like an invalid's. I dragged my fingers across the rough outline of the scars and wondered if my death in the car accident would have been, after what had taken place tonight, a consummation devoutly to be wished. An escape clause presciently added to a contract. A way out.

I swigged from a bottle of lager. The bedsheets smelt stale. Mum and Al were probably still awake in Rosedale, I thought, shuffling around the house, boiling milk or whatever they did as part of their pre-sleep routine. How nice it would have been to be there with them. Yes, how nice.

Later still, I threw back the sheets, disturbed by a knock at the door. I drank warm water straight from the tap, wondering whether to open the door or not. In the end, I crossed the room, and peered through the spy-hole. There was no one there. I unlocked the door, stepping out barefoot into the corridor. Bafflingly, at the end of the corridor, I saw Mrs Green, leaning on her pram, a camera dangling from a strap around her neck, like a medal. Her silver hair was wrapped up in a black head-scarf and her eyebrows were plucked and painted. Her shirt was open so that I could see her bra, and that she was wearing powder and lipstick. Her face was frozen into a mask-like smirk.

'Mrs Green, hey, what's up?' I called out.

'It's cheaper to live in America, you know,' she said, chuckling to herself. I'd heard her say that before.

'I know, Mrs Green, I know. Petrol is certainly half the price.'

'Well, no one told me. No one told me it's cheaper living in America.'

She turned her back on me. Shockingly, she wasn't wearing any knickers and her skirt was ripped so that I could see her bare arse and the black hairs on her legs, squirming like insects beneath her tights.

'So, Mrs Green,' I said, 'are you going to live in America?'

Her head rotated in a full circle like an owl's. 'What, me? I can't fucking afford it.'

Then she pulled out a top hat and a cane from her pram and began a wild, fast-paced jig, leaping energetically from one foot to the other, displaying the agility of a much younger woman. She was singing: 'New York, New York, It's a wonderful town . . .' But her voice wasn't . . . Well, it was a male crooner's voice. Then she began taking photographs of me. Mrs Green opened her mouth and I could feel myself being sucked towards her, and I was powerless. Her mouth was widening all the time like a tunnel and I was sucked into the long dark corridor of her throat, into the kernel of a whirlpool.

*

216

I found myself back inside the hotel room, thinking about Katya, about how much I missed her. I recalled the perfumed scent of her and the excited beat of her heart. I began flicking through the channels, and on MTV I saw an Irishman with bad teeth singing about 'a thing called love', and there was a track by New Order, 'Temptation'. Then, I couldn't rid from my mind an image of Katya being attacked on the Moscow metro, of her being struck so violently by a white-bearded gnome that she'd fallen down, her head splitting on impact with the floor. In my vision, she was lying in a curdled pool of blood and mucus when I found her; yet she still crawled weakly towards me, blood dribbling from her crushed skull. I looked on as she curled up like a small animal on the floor, pleading not to be beaten again. So I cradled her head in my own bloody hands; but it wasn't her head I held, it was Gary Dance's. He told me he couldn't believe how brutal and yet how tender I could be, how much he'd once trusted me.

The sweat had leaked from every part of me and I was trapped in a kind of delirium of rage and regret. I felt dehydrated, nauseous. Searching for something to eat, I discovered the remains of an American hot pizza (now not so hot) I'd bought on my way back from King's Cross. I couldn't eat it then and I couldn't eat it now; opening the box, I smelt the tang of chorizo sausage and felt immediately repulsed. I cackled Mrs Green-like to myself as I threw the pizza across the room and it broke up against the window, a trail of tomato purée running like blood down the glass. Love like blood.

I sat on the bed, lights on, staring at the television, until the darkness began to lift outside.

Time passed. I felt hungry. What sounded like a milk float moved on the road outside, its bottles jangling like distant wind chimes. I closed my eyes.

I don't know how I made it through until morning without ringing for help or medication. As it turned out, my fever began to subside at around nine the next morning. I ordered fresh orange juice, cereal, tea and toast on room service, and spent the morning skipping channels from one confessional talk show to another, from one ironic cookery programme to another, from one item of celebrity gossip to another. And I wondered about who might be looking for me out there on the streets, who might have turned up at my empty flat: Justin, with his newly flattened nose; Katya, perhaps back from Moscow; Binoo John, with his expectations of receiving a long-delayed cheque; Nicholas Dundee, with his deceptions and his games. The only person who wasn't looking for me now was Gary Dance.

I was awoken in the middle of the afternoon by the telephone. I reached for the receiver by the bed but heard only the dialling tone. The ringing continued and it seemed to be coming from the bathroom, from the mobile I'd entirely forgotten about. I found the phone in the pocket of my discarded trousers, still damp from last night.

'Is that you, Gaz?' a male voice said.

'Who's that?'

'Gary?'

'Yes, it's Gary,' I said.

The line went dead. I pressed 'recall' but no number had been retained.

The cell phone had been on all night and the battery was low. I accessed the message service: two calls were stored, both from late afternoon yesterday. The first was from a woman – the name 'Jenny' flashed up on the memory screen – apologizing for a misunderstanding that had happened earlier that week. The second message – 'Nick' appeared on the screen – was from Dundee. His voice was rougher, less deliberate than usual but still unmistakable: 'Gary, it's me. Call me. It's urgent.'

The taste of his betrayal was sour and it repeated on me throughout the afternoon, like an acid reflux. Later, having showered and shaved, I went down to the basement bar. A small group of American men were gathered round a table, dressed hideously in casual roll-neck sweaters, cotton trousers, canvas shoes – just like a gaggle of professional golfers. I sat alone at the bar, drank lager and smoked, and all the time I was writing imaginary letters – of goodbye to Katya Lokteva and Jessica White; of thanks to Killer Kellor and Binoo John; of apology to my mother and Justin Bliss; and one of threat to Nicholas Dundee. As I sat at the bar, replying to the inconsequential mutterings of the Arab barman, I wrote letters to all those who would soon be missing from my life.

The more I thought about my situation the less I understood it, the less I believed in what seemed to be the truth; and yet the more I learned about my father the more I seemed to learn about myself. The solution seemed simple now: either to contact the police or simply to flee.

Gary Dance had been dead now for almost a day. My contacting the police would amount to no more than a confession, if not of murder, then at least of manslaughter; and I wasn't ready yet to turn myself in. I knew, crucially, the intent to murder had been absent. And yet hadn't I also delighted as he'd tumbled – like a scarecrow – down the stairs, all loose-limbed and ragged, and hadn't I felt a surge of keen adrenalin when I'd searched for that non-existent pulse?

'So what, Mr Winter, were you doing in his house then?' the police would ask.

'He'd been following me, Officer.'

'Following you. Right. What makes you think that?'

'I've seen photographs.'

'Photographs. What photographs?'

'Of me, Officer. The photographs of me. He'd taken them as he'd followed me around.'

'Right, OK. May we see these photographs?'

'I don't have them.'

'You don't have them?'

'No.'

'So who does?'

219

'Gary Dance does. They're in his house.'

That was it. I'd lead the police back to the house. If by some chance he hadn't been found or reported missing, then the police would be the first to discover his body; not just the body, but the photographs of me. These would bind the two of us. The letter I was about to write would serve as a further link, this time to Nick Dundee. All that was left for me to do was challenge Dundee directly, accuse him of the murder of Anthony Winter and then watch him squirm and suffer.

I sat down at the dressing table and began to write.

Dear Sir,

I wish to report a missing person. His name is Gary Dance. He lived at 12 Port Poole Lane, King's Cross, London. He works, in some capacity, possibly as a private detective, for Mr Nicholas Dundee of Forest Lodge, High Beach, nr Loughton, Essex. There is strong evidence to link his disappearance with the work he does for Mr Dundee, perhaps as a private detective. Dundee is a leisure and entertainment entrepreneur.

I read what I'd written, disturbed at how easily I'd slipped into the past tense. I'd spoken of Gary Dance as if he were no longer with us – true enough, but not my purpose then. I contemplated embellishing the letter, plumping it out with thick detail. So I crossed out the first line and the last, then began all over again, writing and rewriting something I doubted I would ever send. When I finally settled on a draft – the original copied out verbatim all over again – ragged balls of scrunched-up paper were scattered around the room like so many discarded pages of a novel.

It was after eight and dark again when I refolded the letter and slipped it into a courtesy envelope. The young woman on reception, from whom I bought a first-class stamp, spoke with a soft Scottish accent, had crooked teeth and a small strawberry-coloured birthmark below her left eye from which sprang a solitary white hair. I felt myself shivering again.

'Are you OK?'

'I think I've got the flu coming on.'

'There's a lot of it about,' she said.

I addressed the envelope, crudely, to Holborn Police Station.

'You'll need an umbrella out there,' she called after me.

She was right. It was raining again and the pavement was slippery underfoot. I posted the letter in the first red box I came upon, at the intersection of Dyott Street and New Oxford Street. The next collection was not until seven-thirty the following morning – another long night away. The letter dropped and I imagined it continuing to drop, like a stone tossed into a well, falling through the indeterminate darkness until a faint ghostly splash announces its arrival. Then the glare from the headlights of a passing car lit up the surrounding streets, spraying me with a wet wave of light, and I heard the warm, friendly voices of people passing by.

Once back at the hotel the ceiling of my room seemed even lower than before, just as it had in the YMCA all that time ago, the walls closer together and more oppressive. I'd had very little, if any, sleep the previous night but once again I felt too insomniacally alert to rest. And soon I'd begun to regret posting that letter. The police, I knew, wound be duty-bound to act on it immediately, to visit the house, where they'd discover the photographs, evidence of a break-in, our struggle, his body – the end of a life. There would be the traces of my fingerprints and enough sweat particles from the letter to allow a DNA profile to be produced. Once the body was found they'd inevitably commission a graphologist to prepare some kind of personality profile of the author of the letter – namely, me. From there they would move quickly, to track me down, arrest and charge me with murder. I knew what would follow.

'If it was an accident, Mr Winter, why didn't you report it earlier?'

'I panicked.'

'Yes, but if you were innocent.'

'The man was dead. I'd broken into his house. It looked bad.'

'It still does, sir, I'm afraid. Very bad. Now, how did he happen to fall down the stairs? Can you take us through that again?'

'I told you, he attacked me. I pushed him. He tripped and fell.'

'Why did he attack you, Mr Winter?'

'Because I was in his house.'

'What would you do if you found an intruder in your house?'

'Panic.'

'You seem to do a lot of that – panicking – don't you, sir?'

'No.'

'But you said you panicked when Mr Dance discovered you in his house.'

'Yes.'

'Why were you in his house? Can we have that one again, please.'

'How many more times? I told you, he followed me. He's been following me. You shouldn't be talking to me. It's Nick Dundee you want.'

'Was this Mr Dundee with you in the house at the time of the death?'

'No.'

'So why should we want him then?'

'He put him up to it.'

'Put who up to it? You mean Mr Dance?'

'Yes, Gary Dance.'

'What did he put him up to?'

'To following me.'

'That again.'

'Yes, that again.'

And so it went on, my thoughts against thoughts in groans grinding.

No, what was required was hard evidence to ensnare Dundee: proof and a motive as to why he would have wanted me watched and followed – something more tangible linking him to the disappearance of my father than Justin's unreliable narration, Dundee's postcard to Dance and my own febrile speculations. First, though, I had to retrieve the letter.

The rest of the night lolled and dragged, and I drank more beer, ordered from the night porter, as I sat in darkness on the bed, wallowing in the pale-grey shades of regret.

Just before seven the next morning I roused myself to return to the post box. The city was more than stirring and already the traffic was beginning to congest. I restlessly circled the post box, like a golfer surveying the contours of a difficult green, feeling mocked by its sealed perfection. I pushed my hand into the slit, but could not feel the papery brush of letters at my fingertips. My letter had begun to assume the threat of an unexploded bomb – I had to defuse it. I lit a match, cupping my hands so as to bolster the slender flame against the rain which was now little more than a refined spray. The flame was extinguished, and I retreated, away from the weather, to the doorway of a French restaurant.

The postman arrived in his van, ahead of schedule. I watched him park, gather his sack together and make his way over, jangling his keys like loose change.

'You're early,' I called out.

He stopped. He was wearing the standard uniform of pale-blue open-neck cotton shirt with red piping, navy jacket and trousers. His polished Royal Mail badge shone like a medal. His boots were a tasty pair of scuffed steels.

'I've just posted a letter,' I said, 'forgot to put a stamp on it. D'you mind if I have it back?'

He looked at me blankly, then said, 'Sorry, mate, can't do that, not once something's been posted.'

'But it's important to me.'

'I'm sorry, I can't tamper with the post. If it's a missing stamp there'll just be a charge at the other end.'

Crouching, he punched air into the sack and then opened the box: letters tumbled out in a rumbustious, chaotic flow. So much paper, so many words.

I spoke to him again as he scooped the last few letters into the sack. 'Come on,' I said. 'Do me a favour?'

'There's nothing I can do,' he said.

He locked the post box, and was about to seal the sack by pulling together two stiff threads of rope when, in my frustration, I tried to wrench the sack away from him. It opened and letters spilled on to the damp pavement. I crouched to gather up the nearest pile but released them when a blow caught me on the side of my head, and I momentarily lost my balance. As I put my hands down to break my fall, the webbing between my forefinger and thumb of my right hand split neatly again, like an overcooked frankfurter.

The postman was standing over me, perspiring heavily, and beyond him there were ardent onlookers and beyond them a flickering glimpse of blue sky – the promise of a brighter, better day.

'He tried to mug me,' the postman was telling anyone who'd listen.

'I saw what happened,' said a man with a mobile. 'I've called the police.'

I looked up at the curious faces.

'Are you all right?' a girl asked.

'I think so,' I said, although the pain in my hand was intense.

She was in her late teens and wore spectacles. The buttons of her loose woollen coat were undone. I noticed all this about her before my vision blurred, as if a rock had been dropped into a pool into which I'd been staring, and as the surface resettled itself I was looking up at . . . *Amy*, at my poor lost friend Amy.

'You remind me of someone,' I told the girl.

'Your hand, it's really bleeding badly,' she said, ignoring me.

I sat up and saw, in the background, a cop car pulling into a slot behind the postal van. I watched the postman, accompanied by the man with the phone, approach the car, where I imagined him indignantly explaining how I'd waited for him; how, after calling out to him, I'd grabbed his sack, crazily ranting about a letter. The guy with the mobile would, I knew, support his story with the alacrity of a schoolboy sneak. The girl, meanwhile, was providing tissues to staunch the renewed flow of blood.

There was no point even attempting to flee; the disturbed nights had left me debilitated, without energy. So I leaned against the post box as the girl brushed my face with gloved hands and muttered inconsequentially about the wet morning, asking why I'd not dressed appropriately for it. A few yards away, a shabby pigeon scavenged for food.

A policeman approached. 'Can you get up?' he asked me.

His partner was speaking to the postman. The girl held my arm as I rose, blood showing through the clump of tissues, spreading darkly like ink. The policeman asked me what had happened and I explained about the letter.

'Seems a lot of fuss over a stamp, sir. Did you want to send it first or second class?'

'Don't be facetious, Officer,' I said.

His expression curdled into hostility and he explained how postmen were frequently being attacked by 'desperate people after drugs money'.

'Is that so?' I said.

'How deep is it?' he asked. 'D'you need to go to hospital?'

'I don't think so,' I said. 'It's an old cut reopened.'

He asked my name and whether I had anything to say. I assured him that my intention hadn't been to steal anything, or to attack the postman (I'd never struck *him*); that I had merely wanted to retrieve a letter. It was he who'd struck a blow on the side of my head.

'The bruise on your face, that's old, isn't it?' he said.

I nodded.

'Are you often in trouble then?'

'No,' I said, 'I play rugby.'

The post box was locked and the postie was sitting in his van with the contested sack of letters, like a sullen friend, by his side on the passenger seat. He was talking to the second copper, an Asian woman and the guy with the cell phone.

'Are you going to arrest him?' the girl asked.

'Are you with him then, love?'

'I saw what happened. No one's really to blame.'

The copper repeated his question. 'Are you with him?'

'I've never met him before in my life. It's just . . . I'm sure he wanted to get his letter back, like he says. He seemed to care about it.'

The second copper approached. Lean and angular, he was shorter than his colleague but more officious, and apparently in charge. 'Is everything all right here?' he said.

'There's been some kind of commotion, Sarge.'

'I have an idea what happened,' the sergeant said. 'This young man's going to have to come back to the station with us.'

'Fine,' I said, 'but it's all a lot of fuss over nothing.'

'You'll still need to come to the station,' he said. 'We'll get that hand seen to.'

Some of the onlookers were being recalled, asked to leave names and contact numbers. Watching all this, I felt dull, felt myself slipping quietly beyond despair. Dance was dead, the letter was gone and now, it seemed, I was about to be arrested. The shorter, more officious copper – Sarge – led me to his car, the young woman loyally following a few strides behind. I was told to sit in the back seat.

'I'd rather you didn't come, miss,' he said to the woman. 'We'll contact you if we need anything else.'

The first copper ran his tongue hungrily along his lower lip. I was sure he winked at the girl.

'What about him?' I said, pointing at the postal van. 'I'm the one who's been hurt.'

'Don't worry. He's coming, too.'

I watched the girl through the window as we pulled away. Sarge watched her too, looking up from the notebook into which he'd been writing. From a distance, I was struck again by her resemblance to Amy – it was as if Amy were standing there, her optimistic smile the only source of encouragement on that stalled day. As we lost sight of the girl, an image of Amy became fixed in my mind – of how she'd appeared to me when I found her trapped in the wreckage of my car, eyes open, her face calm, unmarked, but above all serenely dead. That was the strangeness of it: the serenity of her face on that death-haunted afternoon on the way out to Concord. I really can't forget it.

On arrival at the station my hand was inspected by a police surgeon, who said that I was fit enough to be detained – and questioned. Then I was given a cup of coffee and some biscuits, taken to what was described as the 'custody area' – in this instance, a small, windowless room which was hotel-warm and freshened with artificial spray. I could hear the drowsy drone of a vacuum cleaner along the corridor, the thin rattle of teacups, telephones, male chatter, the machine-gun stutter of a keyboard. My lungs felt tight, as if smoked out.

The first policeman asked my name, address and occupation. There were creases of frustration around his eyes and his nose was covered in a film of grease that shone where the light fell on it.

'How long have you lived in Nassau Street?' he asked me.

'Not long. I'm over from Toronto.'

'On holiday?'

'No, I live here now.'

'So how long have you been at your present address?'

'Not even three months.'

'And before that?'

'I was living in Toronto.'

He asked for my address in Toronto and I reluctantly gave him Al's in Rosedale. He asked an assistant to 'check that'. And now my mother would know.

'Mr Winter,' he said, 'you have the right to have someone informed of your arrest, to consult a copy of the codes of practice covering police powers and procedures and speak to an independent solicitor in private and free of charge.'

Well, useful to get that learned, I whispered to myself.

'Sorry?' he said.

I was taken to another room with a phone, offered the code of practice to read. Then, having requested to speak to a solicitor, I was put through to someone called Margot McLaughlin. I explained exactly what had happened, evaded her question about why I'd wanted to retrieve the letter in the first place and asked how quickly I could be out of there. She reasoned that, as I had no previous record or convictions and that I hadn't assaulted the postman, cooperation would offer the best route out, certainly if I wanted to be gone before the end of the day. Yes, I wanted to be gone before the end of the day. There'd been no violence on my part; intent, but no violence. At worst, I would be charged with attempted robbery.

'If you deny the offence,' she said, 'you'll be charged and bailed initially to attend at the local magistrates' court five weeks from the date of arrest. If you admit the offence you're likely to appear four weeks hence. The period of time merely reflects the sort of file that would have to be prepared.'

'So what do you advise, shall I plead guilty or not?'

'Either way, if you're found guilty, because you have no previous convictions, you're unlikely to receive a custodial sentence. You're more likely to be fined, be warned about your future conduct and perhaps you might be put on probation or receive a community service order. In the very worst case, you might be deported. But it's always best to plead not guilty, especially as, if you're telling the truth, you weren't trying to steal anything, although a letter, once posted, is the property of the Royal Mail, not the writer.'

She said that she or one of her colleagues would happily visit the station.

On his return, I explained to the sergeant that I had no wish to speak to anyone else, that I planned to plead not guilty to any charges that were being prepared against me and that I was willing to be interviewed.

Later, during that interview, I was told that the postman was the 'aggrieved party', that he was 'well within his rights to use reasonable force to repel the attack' and that I was being charged with attempted robbery. I pleaded not guilty, and was told, as Margot McLaughlin had predicted, to expect to appear five weeks hence at Bow Street Magistrates' Court. By which time . . .

When I left the station it was already dark, another day lost. At least I was clear in my immediate purpose and set absolutely on revenge.

XI

He used to be called Anthony Winter. Today, stepping off the ferry into the late-autumn sunshine of Santander, after a day-long journey away from the wet darkness of England, he has no idea who he is. He's a man alone, about to walk away from the present and into someone else's past. He hears Spanish being spoken around him. He doesn't understand what is being said but feels the delight of arriving, at last, in a place that he can no longer call home.

The ordeal is over.

Useless Sacrifice

Before returning to the flat, I wandered through the grey-blue expanses of Whitehall and down to the Thames. It was dry and surprisingly cold. The starless sky was irradiated, every now and then, by a soaring rocket, which blazed fiercely before expiring in a powdery spray of dying light. Of course, it was 5 November, Guy Fawkes' Night.

I sat on a bench across the road from Embankment Station, near the footbridge which carried you over the Thames to the south side, to the concrete and grey side. Trains departed at regular intervals from Charing Cross Station, rattling over-head, the faces of some of the passengers pressed up against the windows like excited children as they looked east towards the high-rises and the lights of the financial district. A true urban sublime.

There was a lot of movement on the river. Early-evening commuter hoppers, river buses and commercial vessels all negotiated their ways up- and downriver. I thought of Katya as I waited there – of our evening together in the American Bar at the Savoy, of our weekend in Dorset, the letters she'd since sent, my squalid rejection of her; of how everything in my life had been subordinated these past months to a futile quest for my father. I closed my eyes and conjured up Katya as she'd appeared to me, at first, during the heat and dust of September: her gaze, her little nose stud, the rings on her fingers and thumb, the way the flesh of her thighs had dimpled ever so slightly as she'd walked across the room, uninhibited by her own nudity.

The battery on Gary Dance's mobile was flat, so I crossed the road to a phone box. There was no reply from Katya's flat, not even an answering-machine message to remind me of her voice. From behind the reinforced glass, I watched more fire-works exploding in the sky beyond the concrete, wind-dulled sugar cubes of the South Bank complex.

There was nothing for it, I knew, but to return to Nassau Street, despite my fear of Justin, and of the police having acted on my letter. I wanted to change my clothes before heading out to High Beach. And then what? Feeling hungry, I walked among the swarming masses from whom I felt largely cut off. The broiling days of late summer seemed so very far away now, and everyone was wrapped up in hats, coats and winter scarves. The cafés, pubs and restaurants were brightly lit and heated, and there was the usual fast music, loose talk and laughter. Everywhere you went in the city there were so many people, all striving, all competing, all here and now. The urgent shout of their being. How do they all pass the time, I wondered, what do they do?

I climbed the stairs to my flat, my footfall loud on the bare stone steps. At the bend in the stairs, the lights predictably cut out, just as they'd done all those years ago in Belsize Avenue. I found the switch and continued up to the second floor, hearing the sound of the television in Mrs Green's flat before I even reached the landing. I listened against Katya's door, knocked three times on it. I was about to let myself into my own flat when Mrs Green opened her door.

'She's back, you know,' she said, standing in the shade of her hallway. 'Been away in Russia, she has. Been gone and grown her hair, too.'

'Does it look nice?' I said.

The lights cut out.

'Bleeding thing,' she said, 'it never works when you want it.'

In the abrupt gloom I could no longer see her but could still hear the famished duck's squeal of her laughter.

'They've been back again for you today,' she said, an echo of gathering threat in her voice. 'They brought a big carpet round.'

I ran my hands along the wall, feeling for the light switch. When I turned it back on, Mrs Green was still there.

'What carpet are you talking about? I haven't ordered a carpet.'

She laughed again.

'Why don't you answer me, you stupid witch? What's the matter with you?' I was shouting at her now. Her son appeared behind her in the corridor. 'Come on, Mum. Your tea's getting cold.'

It was the first time I'd ever heard him speak. He closed the door just as the lights cut out once more, but they'd been on long enough for me to have seen the anger on his shy, surprisingly handsome face.

'Both of you, you're fucking freaks,' I shouted, kicking their door. 'You should both be fucking locked up.'

I let myself into my flat, which seemed bleak and cold. At my feet were a couple of flyers, a free weekly newspaper and several letters – from Mum and Katya (I didn't recognize the handwriting on the envelope of the third one). I closed the door, hitting the light switch, but nothing happened. There was darkness still. Perhaps the bulb had blown. In the sad twilight of the flat I began to feel afraid, as if someone was waiting there in the dark spaces of my own home. There was an unfamiliar odour, too, something pungent I couldn't place. Across the room, the red eye of the answering-machine blinked.

I dropped the letters on the bed and opened the curtains. Light spilled into the room, and I saw immediately that everything was as I'd left it: no ransacked drawers, obscenities on the walls or shit-smeared carpets. Nor were there any traces of a thorough police search. Instead, there was only order, calm and familiarity (that smell, though, more than simply staleness). The kitchen and bathroom doors were closed; and then the shuffle of footsteps from the streets below enticed me to the window. I recognized Katya's voice before I saw her, and heard her laughter. A firework exploded in the distance – cloudburst and stardust.

I ran on to the landing, hoping to surprise her on the way up. I heard her voice first, and then there she was, jumping from the last stair on to the landing . . . But she was holding hands with another man. He was very tall, dark, unshaven and had thick wavy hair. He looked Eurasian. She paused, swaying as if tipsy, as if she were struggling to adjust to the light. Or perhaps to the surprise at seeing me there when she was with him.

'Josh,' she said, 'I can't believe it's you!'

I felt an immediate attraction for her, a weakness to succumb. Mrs Green was right: her hair had grown a little, but beautifully.

'What have you been *doing*?' she said, her gaze settling on the lingering bruises on my face and on my bandaged hand.

'Oh, that,' I said. 'I had an accident.'

'What kind of accident?'

'I was playing rugby.'

'I thought you'd given that up.'

'I started again. There's so much more opportunity to play here in England than in Canada.'

'You should take more care of yourself,' she said. 'This is Daourd, by the way. He works with me at Bush House, for the Afghan service.'

'Hello,' he said. 'You must be Joshua Winter. I've heard all about you.'

'Where've you been?' I asked, sniffing the air – the smell had followed me out from the flat, I was sure of it.

'At a leaving party,' Katya said. 'It was only meant to last an hour but went on all afternoon.' They both giggled.

Katya seemed tiny, vulnerable even, beside Daourd, whom she'd never mentioned to me before. She was wearing a short skirt, black thick-soled shoes, tights and a bulkily out-sized leather jacket. Daourd was dressed in a dark suede jacket, sweater and white jeans, gloves and a scarf. I wondered if she'd brought him back with her from Russia. He was handsome. I felt the branding iron of jealousy on my skin.

'How have you been, Katya?' I said, 'I've missed you.'

'I've missed you too, Josh ... But it's not possible to talk about it now.'

'If not now, when?' I said. 'I'm going away tomorrow, to Manchester.'

'Why didn't you reply to my letters?' she said.

'I don't know. It's a complicated story.'

'I was hurt, Josh.' She looked at Daourd. 'Can you let yourself in?' She gave him the keys to her flat. 'I felt foolish,' she said, 'because I'd laid myself open to you.'

'You shouldn't feel like that. Your letters were ... They meant a lot to me.'

She shrugged her shoulders, as if to say that was then. I wanted to invite her in but the smell from the flat was on my hands, in my hair.

'Why do you keep sniffing?' she said, smiling now.

'I've been cleaning out the flat. Used too much fluid.'

'Cleaning, at this time – on Bonfire Night! You're so funny sometimes, Josh, a really maverick person.' Katya laughed again, and attempted to look beyond me and into the flat. 'Who's in there with you anyway?' she said. 'What have you really been doing?'

Daourd let himself into her flat and we were alone together on the landing. Then the lights cut out again and in the darkness I went over to her, pulling her towards me; but I felt the stiff resistance in her shoulders, the reluctance that was newly there, the trust so quickly broken. I kissed the top of her head, smelling the cigarette smoke in her hair, and then, as I tried to kiss her on the mouth, she turned away so that only one cheek was presented.

'I love you, Katya,' I said, 'I really love you. Forgive me for what's happened. I don't know what came over me.'

'Oh, Josh, you're being soppy now. What's the matter with you? You're all pent up about something.'

Words were constricted in my throat. So I saturated her in silence, resting my head on her shoulder.

'Josh,' she said, 'you're being such an idiot.'

I looked at her in the darkness, traced the thick swell of her lips with my fingers, felt her eyes and hands. 'Let's meet. Please, let's meet when I'm back from Manchester. If only you'll give me a chance to explain, it might redeem everything.'

'Josh, what are you talking about? What on earth's happened to you? Come on. Pull yourself together. You seem to have lost all your confidence.'

'Katya, please, don't sleep with him, at least not tonight while I'm here.'

'What are you talking about?'

'Daourd.'

'Daourd! There's nothing between Daourd and me. He's a friend from work, that's all.'

'But I thought.'

She leaned over and rested her hand on my cheek. A door opened simultaneously as the lights came on. Mrs Green was out again.

'They brought his carpet round today,' she said to Katya.

'A carpet? Have you been buying carpets? Is that what you're hiding from me in there?'

'Katya, I don't know what the old witch is going on about.'

'Don't be nasty, Josh. Don't say things like that about her.'

'I'm sick of his face,' Mrs Green said, 'sick of the sight of him hanging around all day, not working.' She turned to me. 'Why don't you get yourself a job? Do something useful instead hanging around here.' She waved her fist, her fingers as twisted as potato roots.

'I'll call you, I really will,' Katya said, her words fresh like new paint. 'There's nothing between me and Daourd, really. But Josh, you've got to understand also. You don't own me, even if you say you love me. I'm not yours to be picked up and discarded like a toy.'

236

I reached out for a hand that felt soft and warm, and as I did so I was overtaken by a memory of another time and place. But it was *rain*, not snow.

Then she was gone.

I went into my flat, watched disapprovingly by Mrs Green.

Back inside, forgetting the bulb had blown, I hit the light switch, but again there was only more darkness. I crossed the room to check the bulb, but there was no bulb, just the complicated hardness of an empty socket. I went through to the kitchen and turned on the light; at least that one worked. The kitchen was also unchanged from how I'd left it. Slowly, my discomfort began to lift and I thought about what I'd said to Katya and felt mildly embarrassed. I filled the kettle with water and flicked the switch; found some instant coffee, spooned the granules into a mug and poured boiling water over them – they fizzed and bubbled. My plan was to bathe quickly, change, and then read the letters on the tube as I travelled east to Essex.

Holding my coffee in one hand, I opened the bathroom door with the other, and was about to put on the light when I saw a human figure slumped in the bath. I dropped the mug, aware of an immediate burning sensation as the coffee splashed over my legs. There were no windows in the bathroom, no access to natural light, yet I could see him lying there. The stench of his body had infiltrated the flat, seemed even to be oozing from the pores of my own skin, like the after-effects of bad food.

I opened every available window and then returned to the bathroom, this time switching on the light; but again there was darkness still. I reached up to the socket to discover that this bulb also had been removed. Still, there was no denying that Gary Dance was lying in the bath, his eyes wide open and stretched oddly, like a Japanese baby's. He wore an expression of baffled wonder, his lips as if frozen in mid-conversation. You could have taken him as being drunkenly asleep were it not that I already knew the truth, knew his life was over. His clothes were unchanged from our encounter, although his trousers and boxer shorts had been pulled down so that they were bunched below his knees. His exposed cock was shrivelled like a strip of uncooked pastry. His right arm hung limply over the side of the bath, the face of his Rolex – perhaps signifying all to which he once aspired – cracked. I held his cold hands, his fingers as brittle as icicles – and as easily snapped. I studied his face: the severe crop that failed to disguise his receding hairline, the swelling of scar tissue around the brows and eye sockets, the open mouth, the hint of puffiness where rigor mortis had begun. It was as if he was smiling even in death. And death was everywhere in that room; I could smell it, taste it.

Turning away, I saw myself in the mirror and was startled once again by the deterioration in my appearance. I left the bathroom and leaned out of a window, as if about to summon a stranger. The night seemed so perfectly harmonious, cold and still. There was the smell of distant bonfires and of what must have been burnt gunpowder. I felt unable to make sense of any of it. Leaving the windows open but closing the door of the bathroom, I changed my clothes, gathered up the letters and fled the flat, this time, I hoped, for ever.

Light was streaming from beneath both Mrs Green's and Katya's doors. The main light clicked on as I hurried down-stairs, self-savouringly imagining myself as an escaping pris-oner about to be caught in the glare of a panoptic searchlight. At the corner of Nassau Street, I looked back to see what I assumed was the tall figure of Daourd leaving the building. So perhaps there *was* nothing between them after all. Tomorrow, I would call her.

On the tube, I opened the letters. Mum, in hers, was 'angry and disappointed' that I'd been out of touch; surprised, too, to discover, on contacting Clifford Chance, that I'd never begun work there. She had considered contacting the British police and would do so unless I responded soonest to her letter. I felt the temptation to disappear altogether, to escape the world and all its dull, imprisoning effects.

The second letter was from Binoo John.

Dear Mr Winter

You worried me running into my office like that. What happened got me thinking you might have landed yourself in very hot water indeed. I can only guess at the extent of your troubles. But let me tell you a little story. Even though you have lived for too long in North America – how vulgar I find North America – you were born and brought up in England and so should have a proper appreciation of cricket and know all about its rules of fair play.

'Now is the time, Perkins, for an absolutely useless sacrifice!' What a very good line – used, I read recently, by Mike Brearley, the captain of the England cricket team in the 1970s, to Phil Carrick, when the hapless spin bowler from Yorkshire was facing the West Indies artillery in, let us say, 1976. Situation thus: silly invitation match, West Indies bat throughout the whole day and mysteriously declare half an hour before the close. Why? To bowl at the speed of light of course at the English batsmen. Dennis Amiss (good, solid opener) is clobbered and shipped off to hospital in the first over; Carrick (a bowler by trade and no batsman) is sent in as nightwatchman. He looks sheepish and nervous (almost as nervous as you did when you ran into my office the other day to be followed by that man with the bloody nose); Mike Brearley, who is batting at the other end (remember, there are two batsmen), approaches Carrick before he has faced the first ball and lets fly with that line about Perkins. Carrick does not understand a word, but makes the useless sacrifice all the same. He was bowled out third ball. The first, a horribly fast bouncer, whistled past his head – before they wore protective helmets! The second ball, an even quicker bouncer, hit him on the chest. The third, a swinging yorker, shattered his stumps.

What all this means is anyone's guess, but please, my friend, don't become an absolutely useless sacrifice.

Now I am settled and forthright. To work, the fount of all happiness.

With my sincerest good wishes to you, I leave you waiting for your rent and other good news,
Binoo K. John, MA

I didn't understand how Gary Dance had come to be lying in my bath. I began to wonder if, psychologically dislocated, I'd invented the whole thing. No, because Mrs Green had seen them arrive at my flat with a carpet. One could only speculate about the macabre journey which had taken him across town, perhaps wrapped in a carpet. So his being in my flat was, then, a final sadistic joke played on me by Nick Dundee, for whatever banal reason. I knew nothing about Gary Dance, nothing about the life I'd taken from him, the people he knew, the places he went to. Nor about the events that led to both of us being so weirdly entwined. But I couldn't pity him, not even in a small way, as one, say, pities a moth as it flies helplessly towards a flame, its behaviour rendered grimly predictable by a crude biological determinism. It was beyond him now, beyond all of us. Dance was, like my murdered father – and I never doubted for a minute now that Dundee had murdered my father – transcendentally out of reach. Only his memory could be bruised, traduced.

The final letter, carrying today's date, was from Katya. She must have dropped it through the letter box that morning. It read like a valediction, her big farewell.

Dear Mr Winter!
I know your heart's in hiding from me. But I'm sick of all this myself. Sometimes I feel attached to you like a tie around the neck, and I don't feel myself free. And sometimes I don't feel like that at all. What I know is that you don't like it, that it's not a rule of yours to make anyone depend on you. You see, I'm really weak sometimes, even though I used to do all the

manual jobs at home when my father left, even mending the coffee grinder when I had to.

'I'm very emotional, but I'm an Englishman,' you once told me. Do you remember? It was a very funny thing to say. But are all Englishmen as emotional? I know this Russian girl, she works with me at Bush House, who once had an English boyfriend – and he used to sleep with his socks on. Can you imagine it! She's not with him any more, of course, and she now sleeps with a toy dog by her side instead. She said to me once, 'Even a toy dog is more emotional than an Englishman.'

Can this be true?

But you stopped writing to me, even little notes, stopped wanting to speak to me. So I suppose this is goodbye, Mr Winter.

Goodbye from you. And goodbye from me.

I'm not a tank any more.

Katya

P.S. I spoke to the law firm Clifford Chance about you, when I was trying to find you earlier this week. It seems you never turned up for work after all. Perhaps you found happiness instead.

From the station I took a taxi to High Beach. I asked to be dropped off about half a mile from the house. I kept to the edges of the forest as I walked down the hill. There were a lot of cars heading that way and as I drew closer I saw a bonfire burning in the grounds of the golf club, and that there were cars pulling on to Nick's drive.

It was by far the coldest night of my stay in England and the people arriving at the golf club had prepared suitably for the sharp change in the weather. The more exotically attired arrivals were all going to Nick Dundee's, who seemed to be having some kind of fancy-dress party. Many of them were tricked up as ghouls, goblins, wizards, black and white witches – all entering into the spirit of the occasion. Others were more conventionally turned out, fancily speaking: I saw a nurse, a cowgirl and cowboy, an Elton John lookalike – *circa* mid-1970s, all flares and preposterous platforms and bright orange specs – a policeman, a couple of clowns and a chimney sweep. An outfit I couldn't fathom was that of an effete-looking man – long blond fringe draped negligently over one eye – who was wearing a white suit, two-tone shoes and spats; he was also clutching a teddy bear and smoking a cigarette in a holder.

There were security guards on the gates, through which the usual smart cars passed; but soon the driveway was congested and people were being asked to park in the surrounding leafy lanes. Beyond the boundaries of the house the forest seemed to press darkly, impenetrable in its thickness and shadows. Quiet and cold, too. And a frost seemed to be settling everywhere. My breath felt warm against my hands.

A chauffeur-driven Mercedes pulled up beside me, although the driver couldn't see me withdrawn there in the trees. Through the tinted glass of the car I saw the huge figure of the local MP, Henry – I'd forgotten his name – and a woman, his wife, I assumed. Neither of them seemed to be wearing fancy dress. Henry had on a long camel coat, a black polo-neck and dark trousers; the woman was dressed in a thick fur coat. I stepped out of the shadows.

'Hello, it's Henry Lewis' – I'd remembered his name. 'You may recall, we met on the *Taipan*, at Nick and Judy's party.'

'Lloyd,' he said.

'No, I'm Joshua Winter.'

'Lloyd,' he said again.

'Lloyd?'

'Lewis-Lloyd.'

'Lewis-Lloyd?'

'My name's Henry Lewis-Lloyd, MP for Epping Forest.'

'Oh, right, sorry.'

'Come on,' he said to his wife, striding hugely ahead of her.

'Are you going to the party?' she said to me.

'You mean at Nick's?'

'Yes.'

'I am, yes. I'm just waiting for someone.'

'You look cold,' she said. 'Are you all right?'

'You don't have a spare coat I could borrow, do you? I am feeling rather cold.'

'They've forecast snow for tonight, can you believe?'

'Come on, darling,' Henry called back.

'Henry, hold on. I want to get something from the car.'

'Oh, God, what is it now?' he shouted.

The chauffeur appeared. 'Is everything all right, Annabel?'

'Charles, can you help us, poppet? I want to get something from the boot.'

'It should be open,' he said, stepping round to the back of the car.

She rummaged in the boot. 'All I've got is this, I'm afraid,' she said, holding up a thick tartan picnic blanket. It was then, as I stepped into the light, that I presumed she saw my injuries, because she withdrew a couple of paces.

'D'you mind if I borrow it?' I said of the blanket.

'No, not at all, but it hardly seems appropriate.'

'It'll do while I wait for my friend,' I said. 'He's likely to have a spare jacket.'

'All right. Just return it to us later,' she said, and a firework exploded behind her.

'Christ, that was a big one,' Henry Lewis-Lloyd called out.

His wife hurried after him. Henry loomed like a tree at the gates. The security guards nodded, as if they already knew him, and he and his wife passed through, not once looking back at the car. I walked round and pressed my hands on the warm bonnet; but the driver, peering over the top of his paper, waved me away as if I were an irritating child.

I wrapped myself in the blanket and approached the gates. The house was lit up and looked quite magnificent in the rimy air, against the darkness of the encroaching forest. A

243

security guard with a gold studded earring asked for my invitation.

'I don't have one.'

'If you don't have an invitation you can't come in.'

'I was invited orally.'

'Ooo, was you now!' his colleague, a black guy, said. '*Orally*. This man likes his orals.'

The other guard came closer. 'Look, mate, fuck off, eh? We don't want any peasants around here. Look at the state of you.'

I pleaded with them to allow me through.

'Try over there,' he said, pointing towards the golf club. 'This is an exclusive event.'

A bonfire was burning in a field beyond the golf club and people were gathering around it, the dim glow of the flames on their faces. Then the frosted calm was broken by a sequence of high-pitched whistles as fireworks took off from Nick's garden, followed by explosions and then a spray of splintering green and red stars.

I was standing locked out from Forest Lodge, where until recently I'd been so welcome, and watched enviously as another couple arrived and were nodded through, like the Lewis-Lloyds, without question. They walked up to the door to be greeted by Judy. Yes, by *Judy* – it was a risk I ought to take if I was to have any chance of exposing Dundee, and at what better event than his own bonfire party, a bonfire of his own vanities?

'Judy,' I shouted, running up to the gate. 'Judy, it's me.'

The security guards grabbed me and were about to drag me into the bushes when Judy, approaching the gates, called out, 'Who's there?'

'Judy, it's me, Joshua Winter.'

She reached the gates. 'Joshua,' she said, 'glad you could come. Oh, what have you come as?' She stared at me through the bars, her eyes on my face. She herself was dressed, I think, as a milkmaid.

I winked at the black guy as I walked through and straight into the white, saturated security lights, which clicked on, as bright as on a film set or at a celebrity opening. Another rocket climbed languorously into the air. Judy's relaxed friendliness convinced me that she was ignorant of what had been happening, although she surveyed me suspiciously. I even felt mild regret for her that her married life would be ruined once she discovered the truth about her husband.

'I'm sorry if it's a bit feeble, Judy' – I searched for an explanation – 'but I've come as a, a . . . Mexican bandit.'

'Oh, right, of course, the tartan blanket and the stubble. Very good. But shouldn't you have a mask?'

'A mask?'

'You know, one of those Zorro things, covering the eyes, like in the Sandeman port ads.'

'Yes, you're quite right, but I couldn't find one.'

'Follow me. I think I might have just the thing. And what have you been doing to yourself? What happened to your hand and face?'

'I've been playing rugby.'

'Oh, not a game I like, really. Everyone seems to spend too much time rolling around in the mud.'

We went into the house. There were guests mingling in the hallway, waitresses carrying trays of drinks and canapés, and through an open door I could see the garden and the brilliantly bright blaze of a bonfire.

Judy showed me through into the study where Nick and I had had our last meeting on his return from the Azores. Our circumstances had changed rapidly since then. I looked out at the surrounding darkness of the forest, and shivered at how hostile and inhuman everything seemed, especially the trees. You could feel the cold pressing against the glass, the threat of snow in the air. I had an idea that Judy was never going to return, that security guards would arrive instead to hurry me away from the party before I'd destroyed everything that Nick Dundee had worked so diligently to create out there on the edges of the forest. But no – Judy returned soon enough, muttering excitedly about a Zorro mask she'd found.

'I knew we had one. Here, put this on.'

The mask, a little tight, was held in place by elastic. I peered at Judy through two narrow slits.

'That's better,' she said. 'All you really need now is a gun and a holster to be a proper Mexican bandit. Come on. We'll find you a drink.'

I went out into the hallway and accepted a glass of champagne, all the time searching for Dundee. I passed through a couple of minimally decorated, brightly coloured rooms and then out into the garden. You could hear the crack of splitting wood and the whoosh of the dancing flames. Away from the bonfire two men, wearing black jackets and white gloves, were in control of the firework display; one of the them, at that moment, had just lit a Catherine wheel, which spun frantically, a whirl of spluttering colours. I searched the garden but couldn't see Dundee anywhere, or his two daughters. I returned to the house, away from the whistles and bangs, away from the cold, where this time I saw Emma, cat's whiskers painted on her face, but she didn't recognize me as she ran out into the garden, holding the hand of a blonde woman who resembled Judy.

'Hello, Joshua,' a voice said behind me.

I turned to be greeted by Wai Lee, the Chinese woman I'd met on the *Taipan*. She wasn't in fancy dress.

'Oh, hi. How are you?' I said. 'You recognized me even in the mask!'

She asked how long I'd been at the party and we chatted briefly about the firework display and the change in the weather. I asked about her husband.

'He's just popped over to the golf club. Thought he better show his face as they're also having a party.'

Had she seen Nick?

'Yes, he was in the garden a minute ago, with his daughter Chloe.'

246

This time, as I turned towards the garden, I saw him, dressed in a long dark cassock, returning to the house through the French windows. He recognized me immediately; there wasn't even a flicker of surprise on his face. Or of guilt.

'Hi, Joshua,' he said. 'Excellent to see you. Nice outfit!'

'Why did you have me followed, Nick?' I said, peaceably enough.

'I don't know what you're talking about.'

'You're lying,' I said.

'I don't understand, Joshua. It's me, Nicholas. This' – he pulled the material of his cassock – 'it's only fancy dress.' And he began to chuckle to himself. 'I suppose this is all part of getting into the role, eh? Zorro and all that.'

'You're a lying cunt,' I said, removing the mask. 'Gary Dance, Justin, the others . . . you can't frame me. I know exactly what's been happening around here.'

'What's been happening? This is quite absurd.'

'Justin told me you wanted me watched. Why, Nick? Why was I such a threat to you? What did you think I was going to find out about you? What have you got to hide?'

'You're mad. This is preposterous.' His eyes were restlessly roaming the room. He nodded at someone. 'If you'll excuse us, Wai,' he said, attempting to steer me away from her. Then more quietly, as if to himself, he said, 'I knew you were bad news the first day I saw you.'

I shrugged his deceitful hand away. There was a long fraught silence and then a firework went off outside. Nick glanced out of the window, gorgeous, jagged patterns of light falling across his pale features . . . his weak lashless eyes, the kink in his nose. Even then, after everything, I was attracted by his appearance, his very peculiarity – Picasso's weeping woman – impressed by how calm he was even at that moment of supposed crisis.

And yet I could feel something moving beneath my feet, like the aftershock of an earthquake. The hatred I felt for him was complete; all sense of self-restraint was lost. I had the chance to expose and destroy him.

247

'Don't fucking lie to me, Nick. I've had enough of your lies.'

My words were spoken, not shouted, but they were still loud enough for people to look round, and for a startled Wai Lee to drop her glass. Nick put his arm around me, in mock friendship, but again I shrugged him away.

'Don't try it on, Nick. You know why I've come. You must have known I'd come. Or did you expect me to run away?'

'Now, Josh, Joshua,' he said, and I could hear his anger and distaste. 'I don't know what's got into you but I'm happy to speak about this in private, if you want.'

'Fuck off, Nick,' I said.

'Come on, old chap. Ease down,' he said, raising his voice for the first time.

'Listen, everybody,' I shouted, stepping back and opening my arms, like a compere introducing his star act. People were being attracted in from the garden, intrigued by the thrilling turn in events. Henry Lewis-Lloyd and his wife were there; so were Judy and the girls, Wai Lee, and several other faces I recognized from the *Taipan*. This was my audience, in thrall to what I was about to tell them. I owed it to my father's memory to get it absolutely right, to crush and humiliate the bastard on his own patch, in front of his own people, in my own way. 'This man,' I began, 'this man, Nicholas Dundee, you see here is a complete and utter fraud. He's a monster. He's a fucking monster. But, worst of all, he's a murderer. He murdered my father, he murdered my father, he murdered him, he did, he did that, he's a murderer, a fucking murderer, he murdered my father, he did that . . .'

I saw Nick Dundee nodding at someone across the room, the hatred for me in Judy's face, her tearful, aghast daughters . . . and then they were on me, the security guards, and I was being dragged out into the garden, where I saw a rocket go up and heard its bang and saw an effigy of a man burning on the bonfire, a useless sacrifice if ever there was one; and then I was being dragged into the darkness and through the garage and out on to the brilliantly lit drive, being dragged across the

gravel towards the gates, kicking my legs out in feckless resistance, and then across the frozen, bumpy pathway and out into
a clearing of trees, where the black security guard punched me
twice in the stomach, and I went down, and his boots came in,
as did other boots, and then abruptly they went and I was left
lying there in the lurid darkness, looking up through the silver-
frosted trees at the soft slide of falling fireworks. I couldn't
move. I couldn't move at all. Nor did I want to. I'd exposed
him. For the first time in my life I'd got something absolutely
right. I'd tracked him down, found him. The relief felt like a
torrent of water bursting through a decayed pipe, all pressure
gone. I began laughing to myself, uncontrollably, but I knew
also that I had to keep moving, had to move before the police
arrived, as they surely would. So I stood; and began walking
into the forest, wandering through the blizzard of fantastic
trees, wrapping the blanket around myself more tightly for
warmth, running wildly now among the trees.

There was pain in my right leg where I'd been kicked but it
was nothing compared to the pleasure I felt at what I'd
achieved in humiliating Dundee; and then as I emerged out of
the trees I saw the lights of a service station and a roundabout.
Without hesitating, I ran across the road and climbed on to the
roundabout, from where I hoped to hitch a lift back to the tube
station.

It was breathlessly cold and I pulled the tartan blanket ever
more tightly around me. There was a muffled bang and
another firework soared into the sky. I saw a car coming and I
ran across the roundabout to flag it down, but the solo driver
sped away without so much as an acknowledgement. There
was another car and then another. The cars continued to ignore
me. The driver of the next car, a Ford Mondeo, seemed unsure
of where he was going. He hesitated at the junction. The car
began its loop of the roundabout and I sprinted towards it,
waving my arms. The driver flicked on his main beams and I
was temporarily dazzled. Even if he saw me coming towards
him, as I'm sure he did, he clearly wasn't going to stop.

'You bastard,' I shouted out as the car sped away towards Epping, 'you fucking unhelpful bastard.'

Eventually I find my way back to Loughton station and then by tube to central London. But I'm feeling feverish now, as if that drenching journey on my return from King's Cross to the hotel has resulted in the onset of flu. I begin walking, for aimless hours it seems, along bright streets, mingling with the competing hordes, through parks and beside a canal, unsure of where I'm going. Except that I have a vague idea I've been heading north-west all this time and recently I've been travelling up an incline. It's so cold now that my lungs ache whenever I take in air. There's no cloud or stars, just the occasional firework. Then I recognize where it is I am, where I'm going . . . Of course, I'm passing Chalk Farm tube station, not far from Primrose Hill now. I pause outside an off-licence, peering through the security grille on the window. An Asian guy gazes flatly back at me through the bars. Our eyes meet and I wonder if this is what being in prison is like: looking out at people looking in at you. There's a TV on in his shop and a clock on the wall; it's around midnight. I cross the road to a pay phone and ring Nick Dundee's number.

He answers after three rings.

'It's me,' I say.

'Hello, Joshua. Have you calmed down now?'

'I'm coming to get you, Nick. You won't escape.'

He chuckles. 'I like your style, Joshua, but it's too late. The police are here now. It's you they're coming to get. Enjoy your fifteen minutes in the spotlight.' He lowers his voice. 'You're trash, Winter, just like your old man. Fucking trash.' Then louder again, 'Would you like to speak to the officer, Joshua?'

I put the receiver down.

From there I move along quiet streets, past parked cars whose windows are thickly frosted, until I reach the perimeter fencing of Primrose Hill Park. I approach the hill from the south side and begin to climb. The lamp-lit frosty grass crunches underfoot, the silvery-blue shimmer of a late-autumn night. I'm breathless by the time I reach the top; but the view works like a shot of brandy: it warms you. I study the map of the defining landmarks of the city: St Paul's Cathedral, St Pancras Station, the NatWest Tower, Euston Tower, Telecom Tower, Senate House, Centre Point. My eye is drawn east to the high modernist glass tower of Canary Wharf, its blink of light a flickering pulse drawing you towards it. A distant rocket climbs into the sky, colouring the empty air.

There's something marvellous about the lights of the surrounding landscape, in all its non-geometric sprawl, so unlike the clinical order of central Toronto or the hard perfection of the Manhattan grid. London is so huge and complex, so much of its growth haphazard and serendipitous, its ever-changing streets like a kind of palimpsest – with successive generations failing quite to erase the influence of those who have gone before – that I know now I will never really understand it, or possess it as a native could; that its true pleasures will never be mine.

I'm so tired that, paradoxically, I no longer feel tired. I've reached a point beyond exhaustion, where exhilaration begins and you feel light-headed, giddy, dazed, lost in blank spaces. It's as if you've slipped into a void. Time dissolves. I've no idea how long I've been up on Primrose Hill, looking down at the small lights of the houses below. There's fine snow in the air, like breeze-blown sawdust. I imagine what the day might be like tomorrow: the roads snow-clogged and almost impassable. Everything seems so much more intense up here: whiter, brighter, sharper, clearer. The traffic is no more than a passing murmur on the roads below and even the low-flying aircraft are of no concern. So I revisit my early weeks in the city, the days spent wandering through the parks and international hotels, the places that had once been mine, the women I followed, the job I spurned, the sunlit evening streets through which I strolled, the restaurants I looked into, the people I

251

hoped to find – the shadow lives we all lead. All that is behind me now.

I turn my back on the lights of the city, which shine with such brightness, and begin my descent from Primrose Hill.

Snow was still falling as I set off, more in hope than expectation, for Euston Station. Whenever I heard the approaching sound of a car I instinctively withdrew or ducked into a doorway, using those moments, such as they were, to catch my breath – moments of repose in a hectic changing world. I wrapped the blanket around my shoulders, the fine snow melting into my hair.

As I continued the long trudge to Euston, the snow falling ever more finely now, I felt as if I were crossing a boundary between autumn and winter, between my old careless life and what lay ahead like a turbulent ocean of unknowing.

I left Euston later that morning at around nine. I settled into a window seat, facing the direction of travel, in a near-empty, non-smoking carriage at the rear of the train, bought a newspaper, a sandwich and a cup of tea. The early morning calm of the carriage was interrupted occasionally by the jingle of a mobile phone. The first time one rang nearly everyone, including myself, reached automatically for their bags or jackets, although the battery of the phone I had was – like its owner, like my father – long since dead. Belonging wholly to the past. And as I slumbered, I began to think that my struggle to find the truth about my father had been, after all, no more than a struggle with memory itself: an attempt to make of the unbearable dross of the past something meaningful and true.

The flat unvarying English landscape unravelled before me: boundless acres of overcultivated fields, housing estates, low grey cloud, and everywhere too many cars.

The snow hadn't really settled anywhere, but many of the passing fields were silvered and glistening. I rang my uncle from a pay phone on the train, told him what time to expect me at Manchester Piccadilly. Then I settled back to sleep, feeling a semblance of peace now that I'd finally resolved the mystery of my father's death. All that was missing was a motive – and his body. One fine day, though, I was confident that everything would be explained . . .

A wood in darkness, empty city streets, a woman alone with her baby in a sombre room, and then the body of a man lying dead in my flat: the events of the past fortnight replayed themselves like a video nightmare controlled by an unseen hand. Since returning to London at the end of August my world had been turned upside down in search of a man I'd never really known. The choice seemed simple now: to run and keep on running, to run somewhere – anywhere – or to take my chance in the courts. The phone in my pocket which I dared not lose was quiet. So I lay there slumped in the carriage of a train speeding north towards Manchester; and lying there I began to mourn the lost warmth of the English summer through which I'd just passed, a summer which had wrapped itself around me so completely – like a safety blanket – that I'd been lulled into thinking that my search was at last approaching an end, that I'd finally returned to a country I once called home. And now? Nothing but the slow desolation of early winter . . . and the mistakes we repeat.

XII: 5 November 1995

They pull off the motorway on the way to visit his wife's ailing mother. The girls are hungry, after the long drive south, and are asking for chips – and because they both missed the school bonfire party he feels he ought to indulge them, at least this once. But there is another reason, too: the sign for Bournemouth has stirred something within him.

'Where are we going, Greg?' his wife says, as he bypasses Bournemouth and continues following signs to Poole and then on to the harbour.

'I thought we might get some chips and watch some fireworks by the waterside,' he says, driving past a cemetery he can't remember, past a pub he can't remember, and down to where the trees become thicker and the road narrows. Here there are no street lamps. Nothing illuminating their way. His twin daughters are singing one of his favourite hymns, 'Lord of the Dance'. As he watches them in the rear-view mirror he's consumed by a happiness so complete he feels humbled by it. He looks at his wife. She reaches out, places her hand gently on his left leg, over which the heater blows warm air. He can see she's tired, but when the headlights of a passing car fall upon her face he thinks how complex and lovely she seems in all her sadness.

He drives on, approaching the roundabout he once knew as the Wake Arms. A sign is lit up by his headlights: left for Sandbanks, right for the harbour. 'There used to be a big pub on this roundabout,' he says, surprised to hear himself say this.

'I didn't know you knew this neck of the woods so well.'

'I don't really,' he says, turning right along the harbour front. 'It's ages since I came here with my parents.' Then he mutters audibly to himself: 'The trivia that stays with you.'

He parks and together the family walks down to the waterside, the girls running slightly ahead. The night is cold and urgent. The sky is so artificially bright. They stand looking out across the trembling water.

'Did you see that one?' his wife says, pointing at a luminous shower of collapsing starlight, at a firework.

'Yes,' he says, but he didn't. For his eyes have been elsewhere, watching the dim glow from the light of a bonfire somewhere beyond Brownsea Island, way out in the deep waters of the harbour – a light that never goes out. Momentarily, he's lost in those rolling hills beyond the dark side of the harbour, and again he feels that something strange stirring within himself which lies beyond mere words, on the other side of silence. He feels ... What does he feel? If only he could say. He begins to say something but his words fragment in the wind, becoming nothing but sounds no one will ever hear.

He reaches out to run fingers through his wife's thick dark red curls. 'So, darling, are you having a few chips with us tonight?'

'Oh, all right, Greg, just this once.'

'Mummy's having chips, too, girls,' he says.

The sisters cheer. The family retraces its steps in the direction of the strip of fast-food restaurants where they have parked just as another firework explodes in the sky behind them, and the night is lit by a magical glow.

Greg says nothing as he drives away from the harbour, drives into the greater darkness of the surrounding countryside, along a wide avenue flanked on either side by frosty trees which are seemingly thickening all the time around him – and it's as if a great, impenetrable fog is coming down from nowhere, settling over this ancient patch of Wessex turf like silence. He recalls once hating the winter darkness of that southern English landscape – the monotony of that watery landscape. But all that seems like more than a lifetime ago. His life has been different since he discovered the consolation of knowledge. He glances at the sticker on the dashboard, *Credo ut intelligentum* – I believe in order to understand.

The
Ghosts
of
Cheshire

by

Muriel Armand

Dedicated to children in need who will benefit from the sale of this book.

First published 1989 by Countyvise Limited, 1 & 3 Grove Road, Rock Ferry, Birkenhead, Wirral, Merseyside L42 3XS.

Copyright © M. Armand, 1989.
Photoset and printed by Birkenhead Press Limited, 1 & 3 Grove Road, Rock Ferry, Birkenhead, Merseyside L42 3XS.

ISBN 0 907768 31 8.

INTRODUCTION

While researching some of the ancient history of Chester, it became apparent to me that history and hauntings go together.

I started by enlisting the help of the Chester Chronicle, asking their readers for true encounters of the ghostly kind. The response was such that the intended book on Chester became the book on Cheshire.

Without further preamble I ask you to read on and sincerely hope that you enjoy discovering who the phantoms of Cheshire are and where they can be found.

ALTRINCHAM
BARTHOMLEY
BEBINGTON
BIRKENHEAD
BOLLINGTON
BOSLEY
BRAMHALL
BRERETON
BRIMSTAGE
BROMBOROUGH
BROUGHTON
BUNBURY
BURLEYDAM
CHELFORD
CHESTER
CREWE
DAVENHAM
DEE
DISLEY
DUNHAM MASSEY
DUDDON
EGREMONT
ELLESMERE PORT
FARNDON
GATLEY
GAWSWORTH
GODLEY GREEN
HOLMES CHAPEL
HOYLAKE
HYDE

KNUTSFORD
LITTLE SUTTON
MACCLESFIELD
MARPLE
NANTWICH
NESTON
NEW BRIGHTON
NORTHENDEN
NORTHWICH
PARKGATE
PLUMLEY
POYNTON
ROCK FERRY
RUNCORN
SALTNEY
SEACOMBE
SHOCKLACH
SPITAL
STOCKPORT
TARPORLEY
THELWELL
THURSTASTON
TILSTON
TOFT
TUSHINGHAM
WALLASEY
WARRINGTON
WEST KIRBY
WHALEY BRIDGE
WILDBOARCLOUGH

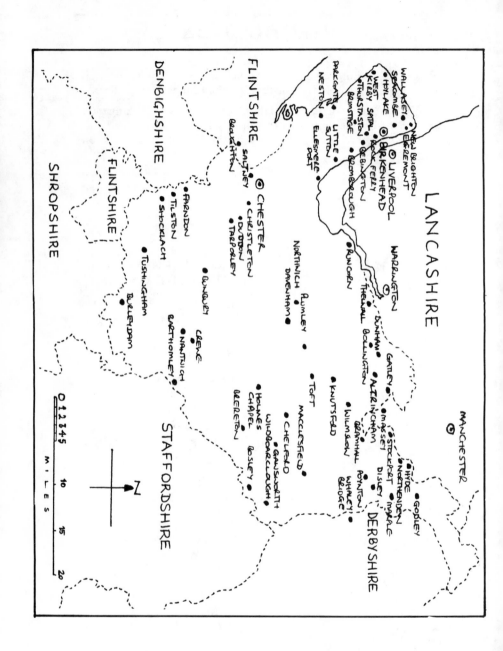

Tour One

CHESTER

We start our Ghostly Tour of Cheshire in the very heart of the county, the city of Chester, the jewel in the Cheshire crown. Few cities can compare with the historical splendour of this once Roman fortress. Seldom can the relics of the past be found to blend so gracefully with the 20th century. The city and it's surrounding countryside are so steeped in history that it is not surprising to discover it has more ghostly visitors than anywhere else in England. You don't have to look for the phantoms of Chester, if you stand still long enough they will come looking for you. The following pages will reveal where they are and in some cases who they are . . .

There will be many more ghosts in the county which have not yet come to light, see if you can unearth one or two for our next edition.

ANCHORITE CELL — CHESTER

It is fitting that we start in Chester with the ancient Anchorite Cell as it's present owner, Mrs. Crossland, was the first person to contact me with her personal account of the monk who haunts the old hermitage.

Between St. John's church and the River Dee stands the ancient Anchorite Cell. It can claim to be one of the oldest ecclesiastical buildings still standing today. It is the reputed hiding place of King Harold the Saxon who was generally believed to have died in the battle of Hastings fighting William the Conqueror. It is thought that after surviving serious injuries he spent the rest of his days as a monk at St. John's, living in the Anchorite Cell. Under the house is a tunnel which runs from the river under the cell and ends at St. John's. On certain nights of the year a ghostly monk appears, he rises out of the river and climbs the path towards the cell. At this point he disappears into the tunnel leading to St. John's. As in the descriptions which follow he is tall and dressed in a dark habit with the hood up. This spectre is seen regularly by the family who live at the cell and was also seen by a group of visitors and their guide from the Chester visitors centre . . .   *Mrs. Crossland.*

The Anchorite Cell, Chester.

Anchorite Cell, Chester.

ST. JOHN'S CHURCH

To my knowledge St. John's church is the haunt of the most active ghost in Chester. It is haunted by a tall hooded monk who appears in and around the church. Six different groups have reported seeing this figure and all descriptions have been identical, so it seems reasonable to assume it is the same monk. Mr. Michael Cooper Porter told me of seeing him way back in 1941 when he and a young priest were walking in the grounds of St. John's. The apparition, dressed in monks habit with hood up, approached the two men. He was a frightening sight, so it was little wonder they moved quickly away but with amazing speed the apparition confronted them again. The

7

Tower — St. John's Church, Chester.

unusual aspect of this encounter was that the ghost spoke to them in a gutteral German accent. Both had a keen interest in languages and later discovered it to be Anglo Saxon, a very old language spoken in England between the 7th and 10th century. The gentleman who gave me this story tells me that his friend is now a Friar in the Franciscan order.

Mr. Michael Cooper Porter

St. John's Tower, Chester.

ST. JOHN'S TOWER

I was fortunate enough to be given yet another eye witness account of the ghostly monk. It was sent to me by Mr. Keith White, a young man who saw the ghost in the tower ruins while playing there as a boy with some friends. As they climbed the tower's sandstone steps, the boys heard sounds of someone praying at the top of the tower. In fright he fell down a few steps and as he picked himself up he glanced behind to see a tall, dark, hooded figure climbing the stairs behind him. The boys ran down and looking back could see a tall monk on the steps close to the top of the tower. This story was verified and printed in the Chester Observer in 1974.

Mr. Keith White

It is my opinion that the same spirit haunts St. John's church, the surrounding grounds and the Anchorite Cell, as the descriptions of a tall monk in grey habit have all been identical.

9

CANAL BANK

In 1959 a young man had been to visit his wife and new born baby in the city hospital. It was late on a sharp clear night as he made his way home along the canal bank. As he approached Griffith's old flour mill he was amazed to see a pale grey figure rising out of the canal. The figure began twisting into different shapes, sometimes opaque and then transparant. To his horror it drifted quite quickly over the water and on to the bank advancing towards him. There was no one around, if there had been, his fear was such that he would not have been able to shout for help. The shapeless form surrounded him, it was cold and clammy like an intangible vapour. He knew he must break free and with an enormous effort he began to run without looking back and did not stop until he reached George Street. There have been other reports of a similar shape seen at this spot, but there is no local story to throw light on who, or what it is.

TOP RANK CLUB — BROOK STRET

The Top Rank Club in Brook Street has not always been a Bingo Hall. It has been a bowling alley and before that was the Gaumont cinema. During the second World War, there were reports of strange noises coming from the top floor. Men on fire-watch duty during the air raids thought that fire bombs had landed on the roof on a number of nights and found nothing. The noises were described as heavy boxes being dragged across the upper floor but on inspection no one was ever found . There have been no reports of the ghostly sounds since it stopped being a cinema so perhaps it was a spirit with a liking for old movies . . .

BANKS OF THE DEE

On the banks of the River Dee close to the Chester YMCA, there are reports of three ghosts walking in this area. Along a path by the river people have told of seeing a ghostly lady who is wearing a long black gown with a black headress. She is thought to be a nun who drowned in the Dee. Also seen is a male figure described as looking like a handyman. The third phantom is that of a young boy who is said to have been a boot black.

CITY WALLS

The old Roman walls around the city of Chester have survived a long and exciting history. It is not surprising then that we hear of two ghosts who are seen walking on the walls. One we know of was a Centurion, who was drowned in the River Dee. Another is that of a Cavalier, who was killed by a Roundhead's bullet. It was probably at the battle of Rowton Moor which took place within sight of the city walls. It is said that King Charles I watched his army being defeated from the safety of the Pheonix Tower . . .

City Walls and Dee Bank, Chester.

MILL ON THE DEE

On a site close to the old Dee Bridge stood the mill that inspired the poet to write the famous Miller of the Dee. The mill eventually burned down, claiming two victims in the fire. Passers by still tell of hearing shrieks and report the smell of burning at times as they approach the spot where the old mill once stood . . .

THE OLD TUDOR HOUSE

The old Tudor house is another old building that can claim to be haunted by a Cavalier soldier said to have had his head blown off by a musket blast. The apparition crawls around the upper rooms, seemingly still searching for his head . . .

Town Hall, Chester.

THE TOWN HALL

The Town Hall is not left out when it comes to phantoms. The store room directly beneath the Tourist Office has something described as a presence which follows the staff when they have to go down there. Those who have gone alone have reported hearing footsteps behind them and a feeling of someone being down there with them. There could be a number of reasons for this as this site was originally occupied by a Roman legionary hospital and much later by an old coaching inn named The Red Lion. In more recent times the basement used to be the local prison cells. With a history like that there is little wonder the Town Hall is haunted . . .

HOUSE IN WATERGATE STREET

A house in Watergate Street is haunted by two spirits from very different times. One is the ghost of a young girl dressed in the clothes of the sixteen hundreds. She has been revisiting the house for over three hundred years. This sounds a long time, but not nearly as long as her fellow phantom — yes another monk. Dressed in the robes of a 13th Century white friar, he is seen moving about the old house from time to time. The young girl, we can assume, once lived in the house but there are no obvious reasons for the monks presence . . .

STANLEY PLACE — WATERGATE ROW

Not much is known about the lady in grey who is said to wander about in Stanley Place. The property is very old, dating back to 1591. Both the house and the lady are believed to have connections with the civil war but both remain shrouded in mystery . . .

THE ROYAL INFIRMARY

The Royal Infirmary has a spirit which is a sad reminder of the first world war. There is a story that a Scottish soldier bearing the proud name of Mackenzie died at the hospital from wounds he had received while fighting in France. It was not always possible to do the proper thing in those dark wartime days and so trooper Mac was buried in a hospital shroud instead of the uniform tartan of which he was so proud. It is said that his ghost is still searching for what is believed to be his proper burial clothes . . .

EASTGATE STREET

A business premises on Eastgate Street that is now occupied by Diner's Den, has one of the saddest spirits of Chester. During the nineteenth century a young girl who lived in the house was jilted on her wedding day. So great was her sorrow that she hung herself from an oak beam in her bedroom. The maid servant who found her body hanging limp, still wearing her white wedding dress, fled the house and was not seen again. The bedroom was emptied and kept locked for many years. Still today she is seen dressed in her wedding finery moving about the scene of her great earthly sadness . . .

DEE HILL PARK

While staying at Dee Hill Park, a local dignitary described seeing yet another ghostly monk in dark habit. The spectre was seen to glide through a room and disappear into a wall. The house stands on the site of a Norman building and goes back still further to Saxon times.

CHESTER TO TIVERTON ROAD

On a calm September night, driving home along a quiet country lane a young motorist saw in front of him on the road, a man walking a dog. The man was dressed in an unusual manner as he wore a khaki coloured smock tied at the waist with string. On his head he wore a type of souwester and his dog was being led on a string lead. Something else strange about them was that they appeared to be battling against a strong head wind. Completely lost by this time, the motorist wound down the passenger window and asked if this was the right way to Tarporley. Receiving no reply, he slid into the passenger seat to be more easily heard and repeated the question. To his horror the man turned his head, which was now only six inches away, he looked with staring eyes and a greenish face and walked on. Terrified, the motorist managed to restart the car and drove off at top speed without looking back. On making enquiries he was told of a farmer who had been run over by a horse drawn coach while walking his dog many years ago. The accident had happened during a bad storm when a high wind was blowing . . .

YE OLD KING'S HEAD — LOWER BRIDGE STREET

Ye Old Kings Head, Lower Bridge Street, Chester.

Ye Old Kings Head is one of Chester's oldest hotels, built in 1520 for the Randall family who lived there for 200 years. It's age is shown in the low ceilings, oaken beams and charming winding stairways. The ghost who appeared there has only been reported once by a lady who stayed in room six five years ago. She was awakened about two in the morning feeling an icy chill in the room. Wide awake and very cold, she was aware of another presence. Suddenly she saw a man dressed in black standing between the bed and the window. Although the spectre stood there for what seemed about ten minutes, the lady did not cry out or try to get help as there was a feeling of great peace in the room. When she did speak the man vanished. On reporting the incident to the manager, she was told they had felt a strange sensation on the narrow stairway leading to room six. A number of maids had told of feeling the icy chill in the room but none had every spoken of seeing anything. Could this be the room James I slept in when he stayed at the Old Kings Head all those years ago?

ST. MARY'S CHURCH

Three women convicted of being witches were buried in St. Mary's churchyard. In those days the custom was that they should be buried in unhallowed ground. However, the good people of Chester did not agree with the Witch Finder General and believed them to be innocent. There is a story that the three fly around the church each Halloween but that sounds rather like a Halloween tale. Something much more positive is that the ghosts of two cats, one black, one white are often seen in the churchyard only to disappear as anyone approaches . . .

The Rows, Chester.

The Rows, Chester.

THE ROWS

The ghost of a sailor who missed his ship many years ago still haunts the Rows and part of Watergate Street. Dressed in the uniform of an ancient sea-farer he searches endlessly for something or someone. Seen recently by a man of the church, he was described as looking so life-like the clergyman took him for a pantomime actor.

THE HOUSE OF BEWLAY

The old house of Bewlay in Chester has seen many changes in it's long history. For a number of years now it has been a tobacconist shop. It was during this time that ghostly happenings were reported and became so intense that the shop keeper found it difficult to keep staff. Reports were of loud noises and heavy footsteps on the stairs. The ghost was generally thought to be that of a woman called Sarah who had hung herself on the premises years before. In 1965 the spirit became so troublesome that the church was asked to help and the Bishop of Chester himself did the exorcising. This proved to be successful for some years, but recently there has been a renewal of unexplained activity. Staff have complained of sweets and chocolate being thrown around the shop at night time. A member of the staff described Sarah to me saying, she is more of a nuisance than a frightening spirit these days.

THE BLUE BELL — LORIMER ROW

The Blue Bell is one of the oldest and certainly one of the quaintest restaurants in Chester. Built in 1494 it has a long and colourful history as a Coaching Inn. The walls are crooked and the staircase twisted, but the most unusual feature is the upper room which extends over the pavement to be supported by pillars in the roadway. Anywhere as old and charming as the Blue Bell should be haunted and it is. The young woman whose spirit is still frequently seen is a sad and lonely figure. She is seen looking through the front upstairs window, searching the street below for her lover who never returned. He is said to have been killed by a horse drawn coach on his way to the Blue Bell. The manager told me they catch glimpses of her moving silently about the charming old rooms. He said there was no definite pattern to her appearances but her shadowy form has been seen by numerous members of the staff.

The Blue Bell, Lorimer Row, Chester.

Ye Olde Vaults, Bridge Street, Chester.

YE OLD VAULTS — BRIDGE STREET

Ye Old Vaults in Bridge Street has a rather distinguished phantom in the shape of a gentleman wearing a top hat. He is believed to be the ghost of a 16th century traveller who hanged himself in an upstairs room.

THE HIGHWAY MAN — EASTGATE STREET

The ghost of a horseman believed to be that of a highway man, has been seen so clearly, that he was mistaken for a party goer in fancy dress. Dressed in a flowing cape, cocked hat and thigh length boots, he appears impatient at being kept waiting. This ghost has been sighted close to one of Chester's smartest stores which is believed to be built on the site of an old coaching inn and it would appear that the highway man is waiting at the door. There is a tale of a highway man being murdered for his ill-gotten gains, but no evidence of the exact whereabout's has been brought to light . . .

BOOT INN — EASTGATE ROW

Built in 1643, the Boot Inn is an enchanting old tavern set in the rows of Eastgate Street. Some 330 years ago the inn had a landlord who practised as a barber surgeon, his wife was "madam" to the local prostitutes of the day. At the dead of night when all is quiet the sound of laughter and the clink of glasses can be heard coming from the empty rooms. The present proprietor, Peter Kinsey, told me that at times the inner front door is sometimes found locked by unseen hands.

MARLBOROUGH ARMS — ST. JOHN'S STREET

The black and white timbered Marlborough Arms was once an old coaching inn. The cellar is haunted by a one time owner who cut his throat amidst the beer barrels in 1886. Psychic researchers have inspected the cellar and felt very powerful forces there. One reported that a large barrel was propelled towards her by unseen hands . . .

OLD SAUGHALL MILL — CHESTER ROAD

The old Saughall Mill on the Chester Road has a long and colourful history. In 1750 two Irish labourers robbed and murdered a traveller on his way to Chester. They were found, convicted and hung fron an Ash tree nearby. Since then it has been known as the Gibbet Mill and, not surprisingly, there have been tales of ghostly goings on, on the road leading to the mill . . .

19

THE VICTORIA — WATERGATE ROW

The Victoria stands on the spot where there has been a tavern since the thirteenth century. Going still further back in time on this site stood the Principal, the Norman centre of Chester. The back of the Victoria looks over the St. Peter's graveyard. The cellars of the inn are actually built over part of the graveyard so it is hardly surprising that a ghost is said to stalk the cellar at night . . .

YE OLD DEVA — WATERGATE ROW

Ye Old Deva is a fourteenth century coaching inn on Watergate Row. Between the bar and the lounge is an original Elizabethan staircase with a quaint inglenook fireplace, and it is where the sad spirit of a small boy lingers. At times it is said he runs from the inn screaming, he appears to be covered in flames and quickly disappears down a side street. The old inn is thought to have been the Roundheads headquarters during the civil war . . .

Ye Olde Deva Hotel, Watergate Row, Chester.

GOLDEN EAGLE — CASTLE STREET

Dating back to the 14th century the Golden Eagle was once the home of the Sheriff of Chester. Going back further still it is built on the site of a Roman camp. The old inn can claim a record for mass haunting as it has regular visits from twenty odd spirits. Both staff and visitors claim to have seen a patrol of twenty Roman soldiers accompanied by an officer in the depth of the dark cellar. They are in marching formation and disappear straight through the wall of the cellar.

CHESTER ROWS —
Also see Ghost of Old Sailor in Chester Rows.

A site now occupied by a well known jeweller in the Chester Rows has a friendly phantom called George. His presence is felt at the back of the shop where he has been known to lightly touch his victims. He is usually accompanied by the smell of tobacco smoke and sometimes puffs of smoke can be seen hanging in the air. Many years ago this building was an old public house so perhaps George is still happily puffing away in the smoke room . . .   *Miss Francis Rand*

The Bear and Billet, Lower Bridge Street, Chester.

THE BEAR & BILLET — LOWER BRIDGE STREET

One of Chester's oldest and most attractive inns, the Bear & Billet was once the home of the Talbots, Earls of Shrewsbury. When the house became an inn the Talbots had a suite of rooms permanently reserved for their own use. Now the B & B is the haunt of an old fashioned lady who is seen in the upper room and on the staircase. A member of staff who saw her told me she is a gentle, silent spirit, not at all frightening. She only appears on the staircase when there is a man around. This is a very gentle ghost who makes no sound and does not seem to move anywhere else in the tavern . . .

THE GEORGE & DRAGON — LIVERPOOL ROAD

As Chester inns go, the George & Dragon is quite modern, but the ghost who marches through the upstairs rooms is very old indeed. Built on the site of an old Roman cemetery, it stands very close to the old city wall. The spirit is believed to be that of a Roman legionary who still faithfully patrols his section. The footsteps are heard loud and clear as the ghostly feet tramp the measured distance of his guard. The upper floor is divided into fourteen rooms and corridors but this does not deter the sentry as he walks straight through walls that block his path. There is a story that he fell in love with a Welsh girl and one night when he should have been oñ duty he deserted his post to be with her. Her countrymen were able to breach the wall and kill many of his comrades. We will never know if this was so, but it would explain his spirit's devotion to duty . . .

THE LEGEND OF THE WHITEHART
of St. John's, Chester.

Legend has it that King Ethelred felt great gratitude to God for all the good things God had bestowed upon him. He decided to show his gratitude by building a church that would teach the people the true - Christian faith. It would be a collegiate church where monks would be taught to pass on their knowledge to the people who worshipped there. He was instructed in a dream to build his church on the spot where he would find a white hart at bay. Following the dream he was led by a vision to a spot where he built St. John's church, Chester. This very old legend describes how it came about . . .

Addressed him where he sleeping lay,
Where first a milk white hart at bay, Thou shalt behold,
There thou mayest build a college church,
Where men may learn in deep researche, To truth unfold,
In Chester suburbs Ethelred,

While musing on his dream was led,
By winding way to wonder by the banks of Dee,
When close at hand beneath a tree, a hart at bay,
Surrounded by the yelping hounds, thous shrilly sounds the
huntsmans horn, King Ethelred surprised espied,
All marred with gore it's milk white hide,
And on the spot in after years, a lordly church the king uprears,
Where still within the walls is heard,
The message of the living word,
The hope of man . . .   *Egerton Leigh*

Tour Two

Our second tour takes us to the south west of the county where we travel through some lovely country areas and visit a few interesting towns as well.

CHRISTLETON

Out of Chester take the A41 south for one mile to Christleton. You take a step back in time as you enter the village over an old humped back bridge. Christleton is an old fashioned village that has become an exclusive dorm for Chester. There is a charming green where the ancient pump still stands.

PLOUGH LANE

For many years passers by have told of encountering two phantoms at the end of Plough Lane in Christleton. They are believed to be the spirits of two Irishmen who were hanged on the local gibbet that once stood here. There have been stories of a haunting at the 18th century Plough Inn close by but a lady member of staff told me she had never heard or seen anything spectral.

DUDDON

From Christleton, take the unclassified road signposted Tarvin for one and a half miles to the A51. Continue along the A51 for five miles to Duddon. Set on the A51 in rural surroundings Duddon is a small pretty place.

THE HEADLESS WOMAN

After defeating Charles I last army at Rowton Moor, the Roundheads began searching the surrounding area and found Hockinghull Hall. The Royalists had left after hiding the family jewels and silver plate. Furious at finding all had fled except for the old housekeeper, they tortured her in the hope that she would reveal the hiding place. When she would not betray her employers they chopped off her head. To this day, her ghost is seen carrying her head under her arm. She walks the path between the hall and the pub which is named after her. Many people claim to have seen her dressed in a white gown as she wanders both inside and out of the inn.

TARPORLEY

Three miles south on the A51 Tarporley is a small pleasant town. The main street is fortunate to have a number of well preserved Georgian houses. These fine examples of the period have stone steps rising to the elevated front doors and some splendid bay windows.

Take the signed, forked road out of Tarporley for two miles down a steep narrow lane which leads to rambling Utkinton Hall. On my visit to the Hall it was interesting to note that the orchard and garden in spring had many blackbirds nesting there.

UTKINTON HALL

Once the family home of the Done family, Utkinton Hall then stood in a forest clearing. It was thought to have been built around an ancient tree which was so enormous the builders had found it impossible to fell. On a rise above the house a healing well was found, it proved to be so powerful that over two thousand people came every day to benefit from it's waters.

The Done family were devout Puritans which made the people who worked for them afraid to go against their beliefs. One of their strict rules was that their employees should not play cards after midnight on Saturdays. Some farm labourers, intent on their game, did not notice the passing of the witching hour. The next day, visibly shaken, they swore that a ghostly horse had entered the stable and asked to be dealt a hand of cards — needless to say the game had gone unfinished. Before the Done family had gone to live there, the hall had been haunted by an unidentified spirit. It was eventually exorcised by the local priest who failed to make it disappear but it was said to turn into a blackbird before his eyes. The spirit bird was reported to haunt the walled garden for over a hundred years. Since then the garden has always had many blackbirds nesting there . . .

Utkinton Hall, Tarporley.

BUNBURY

Take the A51 from Tarporley for three miles, left on a signposted road for a further mile. A large village set in pretty rural surroundings, Bunbury is the proud possessor of a very fine 14th century church. St. Boniface is much larger than the average village church and is very much at the heart of the local community.

Between College Lane and the local school there are reports of two phantoms. In College Lane a ghostly horseman is seen riding his steed across the lane. In the area around the local school, numerous sightings of a spectral hound have also been reported . . .

NANTWICH

Leave Bunbury at Wytch Lane, follow a country lane for two miles. Cross the Shropshire Union Canal, turn right on to the A51 and follow signs to Nantwich through Wardle for eleven miles.

Nantwich is a charming town with many old timbered houses. Standing beside the old stone bridge over the River Weaver is the thatched "Cheshire Cat". This Tudor inn has a flight of mounting steps at the front.

THE BOOT AND SHOE

Built in 1579, The Boot and Shoe survived the great fire which destroyed most of the town in 1583. Part of it's structure is still supported by a huge old tree which props up a corner of the lounge. During the 17th century it was a cobblers shop that also sold ale. When the cobbler died it became a full time inn. It is haunted by a woman who is dressed in the clothes of a Puritan. She has been known to administer comfort to a sick child — the daughter of a licencee. Her footsteps and coughing sounds are heard at night when she is fond of moving small items from one room to another . . .

CHURCHES MANSION

A wealthy merchant by the name of Richard Church built Churches Mansion in 1577. The proprietor, Mr. Peter Tofalos, told me there is more than one ghostly spirit in his restaurant. Customers and staff have told of seeing a lady in a red dress walk through the dining area. Others speak of a lady in white who was seen to walk straight through one of the tables. Also seen is another figure, thought to be male, who sits at a certain table and fades away. Strange thuds and bangs are heard and one or two have been grabbed by unseen hands. One member of the House of Lords who visits Churches regularly, identified one of the upstairs rooms as being haunted. He said he felt the same cold atmosphere that was felt in a haunted room in his own stately home.

CREWE

From Nantwich take the A534 for five miles. Crewe is a large town famous for it's railway junction.

THE LYCEUM THEATRE

Built in 1887, the Lyceum Theatre in Crewe looks interesting enough to be haunted and it is. A young ballerina who hung herself in a dressing room is still seen. Another is an actor of days gone by, usually seen in the vicinity of the stage door. Lastly, a phantom monk who wanders around the old theatre. This is no actor but a real monk left over from the days when this site was occupied by a Catholic church and it's graveyard.

The spirits were exorcised in 1969 but the actor and ballerina have been seen since. Standing together at the back of a theatre box, the cast on stage could see them clearly, both intently watching the play. Since the excorcism the monk has moved on to the cellars of the pub which backs on to the theatre . . .

BARTHOMLEY

Take the B5020 for two miles to Weston, left for two miles on an unmarked country lane. Turn left on to the A531 for one and a half miles.

Once the scene of a Civil War massacre, Barthomley lies tucked away in the heart of a farming community. At the centre of this pretty village stands a group of black and white houses of the Magpie architecture. The "White Lion Inn" dated 1614 is a perfect example of its type. On a rise above the village stands St. Bertolines, a beautiful old church that displays a scroll of its past Rectors dating back to 1303. On the front door in summer, is a notice asking visitors to shut the wire entrance door to stop the swallows from getting locked in the church, a charming place indeed.

White Lion Inn, Barthomley.

Barthomley.

Barthomley can claim to have two spectres, as we are told that a lady dressed in white, haunts the field next to the church. It also has a phantom dog which is quite often seen walking in the road beside the church. It would be nice to think that she was looking for her dog and if they could find each other, they could both be at rest.

COMBERMERE ABBEY

A niece of Lord Combermere who was staying at the Abbey, told of a strange encounter she had there. One evening while dressing for dinner, she saw in her looking glass the reflection of a small iron bed. Standing beside it was a little girl dressed in an old fashioned frock with a ruff at the neck; the child began to run around in a very distressed manner. When the young woman reached out to touch her, both she and the bed vanished. On enquiring, the niece discovered that a small sister of the Lord had died in that very room after playing chasing around the bed with her brothers and sisters. He had become very distressed at the loss of his much loved younger sister. The family became to realise that the spirit child only appeared before the death of one of it's members . . .

COMBERMERE ABBEY BELLS

At the time of the dissolution when monastries were being sacked and destroyed, the bell of Combermere Abbey was thrown into the waters of the mere. From time to time, the muffled tones of a big bell is heard coming from the depth of the water. A story attributed to the ghostly sound of the bell is that when asked to help move them to safety, a blasphemous workman refused. It is said that the large bell moved of its own accord, taking the unfortunate workman with it to the bottom of the mere . . .

COMBERMERE ABBEY MONKS

Before the dissolution, Combermere Abbey was a monastry so it is not surprising that ghostly monks have been seen there. It was believed by the Cotten family, who once owned the abbey, that they could only live there as long as they continued to be as hospitable as the monks had been . . .

COMBERMERE ARMS

Built in the 16th century "Combermere Arms" is known to be one of Cheshire's oldest pubs. David Stockdale, the present proprietor, told me about the monk who still haunts his fine old hostelry. He was believed to have perished when a tunnel leading from the Arms to the abbey collapsed some 200 years ago. He appears in the bar and cellar and legend has it he is buried beneath the front steps of the inn. Apart from the usual door handles turning and footsteps on the floor boards, there have been many mysterious happenings at the old inn.

31

The Combermere Arms, Burleydam.

BURLEYDAM

Take the road to Weston out of Barthomley for three and a half miles, join the A531 through Wrinehill to Checkley for five miles. Turn onto the A529 to Audlem for seven miles then the A525 to Burleydam for three and a half miles.

Passing through the Shropshire border at this point, Burleydam consists of a number of scattered dwellings set in a fine dairy farming district. At the heart of Burleydam stands the 16th century "Combermere Arms" with a sign that claims it is the most haunted pub in Cheshire. Combermere Abbey stands nearby, a large estate of some 2,000 acres with the largest private lake in England.

TUSHINGHAM

Take the A530 signposted Whitchurch, for four miles then the A41 signed Tushingham-cum-Grindley, turn left at Bell-O-the-Hill sign for half a mile.

Tushingham is a small place, a number of farms, the church and the "Blue Bell Inn" dated 1667.

The Blue Bell Inn, Tushingham.

THE BLUE BELL

The Blue Bell in Tushingham was troubled by a ghost of the feathered variety. The story goes that a past landlord kept a little fluffy duckling as a pet. It was much admired by one and all until it grew large enough to peck the customers as they enjoyed a drink at the bar. Afraid of losing his customers the landlord got someone to wring it's neck. He had'nt the heart to cook and eat it, instead he buried his old pet beneath the bottom step of the staircase. Before long the ghost of the duck emerged and was even more savage than when it was alive. It pecked at everything in sight, including members of the family. It was decided to enlist the help of the local vicar to exorcise the feathered phantom. This he willingly did, but things did not go exactly to plan, instead of disappearing, the duck just shrank in size. Not to be outdone, the vicar sealed the tiny ghost in a bottle which was close at hand. The bottle was then sealed up in a recess in one of the pub walls. Even when the Blue Bell was under-going alterations, the owners were careful not to disturb the little spirit duck — just in case . . .

TILSTON

Continue on the road out of Tushingham for 200 yards to the A41 for five miles to Edge Green, two miles further onto the B road signposted Tilston.

Tilston consists of a group of assorted houses and farms, deep in the Cheshire countryside. Two black and white inns, the Fox and Hounds and The Cardon Arms, stand close to the village cross.

CARDON ARMS

The 400 year old Cardon Arms is haunted by a lady who had the misfortune to fall from her horse outside the tavern. She appears as a lady in grey who walks from the lounge bar, through a narrow passage which leads to the stables. After the fall she was carried into the inn where she later died. Proprietor Bill Forrest told me that ghostly footsteps and creaking sounds come from an upstairs room. It is not known if they are connected with the "grey lady".

SHOCKLACH

Follow the unclassified road signposted Shocklach.

Shocklach is a small farming community with fine views of the Welsh hills close at hand. The tiny old St. Ediths church is well worth a visit.

St. Edith's Church, Shocklach.

THE GHOSTLY PROCESSION

The hamlet of Shocklach lies close to the border between Cheshire and Wales. Once it was the ancestral home of the wealthy Brereton family. It is said that the entire family haunts the road leading to the ancient church. The ghostly procession of many carriages makes its way from the family seat towards the village church once a year at midnight . . .

FARNDON

Take the narrow unclassified road signposted Crewe for four miles. Take the road signposted Holt for one mile, then take the B5102 for half a mile to Farndon.

Farndon is a small country town which stands on the Welsh border. It is a most attractive place where the River Dee passes under a fine old bridge at the edge of town.

Farndon Bridge.

FARNDON BRIDGE

The bridge over the Dee between Farndon and the Welsh border is haunted by the ghosts of two young children. They had been entrusted to Roger Mortimer, Earl of Warren by their father Prince Madoc. Unfortunately for them, Mortimer was engaged in treason against his Lord and had the children thrown over the bridge into the fast flowing waters of the river. On dark stormy nights, their screams can be heard by people crossing the bridge . . .

BROUGHTON

Out of Farndon take the road signposted Rosset for five miles. Take the unclassified road signposted Higher Kinnington for four miles. Continue one mile further to Lower Kinnington then one mile on unclassified road signposted Bretton and on to the A55 to Broughton.

Broughton is a village with a stately home and an aircraft factory.

Farndon Bridge.

TARVIN ROAD

A young paper boy living in a house off Tarvin Road, met an early morning phantom at the foot of his stairs. Getting up early to deliver his papers, he saw something move at the bottom of the stairs. Dismissing it as imagination, he was walking through the kitchen to the back door when he heard the sound of a loud scuffle coming from the lounge. Turning, he saw a chair upside down in the centre of the room. Telling his parents, his father admitted seeing a woman walk past him in the hall and that he had noticed that it was very cold on one side of the house. They moved afterwards but not too far away. They watched a steady stream of tenants come and go in their old house, but no one stayed for long.

"YE OLD GARDENERS ARMS"

The two hundred year old Arms is named after the local gardeners who sold their produce on stalls close by. The ghost of a man, known as the Martyr, is said to haunt the cellar. He was the last man to be beheaded in this country and a monument to this effect stands across the road.

SALTNEY

From Broughton take B5129 for four and a half miles to Saltney. A suburb of Chester, Saltney is a small industrial area.

A strange encounter befell a young man employed by the railway to make sure the guards who worked at Saltney Junction were awakened each morning on time. Cycling along Sandy Lane at 3.30 one morning, he saw the light of another cycle coming towards him. As it drew closer, he could see the figure of a man riding it and hear the squeaking of the cycle chain. When it came within twenty feet of him it vanished into thin air leaving him, understandably, shaken. On his return journey the same morning, he was astonished to see the phantom cyclist again on the same stretch of road.

The following morning the lad was too nervous to make the early morning journey alone, so an older relative went with him. Once again, on the same section of the road, the phantom made his lonely way on the squeaking bicycle. The story behind this haunting is that a man who rode to work at a nearby factory was found hanged inside his place of work some years ago . . .

Tour Three

We start the third of our five ghost tours of Cheshire in Northwich. This tour covers ten towns and villages set in the middle and south-east of the county. Northwich is a pleasant Cheshire town situated on the River Weaver.

NORTHWICH

CLOSE TO THE RIVER WEAVER

A ghostly troop of Royalist soldiers are said to ride a stretch of waste land between Leicester Street and the River Weaver. They appear to be in great haste, galloping frantically through the night. It is known to be over this area that the Royalist troops fled the last battle of the Civil War. Their efforts were in vain as they were well and truly routed hereabouts.

DAVENHAM

Take the A533 signposted Middlewich for one and a half miles.

Davenham is a typical Cheshire town situated almost in the centre of the county.

A phantom described as a grey lady is said to float from room to room in Leftwich Hall. There is no regular pattern to her movements except that she always disappears through the same place in a certain wall. In search of a reason the owners had the wall opened and it revealed the skeleton of a woman in a wall cavity. It was decided to give the skeleton a proper burial in the local churchyard and since that time the "Grey Lady" has not been seen . . .

PLUMLEY

Take the A556 out of Davenham towards Knutsford for five miles. Turn right on the signposted road to Plumley, 1 mile.

Plumley is a quiet village with its own railway station and a charming pub, The Golden Pheasant.

TABLEY OLD HALL

At Tabley Old Hall, they tell of two guests fighting because one was jealous of the attention the other paid to his wife. The wife watched in horror as her husband was killed before her eyes. We are not told how, but she committed suicide soon afterwards. Being afraid of the scandal that would follow if the story got out, the owner ordered that the bodies should be sealed up in a secret room. Above and around the great hall runs a gallery and it is here that the ghosts of a man and a woman have been seen. As they lean over the hand rail they seem to be watching some long lost scene below . . .

TOFT

Take the road to the right out of Plumley signposted Lower Peover for one mile. Turn left on to the A5081 signposted to Knutsford for two miles.

Toft consists of a few scattered houses and farms set in lush Cheshire countryside.

THE SEVEN SISTERS

Seven Sisters Farm is so called because of the seven chestnut trees that stand close by at the cross roads. There is a story that an old local woman asked to be buried, not in the churchyard but in a field close by the farm. An even stranger request was that they should place a bag of nuts in her coffin to keep her going until judgement day. It is said that her ghost was often seen sitting on her grave stone eating the nuts in the sunshine. One of the nuts rolled away and when it germinated it grew into a very fine chestnut tree. Soon there were seven trees which still stand today to mark the place where the old woman lay . . .

KNUTSFORD

Turn left out of Toft on the A50 for one mile.

Knutsford is one of Cheshire's most charming old towns. The centre retains a great deal of old, well preserved buildings which stand well alongside the new. Worthy of note is the unusual council buildings on its main street and the quaint old property on the outskirts of the town.

TATTON PARK

Built in the late seventeen hundreds, Tatton Park was the ancestral home of the illustrious Egerton family. Situated in the lush Cheshire countryside, the imposing house looks fit to stand for centuries to come. From Tatton come reports of an up-to-date haunting in the shape of a man dressed in casual, modern clothes. He is seen walking along an upstairs landing which leads to a bathroom, where he vanishes without a trace. There is no story to explain this haunting, so the identity of this phantom remains a mystery.

ROYAL GEORGE

A flamboyant character known as Gentleman Edward Higgins lived in Knutsford during the seventeen hundreds. He was a family man with a wife and five children and neighbours who respected and admired him. There is no doubt he was a rogue but there are stories of him being a charming and courteous villain. He was a highwayman and his favourite place for relieving the rich of their belongings was the Knutsford assembly rooms which was the social centre of the town. Higgins deadened the sound of his horses hooves on the cobbled streets by covering them with woollen stockings. He was finally arrested and eventually hanged after holding up a coach which contained a lady who recognised him. Since his death his ghost is seen in the round room of the Royal George which was one of his favourite haunts.

The present landlord tells of another apparition at the same hotel. A phantom coach and horseman which arrive at the old courtyard of the Royal George. No silent haunting this as the coach arrives to the sound of the post horn and its wheels rattle loudly on the cobbled coachway . . .

A KNUTSFORD ALE HOUSE

A rent collector stopped at an ale house for a drink and it cost him his life. The landlord murdered him for the bag of money he had collected. He then buried the body in a sandpit not far from the inn. He was not allowed to enjoy his ill-gotten gains as the ghost of the rent collector haunted him from that day on. Everytime he went near the pit he saw the ghost walking towards him. This upset him so much that he confessed to the murder and was eventually hanged for the crime.

HOLMES CHAPEL

Take the A50 for three miles signposted Holmes Chapel.

Holmes Chapel is a pleasant town of old and new property.

"OLD RED LION"

Built in the sixteen hundreds the Old Red Lion has a number of interesting points to its credit. The Elizabethan staircase is one of the finest examples of its time, it leads to a secret room on the second floor. There is nothing to indicate why the room was sealed up but it is reasonable to assume that it was something to do with the Brown Lady whose ghost still inhabits the room. Another point of interest in the Old Red Lion is the window pane where John Wesley inscribed a prayer to Bonny Prince Charlie in 1750. Standing close to the Red Lion is St. Luke church, a fine example of 14th century architecture. The church and inn are believed to be connected by a tunnel.

CHELFORD

Take the A537 signposted Macclesfield for five miles.

Chelford is a quiet little place noted for its famous manor house.

CAPESTHORNE HALL

Capesthorne Hall is an historical house which was once the home of the illustrious Bromley Davenport family. The old hall has more than it's share of spirits as there have been sightings of three regular visitors. One is a ghostly figure of a man who is seen descending the stone steps which lead into the family vault below the famous old chapel. Another, rather frightening one, is the severed arm which appears at one of the bedroom windows, this has been seen by numerous well known guests at the hall. Finally they have a more ordinary ghost of a grey lady who wanders around the house from time to time . . .

MACCLESFIELD

Stay on the A537 signposted Macclesfield for five miles.

Set amid rolling hills, Macclesfield is a large town with character. Worth seeing is it's heritage centre and Silk Museum.

THE GEORGE & DRAGON

The George & Dragon has not always been a public house. Many years ago it was a school for refined young ladies. The school has long gone, but we are told that a number of the girls return in ghostly form. A present member of staff told me of one girl in particular who is seen and heard at night in the old pub.

WILDBOARCLOUGH

Take the A537 from Macclesfield to Walker Barn for two and a half miles. Follow the unclassified road signposted "Cat and Fiddle" for four miles, then take the unclassified road signposted to A54 and Wildboarclough for two and a half miles.

A few scattered farms and houses cluster on this high stretch of moorland.

CAT & FIDDLE

Built in 1755, the Cat & Fiddle stands alone on a bleak highway which crosses the moors that stretch north of the county. The inside may well be haunted but it is just beyond the inn where the legend lies. There is a stone bearing the inscription which reads; "Here John Turner was cast away in a heavy snow storm in the night." It does not tell us that the night in question was Christmas Eve. On the reverse side we read. "A woman's single footprint was found by his side in the snow".

The riddle is, who was the woman? Why was she there on such a night when the weather was so bad a strong man could not survive? What was the significance of the single footprint? . . .

BOSLEY

From Wildboarclough take the unclassified road signposted A54 for one mile. Continue through Allgreave for eight miles to Bosley.

A village on the edge of the Pennines, Bosley is close to a large reservoir which supplies Manchester.

GUN HILL GALLOWS

In 1731 John Naden killed his employer at Bosley. The murderer tried to make the killing look like robbery, but this was not believed as his pocket knife was left behind on the body. He could not supply an alibi when questioned and so was hanged at Gun Hill. John Naden's ghost haunted the site of the gallows for some years. When it was taken down and the wood used to make a stile the ghost continued to appear, staggering drunkenly on or near the stile . . .

GAWSWORTH

Take the unclassified road from Bosley signposted Gawsworth for four miles.

Gawsworth gets my vote for the most charming place I have visited on this tour of Cheshire. Fringed by distant hills, it is a pretty spot well worth a visit. The Tudor manor house is a glorious reminder of the England of yesterday. The house has a romantic history where a famous lady once lived and loved.

GAWSWORTH HALL

Once a beauty of the Elizabethan Court, Mary Fitton grew up at Gawsworth Hall and it is there in the garden that her ghost walks on summer evenings. Many titled noblemen fell under the spell of the charming temptress who collected two husbands and numerous lovers. She became friendly with William Shakespeare and is thought to have been the dark lady of his famous sonnet. Her affair with the Earl of Pembroke created a big scandle and caused the family much humiliation. She is seen walking through an avenue of Lime trees that lead from the hall to one of the gatehouses. The Harrington Arms now stands on the site of the gatehouse and is a charming eighteenth century creeper covered tavern . . .

BRERETON GREEN

Out of Gawsworth take the A536 signposted Congleton for five miles. Turn on to the A534 to Arclid Green for five miles then the A50 for two miles.

In a village setting, Brereton Green is where we find the family seat of the great Brereton family who we encountered on our visit to Shocklach.

BAGMERE POOL

The following ballard is based on the legend that foretold the death of the Brereton heir. From the depths of nearby Bagmere Pool, logs and tree trunks would rise to the surface of the pool.

THE HEIR OF BRERETON
Homage to Cheshire by John Leigh

A foolish thing to think that fate / Has come again to rule.
I think it only wind that shakes / The trees of Bagmere Pool.
So spoke the Knight of Brereton / When someone said that trees.
Were stirring in the rush grown mere / And seemed in great unease
Yet he looked gravely at his lad / The heir of Brereton line.
Drooping like a lily in a storm / A sion in decline.
My hearts best hope he shall not die / But trees were rising fast.
In olden Bagmeres reedy pool / Above the sky was overcast.
Then spoke again the Brereton Knight / O God that fate should rule
As an heir that floated down to death / Like trees on Bagmere Pool.
At Brereton others come and go / No more the ancient mere.
But sometimes in a hollow there / A ghost looks on in fear.

One young Brereton heir who would have caused the logs to rise on Bagmere Pool was Sir William Brereton. He was charged with treason and found guilty of conspiring with Ann Boleyn. Sir William, a young Cheshire knight, left behind a broken hearted wife and family when he was beheaded.

Tour Four

RUNCORN

Our fourth ghost tour in Cheshire begins at Runcorn and takes in the north east corner of the county.

Built close to the large Mersey sandbanks, Runcorn is an old town with industrial connections.

THE CASTLE HOTEL

The Castle Hotel was built in the eighteenth century from stones taken from the ruins of Halton Castle. It was formally a courthouse and the present cellar was the courthouse dungeons, since that time the cellar has been haunted by the cries of the prisoners who long ago were incarcerated within its grim confines.

CROWTHERS FARM

A man named Sam Jones who worked at Crowthers farm and lived in Byron Street seems to have been the link between two hauntings. One at his place of work the other at the place where he lodged. Firstly the farmer's wife saw the ghost of her father-in-law standing in the kitchen of the fifteenth century farmhouse. He looked exactly as he had done during his lifetime, even to smoking a cigarette with a long ash hanging from it. Soon afterwards the pigs on the farm began to die and no cause could be found by the vet who was brought in. A black cloud was seen hanging over the farmyard, after which a cow became terrified and never again gave milk. When the cloud entered the farm kitchen drawers rattled and shelves were overturned. Once the cloud disappeared the farm returned to normal. At Byron Street, where he lodged, furniture in his bedroom was thrown violently by an unseen force, when he left the house they had no further trouble.

WILSONS HOTEL

Built almost three hundred years ago, Wilsons Hotel used to be known as the Bowling Green Inn, it was renamed after Job Wilson took it over in 1805. A dashing young cavalier is sometimes to be seen walking through the upstairs rooms of the old inn.

THE WATERLOO HOTEL

The Waterloo Hotel has a playful ghost who delights in turning the pumps on and off. When all is quiet at night the sounds of it playing pool can clearly be heard. The cellar of the hotel seems to be its favourite haunt as its presence is frequently felt there . . .

WARRINGTON

Take the A558 out of Runcorn for four miles. Turn left on to the A56 for two miles then left again on to the A5060 for three miles.

Warrington is an old town standing at the base of the River Mersey. There is an interesting old Tudor cottage where Oliver Cromwell stayed in 1648. From here he is reported to have sent reports to Parliament of his victories over the Royalists.

Almost opposite is another fine old Tudor inn now named "The Marquis of Granby".

THE HOPEPOLE

Close to the Hopepole Inn stood the Hippodrome Theatre, later named the Regent. For many years the actors gathered at the Hopepole, using it as a meeting place, whether it is one of them that causes the disturbances in the inn today is not known. The ghost that haunts it now seems to be a comedian with a touch of juggler as well. He delights in knocking glasses over and a favourite trick is making them jump out of the rack above the bar . . .

HIGHER SEVEN STARS/RUMOURS

The Higher Seven Stars, now known as "Rumours", was a great favourite with the American forces during the last war. It's history goes back much further than that however, as it has been an inn for over three hundred years. This hostelry is claimed to be where Lord Derby spent his last night before being hanged in Chester by the Roundheads. The ghost here is said to be a light hearted fellow who although not seen, makes his presence felt by playfully switching lights and pumps on and off . . .

BLUE BELL

The Blue Bell is a fine example of a 300 year old English Inn. Its traditionally low ceilings and oaken beams remind us of its great age. There is nothing to identify the ghost who haunts the bar area who frequently makes its presence felt. We can only assume that it is male as it enjoys pinching customer's bottoms and sometimes goes as far as pushing them over.

BUTTERMILK BRIDGE — Sankey

In Sankey, during the mid eighteen hundreds, there lived a character known as Buttermilk Bess. She stood on a bridge which crossed the canal and sold buttermilk to the navvies who were working on the building of the canal. Since those days there have been frequent reports of her ghostly figure standing on the bridge. With large staring eyes she is draped in a long black shawl. During the war an American G.I. told of being approached on the bridge by an old woman with a hidious face and a cackling laugh. Reaching out, his hand went straight through her . . .

THELWELL

Travel two miles further on the A56 signposted Thelwell, which is a very pretty village overshadowed by the famous viaduct.

Little Manor Hotel, Thelwell.

"THE LITTLE MANOR"

Built in 1672 The Little Manor in Bell Lane is haunted by the ghost of a girl called Rachel. It is said she hung herself from a tree outside the inn when her lover, a guard in Oliver Cromwell's army was killed in battle. One of the staff at The Little Manor told me that locally it was believed the soldier was in fact a general in Cromwell's army. He had been billeted at the inn for the duration of the conflict in that area and the servant girl Rachel had fallen in love with him.

BOLLINGTON

Take the A56 signposted Bollington from Altrincham for two miles.

Situated beside the Manchester Ship Canal, Bollington is a small farming district.

YE OLD NO. 3

This old coaching inn got it's unusual name from being the third stop on the Liverpool to York road. It claims to have two female ghosts, one being that of a gypsy woman who was drowned in a fast flowing stream while trying to escape from the law. One strange happening at the inn is the icy cold breeze that is said to sweep through the downstairs rooms on nights when there is a roaring fire in the hearth. At other times lights are switched on and off and items such as clothes are moved without explanation. More than once the brasses that hang in the bar have been polished while everyone was asleep. Apart from the gypsy there was no explanation for the strange happenings until one night when the landlord's wife awoke to see a small girl looking at herself in the dressing table mirror. She looked just like a normal child except for the old fashioned dress and poked bonnet. Silently she turned from the mirror and disappeared through the bedroom door . . .

DUNHAM MASSEY

Take the unclassified road from Bollington signposted Dunham Massey for two miles.

Dunham Massey is a picturesque, residential district set in a farming area.

DUNHAM MASSEY HALL

Dunham Massey Hall was built in the 18th century on the site of an Elizabethan moated manor house. Legend has it that the architect fell to his death from the roof whilst inspecting the building. Most people thought he had been pushed by the builder after a quarrel regarding a change in the architects plans. Whatever the reason, the dead mans spirit did not rest as his ghost is still seen to this day wandering about, seemingly searching the building and grounds.

ALTRINCHAM

Take the B5160 for one mile then left on to the A550 for four miles.
Altrincham is a large, pleasant suburb of Manchester.

THE OLD HIPPODROME THEATRE

A cinema in Altrincham that used to be the Hippodrome theatre
was haunted by the ghost of a young man. Since he hung himself in
the orchestra pit many years ago, strange things have happened in the
old building. To the sound of moaning, projectors were switched on
and off, seats went up and down of their own accord. Certain areas of
the cinema were deathly cold and ghostly footsteps would be heard in
the auditorium. He was believed to be the youngest son of the theatre
owners, Hargreaves of Rochdale. He desperately wanted to be an
actor, but his father would not allow it so he took his life . . .

GATLEY

Take the unclassified road for one mile to the A34. Follow the A34
one and a half miles north to Gatley, which is a residential village
close to Cheadle Hulme.

CARR LANE

A man much disliked by his neighbours was a farmer from Cross
Acres. Almost everything he did upset the locals, watering his milk
before sale was one of his crimes. It seemed most people were glad to
hear of his passing. Their relief was short-lived however, when his
ghost soon emerged from it's grave. It wandered Carr Lane moaning
and groaning loudly. The terrified villagers called in the local parson
to help them lay the unwelcome spirit. The parson decided this would
not be an easy task, so he enlisted the support of seven other vicars.
They surrounded the ghost, joining hands to form a ring around it.
The Preacher, Bible in hand shouted until the figure shrank so small
it was caught under a nearby stone. As it has not been reported since,
we must assume it is still there.

NORTHENDEN

Take the M63 to Junction 9, turn onto the A5103 signposted Princes Park for one and a half miles.

NORTHENDEN — Ferry

Close to where the old Northenden Ferry crossed the River Mersey there are sightings of two phantoms. They are believed to be the spirits of Sir Gaulter and the lady he loved dearly. They are seen standing under a Yew tree as though waiting for the ferry to take them to the start of a new life together. The ghostly pair are only seen on dark, stormy nights and legend has it they were drowned when the old ferry boat capsized in a bad storm.

STOCKPORT

Go south to Junction 10 on the M63. Continue on for two more junctions to the end of the motorway. Turn south on the A6 for half a mile.

VICTORIAN HOUSE

A large Victorian house in Stockport had been the scene of some grizzly goings on at the turn of the century. Consequently, the house was haunted by what is thought to be an evil man who lived there at the time. His ghost was seen as a tall man, dressed all in black, who appeared in one of the bedrooms. He would make his way down the stairs, enter the cellar and disappear through a brick wall. At times there were loud disturbances and objects were thrown around by unseen hands. It is believed that the house was occupied by prostitutes during the days when the railway was being built and many labourers lodged locally. When the railway was finished the men moved on but there is no account of the women moving or staying on. During alterations to the house years later, many human bones were found beneath the kitchen and cellar floor. It is now believed that the evil spirit may be that of the man who ran the house of ill repute and perhaps the murderer of the women . . .

THE HAUNTED TAXI

One dark November night in 1974, a Stockport cab driver picked up a ghostly passenger. On his way home from Whaley Bridge to the depot in Lowfield Road, he glanced in his rear view mirror and was startled to see sitting in the back of the cab an elderly lady. The cab had been empty since he left Whaley Bridge and he had not stopped en-route. Never the less, sitting behind him was a very solid looking lady dressed in a black coat and white blouse. Almost too afraid to stop he continued to drive, glancing back to see her sitting there, motionless. Some ten minutes later he stopped the cab only to find the ghostly fare had disappeared. Most of the drivers refused to take that cab out after that so it was sold soon afterwards . .

HYDE

Take the A627 signposted Romiley, turn right on to A560 for one and a half miles, out of Stockport, travel north on the A6 for half mile, turn onto the A560 to Hyde.

Hyde is a market town on the River Tame.

A YOUTH CLUB IN HYDE

A boys club in Hyde was the haunt of an old club leader who had died at the club. He was always seen at the billiard table were he had, in fact, died. Other members always knew when their ghostly visitor had been, as the clock which he had presented to the club was always found to be going backwards . . .

GODLEY

Out of Hyde, take the unclassified road signposted Godley for six miles.

Godley is an attractive village with its own railway station.

OLD NANNY

An old farmhouse in Godley Green is haunted by the ghost of a previous owner, who was known as Old Nanny. Dressed in mob cap and kilted skirt, she wanders the gardens and peers in at the windows. One gardener saw her close enough to describe her withered face, she was waving her apron and making hissing noises at the time. There is no story to explain why the old woman should return to haunt the farm . . .

GODLEY GREEN HOUND

There are reports of a spectral hound having been seen in many parts of Godley Green. Described as being brownish in colour and as big as a bull, it seems to enjoy chasing people and any other animals that crossed its path. With eyes wide and staring and heavy paws that hammered the ground, it would appear in a flash and vanish without trace. One person who saw it believed it to be a large animal escaped from a zoo. One man brave enough to lash out at it, found to his horror that there was nothing there, his hand just went straight through the ghostly image . . .

MARPLE

Take the A626 signposted Marple for five miles. ·

Marple has a great deal of old world charm. With good views over the Pennines it is well worth a visit.

MARPLE HALL

Marple Hall was owned by Henry Bradshaw, a strong Cromwellian supporter during the civil war. His daughter fell in love with a handsome young Royalist who foolishly visited her whilst on the King's business. Henry Bradshaw had him followed by a servant who murdered him and threw his body in the River Goyt close by. The broken hearted girl haunts the scene of the murder by the river . .

John Bradshaw, brother of the above Henry, was also a staunch Republican. When he died, the state afforded him the great honour of burying him in Westminster Abbey. When the Royalists came to power again he was exhumed and his body was hung at Tyburn Hill. It is said his headless ghost haunts the old hall at midnight and is known as "The Martyr" . . .

Marple Hall certainly has it's share of spirits as the ghostly figure of Lady Brabyn has haunted a dark room there for two centuries. She vowed to haunt her brother and his heirs for expelling her from her old home Marple Hall . . .

BRAMHALL

From Marple take the B6103 signposted Bramhall.

BRAMHALL HALL

Built in the 16th century, the ancient Bramhall Hall has a colourful spectre who is said to visit the hall every New Years Eve. Riding a phantom horse he gallops into the courtyard of Bramhall Hall, dressed all in red, even to the long cloak thrown back over his shoulders. There is a story that he first arrived on New Years Eve in 1630, although a stranger, he was wined and dined by his host and given a room for the night. When morning came he was gone but the master of the house lay dead in his bedroom . . .

DISLEY

Take B6101 for two miles, turn onto an unclassified road signposted Disley.

On the east side of the county, in the borough of Stockport, Disley is a pretty place.

THE CONSERVATIVE CLUB

A conservative club in Disley still has a regular visit from an old member who died there one night years ago. He had quietly slipped away while sitting in his favourite chair at the bar. Members began to complain at having him appear among them, still always in his own special chair. The chair was banished to the cellar and much to everyones relief the ghostly member went with it. He can still be seen sitting in the cellar from time to time, so it was obviously the chair and not the bar that was the attraction.

LYME PARK

Built in the foothills of the Pennines, Lyme Park surveys some of the finest views in Cheshire. Within its walls the noble Legh family lived and loved for many generations.

While fighting in the French wars at Agincourt, Sir Piers Legh died of his wounds in Paris. They brought him home to Lyme Park and buried him beneath a hill crowned by Fir trees now known as "The Knights Lowe".

Although married he was much loved by a French lady called Blanche, so loved in fact that she died of grief soon after his funeral. Her body was found in a meadow near the River Bollin and thereafter that place was called "Lady's Grave'. A white lady is said to haunt the house of Lyme, people staying there tell of hearing the sound of a distant peal of bells in the still of the night . . .

Extract from the BALLAD OF SIR PIERS LEGH

Hark what means the sound / The low and murmuring swell Breaking from the neighbouring height / The solemn silence of the night. And see the red deer clustering round/ Half startled, listen to the sound.
And peer into the vacant space / As tho' some strange sight met their gaze.
And shadowy forms now seem to pass / Bearing aloft some lifeless form.
To it's last resting place / And flitting o'er the moonlit scene.
A female form appears in sight / All dressed in white and silver sheen With many a pearl and gem bedight.
And following in her mourners tracks
She rings her hands as one that's fey / And so the vision passes on. To vanish with the light of day . . .

by John Leigh

WHALEY BRIDGE

Leave Disley on the A6 following it towards Buxton for four miles.

Whaley Bridge is a small picturesque place where the grey stone houses climb the steep slopes of the Pennine hills.

THE WHALEY BRIDGE SKULL

On a journey from Eyam to Whaley Bridge, a man named William Wood was murdered for his belongings. He was beaten so badly by a large stone that his skull was broken in two. When his body was found, it was noticed that there was a sizeable hole in the ground where the skull had landed. The body was duly buried but the hole remained, refusing all attempts that were made to fill it in. Nothing would grow in it and so it was left as a grim reminder to all who passed by. In 1859, some thirty years later a man who lived near by filled it with stones many times, only to find that they had gone the next day. He tried filling it with rubble and covering it with sods of earth, but it was empty again when he looked the following day. Strange things began to happen such as the sound of a large bird with flapping wings flying low when nothing could be seen. Once he saw a man's jacket placed on a wall near the hole. Reaching out to examine the jacket it vanished before he could touch it. Since that time many people have tried to cover the hole but no one has managed to do so yet. To this day it will not grow grass or anything else that is planted there.

POYNTON

Take the A5002 for three and a half miles, turn right on to an unclassified road through Shringley to Poynton, seven miles.

POYNTON YOUTH CLUB

A Poynton youth club is reported to have, two unaccounted-for members. Once a school house and before that a church hall, it has two spirits who could answer to naughty and nice. Naughty is not seen, but it makes it's presence felt by moving articles about and often breaking things. Nice is the White Lady who is seen moving about behind the stage in the hall . . .

Tour Five

WIRRAL

Tour Five takes us to the beautiful Wirral peninsular which stands between the rivers Mersey and Dee. Known by the locals as Angels Valley it has a charm all its own.

We start our tour in Ellesmere Port, a large industrial town.

ELLESMERE PORT

On the Vauxhall compound, a number of people have seen a grey shape gliding across the trailer's parking lot. It is said to be a thick grey shape with no apparent arms or legs.

Also on the compound, they have a ghostly airman who knocks at the door of the security guard's office. He is dressed in an RAF flying uniform and disappears when spoken to. It is interesting to note that Vauxhalls stands on the wartime site of Hooton Park Airfield.

Going back still further this was the site of Hooton Hall, home of the famous Stanley family for five hundred years.

LITTLE SUTTON

Take the unclassified road signposted Little Sutton for three miles.

Little Sutton is a residential district with an old world look about it.

THE HAUNTED SEMI

A semi-detached house in Red Lion Road was a frightening place for a small girl who spent her childhood there. One morning while dressing for school the child was terrified to see the solid figure of a man appear in her bedroom. He seemed to come from the wardrobe, walking towards her smiling with outstretched arms. Answering her daughter's screams, the child's mother searched the room but found no one. Shortly afterwards, the girl was in a motor accident and lost a leg, following the tragedy the family moved away but kept in touch with their old neighbour. They were told that the owner had changed the name of the house, but none of the new tenants stayed there for long. One tenant complained that their dog did not like to go upstairs and could not be forced to enter the bedroom where the girl had seen the ghost. On a later visit the neighbour brought a photograph of a man who had lived at the house and had hung himself in the bedroom there. The photograph was identical to the ghost even to wearing a pinstriped suit with his hair falling over one eye . . .

BROMBOROUGH

Take the A41 from Little Sutton for four miles.

The ancient St. Patrick's Well can be found in Brotherton Park.

Dibbinsdale Bridge, Bromborough, Wirral.

DIBBINSDALE

The picturesque Dibbinsdale bridge in Bromborough takes my prize for the most frequently sighted ghost in Cheshire. It would seem to be that of a young nun who it was reported was on a pilgrimage from Birkenhead Priory to St. Werburgh's in Chester. Needing shelter for the night, she is said to have called at the local manor house which stands close by on a rise above the bridge. Here, some say because she would not surrender her virginity; others because of her religious beliefs, she was locked away and starved to death. The apparition is seen very clearly, dressed all in white, she appears to be floating down the hill towards the bridge. There may be two hauntings at this spot, as some describe a headless white form and others a white figure dressed in head shawl and flowing cloak . . .

THE ROYAL OAK

Reputed to be built on the site of a large old house, the Royal Oak Hotel in Bromborough has a visitor who refuses to leave when time is called. Staff and customers have reported seeing what is described as a blue grey mass floating around in the bar. Some years ago a barmaid told of the front door bursting open at ten thirty on a Sunday night. Expecting a late customer, she was amazed to see a grey mass shooting through the back door. A tunnel is believed to pass under the hotel from Bromborough to Eastham . . .

ROCK FERRY

Three miles north of Bromborough on the A41.

As it's name implies, you could once take a ferry to Liverpool from here.

GROVE ROAD

A familiar sight in Grove Road, Rock Ferry is Countyvise publishers where, I'm sure you will have noticed, this book was published. I was therefore intrigued to hear that they have a resident ghost on the premises.

On the sight where Countyvise is situated, there once stood two large Victorian houses. Before Countyvise extended, it occupied only one of the houses, the other remained a private dwelling. The family who lived in the adjoining house, told of seeing a ghostly old lady moving silently about the house. When her visits became more frequent, they sought help from the local vicar at St. Paul's church across the road. Having no experience in such matters, he wisely brought in someone who had. The medium managed to see and speak to the restless spirit, who told him she had been murdered by her two scheming nephews. Being a spinster, she had no close family of her own so the two stood to inherit her money and her house. Becoming impatient they placed a wire across the stairs which caused the old woman to trip and die instantly. In conversation the medium told her that the family who now lived in the house were afraid of her. She replied that they had no need to fear her. Indeed, she watched over them and took great delight in protecting the children as they slept. We are not told if he succeeded in putting the kindly spirit to rest. To add to the mystery my publisher, Mr. Emmerson told me that while working late one night, he actually saw a lady dressed all in white walking down the stairs towards him. An interesting footnote is that someone researching the locality for a book about St. Paul's, discovered an interesting fact about the haunted house. At the turn of the century, it had been a milliner's shop and workroom, the business belonging to several maiden ladies in turn.

The Publishers, Grove Road, Rock Ferry.

BYRNE AVENUE

Three members of the Brethren, a brother and two sisters moved into the top floor of a Victorian house at the junction of Bedford Road and Byrne Avenue. On their first night there, the man was awakened by the terrified screams of his two sisters. Rushing to their bedroom he found it impossible to open the door. He tried with all his strength to force an entry but to no avail. Desperate to rescue his sisters he turned away to get help from his neighbours. As he did so, the doors suddenly flew open to reveal the two women pinned against the wall by a cabin trunk. There was a terrible noise in the room which was filled by an unseen presence. Eventually he managed to release his sisters who had suffered a terrible ordeal. The Elders held a prayer meeting and managed to rid the house of the evil spirit. Later they discovered that the rooms had previously been occupied by a spiritualist . . .

Mr. G.F. Pagendam

BIRKENHEAD

One and a half miles north on the A41.

Birkenhead is a large town famous world wide for it's Cammell Laird Shipbuilders. It still has a ferry service across the Mersey to Liverpool.

BIRKENHEAD HALL

Sir Thomas Powell of Birkenhead Hall fell very much in love with a young maid who worked for his wife Lady Powell. His wife became very jealous and, in a fit of rage, pushed the maid over the banister of the staircase. The girl fell to her death on the stone floor below. Afraid of her husband, the wife ran away and ended her days in a French convent. Sir Thomas was brokenhearted and took the maid's body to be buried in the vault of his country house in Wales. There he lived out his days, a sad old man and was the last of his family to live at Birkenhead Hall. The sad spirit of the little maid was said to haunt the hall for many years after her death . . .

PATTERSON STREET — Birkenhead

The tenants of a terraced house in Patterson Street had the frightening experience of living with a ghost of a previous tenant. They frequently saw the limp body of a tall man hanging from the landing bannister. At other times he would be seen walking from room to room. There were some very young members of the family who told of the tall man watching them. On making enquiries, they learned that a man of six foot four, who had once lived in the house, had indeed hanged himself from the bannister . . .

PRENTON

There have been tales of two hauntings in Prenton. On an old bridge that was reputedly built from the jaw bone of a whale, drowned sailors are said to stalk. On dark nights the two phantoms would lay in wait to frighten unsuspecting passers-by. Over a hundred years ago, the locals used to chant a rhyme about a ghost at Prenton Hall —

When gorse is in bloom and holly is green,
Prenton Hall buggon is then to be seen.

In those days a buggon was the Wirral name for a ghost.

SEACOMBE

From Woodside turn into Canning Street. Turn 1st left into Argyle Street then turn right into Cleveland Street. Turn right into Freeman Street then proceed along Tower Road over the Four Bridges. Turn right into Birkenhead Road to Seacombe Ferry.

Once a busy docks area, Seacombe stands at a narrow point of the River Mersey.

GUINEA GAP SWIMMING POOL

From the Guinea Gap swimming pool there were reports of visitors being confronted by a swashbuckling character of the sixteenth century variety. He rattled his sword and jingled the money in his side purse whenever he appeared. Could it be he only wanted to have a dip and was trying to hire a costume? . . .

EGREMONT

Turn left at Seacombe Ferry onto Church Road and King Street for ½ mile.

This area was once a desolate spot on the Mersey, now a residential district.

MOTHER REDCAP'S

Close to Egremont on the Wirral shore stood a famous hostelry known as Mother Redcap's. Built in 1595 it served as a tavern and meeting place for local smugglers and ship wreckers. In Mother Redcap's day, she had a novel way of letting her customers know if it was safe to visit the inn. Outside stood a tall pole with a weather vane on top. If it pointed towards the building it was safe to enter, if away it meant the Excise men were inside or close at hand. A five inch oak door was a safeguard against unwelcome intruders, if that did not hold, a trap door just inside with an eight foot drop into the cellar was an extra precaution.

Such was their trust in her, that the smugglers left large sums of money with the old woman for safe keeping. When she died suddenly the secret of her hiding place died with her as no one knew where she kept her treasure trove.

It is said that her spirit used to be seen around the old tavern from time to time. We shall never know if she was trying to reveal or conceal her secret . . .

NEW BRIGHTON

Continue on King Street onto Seabank Road for 1½ miles.

New Brighton stands at the entrance to the Mersey. Once a famous holiday resort with a tower to match Blackpool, it can still boast a fine promenade and the imposing Fort Perch Rock.

VICTORIA ROAD

On Victoria Road in New Brighton in the former Woolworths building, they have what is described as the friendly ghost of Fred. The old store is now converted into a work shop for Mersey Advertising and it is here amongst the paint sprays and printing presses that Fred gets up to mischief. Sometimes, as often as twice a day, he has been known to place a ghostly foot on the electric cable to stop the paint spray when in use. He seems to be a constant presence on the upper floor with most of the staff having encountered him at sometime or other. Considering the description of a faceless, shadowy figure in a long coat, the entire staff should be commended for their acceptance of Fred the friendly ghost . . .

WALLASEY

Turn left at Victoria Road onto Warren Drive. Turn right at roundabout into Grove Road for 1½ miles.

Wallasey is a large, attractive residential district.

WALLASEY LIBRARY

At the Central Library, Earlston Road, Wallasey, a phantom presence has been felt in the main corridor leading from the front entrance. It was believed to be that of a caretaker who hanged himself there during the first world war. Although there were no visual signs, the corridor was said to have a very strange feel about it. Another indication was that it was always very cold, regardless of how much heat was on. Dogs have been known to cower at the entrance and refuse to go along the corridor. When a medium was called in to rid the library of the phantom, he told of two ghosts being there, the caretaker and another unidentified presence.

OLDERSHAW GRAMMAR SCHOOL

Oldershaw Grammar School is the only Cheshire school I have found that can claim to have a ghost who once called the register.

The first headmaster has been seen numerous times since his death. Resplendent in his black gown, he moves about the school much as he must have done during his headship. A good deterent for any pupils giving cause for being kept in after school I should have thought . . .

LEASOWE

Turn left at Wallasey Village signposted Leasowe to roundabout, turn right into Leasowe Road for 1 mile.

Leasowe is a residential area on the edge of the Wirral shore.

LEASOWE CASTLE

Built in 1593, Leasowe Castle was originally the summer home of the fifth Lord Derby. During the Civil War, it passed into the hands of the Cromwell supporters. It was neglected and became known as Mockbeggar Hall. It has been home to numerous well known families since then, but later became a convalescent home for railway men. It is now a hotel and is known to be haunted by a man and a little boy who appear together in a bedroom. History tells us that there was a family feud which caused a man and his son to be locked up in a room in the castle. Rather than allow his son to suffer imprisonment, he killed him and then committed suicide. The phantom pair have been seen frequently by many people and are thought to be the prisoner and his son . . .

HOYLAKE

Turn left onto A551, take Pasture Road to Moreton roundabout, turn right onto A553 Hoylake Road. Continue on to Meols, $4\frac{1}{2}$ miles.

Hoylake still bears the signs of having been a popular seaside resort.

THE HAUNTED GALLERY

While converting an antique shop into a gallery, a local artist found he had a strange visitor. Twice, he saw the figure of a lady standing on the stairs which led to the attic. She looked so like a normal person that he made enquiries about who she was, but no one knew of such a lady. No misty, floating apparition this, but a solid looking lady dressed in grey.

The antique dealer who owned the shop admitted to hearing strange noises coming from the attic. He too had felt the gallery room was always very cold, even with the heating on. The young artist enlisted the help of the local vicar and the phantom has not been seen since. There are no longer any strange noises and the temperature has returned to normal . . .

HOYLAKE HOTEL

The old Hoylake Hotel, was haunted by a gentlemanly figure dressed in a tweed jacket, knickerbockers and tweed hat. By those who saw him, he was described as a small, lively character who disappeared each time anyone tried to follow him. A barman told of seeing the tweed clad gentleman walking through the bar, another reported encountering him walking from the billiard room . . .

WEST KIRBY

Take Meols Drive for 1½ miles.

West Kirby stands at the entrance to the River Dee. It is a charming seaside town with lovely views of north Wales across the river. It has a fine marine lake and wide promenade.

HIGHFIELD LANE

Caldy and West Kirby share a ghost which wanders around Highfield Lane from time to time. In 1830 a newspaper cutting described it as a ghost of such bad character that nobody cared to go out at night for fear of meeting it. No details can be unearthed about it so it is not known if it is a man or woman. What is known is that it makes its presence felt as it clanks up and down the lane.

GRANGE HALL

Charles Dawson Brown of Grange Hall, West Kirby, wrote in the early eighteen hundreds about the ghost of Mrs. Glegg who walked the Mount at midnight. There is no local story to throw light on the haunting but the lady must have been connected with the Gleggs who lived at Gayton Hall since 1619. In the article, Charles Brown wrote of stable boys and grooms being terrified of waiting up for the master's horse when he returned late at night . . .

A LANE IN CALDY

West Kirby has a regular visit from the ghost of a lady, again believed to be that of Mrs. Glegg of Gayton Hall. She is faithful to her favourite walk which is a narrow lane near to Caldy . . .

THURSTASTON

Turn left onto Banks Road, left into Sandy Lane, right onto Caldy Road, 1 mile.

A small, enchanting village built of red sandstone. A favourite walking place for many on the high, rocky ridge which affords the best view across the peninsula and over the Dee to Wales.

THURSTASTON HALL

In the nineteenth century, an artist friend came to stay with the family who then owned Thurstaston Hall. On the first night of his visit he was amazed to see an old lady enter his bedroom. Dressed in clothes of a by-gone age, she stood by his bed wringing her hands and appearing to be in great distress. When he asked if he could help, she moved silently towards the bell rope, pulled it and disappeared. She came to his room on other nights and as he was not afraid of her, he made a sketch of his ghostly visitor. On telling the family of his experience and showing the sketch his friend told him a remarkable story. The drawing was of an old lady whose portrait had hung in the hall for many years. She had been a previous owner of the house and had confessed on her deathbed to murdering a young child in her care. Apparently confession had not freed her soul from the guilt of her evil deed as her spirit is still seen at Thurstaston Hall . . .

Thurstaston Hall.

THURSTASTON COMMON

Several of the gullies that run down from the high ground of Thurstaston to the sea are said to be haunted. The spirits are believed to be those of smugglers who were killed by Excise men and they are said to howl on dark, stormy nights . . .

PARKGATE

Continue on Telegraph Road through Heswall shopping centre to Clegg Arms roundabout. Turn right onto Chester Road, A540 for ½ mile. Turn right onto B5135 for 1½ miles.

Parkgate is a picturesque old port on the river Dee. It looks much as it must have done in its hey day, except that the water does not often reach the sea wall these days.

THE OLD QUAY HOUSE

The Old Quay House had stood on the front at Parkgate since 1682. During the nineteenth century, the owner at that time was a Henry Melling who had a bedridden niece, Clara Payne. For a number of years an old lady wearing a long red cloak would silently appear and sit by the fireside to keep the invalid company. Eventually her visits stopped and she was greatly missed by the young girl.

There is nothing to identify the old lady, but the house had endured such a varied history at one time being a prison. Later on it became an inn, so she could have been a passenger awaiting fair winds and a crossing to Ireland . . .

NESTON

From Parkgate front turn left by Old Quay into Station Road onto Parkgate Road for ¾ mile.

Neston is an old fashioned little town where the cross still stands in the market place.

A PRESBYTERY IN NESTON

In 1905, Teresa Higgins was a housekeeper at the presbytery in Neston. One morning when the resident priest was away she was surprised by a visit from a strange priest. He announced that he intended saying mass that morning and instructed her to assist him. This she did believing that it had been previously arranged. When the mass was over, the new priest went into the sacristy which was a small room with no other door beside the one leading from the church. After some time, Teresa entered the small room to find the vestments neatly folded away, but the priest had vanished.

On hearing the story and description, the Bishop recognised it to be the ghost of a priest who had died some years before and was buried in the churchyard . . .

Extract from the ballard SANDS OF DEE

Mary go and call the cattle home
Across the sands of Dee
The Western wind was wild and dark with foam
And all alone was she.

The western tide crept up along the sand
As far as the eye could see
The rolling mist swept down and hid the land
And never came home she.

Oh is it weed or fish or floating hair
Above the nets at sea
Was never salmon yet so fair
Among the stakes at Dee.

They rolled her in across the foam
To her grave beside the sea
But still the boatmen hear her call her cattle home
Across the sands of Dee.

Charles Kingsley

Sands of the Dee.

THORNTON HOUGH

Turn left at Neston Cross into Liverpool Road, stay on B5136 until main Chester to Hoylake road A540. Turn left then 1st right at traffic lights. Continue on Liverpool Road to Thornton Hough.

THORNTON HALL

Thornton Hall, which is now a hotel, has an extra member of staff in the shape of a lady dressed in grey. Sometimes she is seen sitting in a chair in one of the smaller rooms and simply vanishes when disturbed. Both staff and guests have had many sightings of the phantom lady. Judging by her attire, she is thought to have been a serving girl who worked at the big house years ago . . .

Thornton Hall Hotel, Thornton Hough, Wirral.

BRIMSTAGE

Turn left at Thornton Hough Green into Manor Road, turn right into Brimstage Road, $\frac{1}{2}$ mile to Brimstage.

Now a small, pretty village Brimstage once played an important part in local history.

BRIMSTAGE HALL

The little village of Brimstage has a long history, part of which still stands today. The ancient tower of Brimstage Hall dates back to 1398, the rest of the Hall being demolished in 1540 when the present Hall was built in it's place. It was the ancestral home of the Domville family until 1440. Within a few generations, it became the seat of the Earl of Shrewsbury. One of the Earls had a daughter who was disappointed in love, grief stricken, she threw herself from the top of the tower. Dressed in white, she is said to haunt the corridors of the old hall to this day . . .

SPITAL

From Brimstage keep on Brimstage Road over M53 and turn left at roundabout on to B5137 until Spital cross roads, turn right into Poulton Road.

A more up to date haunting occurs on Poulton Road, Spital. There have been many sightings of a young woman standing at the road side as if waiting for something or someone. Wearing a full length top coat she stands at a bend in the road where the housing estate gives way to open countryside. She is seen on dark winter evenings looking normal in every way except that here general appearance is that of the forties era.

Brimstage Hall, Brimstage.

BEBINGTON

Double back over Spital cross roads to Church Road. ¼ mile on is Bebington Village.

Bebington is a charming residential area on the edge of the Wirral green belt.

KINGS LANE

During the first world war, there were reports of a ghostly white figure floating down Kings Lane, crossing Bebington Road and disappearing up Dacre Hill. This caused great distress to many young girls walking this route to and from factory work through darkened wartime streets. Because they were afraid, girls walked in groups, and I have a first hand report from Mr. White, the son of Margaret Langley who did, in fact, see the phantom just a short distance away. While walking home in a group after a late shift, they saw a white shape which resembled a human gliding over the then fields on the left of Kings Lane, it crossed the road and disappeared up Dacre Hill . . .

Mr. White of Pensby

ST. ANDREW'S CHURCH

St. Andrew's Church, Bebington, is built on the site of a former Saxon church. The present building dates back to Norman times and is a fine example of that period. It was a collegiate church where young monks were trained for priesthood. There have been many reported sightings, both in and around the old church. Over many years, people have told of seeing ghostly monks walking between the church and the collegiate house which stood some short distance away up Kirket Lane. In each case the descriptions are of grey hooded figures, gliding along some fifteen inches above the ground. It is interesting to note that the ground surface has dropped just about that much since the monks would have traversed this path. One lady, while kneeling in the side chapel, looked through into the choir stalls and saw two rows of grey hooded figures sitting on both sides of the choir stalls, this is exactly what they would have done in ancient times.

Another ghostly monk is said to walk down a lane leading to St. Andrew's church in Bebington. It is thought to disappear into a tunnel which ends at the church . . .

St. Andrew's Church, Bebington.

ORCHARD HOUSE

Demolished in 1934, Orchard House stood a short distance from St. Andrew's Church in Bebington. For many years it was haunted by the sound of horses hooves, galloping towards the front gate and stopping abruptly at midnight. A local dignitary who lived there fifty years ago said that on inspection, there was never anything there to be seen . . .

BIBLIOGRAPHY

Bebington News.
Cheshire, T.A. Coward; Methwen & Co.
Chesire Pubs, Brewers Society; Good Books.
Gazatteer of British Ghosts, Peter Underwood; Pan.
Ghosts of North West England, Peter Underwood; Fontana.
Further Legends and Traditions of Cheshire, Frederick Woods; Shiva.
Haunted Britain, Anthony Hippsley Coxe; Pan.
Haunted England, Christina Hole; Longman & Co.
Haunted Inn, Jack Hallam; Wolfe.
Homage to Cheshire, Hedley Lucas.
Lays and Legends of Cheshire, Leigh; Haywood.
Legends and Ballards of Cheshire, Christina Hole; Longman & Co.
Legends and Traditions of Cheshire, Frederick Woods; Shiva.
Legends of the Dee, Edward Howell; Longrigg.
Liverpool Echo.
Myths and Legends of Chester, J. Marshall; Chester Blind Welfare Society.
Observer, (Chester Observer).
Romantic Cheshire, J. Cumming Walters and Frank Greenwood; Hodder & Stoughton.
Traditions and Customs of Cheshire, Christina Hole; William Northgate.
Traditions and Customs of Cheshire, Frederick Woods; Shiva.
Wallasey News.
Wirral Globe.

My thanks for contributions and help to — Bebington Civic Library, Mrs. Ruth Blackwell and Mr. Graham Blackwell of Marford Nr. Wrexham, Chester Chronicle, Mrs. Crossland of Chester, Mr. Michael Cooper Porter of Wrexham, Macclesfield County Library, Mr. G.F. Pagendam of Heswall and recently of Lancaster, Miss Francis Rand of Bromborough, Mr. Keith White of Blacon, Nr. Chester and Mr. White of Pensby.

Illustrations by **David Armand.**

Thanks to Derek and Philip Armand for help with mapping and photographs, Christine Kavanagh for encouragement.

OTHER TITLES FROM

Countyvise

Local History

Birkenhead Priory	Jean McInniss
Birkenhead Park	Jean McInniss
The Spire is Rising	Dorothy Harden
The Search for Old Wirral	David Randall
Neston and Parkgate	Jeffrey Pearson
Scotland Road	Terry Cooke
Helen Forrester Walk	K. Rickard
Women at War	Pat Ayres
Merseyside Moggies	R.M. Lewis
Dream Palaces	Harold Ackroyd
Forgotten Shores	Maurice Hope
Cheshire Churches	Roland W. Morant
Storm over the Mersey	Beryl Wade
Memories of Heswall 1935 — 1985	Heswall W.E.A.

Local Railway Titles

Seventeen Stations to Dingle	John W. Gahan
The Line Beneath the Liners	John W. Gahan
Steel Wheels to Deeside	John W. Gahan
Seaport to Seaside	John W. Gahan
Northern Rail Heritage	K. Powell and G. Body
A Portrait of Wirral's Railways	Roger Jermy

Local Shipping Titles

Sail on the Mersey	Michael Stammers
Ghost Ships on the Mersey	K.J. Williams
The Liners of Liverpool – *Part I*	Derek Whale
The Liners of Liverpool – *Part II*	Derek Whale
The Liners of Liverpool – *Part III*	Derek Whale
Hands off the Titanic	Monica O'Hara
Mr. Merch and other stories	Ken Smith

Local Sport

The Liverpool Competition (Local Cricket)	P.N. Walker
Lottie Dod	Jeffrey Pearson

History with Humour

The One-Eyed City	Rod Mackay
Hard Knocks	Rod Mackay
The Binmen are coming	Louis Graham

Natural History

Birdwatching in Cheshire	Eric Hardy

Other Titles

Speak through the Earthquake, Wind & Fire	Graham A. Fisher
It's Me, O Lord	Members of Heswall Churches
Companion to the Fylde	R.K. Davies
Country Walks on Merseyside	David Parry